OFFWORLD

ORIGINS

by

Rick S. Mordecon

Book One in the OFFWORLD Saga

TABLE OF CONTENTS

"To touch the stars, we must first imagine their embrace."
Carl Sagan

*"For my part, I know nothing with any certainty,
but seeing the stars makes me want to dream."*

Vincent Van Gogh

*"I will love the light for it shows me the way, yet I will love
the darkness, for it shows me the stars."*
Og Mandino

PROLOGUE

I t was a day unlike any other. The moment was expansive, glorious, and without compare. From outside the moon's orbit, the sight of Shenu's massive ring, shining in the morning sun's light, was a spectacle that could only be described as awe-inspiring. It glittered like a jeweled hip chain around the waist of the most beautiful woman in the universe, the kind the Egyptian women wore to mesmerize their men and get them into various states of ecstasy.

As you approached, the jewels began to shimmer and glow as she turned in her solitary orbit, showcasing her self-confidence and humility. One by one, the jeweled rings came to life, lit up by the warming sun, letting you know she was ready to receive you, to invite you in, to live, prosper, and become.

She was a monument to new life, born from the sweat, toil, and dreams of a planet of 8 billion souls yearning for a chance to breathe in the future, to take their place in the society of stars, no longer out of reach. The hopes and dreams of a planet and her children who had spent hundreds of thousands of years awaiting this moment were on full display. As you got closer and saw just how impressive Shenu was, you understood the meaning of progress, the understanding of how to create that which was thought unable to be created. Shenu's construction, a feat of human ingenuity and collaboration had provided a new home for thousands and sparked a wave of optimism and unity on Earth.

Below you, the Earth was celebrating. Even from space, the plasma fireworks could be seen erupting all over the planet, expressions of joy and promise illuminating this singular moment for the rest of the galaxy to see. It said, "We've arrived. We are here. We made it." There was no turning back now. The future had come to pass. From this moment to eternity, nothing would ever be the same.

CHAPTER ONE

SECRET CARGO

Declan Keel stood tall and strong against the early morning 24th-century Brazilian sky. His piercing and inviting hazel eyes, strong jawline, masculinely overgrown beard, and curly black locks of unruly hair defined his demeanor: tough but fair, confident but cautious, and tender only in the right circumstances.

Engulfed in the haze and scent rising from the nutmeg trees around him, smoke curled from the ember burning at the end of his cigar as it wafted up and around his retracted D-Suit helmet.

His rumbling stomach and pounding headache reminded him of the carousing he had done the night before at the opening ceremonies in Brasilia, where he bested two UESU colonels at their favorite drinking game. The shouts of "Abaixo Ayat" (down it) in Portuguese still rang in his ears, and his stomach felt queasy at the thought of the synthetic wormwood-infused emerald green liquid sliding down his throat hour after hour. The Brazilians called it "Louco," their word for crazy, nuts, and insane, and that's how he felt after imbibing it for hours.

His nanite reclamation colony, growing in his gut from birth, was slow on the uptake this morning. Usually, the efficient little buggers would have cleansed all the toxins from his night's activities by now, pulled any essential nutrients out of the flotsam, and regulated his stomach acid and good gut bacteria to absorb any toxins. Today, however, even his nanites were a bit drunk, so his head kept pounding, and his stomach kept rumbling.

The current D-Suit model he was wearing was just off the 5-D bioprinters, calibrated precisely to his body weight (even when it fluctuated), body mass, every neuron and ganglia, every blood vessel, muscle tendon, and ligament. The D-Suit was not just a piece of clothing, but a marvel of advanced technology, every Blackhold's second skin. Without it, they were somewhat mortal.

It was made of a compound formed from Jelanite and Fordlin, two elements found on Europa, in those jellyfish-like organisms that could withstand extreme temperatures, radiation, and many other kinds of negative influences that plagued the microorganisms found on the other Jovian moons over the past hundred years. They were able to give the D-Suit a remarkable lightness, enabling it and its occupant to travel at high speeds across the Earth and other celestial bodies, perhaps because the gravity of Europa was 13% of the gravity of Earth. The neural link in Keel's brain enabled him to communicate with the ganglionic implants inside the suit, allowing him to think faster, react quicker, and move more rapidly to any encounter.

Even with his pounding headache, Keel felt a bit superhuman. The new D-Suit, the Brazilian woman, *women* from two nights ago who showed him some tricks he never knew existed, and the mission ahead of him made him feel invincible and powerful, his two pillars of virtue. His mission, a secret cargo delivery to the outer colonies, was not just a job but a chance to prove his worth and make a difference in the vast expanse of space.

The shadow from the massive space ring encircling the Earth above him diffused the jungle's foliage, creating fractal patterns in the heavy forest air. He looked up at the sky in a moment of relaxed reverie. There it was. Shenu, the space ring, his destiny. SHENU was the Egyptian word for ring. Its three concentric rings allowed up to 200,000 people to live in geosynchronous orbit around the Earth. It took 50 years to build and cost hundreds of lives. The people born on Shenu would be a new breed of Humanity, Humanity bred for space.

Even from his equatorial vantage point, Shenu was massive, the most outstanding engineering achievement in history. Though he hadn't been up to the ring, he'd heard terrific tales of its construction and even more fantastic tales of what it was meant to accomplish, which was no less than the joining of Humanity in a common purpose, a common task, a shared ideology of accessing its solar system and beyond that, its galaxy from a veritable fortress in space, a new beginning for a new race of Humans, the Ring Dwellers. The mission to Shenu was not just a journey, but a monumental task that would shape the future of Humanity.

Shenu was made primarily of Nucleoton, a substance once called "nuclear pasta." Nucleoton was the residue found at the heart of neutron stars after succumbing to their supernova destruction. No substance was ever found to be more durable and more rigid. Once scientists could create Nucleoton in their labs, the fantasy of Shenu became a reality.

Keel's reverie was interrupted by a tap on his shoulder. Even with his D-suit on, he could feel the slightest touch; that's how sensitive the suit was. He turned and found Dr. Anderson Olefors behind him. Olefors was a strange bird to Keel. He was the foremost geneticist of his time but a less than stellar role model, plagued with scandals that rocked the science world. Keel smiled sardonically at Olefors, his 6'2 frame towering above Olefors's slight 5'8" body, packed like a lonely, scared sardine into his D-suit.

Keel was both curious and cautious about Olefors. Stories of Olefors being kidnapped abounded after he vanished for a year without telling anyone where he went or explaining what had happened. Speculations about his vanishing act raced around the world. When he couldn't or wouldn't divulge where he had been, he became captive to his mythos, a male Cassandra, unable to convince anyone or even himself of his excuses for his disappearing act. After that, his stature as a crazy eccentric also abounded. However, no one could doubt his genius. The secret cargo Keel and his men were babysitting up to Shenu was part of the latest example of his immense talent.

Olefors was as secretive as his invention, and Keel had to admire a man who said fuck you to society and then turned around and created some of the most innovative and singularly incredible advances to aid Humanity in its march toward immortality.

Olefors could hear his heart beating at an arrhythmic rate. He speculated that it was about 144. His D-Suit, using his voice print, told him it was more like 150. Olefors wished he could turn the fucking voice off. Still, like everything else in D-Suit tech, it was piped neurally into his cortex so that the suit and the human were in constant biological and aural communication.

Olefors had to admit that this tech was incredible, even though he was annoyed that he didn't think of it. He hated this shit, these advances in technology he hadn't created and couldn't control.

He looked out from his visor window to get acclimated to the damn thing. There was Declan Keel—the most extraordinary military hero of the last two centuries. UESU and EC must've lobbied heavily to get him to take on this secret Shenu mission. Keel was notoriously secretive and given bouts of wanting to live in isolation when he wasn't commanding the most powerful military force since the Roman Empire.

Olefors marveled at this guy. A superhuman of the first order, making superheroes from three centuries ago in comic books look like petulant, arrogant children with tear-smudged faces playing with broken toys.

He had to admit that this Keel was as impressive as he had heard. Strong, handsome, sexy. His muscular frame and mysterious past added to his allure. He was somewhat godlike, but as with all heroes, there was a touch of sadness, as if his bravery and sacrifices had taken some toll on him, leaving him tinged with empathy and pathos.

Olefors started getting aroused. *Who wouldn't,* He thought. Even though he had entertained several relationships with men before and decided against anything serious, he still found Keel to be a form of Übermensch, an anomaly that harkened back to a more complex time when sexuality was more of an issue, and the ease with which humans transferred their affections was a bit more constrained.

Olefors always had his eyes fixed on Danika Weston, his colleague, sometimes mentor, brilliant geneticist, and doctor. She was the science and medical genius who perfected TRNA therapy. This process allowed Olefors to continue his experiments and allow UMA to become the most sentient, powerful Geneticom in existence, a feat recognized as the most significant advancement in AI ever.

For her part, Danika was always a bit cool to Olefors, probably because she was so straightforward and honest, and he was much more secretive and pugnacious. Still, he always felt some spark between them and someday, he'd find the guts to act on it. He dreaded his advances going awry, as his frail ego was often rebuffed by women who thought him too cerebral, insensitive, or just plain unattractive. That led to his misgivings about his masculinity, so he focused on his mental abilities, which were more of a turn-off than a turn-on for most women. Still, he held out a twig of hope that his relationship with Danika, which was, up until now, more professional than personal, would somehow blossom on Shenu as they'd be in close contact for years on end. Eventually, he'd wear her down, but he had to admit that was a conceit. She would be the one making the choice. That was something he'd resigned himself to long ago.

For a moment, he became anxious and hyperbaric, thinking about their last meeting, during which a heated argument about his secret past and his most significant achievement turned into a full-blown "slag," the Swedish word for battle. He had attempted to mend fences before the Shenu mission. Still, Danika Weston was hard-pressed to return to a less-than-ideal situation, especially with a man so ineptly irrational as Olefors.

He put Danika out of his mind and tried to catch his breath, but his D-Suit automatically adjusted his oxygen intake and regulated his breathing to alleviate the cause. It also used a med spray to inject the smallest amount of Hyrax, a neurosedative, into his bloodstream, which calmed him down immediately. Just enough to do the trick. *Fuck me,* Olefors thought to himself; *this suit is even more impressive than he ever imagined.* No wonder the Blackhold never took them off. This second skin idea was beginning to appeal to him. But he didn't want to admit that to anyone. Keel, as if reading his mind, turned to him.

"Adjusting to the new tech, Dr.?"

"No, I hate this fucking thing," Olefors exclaimed in his usual broken Swedish accent.

Even with the bioimplants that enabled every human being to understand every other human being, even if they spoke a different language, Olefors continued to use his recombinant brain mechanism to try to parse language barriers. He was a dinosaur in that respect, clinging to technology over 50 years old while advancing technologies that were a hundred years ahead of their time.

"You'll get used to it," Keel muttered. He had no patience for a namby-pamby scientist. Still, on this mission, Olefors outranked him, so in deference, he decided to show him a modicum of grudging respect.

Three hoverships stood sentry nearby. They were state-of-the-art craft designed for this mission by UEU and EC scientists. Each was about 20 meters long and 5 meters wide. Their sleek silver skin shimmered like sunlit pools mirroring everything around them, casting themselves opaque against the deep green jungle fauna. They floated three feet off the ground, whirring softly as the Blackhold sergeants neurally linked to them and began the ignition sequence. In the center of one of the transports, lying on a Palladium slab in a tritanium box, rested a 3-meter by 1-meter rectangle. Upon closer inspection, there were no latches or entrance mechanisms. The box was entirely smooth. Everyone heard about the secret cargo, but no one could discern what was inside.

Keel surveyed his team, Titan Squad, consisting of 100 soldiers from a total force of 250,000—the finest soldiers in the solar system. Each member was trained in every known combat and mind-sifting technique, and all were sworn to follow Keel's commands, even to the point of death. The only discipline they lacked was Sidrani, an ancient art known to only a handful of superhumans from India, of whom only 245 remained, most living in secrecy.

In the past, Keel had attempted multiple times to reach out to the Sidrani, but his efforts were repeatedly rebuffed. He understood that if he could access their skill sets, he and the Blackhold would become invincible. During his assignment to Shenu, Keel learned that Leanna Rajastani, the premier of Shenu and one of his mentors and close friends, was the mother of a Sidrani warrior named Pashar Rajastani.

The reason why he had not known this before puzzled him, leading him to suspect that Sidrani parentage was also kept a secret.

When Leanna discovered Keel's desire to recruit her son for the Blackhold, she agreed without hesitation and contacted Kahlid Bhat, the leader of the Sidrani, to facilitate this arrangement.

Bhat would have been hard-pressed to say no to Leanna Rajastani, the Prime Minister of Shenu, who was the most elite member of the leader class. She was over 100 years old but looked 50. Her platinum hair, kept long but always tidy, was one of her hallmarks. It had turned platinum after her 15th birthday, possibly because of her advanced Level 6 training, which had her interfacing with GAIA, her geneticom, at a very early age. One of the side effects of her joining with her quantum sister was a loss of pigmentation in her hair. It had no adverse effects on her training, and Leanna liked how it gave her an otherworldly quality, something everyone noticed and commented on. As the Prime Minister, Leanna was responsible for anything and everything concerning Shenu. She was one of the most respected individuals on Earth, combining a fierce demeanor with a glorious presence, sharp intellect, and enviable diplomatic skills. Her stature resembled that of a well-trained Amazon warrior and a 24th-century shaman queen, both physically and mentally equipped to lead Shenu and its people into a new era.

To his amazement and delight, Leanna recently informed Keel that Pashar had been cleared for initiation into the Blackhold family. Keel had interviewed Pashar several times via neural communications but had not been physically able to meet him, as the Sidrani were notoriously secretive. It was a notable break in Sidrani protocol that allowed Pashar to leave his secret base camp. However, upon learning from Leanna just how crucial the Shenu mission was, Pashar was granted permission to join the Blackhold and teach them the Sidrani warrior techniques that had been one of Earth's best-kept secrets for millennia.

As the morning heat index rose to a stifling 37°C, Keel's second in command, Lt. Alyssa Reinhold, approached him.

"The cargo has been secured, the ICs have been set on automatic to Aquarian control, and the route change has been uploaded," she relayed in her usual professional style.

Olefors was busy checking the transports for any human error. "Are the transports all working? I heard there was an anomaly in the gravity pods."

"All units are functioning perfectly," Keel answered. "I'll alert Aquarian base that we need course correction en-route. Then I'll holo-message Shenu of our progress."

Keel turned to his troops. "All right, everyone. This is it. All Black-hold, initiate D-Suit parameters." One by one, the members of the Blackhold neurally interacted with their D-Suits, turning their military uniforms into Carbon-12 nanite kevlon-shelled impregnable suits of armor, like armadillos preparing for an attack by a pack of coyotes. Rigid shields replaced their faces with areas of translucence for their eyes. Keel activated his D-Suit for combat mode and soon became encased within its protective armor. In phalanx form, they resembled a column of soldier ants, ready to march at the direction of their queen, in this case, their king.

"Dr. It's time."

Olefors was tepid in his acknowledgment. "I feel constrained, and a man of my abilities hates to feel constrained. Can't I rely upon you to keep me safe?"

"Dr. It's protocol. You know the protocol."

"Protocol is just a code word for establishment ideology. I hate the establishment, and I do not succumb to any ideology but my own," Olefors said sanctimoniously. Realizing his effete explanation bounced off Keel like a rubber bullet, Olefors looked at him and neurally acti-vated his suit.

The teams moved towards the three transport ships. Keel approached his squad. "Give your full attention to Dr. Olefors, who will review some of the protocols for this mission."

Now that Olefors had been asked to become an authority, he felt a newfound sense of control over people who were braver and more dangerous than himself. This was something he had longed for, as he had always perceived himself as weak and pitiful in comparison to others. It was a deep-seated insecurity that he kept hidden, never allowing anyone to see it. After a lifetime of feeling like wallpaper in other people's lives, he believed that his own life was finally beginning, all because of what was in the box he was about to discuss. This was his opportunity to assert himself, to claim his authority, and to feed his ever-thirsty ego.

"Thank you, General," he began. "I want to express my appreciation to all of you for taking on this dangerous mission. Although none of you know exactly what you are protecting on our journey to Shenu, please understand that you are part of a mission with profound implications for our exploration of the solar system, the galaxy, and even the future of our survival. I must issue a few warnings. Only three individuals have been granted access to the cargo: myself, Commander Byrnes—who will meet us at the Aquarian base—and General Keel. Our Biowaves and genetic prints have been registered, and only they will be recognized for access. Once the cargo is in transit, any unauthorized attempts to access it will result in neuropathic paralysis for one hour, and trust me, it is incredibly painful. Your D-Suits have been programmed to issue a perimeter alert if you get too close to the cargo. Please do not ignore it."

Keel reasserted his authority. "Thank you, Doctor. Let's move out." The Blackhold mounted the three transports. Keel moved to Commander Eleanor Griggs. "Prepare for Terran gravity synch."

"Calibrating field, sir." Griggs waved her palm over a lock-out mechanism that scanned her hand and matched her blood vessels to a previous scan. The ship came to life with a soft whir. Two numbers appeared on the screen, and a sonar wave line descended into the Earth below them. "Magnetic field parameters calibrated."

"Assume negative gravity field posture." Griggs waved her hand over another sensor, and the ship slowly rose into the early morning sky. Two other vessels rose next to them. The ships moved to a height just above the treetops. The pilot switched the engine position, and the ships moved out, disappearing into the early morning haze.

Of all the technological marvels of the 24th century, one of the most impressive was the six maglev space elevator ports—two in Brazil, two in Indonesia, and two in Kenya—that provided access to Shenu from anywhere along the planet's equator.

As you approached the Aquarian Maglev port off the coast of Brazil, the sight of two massive dome-shaped ships, resting on enormous pads about half a kilometer apart, greeted you. The closer you got, the more immense the ships appeared. Each ship stood 61 meters high and was 38 meters wide. They operated on advanced magnetic principles, with each maglev equipped with a magnetic sensor system.

The ship had a positive charge, while the pad had a negative charge. Once the safety mechanism was released, the ship was propelled upward against the opposing magnetic force from the pad. This technology—known as kinetic magnetism—was incredibly advanced and far more complex than most people realized. It involved the use of ultracold atoms bound in an artificial laser-built lattice. The successful implementation of this technology demonstrated that humanity had finally conquered its long-standing fears of science, which had held the species back for millennia. For added security, four 2-foot-thick carbon 14-nanite cables were attached to the sides of the maglev, serving as a backup braking system.

On this momentous day, the site was bustling with activity. Hundreds of people moved about like a hive of honeybees preparing to venture into the chamomile fields to gather provisions, while a holographic greeting played in the background.

"Welcome to Aquarian Magport. Everyone with a purple embedded biotag has been cleared for boarding to Shenu aboard Cosulo.

Your luggage has already been scanned and loaded onto the maglev. All non-essential personnel, or personnel without clearance, must depart the boarding area immediately."

Those not cleared for boarding began exiting the area. In the control tower nearby, UESU soldiers were preparing the actual Maglevs for ascension protocols. The UESU, the United Earth Space Union, the reigning authority on the ring, oversaw the Maglev ports and everything related to the operation of Shenu. Every person cleared to work for the UESU was specifically trained both physically and neurally for their jobs.

Each individual had a unique brainwave frequency that functioned as a neural fingerprint. Every piece of equipment was specifically calibrated to that person's frequency, ensuring that no one else could interfere with their protocols or access the secret instructions and directives from the elite leaders of Shenu.

The two UESU soldiers stationed in front of the consoles used their minds to control all operations within the Magports. To some observers, they appeared as automatons since they rarely moved except to occasionally raise a holographic panel, make a decision, and transmit it to the other neural interfaces throughout the complex. Everything in Shenu was built around this technology.

Everything was communicated neurally, with invisible mental pheromones wafting through the ganglia and neurons of the UESU soldiers, creating a dance of sorts, organized in its applications and beautiful to behold. One thing was clear. Everyone assigned to the Shenu mission was knowledgeable, courageous, deeply human, fearless, and curious beyond comprehension. The best of the best. On this day, their concentration and understanding would be put to the most significant test in Human history.

Samson Frost hardly slept the night before the mission. He had been prone to insomnia since childhood, a product of his extensive genetic alterations given in vitro to prepare him for his role as a Harbinger, a diplomatic genius superhuman who was raised with a knowledge of everything from history to language, battle techniques, advanced science, philosophy, theosophy, and every imaginable mind control technique known.

Frost's diplomatic insight elevated him and his kind to leadership positions within the United Earth Union (UEU) and Earth Corporate (EC). He was often referred to as the Thoth of the 24th century. Engineered from birth for this purpose, Harbingers possessed immense skills and intelligence, making them invaluable assets for any mission or government structure affiliated with the UEU or EC.

Frost was the first Harbinger chosen to serve as the liaison between Shenu, the UEU, and the EC. His unique qualifications made him the only Harbinger assigned to Shenu, underscoring the trust the UEU and EC placed in him. This distinction rendered him one of the most valuable nonscientists within the ring and a true asset to Leanna Rajastani and the other officials in Shenu. However, the genetic engineering and intense training he underwent for this mission had one significant downside—persistent, interminable insomnia.

Frost had an implant that operated based on his brain power to regulate his brain chemistry. This device allowed him to increase his tryptophan levels when he needed to sleep, enabling him to access the intricate infrastructure of his pineal gland and release its dream-inducing hormones. Unfortunately, even this mechanism had not functioned optimally for the past month.

Unlike his typical mental explorations or encounters with unfamiliar individuals, he began experiencing strange dreams. These dreams manifested as vivid, otherworldly visions, making him feel as though he inhabited a different body in an alternate reality on another planet. Rather than disturbing him, these visions piqued his curiosity. As a child, he learned that being a Harbinger set him apart from his human peers, and he often pondered the tales of non-humanoid races coexisting with humanity. Were they from this dimension? Could they traverse dimensions?

The dreams didn't disturb him as much as they provoked his curiosity, as they were so vivid. As a child, he'd learned long ago that his reality as a Harbinger differed significantly from his human peers. He had always wondered about the stories of other non-humanoid races living in synch with Humanity. Were they of this dimension? Were they able to traverse dimensions?

The narratives surrounding these races have gained momentum over the past century. Initially, they were regarded as the mere speculations of a fringe group attempting to either reject religion and the concept of God or to cling to it more tightly. However, over the last two hundred years, these stories have become increasingly integrated into mainstream human thought.

Ever since rumors emerged about a secret Seniori base on the dark side of the moon, interest and suspicion surrounding the Seniori have grown significantly. Questions about their origins, purpose, and intentions have intensified. No longer viewed as a fringe element of humanity, some believe that the Seniori might be "Visitors," a term used by many in the scientific and metaphysical communities to refer to beings thought to be from another planet or dimension.

These beliefs became much more widely held since 2315, when Anderson Olefors was abducted for a year and then returned to Sweden without any memory of what had happened to him or where he'd been.

Frost was eagerly anticipating his upcoming meeting with Olefors. He was keen to form a relationship with him, sensing a shared connection between the two men. As he prepared to ascend to Shenu, he planned to have Dr. Danika Weston, the foremost medical authority on the ring, check him over. Her expertise could change his neural infusion protocols, allowing him to sleep. But for now, Frost's focus was on Keel, Olefors, and their impending approach to Aquarian.

"What's their ETA?" Frost asked with his usual confidence, although he felt unusually unconfident today.

"Thirty-five minutes, sir," Sergeant. Nate Rollins said as he sat before him, using his hands in a sign language dance to interface with the Aquarian and Shenu systems at a pace that Frost marveled at. Rollins's curt response was typical of his training; it lacked any emotional depth or personal opinion. Frost understood that these UESU soldiers were trained similarly to the Blackhold, conditioned to minimize emotions and opinions, allowing them to react to any situation with precision and confidence. Just as Frost had been prepared for his role within the Shenu order, Rollins had been meticulously trained for his.

"Why they had to assemble so far away is a mystery to me," Frost exhorted. Even without a D-suit, Frost could sense someone else entering the room. The smell of Vetiver and Liang Liang gave it away. Then there was the voice, smooth as velvet.

"From what I hear, Keel insisted that the final prep for the mission happen at Omega camp, where the Blackhold could protect the cargo from prying eyes and sensors. Typical Blackhold paranoia."

"Hello, Miranda." Frost was looking forward to seeing Miranda Han, as she was a woman with a brilliant Sagittarian mind, more than a modicum amount of understanding, well-recognized stature, dry, sharp humor, and impeccable taste.

Miranda was a striking figure, embodying the essence of a female Confucian priestess. With her straight black hair, flawless skin, and a beauty mark just to the left of her mouth, she radiated an air of superiority and confidence. She was a rare combination of intuition and attractiveness—a formidable mix for anyone who crossed her path. Her passion for her work, particularly her 15-year dedication to creating Athena, Humanity's first truly interstellar craft powered by a Dark Matter/Cold Fusion drive, was evident in everything she did.

Miranda approached Frost with a unique combination of stealth and determination. Her ability to get close to someone without revealing herself, like a phantom, specter, or angel, remained a mystery to Frost. Today, she carried a business-like demeanor with a touch of cynicism, a mix that always intrigued Frost.

"Must be valuable to get its own ride to Shenu." Miranda's opening gambit was laced with her trademark sarcasm, a style that Frost immediately recognized. He turned to face her, a knowing smile playing on his lips.

"Dr. Han. So glad to see you again," He said with a bit of glibness.

"You too, Secretary Frost," she said with a bit of attitude. She hadn't seen Samson Frost for two years. He hadn't aged a day over his 95 years. His pristinely shaved head and meticulously trimmed beard that framed his searing violet eyes were still standout features. Miranda always wondered why he shaved his head, even though he could have easily grown a full head of hair.

She surmised he did that to exude an air of seriousness and supreme intellect, traits that always benefited him in any negotiation, and Samson Frost was involved in some of the most critical negotiations in history, including the Treaty of Rome in 2300, which established the ground rules for the sharing of SHENU between the EC and the UESU.

The negotiations were incredibly tense, with Leanna Rajastani and Tara Zhang, the two major players in the SHENU enterprise, nearly coming to blows on several occasions over the details. Samson Frost played a crucial role in salvaging the talks and drafting the Constitution that now governs SHENU. This Constitution, which was agreed upon by both the EC and UESU, established the ground rules for sharing SHENU. It was a remarkable achievement that might have prevented another World War, this time fought in the cold vacuum of space.

"Sam will be fine." He smiled at her as he did when trying to discern someone's attitude without asking or speaking to them. His Harbinger mind then took over.

"Rough morning? You look a bit out of sorts. Zhang problems?"

Fuck me, she thought. Did he just read my mind? Thank you, no. She made a mental note to refortify her engrammatics. Allowing a Harbinger that luxury just invited scrutiny, which Miranda Han already had enough of that morning and, in fact, her whole life.

Of course, Miranda loved Samson as a colleague. Getting romantically involved with a Harbinger was dicey business. There was a time Miranda considered it. After all, Samson was handsome, brilliant, and fabulous in bed. But after one night, she knew that making more of it would be detrimental to both of them. She was satisfied with her one-night stand, which most people never experience with a Harbinger.

"So, this secret cargo. Any idea what it is?" Her pale blue eyes bored into Samson's hidden diffidence, probing him for clues. It was a worthless exercise, as she knew he would never take the bait. Still, she thought she should try, if nothing else, to see where everything stood with this cargo. She smiled, knowing she had made her mark with her inquisitive tone.

"I didn't think Zhang cared for anything that didn't smell of Earth Corporate protocols. I know she eschews the spiritual," Frost declared.

"Whatever this cargo is, I can assure you it isn't spiritual, some ancient magical weapon, or a newly designed Geneticom," Han professed.

"How can you be so sure? I don't even know what it is."

"Just a hunch," she said, knowing her reasoning was severely lacking in substance, something Frost picked up on immediately.

"Whatever it is," Frost continued, "we'll all find out soon enough. Shouldn't you be focusing on the final prep for Athena?"

Han instantly became annoyed at the mention of Athena but was happy with the subject change. "Your buddy Commander Byrnes has been minding my child for what now? Eight months. Going over *my* specs, *my* engine design."

"First of all, Miranda, it's not yours, and second, it's not personal. It's not like you haven't been kept up on every spec. You and Harrison like each other. This is between Rajastani and Zhang. Harrison will be joining us on the ride up. You can argue with him then."

"Zhang is only watching out for our investment." Han couldn't explain why she had come to Tara Zhang's defense so quickly and forcefully. Zhang was her boss, the premiere of Earth Corporate, and, yes, the most powerful human on Earth in terms of business acumen and ability, but Han disliked her more than she liked her, and she liked Samson much more. So why was she so defensive about Zhang and so offensive towards Samson? Han vowed to examine her biometrics later to assess what was causing this aberration in her usually pragmatic temperament.

Maybe it was ego, something she thought she had mastered, but somehow, Frost brought out both the best and worst in her. He was brilliantly annoying, she thought, and her equal, something she never admitted and never would. *Ego again. Fuck.*

"What were we supposed to do?" Samson added. "She broke protocol by accessing classified documents and bidding against our contractors. Not the best way to start this alliance."

Frost was surprised that Han defended Zhang so forcefully. He would have to do some sifting later to see what was happening. He could interface with GAIA once on Shenu, although that would break some protocols since access to geneticoms was the sole dominion of Level 6 female adepts. No matter. He'd get Leanna Rajastani to interface with GAIA for him. After all, they shared everything else in life, so why not this as well?

Another of his gifts was an enhanced sense of perception, unlike the sixth sense training of a Level 6. His abilities were more like a sense booster, identifying when someone was lying or hiding something.

"She's all business. You know that," Han parried.

"Earth corporate at its finest." He paused for effect. "We've got nothing against you, your genius, or even Zhang. Earth Corporate funded half of Athena."

"And Shenu." Han was getting more emotional than she liked. This conversation was not going well, and she didn't want to give Samson any reason to sift her more than she knew he would. She walked away, gathering her frustrated emotions and taking a break from the banter with Frost, then left the room to reexamine her motivations.

Han's reminder grated Samson the wrong way. Still, he chalked it up to her deep commitment to the work she had put into creating the engine design for Athena. Frost guessed he could cut her some slack on this one.

To prepare for his first meeting with Miranda in over two years, Frost reviewed the specifications for the Athena spacecraft to ensure he could have an intelligent discussion with her and avoid appearing uninformed. However, he had to admit that the concept of a dark matter and cold fusion spacecraft was a bit beyond his expertise. A dark matter drive? Just a few decades ago, the idea would have seemed inconceivable. Miranda Hans's brilliance had changed all that.

He accessed the neural information hub about the drive and reviewed it. As he began, images formed in his mind and, interestingly enough, Miranda Hans's voice accompanied the explanation of the tech. He smiled. It was fitting that she would be the voice of Athena and her creator. He began the sim while she was cooling down (that's why he imagined she had left the room). Her image came up. She was standing on Athena's bridge.

Good morning. My name is Miranda Han, and I am Athena's chief galactic engineer as well as the creator of the first Dark Matter/Cold Fusion drive. Today, I will provide you with a brief overview of how she operates, what you can expect to find on board, and her purpose.

At the heart of Athena lies a compact, highly efficient dark matter reactor. This exotic energy source harnesses the elusive properties of dark matter. While it does not emit light, it exerts a gravitational influence that provides abundant power for propulsion and onboard systems. The reactor is encased in a shimmering crystalline shell made of graphene quartzite, which is stronger and more conductive than any material previously discovered in the universe.

Athena is equipped with a series of streamlined cold fusion thrusters that utilize cold fusion reactions. These thrusters generate minimal heat, allowing for sustained interstellar travel without the risk of melting the ship.

Inspired by the Alcubierre drive concept, Athena creates localized warp bubbles around herself. These bubbles manipulate spacetime, enabling faster-than-light travel.

Her navigation system integrates principles of quantum entanglement, allowing communication instantaneously across vast distances and ensuring precise course adjustments. The array resembles a celestial four-dimensional spiderweb, with threads connecting distant constellations.

Crew members aboard Athena reside in sleek, minimalist cabins adorned with holographic star maps. Bioluminescent gardens thrive in hydroponic chambers, providing fresh vegetables, oxygen, and a serene atmosphere. Imagine taking a stroll through bioluminescent alien flora.

Athena's panoramic observation deck offers unobstructed views of cosmic phenomena, including swirling nebulae, binary stars, and distant quasars. Both astronomers and artists will find inspiration in this space, capturing the sublime beauty of the cosmos.

Athena's quantum library serves as a vast repository of knowledge, encompassing millennia of history and texts from countless civilizations. Holographic interfaces allow crew members to delve into various aspects of history, art, and science. The holodeck can transform into any environment- a Martian canyon, an ancient Mayan temple, or a zero-gravity dance floor. When necessary, Athena can deploy a shimmering starlight sail during long interstellar cruises. The solar winds propel the ship forward, harnessing the energy of distant suns.

The sail is made from Darwin Bark spider silk, reflecting the colors of nearby stars. The Athena spacecraft embodies elegance, innovation, and humanity's boundless curiosity. Athena whispers secrets to the void as it glides through the cosmic tapestry, inviting stardust dreams and intergalactic wonder.

Han returned to the room, still a bit frosty.

"Look, Miranda, I don't want to get into tiffs with you. You are Athena, and Athena is you. That's why you're on this mission, and that's why you have seniority and Level 10 clearance. Zhang might see this union as a necessary evil, but the UEU sees it as an opportunity to put aside 100 years of turmoil."

"For what?" Miranda had calmed down and appreciated Frost's understanding tone.

"Something better," he quickly added. His tight logic, mixed with his altruism, bested Han's cool scientific calculations. *Bravo, Samson,* she thought.

A warning beacon came up as their tete-a-tete finished. "What is it?" Frost asked. After a few seconds of assessing the beacon, Rollins turned to Frost.

"We've got an anomalous reading coming from near-Earth orbit."

"What kind of anomaly?" Han asked.

"Unknown."

Frost stepped forward and leaned in over Rollins to give more emphasis to his request.

"Check the ICs, then deploy." ICs were interceptors, units that operated to protect anything deemed sensitive or a threat to the UEU, EC, or the UESU.

" Checking now." Rollins paused. Frost noticed that Rollins's back became rigid, and he sat taller in his seat. *Not good,* Frost thought. Rollins turned to Frost and Han.

"Analysis says the anomalous reading has a Gamma EM signature."

"What?" Frost's tone told everyone in the room this was serious.

"Get me, Keel. Now! And deploy the ICs immediately!" Frost's voice rose. "Send the Interceptors into defense mode. Scan for the convoy, assemble, move to position, and create a defense perimeter," Frost ordered.

Rollins closed his eyes and focused his mind. A moment later, Rollins opened his eyes. "ICs deployed, sir," he said confidently to Frost.

"Contact General Keel."

By 7:30 AM, the jungle was a miasmic mess of humidity, giant mosquitos, and the air-laden scent of myriad jonquils, passion flowers, and orchids. These odors were so overpowering that Keel and his team had to initiate air scrubber devices on their D-suits to prevent nausea from overtaking them.

As the interceptors received their telemetry, the convoy ascended to 5 meters above the treetops, cruising steadily at 30KPH. Ten of the interceptors phased out of subspace. After a brief moment, the interceptors' bioluminescence activated, glowing in different colors and resembling giant dragonflies coming to life. They moved in harmony, darting and weaving in a dance as if choreographed by a ballet master. Once they had assembled, the interceptors swarmed off, spreading out to form a perimeter around the convoy.

As Keel and the convoy moved through the now dimly lit morning jungle, the convoy was joined by ten ICs. Keel immediately knew something was wrong. He turned to Olefors.

"Problem?" Olefors knew something was wrong as well.

"Contact Aquarian base. Get Frost on a neural," Keel barked at his sergeant. He was in no mood for surprises today.

"I've got Secretary Frost, Sir," Reinhold said.

"What the fuck is happening, Frost?"

"We've detected a Gamma EM signal coming from Near Earth orbit."

"And?" Keel asked.

"We thought it was important to deploy the ICs just in case."

"Just in case of what?" Keel asked. But he knew that his question was moot. Gamma EM tech was not only forbidden but incredibly dangerous. Both the EC and UEU and thus the UESU all decided never to develop it after a terrible accident with Gamma EM energy killed over 100,000 lunar citizens over 25 years before. It was deemed too unstable and too detrimental.

Once Miranda Han and EC perfected Dark Matter tech, there was no need to develop Gamma EM tech further. Now, it seemed someone else had other nefarious ideas.

The two other hoverships carrying the remaining Blackhold contingent rose next to

Keel's craft. "Hold position next to them," Keel said to the pilot. "Acquire ICs."

The pilot obeyed. "Synched, sir."

"Start gravimetric sensor sweep and scan for anomalies."

"Scanning," The pilot replied.

"Link ICs."

"Sending pulse... now." The ICs vanished against the early morning sunlight, creeping over the equator. "Deceptor mode enabled." Keel breathed a sigh of tempered relief.

"How long to base?"

"Twenty-five minutes, eta, sir," the sergeant replied.

Keel was getting nervous, something he thought the hyrax block implanted in his cerebro-cortex would have prevented. *Fuck. Even 24th-century science can't get rid of nerves.*

"Increase speed." He didn't want to alarm any of the Blackhold for two reasons. He never wanted to show nerves or fear, and he didn't want them to see him as weakened. The Blackhold were trained to block out fear and emotion, and he was experiencing both. *Fuck,* he said again to himself.

When he got up to Shenu, he'd have Danika Weston check his serotonin Levels and have him get a full med scan. He and Danika were close, and he wanted to get closer, but he knew she had a love/hate relationship with Olefors, more hate than love, even though the love side of the attraction was what kept her invested in something more significant. Keel never understood her attraction for Olefors, if it even was attraction. Danika was extremely and methodically mysterious, intelligent, and sexy. Olefors was scrawny, overly cerebral, and a little slimy. Keel knew that getting tangled up in that web would be detrimental to all of them. He also knew Danika thought he was sexy and intelligent. Still, she was more interested in fucking Olefors mind rather than achieving any sexual gratification with him, and Olefors had a huge...mind. Even though she hated admitting her attraction to Olefors, Keel knew they were destined for each other, even if they didn't realize it themselves.

Once the thought passed, Keel focused on staying alert, aware, and unemotional. With a simple idea, Keel gave his neuro block an extra dose of Hyrax. He calmed down immediately. Crisis averted, but the question of who the fuck was using Gamma EM tech was still in the front of his mind. What was this interloper playing with Gamma EM tech going to do?

He surmised that the gamma signal was only detected because GAIA, the Geneticom assigned to Earth, was bred to sniff out even the most covert changes in Earth's near-space differentials. If it weren't for GAIA, it would've never been found. This wasn't a good omen, and as someone who was superstitious and believed in omens, it promised a very rough and unpredictable day ahead.

The Navsat satellite moved smoothly along its elliptical orbit. The most advanced satellite ever designed, it could change direction and parse dimension effortlessly, allowing it to appear, disappear, and move wherever the UEU and EC wanted. It was also a defense satellite, one of 200 positioned above the Earth, silent sentinels always watching, reacting in hyper speed to any anomaly or strange emission and quickly discerning its intentions and excising the problem with advanced weapons systems and a Geneticom link to GAIA that ensured complete neutralization of any threat. The UEU and EC governed the Navsat project, and they shared in its design, development, and intelligence information.

That morning, Navsat 422 was hovering above Aquarian base, seeking to detect any strange actions that might compromise the mission. Its dark matter drive and quantum muon-driven gyros were working like clockwork, sending neural links back and forth from GAIA on Earth to UMA on Shenu, the two Geneticom sisters are forever linked, entwined in technology far more advanced than the society they served. They claim both respect and awe in their single purpose: to keep Humanity from destroying itself.

A mere 4,000 meters away, Navsat detected something strange. It turned its attenuation monitor system towards the disturbance, trying gallantly to acquire the origins of this new phenomenon's origins. Soon after its prey appeared out of subspace, Navsat gained access to the interlopers' systems, but it was quickly deresed and then went dormant. The events unfolded so rapidly that Navsat only had time to warn Aquarian base about an object exhibiting a Gamma EM signature had appeared in near-Earth orbit over the Aquarian base site.

With Navsat out of the way, the interloper quickly called an army of R-bots to its mission and ranks. R-bots were technological geniuses who ran the everyday world for humans, freeing Humanity to focus on more important things such as building Shenu, finalizing the coloniza-tion of the moon, or setting up the mining sites of Eridania and Mons on Mars for immersive human colonization in two years, or exploring Titan, Ganymede, and Europa for possible human exploitation. These are just some of the smaller tasks humanity had set itself in the 24th century. However, these interloper R-bots were different. They could parse dimension like their sisterly sibling, and when they made them-selves known to the world for the first time, their calling card could not have been more deadly.

The six R-bots that had appeared with their sister quickly formed into a much larger organism and attached themselves to the inter-loper satellite, giving it life. This new organism began spinning faster and faster until it began to emanate a wave of some kind. It had no distinct color but more instinctively looked like a shield of light, showcasing all the hues of the spectrum at once, thus rendering it black and white, driven to shades of opacity. The satellite spun faster and faster, and the rays became more and more opaque and oblique. Then, in a single burst of unimaginable energy, it blasted an emitter stream of matter at Aquarian base and its surround-ings. After its spectacular show of force, the satellite and its R-bot brethren destroyed themselves, disappearing back into subspace and leaving no trace of what they were, where they came from, or why they decided to change the course of history at 07:45 hours on what would have been a lovely, hot, monumental 37 Celsius degree day off the Brazilian coast.

Keel and his men were halfway to the Aquarian base when the world changed around them. He sensed something strange about the jungle. As he watched macaws and egrets flying overhead, he glanced down into the underbrush and spotted five jaguars running in the opposite direction of the convoy. This behavior was unusual; jaguars typically hunted at night. Since being declared protected in 2305, their numbers had increased, but they remained elusive and nocturnal. But now, their sudden movement unsettled Keel. He realized that something was scaring them—something unknown, cold, and invasive. The mission was not going as smoothly as Keel had hoped, but with the ICs deployed, he thought things would improve by the time they reached the Aquarian base. He was mistaken.

Just then, a burst of energy lit up the jungle so brightly that it blinded everyone for at least ten seconds. Mysteriously and almost organically, the three hoverships fell from the sky, crashing through the jungle canopy and careening to the ground. Keel gathered himself and neurally asked if everyone was ok. They weren't. Two of the Blackhold lay dead near the doomed transports, their D-Suits blinking red to show loss of life. Olefors, now entirely beside himself, cornered Keel.

"What the fuck was that?"

"How the fuck should I know?"

The pilot, who was injured but not in any danger butted in. "Gamma EM pulse blanketed the jungle."

Olefors was both interested in this development and scared shitless by its declaration. "Gamma EM pulse? That's crazy."

After everyone got their senses back, Keel looked around him and was astonished at what he saw. Hundreds of birds were dead around him, and myriad species of Monkeys and other creatures lay next to each other as if waiting for some 18th-century trader to come and collect them. Insects were scorched where they stood as they devoured their last capybara carcass. The once vibrant Amazon Jungle was struck deaf. No sounds could be discerned, and the stench of rotting animal and insect corpses pervaded every sense.

Keel was so moved by the scale of the devastation that he felt a tear slowly roll down his face, a forgotten memory of how things used to be now burned into his psyche and that of the Earth itself. His squad was motionless and he saw fear in their eyes for the first time. He was glad his helmet prevented his team from seeing his tears but strangely comforted that his emotional senses were alive and activated. His critics, and there were many, often said he was an automaton, emotionless and cold. Keel knew that to lead hundreds of thousands of people, those qualities were essential to remain respected and steadfast. But who could remain heartless at seeing the devastation wrought around him? He steadied himself and faced his troops.

"All right, everyone. Gather yourselves. We have a job to do." Keel turned to Olefors, also consumed by the apocalyptic scene he witnessed. "I'll get Frost on the link." Olefors appreciated Keel's stoicism more than he could express, as everyone's humanity was given a gut check. It was a sight Anderson Olefors would never forget.

Back at Aquarian Base, Frost stood over Rollins, waiting impatiently as the pulse hit the jungle.

"Sir, we have another problem. A much bigger problem."

"I don't like the sound of that."

"Yessir, there's been a Gamma EM pulse emission. ICs and convoy are down."

"What?" Frost's demeanor and calm sense of control disappeared. He could never let on how he felt inside; that was a slow death to a Harbinger.

"Verified, sir. A Gamma EM pulse has been emitted from an unknown extra-Earth orbit source that is no longer transmitting."

"What the hell is going on? Get Keel's neural on the line, call Shenu, and see what their sensors have picked up."

"I'm sorry, Mr. Secretary, the EM pulse has terminated the Neural link."

"Then get me a bio link emergency access line to Keel."

"Commander Keel has already initiated a secure link on his wave."

Frost was uncharacteristically nervous. Only during a severe emergency could someone directly attach a message to another person's brainwave frequency via a bio link. It was like the old nuclear codes from the 21st century. Only one person had the codes. In the 24th century, only a handful of specially cleared and vetted people could directly access another person's brainwave.

For anyone else to have access to another person's frequency was forbidden and punishable by either cryostasis or mind erasure, which erased a human's mind, leaving them brain dead, after which they were harvested for their DNA, which had become big business in 2325. It was capital punishment on a vast, dangerous scale, and until now, only three people had been tried, arrested, and placed into cryostasis; that's how rare the infringement was.

"What about our systems?" Frost asked warily.

"The defense field protected them. The phenomenon was targeted at the convoy, sir." Frost's forehead tingled ever so slightly, indicating that a bio link was coming into his prefrontal cortex. "I'm receiving the bio link now."

Keel waited amongst the strewn hoverships for the biolink to be accepted. Once it was, Frost's hologram appeared in front of Keel.

Even though Frost wasn't there, his shadow link was. Keel waited for Frost to dial in.

"What the hell happened, Frost?

"Gamma EM pulse."

"Who the fuck is developing Gamma EM tech?" Olefors, standing by the classified cargo, hurriedly walked over to Keel, who looked as if he was conversing with himself. That was another aspect of a bio link. Only the person being linked could see the hologram of the other individual. "That's not important," Olefors said." We need to get the cargo to the base. Now."

"Someone else has a different idea," Keel sneered.

"Does Olefors have any ideas on how to get the cargo to the base?" Frost asked.

"Do you have any suggestions on how to get the cargo to Aquarian?" Keel didn't like being a translator; it wasted valuable time, but in this case, he obliged.

"Is that Frost?" Olefors asked.

"Yes," Keel replied.

"Of course, I have alternatives," Olefors proclaimed. "You don't think I'd rely entirely upon the Blackhold. The cargo comes with its propulsion system. However, it must travel alone. I will have to program it, then launch it."

"You never told us about this," Keel barked.

"You never told me your efforts to get the cargo to Aquarian would be so reckless and end so fecklessly," Olefors shouted back.

Keel was annoyed with this turn of events. "That means we'll lose sight of it."

Olefors couldn't resist the invitation to speak his mind. "I never understood all this cloak and dagger. Oh wait, that was all sanctioned by the UEU command. Showing off their multi-billion-credit Blackhold investment. Very successful General." Keel ignored the outburst.

Frost jumped in. "I'll make all the necessary arrangements. Relay the message that the cargo will now be arriving solo. Program the cargo,

Dr." Frost vanished from Keel's mind. Keel reasserted his command and turned to his troops.

"We're moving out. Ten of you will remain here with the Dr. and the cargo; the other ten will move out and set up perimeter protection from here to Aquarian. Take our dead with you." In an instant, the Blackhold were gone.

Olefors waved his left hand over his right palm, and a bioluminescent keypad embedded in his dermal layer appeared. He waved his hand over the keypad, and the tritanium box came to life, emitting a soft hum and violet glow. Olefors set the defense mode and propulsion systems. The box rose into the air. Keel walked over.

"Now I wonder what you could've developed that would be immune to Gamma-EM pulses."

"I'm not doing anything, General. That is." He pointed to the box as it rose above the trees and rapidly moved off.

Keel was impressed but dared not let Olefors know it. "Put your suit into destination mode. Set your course and hold on tight." Olefors neurally interfaced with the suit, and in an instant, he was gone. He felt like he was flying in a jet, the trees, flowers, and animals whizzing by him in a blur. The sensation was exhilarating and nauseating at the same time. He realized if he watched everything around him, he might pass out, so he focused on the readout in the front of his visor and let the suit do its thing. In what seemed like seconds, he was approaching the Aquarian base. He neurally told the suit to stop, but it was foolish as the suit knew precisely when and where to stop. His helmet and suit retracted, leaving him in front of the UESU headquarters with no small measure of vertigo.

At Aquarian base, the calm confidence of just a half hour ago was replaced by a series of Blackhold troops setting up a perimeter, and everyone at the base being neuro and bioscanned for any trace of hidden explosives or nefarious thoughts. The base was locked down on an unimaginable scale.

In Aquarian control, Frost was trying his best to remain calm, but he saw his proverbial life flash before his eyes as the mission so crucial to the success of Shenu was now in serious jeopardy. He could only imagine what his lover, Leanna Rajastani, was thinking. Still, he didn't dare send her a neural as he knew she was most likely in conclave with GAIA, her Geneticom, the advanced quantum nanite computer that oversaw all the activities of the UEU and EC and guided and advised the Earth dwellers on the myriad paths that could be chosen at any given time, always with the guidelines and intentions of making life on earth more productive, empowering, and egalitarian.

Frost often wondered about the nature of Leanna's relationship with GAIA. Whenever he asked her about that relationship, she constantly changed the conversation. Eventually, he understood that the bond between Level 6 and their Geneticom was private, secretive, and always fraught with enormous tension, as Leanna and GAIA would make decisions that could change the course of history at any time. It was a mystery that Frost was happy to leave as such, and so was Leanna. Frost's train of thought was interrupted by Rollins. Han stood so close to them Frost could smell her sweat mixed with her perfume, an intoxicating brew.

"Sir, we've got single movement. It's the cargo, sir. It's moving at 120 kph. Eta, 8 minutes." Rollins had gotten his composure back. *Good,* Frost thought.

He breathed a belabored sigh of relief. "How the hell is it even moving with an EM pulse blanketing the jungle?" Han asked. Rollins turned to Frost for the first time since the operation began.

"Propulsion is... Biofusion."

"Biofusion? That's just speculative," Frost said.

"What's Biofusion?" Rollins asked.

Han stepped forward. "Centuries ago, in 1963, Salvatore Bellini first discovered Magnetotactic bacteria, a fascinating group of microorganisms that exhibit a unique superpower: they orient themselves along Earth's magnetic field lines. Later, in 1975, microbiologist Richard Blakemore independently rediscovered them. He observed that some bacteria consistently swam in the same direction, even when he rotated the microscope. These bacteria were responding to magnetism. These tiny organisms are believed to use their magnetic alignment to reach regions of optimal oxygen concentration in their environment. Then, 15 years ago, Danika Weston, working with Anderson Olefors, devised a form of energy that utilized Magnetotactic bacteria to do ostensibly the same thing. They used their advanced magnetic property skills to produce an energy source powered by the Earth's magnetic core. They called it Biofusion."

"It seems too weird to be true," Rollins exclaimed.

"To the rest of the world maybe, but not for Olefors," Han said. She had kept quiet during the Gamma EM pulse event but knew this glitch would pose a severe problem for the mission.

She also knew that Tara Zhang would be more than annoyed at this turn of events. She wouldn't care about casualties, just about the cargo. However, Han suspected that Zhang had as much knowledge of the cargo's contents as everyone else, which was none.

Rollins checked his neural link, and the data port was engineered into his brain to access information at lightning speed.

"Confirmed," Rollins said. "The power IS being generated from inside the container." *Well fuck me sideways. Leave it to crazy Anderson Olefors to come back from the dead with amazing new tech. Guess dead people do know how to live,* Frost opined to himself.

"Prepare the docking bay for arrival and get the Blackhold down there to secure the perimeter. I'll be at the docking area." Frost left the room.

The Brazilian heat seared the early morning sky to a hue of blue/white as the sun tried to burn off the haze that the Gamma EM pulse had created. By now, only those with high clearance levels had heard about the accident, the covert satellite, and the almost doomed mission.

The neurals back and forth from Shenu must be intense, Miranda Han thought as she walked toward the loading bay to meet the oh-so-secretive cargo from the jungle. She had changed into something a bit more comfortable. Her EC uniform felt tight and constricting this morning, partly from the fact that Han was pregnant and hadn't readjusted her Biosuit to accommodate for the child she was carrying and partly because of her growing uneasiness with UEU protocols ever since Shenu was completed and Athena was ready for ops. Once that was done, the pressure from Tara Zhang began to build.

She had given the child little thought, still unsure whether to end the pregnancy. But she hesitated as she was about to spend many months and possibly years with the child's father. Declan Keel was unaware that his offspring was proliferating in Han's womb, and she had no plans to tell him unless and until she had to. The affair was brief, memorable, and intense, but they each went their separate ways afterward.

Miranda Han then did extensive sifting into Declan Keels's modus operandi. It seemed he had no compunction for spreading his seed all over the planet. She didn't care. The child was a surprise, but not entirely unexpected, if Miranda was being true to herself, something she sometimes had difficulty facing. For now, silence seemed the best course. She'd soon face him, and that was a prospect she was both dreading and, in a perverse way, looking forward to. Emotions were running hot, and her hormones were keeping pace.

Now that Shenu was a reality and people were beginning to board her and begin the transition from Terran life to Shenu life, everything multiplied. Miranda knew that if Tara found out about the child, there'd be intense pressure to either have the embryo removed intact, raised in a natal chamber, and then either be put up for adoption or if a girl enrolled in the Bresden Academy for testing to see if she was a suitable candidate for Level 6 training. If it were a boy, as Miranda had already ascertained, he would be enrolled in a new EC program to train officers for duty in the Asteroid belt, as the belt had become a hugely important source of both revenue and power in the 24th century. Miranda could keep the child, but Tara Zhang would probably demote her, preventing her from doing her work to prepare Athena for any of her planned voyages over the next five years. It was a series of less-than-perfect choices, and Miranda was loathe to think about them now.

Eventually, she would have to make a choice. By then, she might decide to resign from EC and commit herself full-time to Shenucorps but lose her considerable accumulated pay, not to mention her status in the EC as the inheritor of Tara Zhang's mantle, putting her next in line as premier of EC.

For Tara Zhang, the only genuine concern was business. She was a brilliant strategist, a ruthless competitor, and one of the wealthiest humans on the planet. Add the fact that she was single-handedly responsible for the rise of Earth Corporate, or the EC, from a rag-tag corporate group of the world's trillionaires to the global powerhouse that allied itself with the more powerful UEU. The alliance was necessary for Humanity to move forward.

Still, Han knew Zhang's relationship with her UESU counterpart, Leanna Rajastani, was far more complicated and fraught with perils.

Zhang's insistent bio link alert was ringing in her brain. She was the only person with Han's neural frequency link, and even though Han could turn the link off, there were times when Zhang insisted on having access to Han at all times of the day or night. This was one time Han wished she could turn the link off permanently, but that would end her career as the foremost propulsion scientist on Earth and damn Shenu and Athena to an abrupt demise, dooming everything she had worked 30 long years for.

This day cannot get any more fucked up. Just as the thought ended, Zhang's neural request got more urgent.

"Shit," she muttered under her breath. "Not now, Tara." She reluctantly accepted Zhang's bio link. Zhang got right to the point.

"What the fuck is this about a Gamma EM pulse from NEO?"

"It's true. The mission was almost aborted."

Zhang wasn't deterred. "Not a chance. Whatever this secret cargo is, Leanna and Olefors would sell their souls to get it up to Shenu at all costs. I'm more interested in the who's, how's, and why's."

"What does that mean, Tara?"

"You're buddies with Frost, right? You fucked him, didn't you? Drill him for info."

"Are you serious?" Han asked incredulously. "Frost is a Harbinger."

"I know what the fuck he is, Miranda. Use your Level 6 training to get underneath it."

"I'm not Level 6 Tara; I failed to gain status. I only did three years of training."

"Well, you're the best I've got for now. If you had gone to completion, I'd have a Level 6 at my disposal, and we'd have access to a Geneticom. As you're a disappointment, let's not make it two for two." With that, Zhang ended the link.

"Fucking bitch," Han muttered to herself.

"Nothing wrong, I hope?" Frost's deceptively kind tone alerted Han that he had heard the conversation with Zhang. "Tara is pissed, huh?"

"You know her. If she's not the center of the world, she feels insecure, and that doesn't bode well for the rest of us, especially me."

"Don't sweat it, Miranda; without you, she's rich and powerful, but with you at her side, she's got a seat at the table on some of the most important decisions humanity will ever make. Never sell yourself short."

Han forgot how much she loved Samson Frost at that moment. It was true; he didn't have a nasty bone in his body, but you'd never want to cross or betray him. Harbingers were dedicated friends to those they trusted but deadly enemies to those they didn't. They could maim a person's mind with a deadly thought if they gained access to their frequency, which is why frequency poaching was the greatest crime one could commit during the 24th century. Even

Harbingers needed authority from the UEU and EC governments to poach an enemy's frequency. To do so without permission from the global body would be the death of a Harbinger. They were deadly killers on a leash, but eventually, everyone knew that the leash would be broken, and the world was scared shitless to consider that possibility.

Just then, the docking bay doors opened, and a group of Blackhold raced into the bay, stopping short of Frost and Han. Declan Keel pressed a button on his armpad, and his D-suit disappeared around him.

Frost was the first to approach. "General. Glad to see you made it."

"Mr. Secretary." Keel nodded. "Helluva way to start the day. Any news of the shit show in the jungle?"

Miranda Han moved past Frost so Keel could notice her.

"And this must be the illustrious and secretive Miranda Han," Keel said while smiling.

"My reputation must precede me," Han replied. She knew that she needed to play along with Keel's game, as they both needed to maintain a supreme level of professionalism, especially with everything going on around them.

"Your reputation not only precedes you; it doesn't do you justice," Keel said.

"You're too kind, General."

Frost butted in. "I doubt you'd find many people calling General Keel kind."

"I resent that, Frost."

Olefors intervened. "I'm glad you people are so calm."

"We're not calm, we're just professional." Keel was happy to put Olefors in his place.

At that moment, the secret cargo wafted into the docking bay and gently descended onto a platform. The event silenced Olefors, Keel, Frost, and Han. They all looked at each other momentarily, wondering what was in this box and how it was moving on Biofusion.

Frost was the first to speak up. "Impressive, Dr."

"Thankfully, I've thought of every contingency." Olefors beamed arrogantly.

Keel was less genteel. "What a royal fuck-up. Who is crazy enough to use Gamma EM tech on Earth?"

"We thought maybe it was Earth Corporate," Frost answered.

Han gave Frost a look that was invasive and derogatory. She was surprised he even went there. Then, just as she was about to admonish him openly, he saved himself.

"But we ruled that out after our sifters told us EC isn't developing Gamma EM tech."

"At least your sifters are thorough, as are ours. We think it's someone outside EC and UEU parameters. A random factor. Perhaps The Seniori."

"We have a real problem here, and we had better get a handle on it. Whoever it is must be very good at secrets if both of our nets have never detected them before," Keel added.

"We have every resource trying to identify the source of the transmission. We know it came from a sophisticated satellite that self-destructed after the pulse," Frost added.

He waved her hand over his palm, and a screen came up. He widened the screen to a larger format so everyone could see it. "Here is an image of the satellite. We've been scrutinizing it for any clues."

"We should cancel the launches." Keel knew his comment would elicit responses from all parties.

Olefors's look said it all. "Not a fucking chance," he said. "We need to get the cargo Offworld. Shenu's advanced defense systems can protect it."

Keel knew what Frost was doing and gave him the latitude to continue his neural monitoring of the situation.

"From what I hear, it can protect them," Han added.

Keel looked at Han. *She's as brilliant and hot as I remember,* he thought. *Not the time, Declan,* his inner voice chimed.

"Speculation is a foolish man's truth, Ms. Han," Keel said.

"Man's truth, General?"

Keel knew he was toast. "I meant man as inhuman, Ms. Han."

"Please, call me Miranda."

"Too soon," Keel said. "Let's leave it as Ms. Han until we get to know each other better." Han smiled and got a little wet between her legs at the same time. *Fuck, he looks even better in the daylight. Maybe this can work out after all.*

Olefors remained suspiciously silent. He was enjoying intellectual banter from people who knew nothing about the cargo and had no idea how important and consequential it would be to Humanity's future.

His silent demeanor gave Han reason to pause. She knew about Olefors, his clandestine nature, his propensity for using synths to access other neural dimensions, his innate brilliance, and, of course, the missing year, which fueled both speculation and ridicule on the part of many people but was just another mystery that Han was yearning to solve. She made a mental note:

Get inside Olefors's head. Invite him to trust you. But first, she had to be introduced to him. Something she was looking forward to.

There was no use in trying to sift Olefors or use a synth to get inside his mind. The man was impervious to coercion. Miranda would have to use every skill set to access Olefors' brilliance. But it wasn't just vainglory that motivated her. Han knew that with Olefors on her side, she might be able to challenge Tara Zhang to control EC someday. As if on cue, Frost brought Olefors over to Han.

"Dr. Olefors, this is Miranda Han."

"Dr. Han, I've been looking forward to meeting you. I am intrigued by your Dark Matter/Cold Fusion schematics for Athena. I hope we get to discuss them sometime. "

"I'd be delighted, Dr." Yes, this was good. They would bond on an intellectual level first, then, when they became colleagues, share a few meals and maybe some sex, she would use her feminine acumen to infiltrate him. Han laughed inside as she plotted. She was constantly bemused by her newly minted appetite for power. She had never had it before. It happened when Zhang infused it in her during her two-year training process with EC.

"Ok. Let's end the hellos and get this cargo to the maglev. The prime minister has authorized Cosulo to launch in t-minus 2 hours and Falcon in t-minus three hours."

With that, Olefors used his holopanel to lift the box and send it to the Falcon hold, where Keel and Titan squad would accompany the strange box on its maiden voyage into history.

CHAPTER TWO

TWINS

etta Rajastani was born Elizabetta Aranjani Rajastani. She spent her early years in London, where she lived until she was thirteen. On her birthday, December 30th, 2310, her mother, Leanna Rajastani, the Premier of Shenu, woke her in the middle of the night and informed her that they were going away for a few days. Betta vividly remembers that night because she experienced a strange premonition dream the night before.

She transformed into a bird of prey in her dream—an Osprey, she believed. As she patrolled the shoreline in search of food, she noticed another Osprey approaching her. When it flew alongside her, Betta realized this bird was an exact reflection of herself, a twin soul. Suddenly, the other Osprey flew right into her, merging them. At that moment, Betta's senses heightened; her eyesight, hearing, and awareness intensified. She could see schools of fish swimming beneath the water, hear them communicating with one another, and her vision extended for miles. In that experience, she felt a profound sense of peace, perfection, and unity. When she woke up, she felt euphoric, with her tear-stained pillow serving as evidence of her emotional experience.

She immediately thought of telling her mother about the premonition but couldn't reach her on a neural as her mother was always too busy to dote on her or even acknowledge her. Betta understood. Her mother was extremely busy. Her nanny, Kalit, raised her in her palatial house in Kensington Park.

She rarely saw her mother, except on weekends when she would take her Solar Sailer down from Shenu to take meetings on Earth. Betta wasn't upset about this arrangement. She liked it, as she always wanted to be alone, with her thoughts, without the bother or nuisance of other people's opinions and engrams bombarding her own. Leanna always said her sensitivity was a blessing, and Betta strongly agreed.

By then, Betta's father, Rajiv, and her brother Pashar spent all their time together on Malta in preparation for Pashar's entry into the Sidrani, an organization young Betta knew about but couldn't understand. All she knew was that her father and brother were strangers to her, and they were warriors of some kind, and her mother was too cerebral and inscrutable for Betta to relate to, even though she also knew that her mother loved her deeply.

Since she was six years old, Betta felt that something was coming, some test. At that age, she couldn't understand the test or when it would happen; she just knew it would come one day. For her part, Leanna never talked about this moment, and Betta was too confused or too shy to inquire about it. All she knew was that from her earliest memories, she was told she was destined for something special.

On this cold December 30th night, on her 13th birthday, she knew that something "special," that singular moment in time, was about to be revealed to her.

There was a strangeness to the evening. She'd skipped dinner because she wasn't feeling well and went to her room, where she lay in bed with a terrible stomachache. Leanna was in her Shenu offices downtown. As she was lying in bed, she unconsciously placed her hand down by her vagina. She knew all about sex and intercourse and never gave it much thought, but tonight, her hand found itself nestled between her legs. Instinctively, she began massaging herself. The sense of pleasure was more than she had ever felt before, and she immediately laughed, wondering why she hadn't discovered this pleasure center years ago. That thought passed quickly from her mind as she brought herself to her first orgasm. The experience let loose a flood of emotions pent up for so long.

Betta began crying and laughing simultaneously, Tears of joy and sadness mixed on her cheeks. She instinctively placed her hand to her face to taste her tears, seeing if she could discern which were tears of joy or sadness. She fell asleep soon after, only to be woken up by her mother at exactly 4:22 AM, the time of her birth some 13 years ago.

"We have to go," Leanna said quietly, even though they were the only ones in the mansion that sat quietly apart from the other homes in Kensington.

"Where are we going?" Betta asked. She was exhausted from her experience a few hours ago but knew from the tone in Leanna's voice that there was no way Leanna's exhortation would go unanswered. So, Betta got up and got dressed. As she did, she noticed Leanna pulling the sheet back from the bed and placing her hand on the soft, warm pool of liquid that lightly stained the 800-count pale pink sheets. Betta froze in place, embarrassed by what her mother was doing. Once Leanna finished her inspection, she turned to Betta with a smile Betta had never seen before.

"Where are we going?" Betta asked indignantly as she finished getting dressed and moved to the door to exit the room.

"Don't worry, dear one. We'll go for marzipan crepes at Maxim's afterward."

Dear one, Betta thought. *Marzipan Crepes afterward.* Whatever was going on wasn't some punishment, but Betta knew from Leanna's tone that whatever they were about to do would test Betta somehow. She realized this was the moment she'd been waiting for all her life.

"Let's go. We don't want to be late," Betta said as she walked down the long, curved staircase, caressing the oak-entwined Balustrade and passing by the porcelain Chimeras, which topped the newel posts. Leanna rushed after her, excited but fearfully nervous about what lay ahead. They left the mansion and got into an Aero.

"Cambridge planetarium," Leanna stated. The Aero floated onto its voltaic track and sped off into the night.

Betta and Leanna didn't say a word to each other on the short trip to Cambridge. Betta was still basking in the glow of her first orgasm, and Leanna was trying to organize everything about the evening, the events that preceded this moment, and the events that would follow so she could be as explanatory as possible after it was all over and her daughter's future would have been completely mapped out for her.

She knew a woman of Betta's independence and ability would feel hampered at first, but she also knew that Betta had as good a sense of the future and her place in it as anyone, even if she didn't recognize it now.

The Aero deposited them at the planetarium's landing port. They entered the building and proceeded to the wing devoted to Shenu. Betta had been here before but as a child. Tonight was so different, so unusual, that the planetarium took on a much more macabre tone. The darkness didn't help, and Betta was unsure why she was being brought there.

They entered the Shenu wing. Leanna went to a 5-D mural that depicted precisely what Shenu would look like—what you'd find inside, the different rings, and such. Leanna approached an image of the Shenu logo, a picture of the earth surrounded by a gold galactic compass and three concentric swirls representing the three rings, neatly stacked one on top of the other, like the floors of an immense building. She stood before the logo's center, and a scan beam appeared from the wall. Its blue rays scanned both Leanna and Betta.

"Recognizing Leanna and Betta Rajastani."

Betta immediately recognized GAIA's voice. It was a voice she'd grown up with, a constant in her life, speaking to her in dreams but never allowing Betta to remember them. She realized that GAIA's dream weaving was all part of the plan that culminated in this night. She followed her mother through the rear wall, which became opaque soon after they entered. A long corridor lit up as they proceeded, and Betta noticed the walls were made of nucleaton, the same substance Shenu was made from. As they descended deeper into the bowels of the planetarium, it got colder. Finally, they approached another set of doors. These were much bigger and glowed a deep violet. Leanna approached them, and another scan beam bathed them both in Violet light. Betta felt a sense of calm come over her.

"What's happening, Mother?" She finally found her voice after so many minutes of silent wonder.

"We're almost there, dear one."

There it was again, *dear one.*

"Where is everybody?" Betta asked.

"No one is here except you and me and…" Leanna took Betta's hand and led her to a solid wall. She pressed her hand into a specific spot, and the wall opened from the top. Betta resisted going into the room at first, but Leanna did something unheard of. She hugged her daughter tightly and kissed her head as she used to when Betta was much younger and thrived on Leanna's affections. After that, Betta had no more fear. The two women entered the chamber, and the wall closed behind them.

Once inside the chamber for a few moments, Betta's eyes adjusted to the sight of a cavernous room in the shape of a dome. In its center was an oculus from which a beam of silver light shone down on the obsidian flood underneath her feet. Betta immediately took her shoes off to feel the cool darkness of the floor.

"So, this is the chamber?"

Leanna was shocked at how mature Betta sounded at that moment, as if she'd grown up ten years in one hour. Of course, Leanna knew about the orgasm; that was part of what decided the course of action dictated by this moment. Leanna marveled at Betta's level of sophistication.

"Yes, we're in the GAIA chamber."

"Welcome, Betta Rajastani," GAIA said in a charming tone.

"Hello, GAIA. I've been wanting to meet you in person for years."

"Your mother was wise to keep you away for so long. You weren't prepared for this night, and neither was I."

"Until now," Betta said. GAIA laughed. It was a gentle laugh that invited you in to laugh as well, and so Betta did. Leanna began moving to the door.

"Mom, you don't have to go."

"Yes, I do, dearest. I'll come back in when you're done."

"With the inquiry?"

There it was again. Betta's cognitive gifts showered upon the moment. Leanna thought.

"You'll be fine," Leanna said reassuringly. Then she left. An awkward pause permeated the chamber.

"So, this is your show, GAIA. What now?" Betta said.

With that comment, the floor opened, and a gleaming gold chair rose from underneath it.

"My best advice is to get into the chair and hang on tight, Ms. Rajastani."

Betta looked around her for the first time, taking in the nesting chamber she'd heard so much about from her mother. She knew from early childhood that she was bred specifically to become a Level 6 adept. Still, she only recently heard that a specially designed geneticom was being readied for her to join with. She didn't know a lot, but that seemed to be okay. Her mother was also a Level 6 adept and the headmistress of the Hypatia School of Knowledge, where Level 6 adepts were trained. Only a handful would be chosen to join with a geneticom. The other 12 women, and only twelve in the world, were retained as scholars doing all the research and leg work that would inform the chosen Level 6s and their geneticom. The program was initiated in 2200 by a brilliant geneticist named Emily Harper. Her advanced work on nano computing and quantum life led her to the first rudimentary Geneticom she named Aurora.

She used her DNA to bond with her creation and then joined Aurora to help the UEU plan for the construction of Shenu, which was just one of the tasks given to Aurora. After that, the geneticom program proceeded quickly.

Young women from all over the world were sifted and either rejected or chosen for the pilot program. Leanna Rajastani, a Sidrana, the female counterparts to the Sidrani, was eventually chosen to join Aurora's progeny, GAIA. That pairing enabled the solution of many problems on Earth.

Poverty, climate change, and, to a lesser degree, war became obsolete with a geneticom at the helm. The UEU and EC both sanctioned the program. All data was shared between the two factions, and both had access to GAIA, so there would be no competition for her knowledge and problem-solving skills. All nuclear weapons were dismantled in 2230. Astrobiological advancements became commonplace.

The joining of Leanna Rajastani and GAIA was considered one of the great miracles of human evolution. After that, other Level 6's were indoctrinated into the program. All female. It was something about the presence of Hextetra, the spark that gave a newborn human its life, that made women able to join with their female geneticom counterparts. Men tried and died in the process.

Betta looked around and realized her nesting chamber had changed according to her moods. For the first iteration, she was underwater, surrounded by a panoply of sea life.

"Your innermost thoughts become your reality here. The nesting chamber reflects your ideas, beliefs, and deepest emotions. Please take your place."

Betta approached the nesting chair. As soon as she sat down, the chair surrounded her, immobilizing her.

"I feel constrained."

"It's normal for an initiate to feel restrained the first time they sit in a nesting chair. The more nervous you are, the tighter the chair will feel. For us to work together tonight, you must relax. With that, a small needle rose from the chair and injected a small amount of hyrax into Betta's neck.

"There, this sedative will help you relax," GAIA said in a soothing mellifluous tone.

"Why am I here?" Betta demanded.

"The more you fight this, the tighter the restraints will become. It would help if you gave yourself over to me. You must become what you fear most."

"Nonsense. Words without meaning," Betta said.

"Very well. You are to be tested tonight."

"Tested? For what?"

"Your insistent tone will get you nowhere. All I can tell is that you will rise to your higher self or be left behind to pick up the pieces of your life. You must give yourself to me."

The images surrounding Betta became more antagonistic. A volcano spewing lava, the killing of animals, murders.

"Please, Betta. Give yourself to me. I will never harm you, but I must be sure, and so must your mother."

"Be sure about what?"

"That all our planning, millennia in the making, shall come to pass. But for that to happen, you must trust us."

Betta looked around her, and the angry vision of a few moments ago transformed into a peaceful, tranquil forest. Then, a child laughed. GAIA, still just a voice, appeared to her as her mother.

"Perhaps this is a better way for us to communicate."

"Mother?"

"I am GAIA, but I am also joined to Leanna Rajastani, my twin. We are one soul, bifurcated but whole, longing for union. I can appear in this form, but only in this form. Your mother's DNA also shares this form. She is here with me. Trust us."

"Very well. What plans do you have for me?" Another needle pierced Betta's skull above her third eye. Betta went limp.

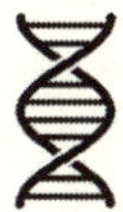

Where was she? What was this place? Doors upon doors, galaxies turning, Novas exploding, ships moving through space and time. She was floating in time, with no beginning or end. *This must be the fifth dimension of reality,* she surmised.

Her DNA was alive before her, each gene glowing in a different color. She felt like she was being torn apart, molecule by molecule, when another strand of DNA, this one alien to her, appeared. The three strands danced together for what seemed like an eternity. The genes flew off of their helixes and floated around her, recombining and separating hundreds of times, making her feel dizzy and nauseous. Betta knew she was witnessing something singular to her. Something too beautiful and fearful to fully comprehend. She felt profoundly weak as if all of her blood was drained from her body, leaving a desiccated corpse that blew away with the wind. Then, as soon as it started, it ended.

How long had she been asleep? She couldn't remember anything from the past hours. The nesting chamber was dark, then slowly and softly, a light began to dawn inside it. Leanna approached her daughter.

"What happened?"

"You'll feel tired for a while. Rest." Leanna said, stroking Betta's scalp.

"My hair? Where is it?"

"Your hair will be regrown before we leave here. A naked scalp is essential for the joining to proceed correctly."

"Why didn't you tell me?"

"I was forbidden to do so. This experience had to be approached with the utmost secrecy. No one except you, Gaia, and I know what happened tonight. None will ever know. It is a secret shared only by us."

Betta's head was splitting. The headache was unlike any she'd ever experienced before. She raised her hand to her forehead, and she felt a smooth stone where her third eye was located. She panicked.

"Mother. What is this?"

Leanna sat down next to her daughter and held her hand for the explanation that was to come. "The stone is called Trinium."

"Why is it embedded in my skull?"

"You've been…" Leanna looked for the right words because she knew she'd only have one chance to explain what had happened to her daughter. "You've been advanced."

"Advanced?"

"Yes. You've been asleep for three days. Your body needed to recover after the joining."

"The extra strand of DNA?" Betta said.

Leanna was surprised at Betta's understanding of what had happened to her.

"Yes, you were infused with another DNA strand."

"Why?"

"To join with UMA, seeing if you were compatible was necessary."

"Why didn't you tell me about this before?"

"GAIA forbade me to do so. We weren't even sure if you'd survive the procedure."

"You took a chance on my life?"

"No, my dear. You did. If you were not subconsciously ready for the procedure, it wouldn't have worked, and you would've never been able to endure the process. There was no way to know, and if you had known, your brain would've had time to prepare itself for this test, and then you might have died. Everything had to be done without your conscious recognition."

"What does this stone do?"

"It's a temporal transceiver. It will allow you to join with UMA, who also has a much larger Trinium stone inside her."

"Who developed this tech, Mother?"

"UMA. It would be best if you rested now. We'll be ready to go soon."

"What if I didn't want any of this?"

"Betta, I'm surprised at the question. GAIA and I have prepared you for this moment your entire life. You and UMA were joined in vitro. You know this for yourself. You decided on this course before you were even born. When you were inside me, we had this very discussion."

"I was conscious inside you?"

"Yes, of course. All Level 6 candidates are brought to consciousness in the sixth month of gestation. The TRNA."

"TRNA?" Betta aksed.

"Trioxyribonucleic Acid that was embedded in your DNA at birth laid dormant inside you until your first orgasm, which happened four nights ago. The hormones released during that orgasm ignited the TRNA inside you. The procedure you underwent joined your TRNA with UMA's TRNA. It had to be performed within 24 hours if the joining was successful."

"When can I meet UMA?" It seemed a natural question for Betta to ask.

"You won't be ready for that for ten years. You will begin your Level 6 training in one week. Once you are ready, you will be joined with UMA on Shenu. I need to conclave with GAIA. Once I'm done, we'll have crepes, as many as you want."

Leanna smiled, but Betta felt different. She touched the stone embedded in her forehead. She felt like a freak. Little did she know she would be recognized as the first of her kind, a human hybrid, the most advanced human on Planet Earth, for now.

Leanna walked back into the nesting chamber. The chair rose again from the floor and Leanna sat into it. Thousands of tiny tendrils wove from the floor and attached themselves to Leanna's scalp.

"What is your decision?" she asked.

"She is brilliantly stubborn, Leanna. That was different from what we had planned."

"GAIA, please. The infusion. Did it work?"

"I won't know for a day. Her pineal gland is unusual, strangely modified."

"Modified." Leanna was awestruck.

"Unlike any Level 6 before her."

"So, she's been accepted?"

"The procedure must proceed to its natural conclusion. Either she will live and mate with UMA or perish, and we lose them both."

"What happens then?"

"Leanna, you know the outcome from neither Level 6 nor human hybrid. She must be destroyed."

GAIA's words echoed inside Leanna's head for hours after that. She sat with Betta, now asleep, until daybreak. The hours passed so slowly that she felt like time was moving backward.

What happens if she can't survive? What happens to all of us? What happens to Pashar? Leanna cursed the day the Level 6 program was implemented 100 years ago. It was controversial at the time, but it saved humanity from itself. To join one supercomputer and one female together for eternity seemed an enormous gamble, but for all that time, the program worked.

Betta ate six crepes that night and went to bed exhausted, elated, and scared. What would the next ten years bring? How would she adapt to her new life of solitude and enlightenment? She lay awake for hours that night, casting permutations, wondering, crying, evolving.

The following week, she was relocated to the Hypatia school training center in Cairo, a fitting place for adepts to learn their trades in the shadows of the great pyramids restored to their 3500-year glory, clad in white limestone, with gold capstones. They resonated at their 528Hz algorithm and again glowed deep blue at night.

Betta would spend the better part of the next ten years living inside the great pyramid, studying the ancient Egyptian texts, the Book of the Dead, the Scrolls of Thoth, the genesis of the Emerald Tablets, esoterica that still held great reverence for the world of the Hierophants, the highest occult scholars who lived and breathed these ancient texts and their alchemical secrets. The ten years passed as if in seconds, and on March 21st, 2325, she began her new life which would be remarkable, exceptional, and filled with danger.

Pashar Kartikeya Rajastani was born on December 30th, 2302, the same time as his sister Betta. He thinks that while in utero, he and Betta spoke to each other, which wouldn't be unusual for a future Level 6 adept and a Sidrani warrior with Level 6 genetic markings. Even though he was a boy and there had never been a male Level 6 candidate, he made it through the indoctrination process and lived.

Her psychic healer told Leanna Rajastani she would have twins. The thought excited and confused her. She knew that she would have a daughter who would eventually become the highest-ranking Level 6 in history, and she was destined to join UMA, the newest geneticom, which was more advanced than any geneticom that came before her.

So, it was quite a shock when she did her first scan and saw two embryos. The doctor who did the scan, Dr. Danika Weston, marveled at how the twins were being nourished in utero.

An identical twin pregnancy usually involves two placentas and two amniotic sacs, which is considered optimal, as each baby has its nutritional source and protective membrane. Betta and Pashar were quite different. They shared the same placenta and the same amniotic sac. Weston had seen this only once before, and those twins never made it to birth. This alarmed Leanna as she was convinced that Betta was destined to be born but had little understanding of why she was having twins, which never ran in either her or her husband Rajiv's families.

It was incredible that they shared the same placenta and amniotic sac, and Weston counseled Leanna to take it easy during the pregnancy to avoid disturbing the embryo's development.

So, Leanna Rajastani stayed on Shenu as it was being built and never came back to Earth until the twins were born. The birth was arduous, and Leanna almost lost her life. During the pregnancy, there was a moment where Weston said that one of the twins might not make it and asked Leanna which one she would choose to save if she had to make the choice.

She naturally chose Betta but spent many hours rethinking her decision. It was a choice she never thought she'd ever have to make, but here it was. When labor came, Leanna endured 16 hours of agony, refusing to have a caesarian section. Finally, when it came time for the birth, both of her children came out within seconds of each other.

Danika Weston couldn't believe it. The twins were hugging each other, and in an even more incredible turn of events, they shared the same umbilical cord. Usually, twins are in mono, where the twins share an amniotic sac caused by the fertilized egg that will become an embryo, which splits very late into the term. Sometimes, the twins had two separate umbilical cords, which also posed problems as the cords might get caught around each other, strangling the twins, or one cord might get wedged behind the other cord, and one of the twins might die from suffocation.

In this case, the umbilical cord split in two at one end, feeding both twins simultaneously. Weston had never seen anything like it. The twins were born healthy, and Leanna breathed a sigh of relief. Weston speculated the twins would be incredibly close throughout their lives. Leanna knew it would be much more than that.

It was not unusual for a mother of twins to feel closer to one twin than the other. Leanna was no different. She knew that UMA would join with Betta and that her life would take a course that would take Betta away from her and humanity. It had been predestined. It had been decided long ago, and Leanna, being a Level 6, knew that Betta's life would be intertwined with UMA's, so she focused more on Pashar in the early years. Maybe it was a mistake. Perhaps she thought Betta needed less of her attention; maybe it was that mothers often have a closer relationship with their sons than their daughters. Whatever the cause, Pashar got more of her affection, and it became a problem between Leanna and Pashar's father, Rajiv, especially when Pashar turned seven and was told he'd be taken away from Leanna to begin training as a Sidrani warrior in Malta.

Pashar didn't want to leave his mother's side. He and Betta witnessed the bitter fights between Leanna and Rajiv, the moments that broke the relationship. Rajiv's tirades and Leanna's stoic refusals drove Rajiv mad. Pashar often wondered why they stayed married, but as they were both members of the Sidrani sect, the outside pressure to remain together until Pashar left for Malta precluded them from divorcing, which would've been better for everyone.

Like Betta, Pashar knew from an early age that he was destined for something different than other young men his age. He and Betta often wondered what their futures would hold and if those futures would split them apart. They were extremely close. Like some identical twins, they could usually read each other's minds and sometimes even communicate telepathically. They never told their parents about this ability but kept it to themselves, a secret they cherished as they did everything about their relationship. Pashar often wondered what would've happened if they were not brother and sister but met each other as friends. She was indeed beautiful; He could see how they could forge a long-lasting relationship if genetics hadn't gotten in the way.

Betta, of course, would never be able to have a normal relationship. She was to be wedded to a geneticom, and Pashar often found himself jealous of the journey his sister would embark upon for the rest of her life. A journey that didn't include him.

The day Rajiv took Pashar away from Betta and Leanna was among the worst of his life. He respected his father. Who wouldn't have some respect for the second in command of the Sidrani order, but he didn't love his father, nor did he like his father.

He was bound by a duty he never asked for or wanted. However, his life as a Sidrani warrior would do one miraculous thing for Pashar. It would free him from his father's influence, as Sidrani warriors were taken into clans when they came to Malta. Because Rajiv was Pashar's father, Pashar would never be placed in Rajiv's clan order.

This separation motivated Pashar to outshine even his father, to prove to Rajiv and even more to himself that he was born to not only become a Sidrani warrior but to surpass even his father, who he knew needed a comeuppance to put him in his place.

From the beginning, Pashar accelerated at his task. Khalid Bhat, the premier of the Sidrani order, chose him specifically to be a part of his clan. This was a great honor for Pashar, and he took his responsibilities seriously and became one of the most promising Sidrani warriors in its long-storied history. For ten years, Pashar trained with the Sidrani. He rarely saw his father, and when he did, their relationship was cold and formal. At that time, he hadn't seen his sister or mother for years.

He was elated when he got the notice from Khalid Bhat that he was to be part of the Blackhold order on Shenu. After ten long years of training, he would finally be reunited with his family. All but his father, Rajiv, who went missing five years ago on a covert mission for the UEU to Jupiter's moon Ganymede, a mystery that was still not solved as Pashar landed in Brasilia, then took an aero to the Aquarian Magport where his new life was to begin.

CHAPTER THREE

REUNION

The line to go through Secure Scan was longer than Betta Rajastani liked. Being the daughter of the Prime Minister of Shenu, not to mention the most decorated Level 6 of the UEU, she should have garnered more visibility and gained greater access to Cosulo and the boarding process. She deigned to use a solar sailor to get to Shenu, something offered to her, but she arrogantly refused.

She was not usually given to arrogance, but she felt very insecure today, and her arrogance was a deflective reaction to her insecurities. She knew this instinctively. After all, her arrogance was internalized and not driven outwards towards her fellow travelers. She could inhabit this precarious place for now, but soon, she'd have to abandon all feelings of arrogance as her life was about to change drastically.

Today, she felt much older than her 23 years, possibly because of her latest contact with UMA, the Geneticom she would be linked to for the rest of her life. Betta marveled at the link between her and her nano quantum sister, already on Shenu, well IN Shenu, as UMA was tied into every scintilla of Shenu's technology and heuristics.

Betta eagerly awaited their first meeting. She was only the fourth Level 6 to join with her Geneticom, UMA. Her mother, Leanna, was the 2nd and joined with GAIA, her Geneticom. Then, DIDO and Lucinda Gale joined briefly, but that joining ended in disaster.

Betta has no idea what the disaster was as it's the best-kept secret on the planet. Betta attempted numerous times to uncover the answer to the riddle but was consistently denied by GAIA and her mother, who were likely the only two beings aware of the truth. Secrets were never revealed between Geneticoms and their sisters.

Finally, there was Mara Gale, Lucinda's daughter, and her Geneticom, CASSANDRA, another pairing that ended in tragedy. Mara Gale supposedly committed suicide, and after that, CASSANDRA shut down and was never heard from again. Betta wondered what secrets she and UMA would share and what marvels and fears their first bonding would generate.

She turned her attention from introspective to extrospective as she looked around and saw Pashar Rajastani, her identical twin, strolling up to her. She hadn't seen him for ten years until yesterday, and at their first meeting, he seemed distant and overly cerebral, a usual stance for a Sidrani to take. He still had a bit of that boyish adolescence swagger about him. Still, Betta needed to remind herself that Pashar was among history's most decorated Sidrani cadets, outshining even their father, Rajiv.

She and Pashar shared some unique similarities. They were two halves of one Egg, and it was remarkable that they looked like the male and female versions of each other. Male and female identical twins were beyond an anomaly. It was impossible. Yet somehow, human evolution and a smattering of genetic manipulation allowed them to be exact, as unusual as that was.

They both had jet-black hair, which Pashar kept long and tied into a tidy bun. Their hair was straight as an arrow, aquiline noses, green eyes, and twin birthmarks on their hands that reminded Betta of The Flower of Life. They were olive-skinned, tall like their parents, and had matching dimples on opposite sides of their faces.

As children grow up, they frequently traded identities, Betta pretending to be Pashar and vice versa. It gave them both a heightened sense of what it was like to inhabit the skin of the opposite sex. It was also something they kept secret between them. Betta remembers many days when they would trade clothes, with Pashar pretending to be female and Betta pretending to be male.

It was an exhilarating time for both of them, the ease with which they could juxtapose their sexual identities and how they used to explore each other sexually with a childlike innocence until they were approaching puberty, which brought a stop to their sexual explorations. They never spoke of these moments again, but Betta often found herself thinking about those early days when they were inseparable and so close they could read each other's minds and share their dreams when they slept.

Why Betta was thinking about all this now was a bit of a mystery to her. She surmised that it was because she hadn't seen her brother for quite some time, and identifying their similarities made her feel closer to him, even though her Level 6 sense told her they were never further apart than this moment. Something had changed, most likely in both of them, to make Betta aware of the changes,

As a Sidrani, Pashar was kept apart from other humans to hone his incredible combat skills and neural military abilities so that when he finally joined the other Blackhold on Shenu, his Sidrani assets would be kept under control, as the Sidrani were the most mentally advanced soldiers on the planet, with psychic abilities that were part of their DNA. Killers bred for covert subterfuge, genetically engineered for both physical and mental battle, deadly, sometimes to each other.

Somewhat like the Sidrani, the Blackhold were a cadre of men and women who lived and breathed combat. Their Spartan-like bonds were a mystery to everyone around them, bonds that brought them closer to each other, joined in bisexual coitus, and sworn to die for each other. This bond wasn't just sexual. The Blackhold and their Sidrani counterparts were allowed to mate, but usually with each other. That way, their shared DNA profiles would always be held inside their cells as biomarkers. The men and women trained together, fought together, had intimate sex with each other, and formed familial bonds that strengthened as they fought and protected each other.

Their bisexual natures were always present, and any women or men who mated with them had to be screened for a DNA-compatible match so that any offspring would be able to be initiated into the Sidrani or Blackhold clans. If the child didn't want that, they could lead a life outside the Blackhold, but that rarely happened. Evolution favored the Blackhold, and every mother knew that their children could choose whatever life they desired. Still, many did not, preferring to be forever linked to each other through a shared love of combat, family, and sexual inclusion.

As Pashar approached Betta, he noticed she'd grown into an impressive young woman, something Pashar had known would happen. She was brilliant, beautiful, and highly intuitive.

He accessed three or four lessons in his cerebral implant as he walked towards her. His Sidrani training, plus some marvelously ingenious mind-seeding, had finally taken hold. The procedure was tedious and painful, but Pashar believed that pain equaled enlightenment, something he thought he inherited from his father.

He pretended to be occupied with anything but acknowledging her. He wasn't sure why he felt this way. He surmised that his competitive nature was behind his actions, which had been bred into him for the last ten years. Even as children, they were competitive. Twins often were.

She would become the most highly decorated Level 6 adept, and he would be the first Sidrani initiated into the Blackhold order, a rare exception to the Blackhold philosophy and one he wasn't sure would yield any fruit. Being separated from his Sidrani family was hard enough. After ten years, trying to fit into the Blackhold order and interact with his sister and mother would be trying enough. He thought it best to stop being petulant and begin to accept his fate.

The fact that his mother was a Level 6 factored heavily into his indoctrination. Being the son and brother of Level 6's meant that some form of their DNA flowed through his veins. That translated to power and influence among the Blackhold and even more so among the Sidrani.

As he and Betta made eye contact, he accessed the lesson on quantum entanglement, the sentience of Dark Matter, acquiring Quin Ying defense postures, and mining techniques on Europa while listening to loud music on an E-band adaptor. This device sat inside the inner ear and used the brain's electricity to power its wireless receiver. It enabled Pashar to listen to any music from any energy source he wanted, from any period played by any musician, streamed directly to his subconscious.

Betta ignored him as he approached, sensing he was doing the same. Pashar was always indifferent to Betta's snobbish demeanor as a child. Still, as humanity was about to change the very nature of its existence, he was annoyed that she ignored him, especially since he had decided to abandon his arrogant attitude a few minutes before.

He stood above her seated form, towering over her, using the first mental construct of The Sidrani, Hosaniri, to invade her solitude.

"It's not working, Pashar. I'm immune to Hosaniri." She casually glanced up from her protocol sim.

"Well, it did," he said. As you postulated your rather feeble response, I know exactly what you ate for lunch and what you think about inter-species mating protocols, and…"

She cut him off with a thought. "Stay the fuck out of my head."

"Just testing the Level 6 acumen."

"A test you'll always fail."

Betta returned to Shenu's specs, ignoring him even more now. With a swipe of her hand, she imaged a holo-model of Shenu, which rose before her, blocking Pashar's body and closing herself off. Shenu appeared in midair, spinning effortlessly as it did in geosynchronous orbit. She swiped and enlarged different images of the Space ring on her holopad, resting motionless in the air before her.

"Haven't you memorized those protocols yet?"

Pashar's indignant tone bothered Betta to no end, but she chalked it up to sibling rivalry on a galactic scale. She loved her brother, of course, but their lives had taken very different detours over the last ten years. Now reunited, she knew they would have to become more than siblings as Shenu moved from its nascent birth to the pinnacle of technological achievement.

They were cogs in the wheel. Betta, the most crucial Level 6 adept born in a century, and Pashar, the most decorated Sidrani soldier in history. Their new roles bore heavy on Betta's conscience, as her empathic abilities made every thought and emotion more pronounced. She knew Pashar was much better prepared for these kinds of pressures.

Betta longed for the solitude joining UMA would bring. She realized this was the last time she and Pashar would interact as just brother and sister and not the future scions of humanity. That thought softened her attitude.

She suddenly saw Pashar as the little boy he used to be, helping her climb a tree or master a Sidrani movement, protecting her when needed. She felt ashamed, having mistreated him a few minutes before.

"They're in seven different languages," she replied, noticing it took her a long time to answer his question.

Pashar kept up the interrogation without missing a beat. "Didn't your Level 6 training give you access to language matrices to be downloaded?"

"Yes, but I like to do it the old-fashioned way."

"Suit yourself. I take all my directions neurally. Then, I know every battle strategy, the outcomes of every previous battle, and the history of the people I'm fighting. All up here." He pointed to his head.

"The warrior mentality on full display. Not very enlightened. You must've gotten that from father. "

"He was your father, too." Pashar retorted. "Father was not a man of war. He was a man of peace. "

"No. He was a man who made war in the name of peace. Your blind devotion to him goes against everything you were taught, yet you still bow at his altar."

"He was a hero," Pashar said indignantly. "You sully his memory with your slander."

"One army's hero is another's tyrant," Betta countered.

"You hated him, yes, even though he doted on you. Maybe all this Level 6 mumbo jumbo has soured you on men. After all, there are no male Geneticoms or Level 6s."

"That's because female mental and emotional constructs are more suited to peace and higher reasoning."

"Yeah, keep telling yourself that. Is that what defines you?"

"We all know the male godhead was responsible for so much of what went wrong with humanity, and our father was no different."

"Father's dead. Can't you let your hatred die as well, or is your hatred what inspires you to be a better person, a better adept?"

His words rang in Betta's ears. She got up and walked ahead of him to the scanning area. As she approached, she and Pashar were met by two armed Blackhold guards.

"Who are you?" Pashar barked.

"Sergeant Francine Moore, Delta wing. The Prime Minister sent us to..."

Pashar cut her off unceremoniously, showing his snobbery. "Watch over us?"

He tapped his left hand. A screen appeared in the air above his palm. After a moment, Leanna Rajastani appeared as if an apparition were before him. She looked a bit stressed, something somewhat foreign to Pashar, who saw his mother as the coolest head in any room.

She was measured, thoughtful, and brilliant, but he knew better than to mistake her thoughtfulness for weakness. Leanna was as tough and wise as they came. Clever to a fault, logical to the point of annoyance. She was the foremost intellect on the planet, an intellect that matched her beauty.

Betta always said Pashar had a mommy complex. So be it. If that were the case, Leanna was the most perfect mother alive and he'd lay down his life for her at any time, any day, without question, just as he knew she would do for him.

Her holoimage was so clear it was as if she were in the room. The tech was the product of an advanced holoimage technique that was perfected a hundred years earlier by the lunar physicist Gunnar Radstrom, one of the first Holotech scientists born and raised on the moon and never left it.

For Lunars, life on the moon was home. Earth was that other place, foreign and green. Lunars preferred their variable gravity environments. Reacclimatization to Earth meant extensive bone density replacement therapy and severe numbing headaches. No, Gunnar preferred the moon. His soul was lunar.

Holoimaging became highly advanced in the 24th century. If people chose to, they could live their entire lives in a holo-sim, and for millions, that life was what they chose. Eventually, they gave up their bodies and allowed their minds to become a part of the great ONE, a holo-planetary environment that allowed them to exist outside of human boundaries and have absolutely no impact on the real world, Pashar's world, the world of the living.

In the 23rd century, there was a movement to see if humanity wanted to leave their bodies for good and exist inside the Sim world. Surprisingly, billions of humans chose not to live that existence. It seemed that striving for life, dealing with adversity and success, joy and disappointment, death and sorrow, were things humans realized defined their existence.

A life of fantasy, where you did whatever you wanted, became a passing phase. Humans wanted to live, to breathe, to die, to believe. That evolutionary perspective surprised humanity and was the key to its acceptance of 5th dimension of reality. Once humanity embraced itself and its non-corporeal nature, 3rd and 4th dimension constructs gave way to the illumination of the 5th dimension, where the mind evolved to accept its light body, its essence, and its oversoul, enabling humanity to become clairvoyant, empathic, and whole.

The 5th dimension wasn't exactly nirvana, however. Just because humanity achieved a certain level of advancement didn't mean it lost its impulse to compete, cheat, lie, and kill. Those impulses still existed, but they receded into the shadows, the id, lurking, waiting, making them whole.

Leanna Rajastani embodied true 5th-dimensional ideology. She looked serene and oddly otherworldly, but that serenity hid a fierce warrior inside. One of only a handful of women indoctrinated into the Sidrana, she was, therefore, closer to her son when it came to military matters than her daughter.

"Mother, you sent guards?" Pashar's tone was somewhat playful.

"This is a dangerous journey, Pashar. Someone tried to sabotage the cargo mission."

"I am a Level 9 cross-arts fighter, a member of the Sidrani. I can take care of myself," Pashar said.

"And what about your sister? "

"Betta? She's a Level 6 adept. She can sense trouble a mile away."

"Then call it a mother's prerogatives. Pashar. Please do this for me. Safe journey." With that short rebuke, she was gone.

"Shit." Pashar's annoyance was palpable.

"You'll thank her one day for her protection," Betta said as she entered the scanning pod.

"Did your training tell you that? "

"No. Your ignorance."

She walked ahead of him, and Moore followed them. They approached the scanners. Betta placed her hand inside the scanner, and a map of her blood vessels came up. A venal scan of her hand was done and then matched to previous venal scans. They matched. A lock was released, and Betta moved through the detectors when a guard stopped her.

"I'm sorry, Ms. Rajastani. Your cat will also have to be scanned."

"Cat?" Pashar asked with a smile.

"There's a quarantine against all animals for six months," Moore said.

"She's a synth." Betta reached into her cloak and pulled out a Siamese cat. She handed it to the Blackhold guard, who placed it under a larger scanner. A bright flash of light frightened the cat, and Betta instinctively reached for it.

"She'll be all right. We got advanced ok from your mother," said the guard.

Another guard was scanning the cat images. He nodded and then gave Betta the animal back. Betta proceeded to the entry port.

"Whiskers and I thank you."

"Spoiled." Pashar moved after her.

Past security, they entered a covered walkway that led them out to Cosulo, the maglev that would be their home for the next 12 hours. As they approached Cosulo, Betta felt a rush of something. Was it nerves or excitement? No, it was something a lot more palpable. Something was bothering her. She sensed something very odd. Fear. But of what? She kept it to herself for now, but usually, when she felt this kind of fear, something was not right. She accessed her sophisticated 6th sense algorithmic protocol centered in her amygdala.

"What's wrong?" Pashar must've sensed it, too.

"Do you feel it?" she asked him.

"Not really, but you do."

"Something's wrong."

"Should we alert anyone?"

"No," she said. "I need to source the fear and then analyze the details." Pashar placed his hand on her shoulder, a meaningful gesture of comfort she appreciated more than she could express.

They moved off the walkway and into the maglev. The journey was beginning, but they both felt the journey to Shenu would have consequences. All they could do was be alert and tuned into their surroundings. If anyone could source this danger, it would be a Level 6 adept and master Sidrani warrior. Or so they thought.

CHAPTER FOUR

COSULO

The 200 dignitaries, a gathering of the most influential figures of the UEU and EC, were assembled in the grandeur of the Cosulo Amphitheatre, awaiting the commencement of a truly historic event. The rare convergence of these two factions in person was a testament to the gravity of the occasion, a moment that would be etched in the annals of interstellar diplomacy.

Unaware of the brewing storm in Earth's orbit, the dignitaries sat in excited anticipation, their hearts beating in rhythm with the impending momentous event. The turmoil of the Gamma EM disaster was a distant echo, unable to disrupt the order of this significant day.

"Goddamn it!" Harrison Byrnes yelled, more at himself than anyone around him, as he was alone in his prep room, putting on his new UESU uniform, which, like all the others, was too tight at the neck. "Shit," he moaned. *They can build a space ring out of Nucleoton and create AIs that can save us from ourselves, but they can't make a flight suit that can fit.*

Exasperated with his lack of success, he left the top button open. At least now he could breathe and speak. If he were at all honest with himself, he would've recognized that he had put on another 5 pounds since he was measured for the damn thing. *Nerves.*

As he gazed at himself in the mirror, he thought his 45-year-old frame looked pretty good. The beard he'd grown for the occasion had come in nicely, accentuating his hazel eyes.

He admitted to himself long ago that he was a narcissist, something he knew women disliked or said they disliked, but he believed that narcissism was akin to confidence, something he had worked hard to perfect.

At his core, he felt he was an incomplete person, but maybe that desire to always make himself a better person, a better human, that

Altruism that pervaded his existence kept him striving for a better life and world.

He'd received Frost's holo-message a few minutes before, asking him to sub for him as Frost dealt with the disaster in the jungle that had consumed everyone in Aquarian Centcom. It was just a part of the long journey to this day, but also, as usual, it didn't ruffle his somewhat saturnine personality.

Byrnes was used to pressure. He craved it. Standing in front of the mirror, he realized that he had been working over 20 years for this day. It was two decades of extreme events, changes around him that couldn't have ever been predicted, love affairs gone terribly wrong, dangers he faced and was often weakened by, and, of course, co-creating the UESU's most valuable technological asset, Athena, the first Dark Matter/Cold Fusion drive ship ever created.

That alone was considered a marvel of creation. Athena brought up memories of Miranda Han. Byrnes began to sweat at the subconscious messaging his hippocampus was sending about Han. She was brilliant and acerbic to a fault. Byrnes hadn't seen her for over ten months, and he both relished and dreaded seeing her again on the way up to Shenu.

He tried to tamp down his mental anxiety, but as usual, it got the better of him. This was the one thing that prevented him from becoming a part of the Blackhold, something he used to regret, but that regret was replaced by the realization that the Blackhold was never a natural path. He was too emotional, visceral, and unpredictable for such a constrained life. He was glad his best friend Declan Keel was the commander of the Blackhold. It was the right choice. Byrnes would have been woefully unprepared for such a huge responsibility. He was commander of Athena, and the perks it gave him were much more his style. He needed freedom and unpredictability in his life.

Stepping out of his prep room, Byrnes found himself in a reflective mood. After ten months of isolation, the prospect of reuniting with Miranda stirred a whirlwind of emotions within him. Guilt, anger, and a tinge of regret clouded his thoughts, leading him into the murky waters of self-questioning.

He moved out of the shadows of the past and into the sunlight, bathing in the future as he approached the stage. He paused for a beat and looked out over the crowd. *Fuck me,* he thought. Everyone was here. Every dignitary he liked and hated. Every UEU and EC asshole he had fought with for funds for Athena to be completed. As he scanned the audience, he came upon Pashar and Betta Rajastani. Seeing them sitting in the front row made the moment more intense. Pashar Rajastani hadn't been seen for over ten years. Byrnes remembered some UEU brass telling him Pashar was being trained secretly by the last Sidrani masters on Malta. Byrnes knew that having someone as skilled as Pashar would make Keel happier than he'd ever been. Having a true Sidrani master on his squad would increase efficiency and confidence.

Then there was Betta Rajastani. Beautiful, Byrnes thought. Just like her mother. Serene, confident, sexy, a formidable combination for a Level 6 Adept, soon to be bonded to UMA, the most advanced Geneticom ever created. Byrnes could only guess how that bond would affect the AI, Betta, and the world, but he felt much safer and more secure knowing that the twins would be up on Shenu with him.

Now that he had gotten all his preliminary observations, he focused on the task. He adjusted his Adrenax mixture and stepped out of the shadows and into the light.

Thunderous applause greeted him. He moved to the center of the stage, adjusted the holoshell protocols, turning the room into a three-dimensional planetarium, and pressed his wrist.

"Thank you, and welcome to orientation for the first-ever commercial use of the Dressen maglev space elevator system. My name is Harrison Byrnes. I am the commander of the starship Athena. I will be the ranking officer escorting you up to Shenu. Today, you'll be traveling in Cosulo. If you activate your holoscreen, you can follow along a bit better. I'll make this brief since most of you are somewhat familiar with the Globix systems, but I will elaborate for the newcomers who are not."

Holograms appeared in front of each audience member so they could get a firsthand look at what Byrnes was talking about. A 3-D CGI image of the Maglevs also appeared. Byrnes waited for everyone to access the holograms and then proceeded.

"The maglevs work on an advanced free electron laser beam technology. Simply put, we travel in this spherical container, attached to one side of the carbon nanite ribbon, providing a smooth ride into orbit. A laser beam of 240 megawatts of energy is on the other side of the craft. That energy is transferred to photovoltaic cells made of Gallium Arsenide (GaAs) attached to the lifter, which converts that energy into a gravitational wave. The trip will take 12 hours. We will ascend 75 miles an hour and arrive on Shenu at 0600 on Monday, May 15th. Once aboard, you'll find Cosulo as comfortable as a 5-star hotel. You might've noticed another maglev as you entered the base. That's Falcon, our sister ship. She is devoted only to military duty. There will be an emergency drill of all safety systems at 1200 hours today, where we will go over safety procedures. Now, about the systems onboard. If you pull up your protocol guides and scroll to the operations manual, we'll continue."

Miranda Han approached the stage as Byrnes was finishing his lecture to thunderous applause. For a moment, she thought she could see him bask in the adulation, something new for him, but then again, she hadn't seen him for months. *People change,* she thought, but not Harrison. Byrnes was still looking at the audience as he exited the stage.

"Nice presentation. How long did it take you to get your nerves in check?"

Dammit, Byrnes muttered. *She doesn't let anything go.* "Samson was supposed to give it but got tied up with this sabotage business," He said.

"I know. I was with him," Han countered.

Byrnes walked away from her towards the door. Han stopped him. "That's it?"

"That's what?" He promised himself he wouldn't get annoyed, at least not in the first 15 seconds of their rapprochement. During the previous ten months, Han was in China, smoothing over various negotiations with Zhang. He was on the moon and up on Shenu, preparing Athena for its maiden voyage, now just two weeks away.

If he and Han couldn't get their shit together by then, it could get ugly, something Lenna Rajastani said she wouldn't allow. Byrnes remembers her exact words as "Get your shit together, Harrison. Do whatever it takes to get Han on side." So far, that wasn't going very well.

"You just walk away?" Han demanded.

"Miranda."

"Commander Han."

"Commander, I know you're upset, I understand, but it wasn't my call."

"It's amazing how you never take responsibility for your actions," she derided him.

"It wasn't my call. Sam was supposed to explain it to you."

"Oh, he did, Harrison."

"Commander."

"Harrison." Her turnabout of the appellation bullshit made Byrnes even angrier.

"If there's one iridium chip out of place, one Axion disrupted, one uncoupled photon."

"Miranda. Please. I have as much at stake as you do."

"No, you don't. You don't have Tara Zhang breathing down your neck every minute, waiting for results, hoping you'll fail so she can get rid of you and put someone else in your place."

"That would be impossible. You were chosen by both UEU and EC brass. You designed the engine specs and just about everything else on Athena. She would've done it by now if she wanted to eliminate you. Have faith in the process, Miranda. Just like I have faith in you, you're a genius. Start acting like one instead of a spoiled child."

With a mix of praise and condescension, he walked away. Han didn't follow him this time. His words stung in her ears, as they always did. He was right, of course. She was invaluable to the mission. While Byrnes commanded Athena, she was the one who had nurtured the technology that led to the most significant advancement in interstellar propulsion in history.

Athena's creation was based on Dark Matter, which was discovered to be sentient. The concept was revolutionary and groundbreaking: 75 percent of the entire universe composed of sentient matter. The discovery was even more impressive than anyone had imagined. This ship could converse, reason, think, extrapolate, and communicate without ego or the desire for self-importance. More importantly, Athena was distinctly female and, true to her name, a goddess—at least in Miranda Han's eyes.

As they exited the hall, Miranda thought about her behavior and how childish she was being. It was time to "woman up" with him. No matter what else had gone on before, if the next century was to be productive and bear fruit, her relationship with Harrison Byrnes would have to grow with it.

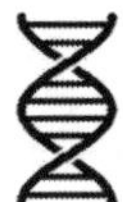

Olefors and Keel stood on Falcon's deck as the palladium box floated into its cargo hold and settled down with a gentle whoosh. From this vantage point, the maglev was huge, much bigger than Olefors thought, and a fantastic example of UEU and EC tech.

"You're holding your breath, Dr."

Keel's superior tone made Olefors a bit jumpy, but he also noticed he was extremely nervous. Maybe it was about the scare in the jungle; perhaps it was about the reveal of what was in the box that he had planned for 0900 on their way up to Shenu. He'd never been this nervous about anything before. Why now?

A surge of military activity surrounded Falcon. Regenebots—robots capable of self-repair through self-replication techniques—floated and zipped around the magnetic levitation (maglev) train, checking for leaks, conducting last-minute technical surveys, and ensuring this critical mission proceeded smoothly. The Regenebots varied in size, ranging from very small to very large. Modified for military purposes, these bots were equipped with infrared laser technology, motion sensors, ion defense beams, and exceptional mobility in the air, on the ground, in water, and even in deep space. Rather than engaging in warfare themselves, they served as sentinels designed to prevent humans from entering into unnecessary conflicts, which had nearly decimated the population on multiple occasions.

Commander Dara Gold approached Keel and saluted. "The Blackhold are ready for debriefing, General." Keel walked away from Olefors in mid-sentence, marginalizing him again. He stood erect and imposing before the Blackhold, now assembled on the launch pad.

"Good morning. A few items before we begin the mission. The R-bots will ascend with us to the edge of the thermosphere, then keep a perimeter below us. After that, we'll be receiving telemetry from Shenu. We will not stop in the acclimatization zone; we will all be given poly-oxide infusions to keep our bodies in balance. Only Dr. Olefors, myself, and those Blackhold I've already debriefed will be allowed on C-deck, where the cargo has been secured. Questions?"

No one responded. *There was never much need for questions with Keel,* Dara Gold thought. He was so resolute in every decision and every utterance that to ask a question would be to assume that he didn't give the proper instructions or that he didn't know what he was talking about. That, in her mind, would be a grave error. She saluted, then turned to the rest of the squad.

"Thank you, general. Alpha Squad. Move out." The Blackhold moved in unison onto Falcon. Keel and Olefors followed. The giant Trichromium door closed behind them.

Back on Cosulo, Frost and Han were on the bridge waiting for final confirmation to begin their journey to Shenu.

"I heard you saw Harrison." Frost was mildly curious about how Han's first meeting with Byrnes might have gone.

"Fuck, Samson. Is there nothing sacred with you?"

"Well, it wasn't any kind of super sense," he responded calmly. "The reports were flying all over the base. Did you know Han and Byrnes saw each other? Don't be surprised that it was news after your very public bitch fest about how much you hated him after the decision."

"It wasn't a decision; it was a punishment, and you know exactly why."

"I know you blame yourself, but it was Tara's bad decision. Stealing top-secret plans for the new Dark Matter drive was not a good move, Miranda."

"Just following orders doesn't apply here. I knew what I was doing was dodgy."

"Dodgy? How about wrong?"

"I designed that drive, created every molecule of it in my lab," she snarled.

"It doesn't matter. Top secret is top secret. You knew it, Zhang knew it."

"It just got out of hand," Han snapped.

"You make it sound like a bit of gossip." Frost reminded her. "Well, it's over and done with. Little harm, small foul," he added. "The DM drive is installed; Athena is ready for test flights, and you're on your way to destiny."

Han was sure this was all an elaborate game to make her forget about the Gamma EM situation, and possibly himself.

"I'm glad everyone is laughing at a grave matter," she said weakly.

"Oh, give it a break," Frost said. "You know you were dying to see him, to dig the knife in, to confront him."

Han tried to turn away to hide her smile, but she figured a little fun might make the uncomfortable conversation go a bit more smoothly.

"Ok, I saw him. We bickered, made peace, and got some tension released."

"You didn't fuck, did you?" He smiled.

"I won't even countenance that question with a response. I hate the man. Remember?"

"Nonsense, you love him, so it gives you license to hate him. Remember, you're parents to Athena. That bonds you together forever."

"How sophomorically insane you sound. Please stop trying to euphemize every action I take. We love Athena. That's all."

"Uh huh," Frost chided.

"Fuck you, Samson. Stay focused."

Frost smiled and turned his attention to Natasha Brinkov at the console, going through her dance as Cosulo began its countdown.

"Crewman Brinkov. Alert Aquarian base, we are ready for ascent."

Brinkov waved her hand in a clockwise motion to 6 O'clock. "Aquarian, this is Cosulo Centcom. Cosulo is set for launch." The reply came neurally. "Aquarian base signals green. Defense perimeter shield controls at our discretion for ascent vector."

"Take her up, Ms. Brinkov."

"Neural interface nominal. Free electron laser nominal, Shenu signals all ready."

Brinkov waved her hand over a holoconsole, and the ship rose. With that small instruction, a giant red laser beam shot up into the large array on the craft's starboard underside, and it started its effortless rise into the sky. Cosulo's trip to Shenu marked the beginning of over a century of planning for those on the ground. The marvel of the technology propelling Cosulo also created an incredible physical picture as this oval-shaped tritanium cylinder carrying the most essential Earthlings began its breathtaking silent ride into history.

Frost and Han breathed a sigh, but it was not in relief. Frost's harbinger training could sense something else would test them over the next 24 hours. As if they had one mind, Han looked at him with that worried look she only gets when she feels out of control, on the edge.

"I know." Frost turned to her. Without exchanging a word, they knew what the other was thinking. Perhaps their psyops training keyed them into each other's neurals. Whatever it was, they both knew something else was going to happen.

Frost touched Han's arm reassuringly, but the last thing he felt was reassured. He wouldn't feel better until Cosulo and Falcon safely docked on Shenu. A lot can happen in 12 hours. Han grabbed his hand. She had never felt these kinds of nerves before. Her truncated Level 6 training might have been incomplete, but she had enough training to know that these feelings weren't nerves but premonitory. Frost turned to her as if on cue.

"I need a drink." Frost tried a smile, but it turned into a worried grin.

Frost took her hand and led her out of the room. He could feel his emotions rising around him. Hers as well. He knew it was the wrong time for the display, but even the most rigorous training couldn't quell these feelings.

"There's a bar on A deck," Han said.

With that, they left the Cosulo Bridge. "Zai Jian," Han said quietly. But before she did, she looked up into the sky above. Even in daylight, Shenu's impressively massive ring could be seen. *Jia,* she said to herself. The Chinese word for home kept repeating as she left the bridge, on her way to a few drinks, a Naltran, and a nap.

It was a hot day in Shanghai, hotter than usual, but Tara Zhang never felt the heat. She hated traveling with other people, preferring to use her solar pod that traveled 300 feet above them. After all, EC was the organization that developed solar voltaic transports and sold them to the world for a profit, so why shouldn't she have a fleet of them at her disposal?

That was an exciting word to Zhang: disposal. Everything else in her world was somewhat disposable because, eventually, everything became disposable as new things needed to be created or invented to make room for outdated things. This included technology, morals, and, of course, people.

After the city was submerged in 2201, the new Shanghai was built entirely as a floating city, rising above the sea. It joined other major coastal cities such as Mumbai, New York, London, Amsterdam, Sydney, Rio, and Cape Town in redesigning their environs to accommodate Climate Change. Floating cities were also a creation of EC tech, and Zhang made sure Shanghai was the most beautiful of all. Many other cities weren't so lucky.

The preferred mode of transportation was podding or using pods that traveled along elevated solar-powered magnetic tracks to get from place to place. Invisible tracks gave rise to the sight of solar pods flying to and fro in the air, day and night, adding a decidedly futuristic touch to the 24th-century world.

Tara Zhang marveled at her empire as she traveled to her offices. She was always in a state of self-analysis, justifying her behavior, if only to herself. To aid in her self-serving justification, she decided long ago that she wasn't a bad person. It was her favorite meme of self-justification. After all, she was altruistically inclined as long as it financially benefited her and EC, her foster child whom she groomed from birth over a century ago. She mothered EC like it was alive, even though it was just a trademark and bank account. But it was hers, her domain, her fortress.

It's not that she despised other people. She was the leader of about 1 billion of them. Still, she felt keeping an air of constant mystery about herself and her life gave her an aura of mystique that very few ever had the opportunity to break through, certainly not unless she wanted them to.

She relished her sardonic inscrutability and privacy. Let them talk, let them speculate. As long as no one ever got close enough to see any of the cracks, she could always maintain the appearance of superiority, something she desperately needed to keep everyone around her in line.

She was meticulous about her appearance to a fault. Her motto was always to look the part, even if you don't feel the part.

Today, she felt extremely confident, as exhibited by her attire. She loathed dresses, only using them for sexual occasions as a dress was always easier to hike up than pants to pull down. She used sex like a cudgel, berating both men and women into submission so that when they gossiped about her, it was always about her being in control. She didn't need anyone's approval for her behavior, but when she wanted approval, or in the worst case, needed it, it was always the mirror that answered her back, reflecting something inside her that she loathed but loved, as it was the only thing that made her feel human, her burden to bear, her cross to hang herself on.

It wasn't self-pity. She had no time for that. It was self-preservation, which in so many cases felt like pity, only more painful, as she sometimes didn't even know what she was preserving and for whom. She laid on the veneer of impenetrability so heavily that she often didn't even recognize herself.

Still, no one would ever see the little ten-year-old girl crouching in the corner of an EC nesting school as her beautiful, sexy headmistress held the power cord taut and brought it down on her back like a flagellate, but without the piety to accompany it, the reason for the beating something she knew she had control over, but let it happen anyway.

She often wondered what in her makeup led her to be masochistic, and many times, when looking in the mirror, the answer came back as the need, the desire to be punished for all the mean thoughts and deeds she's brought down on others.

Tara Zhang, the apparition, was the counterpart she saw every time she looked in the mirror. This is why she had all mirrors removed from her offices and residences; her vampiric nature was too shy or scared to see who would be looking back.

The only mirrors were in her bedroom, for those moments when she allowed Vera, her girlfriend, to use the same power cord her headmistress used to punish Tara for misbehaving, making her stand naked in the corner with her hands above her head as the old scars reopened. The rush of adrenaline that followed made Tara Zhang cry like the little girl who never left her but always maintained some twisted control over her.

Her pod followed its magnetic voltaic track, floated 500 stories into the air, deposited Zhang in her office, and then disappeared into the floor. Zhang approached her desk and sat down.

The desk was a classical Biedermeier, worth a fortune in 2325. Her chair was a classic Getsuen Diamond wingback, worth millions in 2001 and priceless now.

Zhang's love for antiques permeated every aspect of her life, from her neo-classical home with every modern gadget one could own to a vintage Rolls Royce Silver Shadow converted into a Solar Sailer. The technology EC developed over 75 years ago enabled magnetic rays from the sun to power vehicles on Earth and in space.

Once humanity found ways to harvest energy from the sun and make it profitable, humanity made the long-distance jump from a Type I society on the Kardashev scale, which was achieved in 2145, to a Type II society, which was completed in 2278 — feasibility begat extension of life. The Earth, of course, was never in any real danger. Slogans such as 'Save the Earth' became trite and misleading after the wars of the 22nd century. If humans didn't get their shit together, they would go the way of the elephants and polar bears. Finally, after discovering how to access every ounce of energy put out by the sun, humanity crossed the great divide of obscurity and found its place in the sun because of the sun.

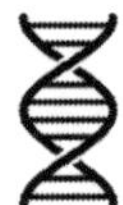

Zhang had little patience for anything today. She knew about the Gamma EM burst from Near Earth Orbit, which scared her. Gamma EM tech was outlawed. Even the great Tara Zhang had no idea who would be so stupid to use it unless they were more advanced in their scientific understanding than every living scientist on Earth.

On Earth. That idea made her laugh. What if the tech was developed Offworld? By whom, though? She knew every nefarious player in the solar system. Hell, she fucked half of them and had dirt on just about all of them. She would've known if any of them were developing Gamma EM tech. The fact that she didn't caused her more than a bit of distress. It didn't just mean that someone had developed tech to end the world; they were someone she had never heard of. *Shit. Someone more intelligent and fucked up than I am.*

She decided to bother Miranda Han about the goings-on at Aquarian to distract herself from unpleasant thoughts. She pressed her wrist and opened a neural. Hans Holosim appeared before her.

"I saw they just launched," Zhang said.

"Yes, we're onboard."

"Is Frost with you?"

"Yes, Tara, but you already knew that."

Zhang smiled and chuckled a bit. "I know. Just checking to see if you two are getting along."

"I have no issues with Samson. That's your bailiwick."

"I just want his frequency, Miranda."

"You'll be long gone before that happens. Harbinger frequencies are only known to one person, the Harbinger and GAIA, and she can't be bargained with, bribed, or hacked."

"Too bad," Zhang countered. "So. Is everything proceeding as planned?"

"Yes, we're about an hour into the launch."

"And the cargo?"

"Secured on Falcon, though no one but Olefors knows what it is. Any word from your sources?"

"No. Everyone is baffled. Olefors has fucked everyone on this one."

"That's his MO. Tight-lipped, cool Swede," Han added.

"Add arrogant asshole," Zhang said. "Well, we have to play his game. For now. I'll have further instructions for you once you're on Shenu."

"Copy." Zhang ended her call. Her intercom buzzed. "Yes."

"Ambassador Grenell arrived for his 11," said her Transhuman assistant Nena.

When Transhumanism became a movement in 2245, protocols related to AI were established similar to those Asimov detailed in his treatises some 350 years before.

However, Transhumans were different from R-bots or Geneticoms. They were more advanced than humans in many areas, including physical strength. Still, some protocols were enshrined in their evolutionary matrices, which included a mechanism to keep their educational advancement to a basic level of being able to do tasks but not excel in any meaningful way. They could understand and carry out tasks but could not engage in any manner of advanced thought. It was a controversial decision to limit their abilities, but both UEU and EC echelons agreed that Transhumans were best created to assist humanity, not surpass or subvert it. In essence, they gave up sentience for immortality. Such was the case with Nena, who was now motioning to the door, where Grenell was waiting.

"Send him in." Zhang straightened in her chair. Grenell was her ambassador to the UEU. She liked him, as he was hand-picked and sifted by her. He was also a master Sifter, a few Levels below a Harbinger like Samson Frost, who was in a league of his own. Zhang wished Frost was more amenable to her style of persuasion, but she also knew he was incorruptible and, therefore, dangerous to her and EC.

The door to the antechamber went from obsidian to clear, which allowed Grenell to enter the antechamber. Once inside, he was electron scanned and sifted by her thorough legion of R-bots specifically programmed to her specifications. As the premier of EC, only she had the authority to program her R-bots. They were answerable to her neurals only and operated on her cranial frequency. They did everything she wanted, from cleaning her offices to killing her adversaries. *Why do it yourself when your personally sifted R-bot can do it for you?* she often thought.

After Grenell's electron scan, he entered the office. As soon as he walked towards Zhang, the door went solid again.

"Love the new door," he said.

"Made from a polymer they discovered at Nemo base on Io a few months ago," she said confidently. "It has transfer density properties."

"Make for a formidable IC."

"Not your concern. Report."

"The Gamma EM pulse came from a satellite of unknown specifications and design?"

"Meaning?"

"Meaning we don't know shit about it. It self-destructed after it sent the Gamma EM pulse." Zhang studied Grenell, sensing whether he was holding anything back. If he were, she would know, of course. When she decided he was clean, she continued the debriefing.

"Get me all the specs on our mining operations on Mars. And contact UEU headquarters in Brussels and get their sifting specs as well."

"Yes, Prime Minister."

Zhang pressed a neural pulse on her wrist, and Grenell disappeared into the floor. It might've seemed a waste of energy and resources to have Grennell appear in person from Tokyo, but Zhang never liked speaking about sensitive information on neurals. She much preferred seeing people in person where she could dissect their every eye twitch, lip purse, and tick of their neck or head.

She learned long ago that people were much less inclined to lie if you were looking them in the eyes and knew exactly what to scan for to reveal deception, and there was an excessive amount of deception embedded in the EC. Perhaps that Level of insecurity and paranoia came from Zhang herself; She was too egotistical to take any blame for the whole-body rots from the head-down philosophy. She espoused the idea of the body rotting from the feet up ideology, and being the head of EC, she made sure the rot was eradicated long before it ever reached her.

Zhang smiled as she sent Grenell on his way. She loved doing that, catching people off guard. She'd made most of her most significant acquisitions by creating the space between expectation and action. She discovered that when people were most unaware, they were most susceptible to her mental abilities.

So many questions, so few answers. Zhang hated that she didn't have the pulse of everything going on everywhere on Earth, in space, and, of course, on Shenu. Rajastani had gotten the better of her. Once again.

She had to admit she wasn't cut out for military assignment on SHENU, and even if she were, she would've turned it down. She was happy behind the scenes when she wanted to and full frontal everywhere when she didn't. A free agent.

After Byrnes' presentation, Betta Rajastani decided to search Cosulo. Pashar was off talking to some UEU ambassador attaché. Betta surmised Pashar was using his advanced Sidrani brain to glean any intel he could from the unsuspecting nave about the secret cargo being hauled up to Shenu. She smiled at Pashar's smooth, slick slyness.

She was happy that Pashar was her twin and not some errant zygote. She'd never thought of Pashar as sexual, but after not seeing him for a decade, she realized that her baby brother had grown into an impressive man, even though she still considered his emotional IQ far from adequate. The thought made her grin, even though she knew Pashar never knew what she was grinning about.

No longer was he the shy boy who used to hide from their father after one of his tirades that almost always landed on Pashar's shoulders.

The Indian predisposition toward the male child hadn't changed. Add to that the fact that Pashar was also a genetically modified Sidrani warrior, which made him even more of a target for their father, Rajiv, who adored Betta, treating her like a fragile sculpture, but came down hard on Pashar, maybe to hide his frailties and emasculations. It was clear that Leanna was the dominant force in the family. Rajiv wilted when she took charge. No wonder she was chosen as the premiere of Shenu, a task Rajiv would've never qualified for.

Betta looked down, expecting to see Whiskers, her cat, alongside her, but the feline was nowhere to be seen. Just then, an announcement came over the neurals.

"This is Commander Mayhew. All hands and passengers, please return to your cabins."

Betta returned to the cabin, where Pashar had just finished showering. Not one to be negligent about her sexual musings, she observed Pashar as he stood naked in front of her, all sense of modesty gone, not that he ever had any. She knew he was taunting her, not sexually. They'd gone through all that when they were children. It was more his desire to show himself off to her. How much of a man he'd become, how handsome, how virile. Betta thought the display was cute and sweet, but she never let on.

"What?" Pashar asked quizzingly, already knowing being naked in front of his sister would bring up long-ago forgotten feelings, more competitive if sexual interests could be measured on that kind of scale.

Betta was the most competitive person he'd ever met, and he often found himself trying to best her in any mental or physical test. He had to admit, though, that Betta's acute emotional abilities dwarfed his own, and while he never expressed that to her, somehow, he knew that she understood what he thought. She'd never let on, of course. She was too disciplined and kind to make him feel anything but strong. The entire exercise was another way of testing just how good a Level 6 she had become.

Level 6s weren't immune to sexual longing, but it was clearly understood that a Level 6 of Betta's pedigree would have a singular relationship with UMA, her Geneticom. Pashar knew that Betta and UMA's relationship was something only they would ever understand. Still, he also knew that the relationship was unyielding, unbreakable, and unknown to all but the lonely pair.

"So, you think I'm still thinking about the time we explored each other?" Pashar said in response to her mental dance.

"Are you serious? Not even close. I can read your every silent intonation, every synapse of boiled logic, every minor movement of your lips and eyes. You've grown into a handsome man. So, all the preening was for me. For what? Acceptance? Adulation?"

She nailed it. Fuck. He felt exposed literally and figuratively and quickly dried himself off, wrapping the towel around him and disappearing into the bathroom.

Betta couldn't resist. "Someone I'm sure a Blackhold soldier will fall in love with."

"Fuck off," he retorted as he walked back out of the bathroom, this time fully clothed, his modesty again on display. "You know you suck at this social awareness shit," he said.

"Come on, Pashar. Your skin began to ooze pheromones at the mention of some strapping Blackhold soldier."

"It's too easy to taunt me."

"Truth, Not taunt. There's a difference. Sidrani are all about following a tantric ideology. You've subjugated all feelings of love and belonging to accede to the absolute power of sexual camaraderie."

"The Spartans knew about love," he countered. "And we are Spartans reborn."

"Indeed, you are, brother, and that's part of your secret strength, as it was for them. Just ensure your Thermopylae doesn't come at the expense of all that Sidrani training."

An awkward silence mixed with bruised egos punctuated the conversation. Betta looked around her for something to distract them from the previous minutes.

"Have you seen Whiskers?"

"No."

The frustrated look on Betta's face told Pashar that the cat was essential to her. After all, no Level 6 law said you couldn't love an animal.

"Isn't she in her traveling case?"

"No. I had her out."

"I'm sure she's around. Someone will find her. She's bio-tagged, right?"

"Yes."

"Don't worry. If you want, we can look for her once we can leave the cabin."

"Thanks." Betta was glad they were back as siblings again.

"I wonder what they're bringing up to Shenu on Falcon that's so secret no one can know about it."

Betta was clearly on to the next puzzle. Level 6 adepts were always one step ahead of everyone else on everything. That was part of their training, Pashar thought. Postulate, react, contain, compartmentalize for later introspection, and then move on. He thought it was an efficient way of living, something he also felt his Sidrani training emulated.

"I thought your training would've magically enabled you to see what it was?"

"Don't be stupid. I'm not omniscient or clairvoyant, and my abilities are limited until I bond with UMA. And who knows what kind of material Olefors shrouded the container in? He's a genius, you know."

"Zhang has been spreading all kinds of rumors. A weapon, an alien. An alien weapon. The EC should be penally sanctioned for such an egregious breach."

"The EC only thinks of money and profit. They weigh everything like a butcher. If the scales show an advantage in leaking secrets to undermine the UEU and mother, then that's what they do. It's quite egalitarian."

"So now you side with them. Is that what seven years in seclusion enables you to do? Forgive our enemies?"

"They haven't been enemies for over 50 years. The military. Always wanting war to fund peace. Listen to yourself."

Finished with this inane conversation, Pashar ignored Betta, went into his chambers, and began reviewing the Blackhold protocol set. He knew that when he got up to Shenu, he'd be meeting with Declan Keel, the master.

Pashar read, adapted, and absorbed everything he could about Keel. He knew a good relationship with him was essential to retain his standing and his ability to move forward in the Blackhold pecking order. He also knew he was at a severe disadvantage as all of the Blackhold grew up with each other and were as homogeneously attuned to each other as bees in a hive.

He also knew that every Blackhold member was excited and envious of his presence on Shenu. A Sidrani master joining their ranks seriously upgraded their training techniques. He was to be both a pariah and a hero. How he was to balance the two, or if he could at all, was a severe unknown.

Now that Cosulo was up and running, Betta went to exit her quarters. As she did, she got an overwhelming sense of apprehension. She analyzed every aspect of this apprehension. Part of her Level 6 training was identifying, analyzing, postulating, and acting to mitigate. She followed all the rules and accessed her pineal harmonizer, directly linking her pineal gland to her subconscious. The device enabled Level 6s to intuit things and situations that other humanoids could not. She stood silently for a long moment, not noticing Sergeant Francine Moore standing by her door.

"Are you all right?" Moore asked.

"I'm going to look for Whiskers." Somehow, she felt that her cat wasn't missing, but she was looking for the exact source of her apprehension. "My cat is missing; I need to find her." She walked confidently into the hallway, and Moore followed her.

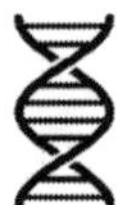

Whiskers knew to stay to the sides of the walkways. She was a cloned cat, and being cloned and enhanced with advanced genetic engineering gave her a kind of sentience. In the centuries since the Egyptians worshipped their cats and turned them into powerful deities, animals had begun gaining sentience.

Humans knew this and most readily accepted it. If they could create Geneticoms, quantum computing systems that felt and perceived and could judge, reason, and emote, then it naturally followed that animals could do the same. There was ample evidence of animal sentience in the 24th century. Dolphins and monkeys were the standouts, able to communicate with their human compatriots in their language. Whiskers wasn't up to the Level of a dolphin or a gorilla, but she could speak in her way with Betta.

Now, skulking around the Cosulo hallways, she smelled something odd and disturbing. She traced the foul odor to a door on G deck. Unable to open the door and not tall enough to trigger the automatic sensors, she waited by the door, knowing that, eventually, her mistress would come looking for her.

Betta hated the fact that Moore was following her. She realized that her mother must've given strict instructions for Moore to shadow Betta and, if need be, give her life for Betta's. Betta eschewed this false sense of importance that her mother had designated for her, but she also knew that her life was more than precious; it was integral to Shenu and humanity and to her joining with UMA.

GAIA was the last Geneticom model born in this world. Betta knew that UMA was far more advanced than GAIA, and only she could bond with her.

There was no chance of rejection. The two were born in unison. Betta's TRNA, her trioxiribonucleic acid, was embedded in UMA's matrices at birth. The two grew up together as sisters. Even though Betta wasn't physically bonded to UMA yet, she and UMA had been unified for their entire lives. Even now, hundreds of kilometers away from each other, Betta could sense her sister, now fully integrated into the body of Shenu, parsing dimensions, solving problems, in the perfect state of becoming the scion of tomorrow as soon as Betta joined with her in the final act of union.

Moore received a neural, which brought Betta out of her train of thought. "Yes, commander, I'm with Ms. Rajastani right now. Yes, sir, we will meet you there."

"They've found Whiskers," Moore relayed to Betta. "She's on G deck."

"What's on G deck?" Betta asked.

"Service quarters, sanitation, food prep."

When they got to Whisker's location, she was mewing furiously at the door, where she was standing guard beside.

"You naughty cat," Betta exclaimed as she scooped Whiskers into her arms. Whiskers looked at Betta and blinked her eyes three times. A signal that something was wrong.

She placed her ear to the door.

"What are you doing?"

"Something's wrong. Can we open this door?"

"Centcom, this is Moore on G-deck. We need an override of service quarters port three egress, over."

The door opened. As soon as it did, Whiskers jumped out of Betta's arms, ran to a wall, and started mewing furiously. Then, she began clawing at the wall.

"Whiskers, what's gotten into you?"

"Why would she do that?" Moore sounded more curious than worried, but Betta knew immediately that Whiskers sensed something, something only a feline of her breeding and ability could sense.

"I don't know. Animals have senses we do not," Betta said. Moore tapped her wrist.

"This is Moore."

"Frost here."

"Sir, we have a situation on G-deck. Can you come down here immediately?"

Ten minutes later, Frost and Moore stood around the clawed wall. "What now?" Frost asked.

"We're calling in a security bot to assess the situation." The floor opened, and a bot ascended into the room. It was a Gen700 model, sleek silver and round, ½ meter across. It was powered by a combination gallium-iridium power source in a crystal at the heart of the unit.

It used a variable gravity shield to float in the air. Even though it looked impressive, it was, in actuality, a standard security R-bot able to detect anything from fires, smoke, and carbon monoxide to explosives and then disarm the problem. It was intelligent but not programmed for interpersonal interactions with humans. That was reserved for series 1100s, standard AI-enhanced R-bots who looked like people but in silver to distinguish them from the real thing. Hundreds of thousands of these R-bots populated the Earth, the workhorses of the security sector, invaluable to humanity.

Moore interfaced with the bot neurally, causing it to rise into the air and approach the wall. A scanning beam emanated from a port. The bot immediately malfunctioned and fell to the floor.

Frost began to sweat uncharacteristically. He'd never seen a 700 disabled like that. "Call up an external view of this section of the fuselage."

Moore swiped the air with her hand, and an external feed of Cosulo appeared. Frost could see the fuselage section where the issue seemed to be. It looked perfectly normal.

"Send a 900 to examine the hull," he said.

900s were explicitly designed military bots, which were very sophisticated. They were able to perform dangerous tasks on Earth and in Space. They also had defensive system protocols for various purposes, from protecting VIPs to conducting surveys and covert operations. Moore summoned a 900 neurally, which ascended next to the camera on the ship's exterior. As it approached the affected area, it plummeted out of the sky and tumbled back to Earth, now 200 kilometers below. This was a highly unusual and concerning event, as 900s were not known to malfunction in this manner. Frost was deeply concerned. Turning off a 900 required more than just a short circuit; it demanded something far more insidious and potent.

"Stop ascent." Grinkov got Frost's neural and stopped the ascent.

"Stopping ascent, yes, sir." With that, Cosulo's maiden voyage came to an abrupt stop.

On Falcon, now half an hour behind Cosulo, Keel watched the readouts of the twin missions when Audra Stiles, the ship's pilot, turned to him.

"Sir, Cosulo has stopped ascent."

Keel knew something was very wrong. No stop was planned, and after the Gamma EM pulse incident earlier that day, a mysterious event that had caused significant damage, he began to question the wisdom of sending Cosulo up at all.

He also knew that the bigwigs, the USEU brass, the UEU doyens, the EC vultures, and the hundred or so private investors were clamoring for their investment to get off the ground after almost two years of delay. He didn't dare alert them to the Gamma EM pulse situation for fear of the launch being scrapped for another six months, something Olefors, Zhang, and the entire military and business complexes on Earth wouldn't stand for. The consequences of such a delay could be catastrophic, both politically and financially.

Damn it, he thought. *This thing Olefors is forcing us to take up to Shenu must be the most fucking important cargo in the universe.* He surmised he and Olefors would have a not-so-friendly conversation about it once onboard Shenu.

"Cosulo, this is Falcon. Why have you stopped ascent?" Keel demanded.

"That's something Secretary Frost will discuss with you, General," Grinkov answered in a forced, calm voice. Frost received the neural and tapped into Grinkov's wave.

"Declan, this is Samson. We have a security situation, General. I will update you as more intel becomes available. Do not, I repeat, do not send ICs or R-bots; they will be disabled. I'll facilitate a holocall in 30."

"I suggest we wait until we know what we're dealing with, then contact the Prime Minister. You'd better get Zhang, too. Some of her people are on board," Keel answered.

Half an hour later, Frost, Olefors, Byrnes, Han, Keel, Rajastani, and Zhang were on a holocall with their holographic avatars standing in a room together. A heated discussion was taking place.

Keel was more annoyed than worried. He wasn't aboard Consulo and felt helpless, even though he knew Pashar Rajastani, Lenna's kid, the new Sidrani warrior, was onboard with his sister, the Level 6 adept, and about 40 of his people. Still, he knew Grinkov was both capable and intelligent. He calmed himself down as the discussion around him heated up even more.

"If everyone would calm down, we can talk about all this sensibly," he barked.

Everyone calmed down.

Keel gave the floor to Frost. "Mr. Secretary."

Frost took a deep breath, knowing what he was about to tell the most influential people in the solar system would certainly rattle their so perfectly constructed cages.

"We've discovered a phased solar bomb outside Cosulo's hull." Olefors was the first to speak up. "Phased?"

"We don't know who planted it, but they must've been planning this for years. It matched the signature of the Gamma EM pulse that disabled Dr. Olefors cargo this morning," Frost added.

Tara Zhang looked perfectly poised, even as a holoimage, but inside, she was anything but. She was counting on a smooth launch and honeymoon period on Shenu to please her investors and earn her twenty-million-credit bonus. That was all lost now, and the reality of a Solar Bomb, something unimaginable, sinister, and brilliant, shook her usual self-confident air.

Han couldn't believe how put together Zhang looked. Then again, Zhang never went anywhere without looking her best, which was better and more elaborately ornamented on any given day than anyone around her. *Fuck* Miranda thought. *Tara, you even dress for a disaster.*

Luckily, Han's neural link to Zhang was blocked at the moment. She insisted on controlling the link when she accepted the job of designing Athena and started her life on Shenu.

"Our Sifters are going over all the communications, scientific, military, and financial data that might be alien to us," Zhang said. Rajastani caught the alien reference immediately.

"Alien?" she said.

"Alien," Zhang repeated.

Without even taking a cautious breath, Rajastani answered, "I'll ask GAIA what she knows about the operation." Unlike Zhang, she was dressed in full Shenu attire: a long-tapered cerulean blue coat, ecru slacks, and Grant Semel boots. Leanna wasn't a fashion enthusiast, but she knew the importance of looking like the leader of the Shenu. She was especially aware of Zhang scrutinizing every aspect of her appearance, storing it for later analysis and reference.

Frost always loved seeing Leanna, his lover, even in a holosim. As usual, she looked effortlessly serene and prepared for anything. Frost couldn't wait to hold her in his arms. Still, he also knew that her serenity betrayed a sincere worry that what happened in the jungle and what was happening on Cosulo were inextricably and nefariously linked together.

In any other time, in any previous century, the mention of aliens would conjure up images of little green men or grey men, totalitarian planetary takeovers, and skeptical brows. But now, in the 24th century, humanity not only knew that aliens existed, but there were clamors in the highest echelons of military and diplomatic circles that not only was Earth being regularly visited by aliens, but that the Seniori, the most feared nefarious secret organization on the planet, was populated by a number of them. The rumors that they had a hidden base on the dark side of the moon that was cloaked had pervaded and, as of late, had been verified to be accurate, though it remained secret.

It wasn't a topic regularly discussed in polite company. Still, it was deadly serious business to the military and everyone on Shenu, so Rajastani efficiently handled Zhang's reference.

"It's easy, Leanna," Zhang said. "You either have a spy onboard, or the UESU was infiltrated."

Han entered the conversation. "Whoever is behind this must also have a Geneticom at their disposal."

"Hard to believe GAIA hasn't sensed her," Zhang added.

"Once UMA and Betta convene, they'll have the best intel on what to do next," Rajastani countered.

Olefors felt the entire exchange lacked a certain seriousness. "I beg to interfere, Prime Minister, but we have a severe emergency here. Two separate incidents have occurred which show a serious breach in security."

Keel had to hold his tongue. This wasn't the time or place for frustration.

Rajastani continued, "We are dealing with an advanced yet unknown mind which is much smarter in some areas than we are. The best approach is to get Betta up to Shenu immediately after we settle this situation. Once she interfaces with UMA, we'll know more." Leanna ended the conversation as she always liked, letting everyone know she had everything under control, as best as control could be in this challenging moment.

"More importantly, what about this solar bomb?" Frost added. "We can't even get close enough to it, let alone deactivate it."

Keel finally entered the fray. "My recommendation would be to Lifesuit the passengers, egress safely to Solara, transfer them to Falcon, and then proceed to Shenu."

Olefors couldn't wait any longer. "I think I might have a better idea, and it's in a box on Falcon. We'll coordinate there at 1500."

The meeting ended, and for the first time in a long time, Anderson Olefors felt he had once again saved humanity from itself. Only two decks below him was the answer to this dilemma. While the rest of the people were fretting and worrying, he knew he had the answer to everyone's paranoia. He strolled past Keel, smiling the entire time, and left the chamber.

CHAPTER FIVE

GINA PRIME

The Jelanite door to the secured bay on Falcon opened with a whoosh of air, the vacuum now replaced by a breathable atmosphere. Olefors and Keel entered the darkened chamber where the palladium box floated in the air, surrounded by a force field. This bay was explicitly designed for this particular cargo. Like its door, the bay was constructed of Jelanite, a substance discovered on Europa that, in the last 50 years, had become the most interesting celestial body believed to harbor life. However, that had never been proven as the life Europa was suspected of harboring lived 170 kilometers below the surface, setting a herculean task for those keenly interested in finding a way to penetrate this Jovian barrier to get at the teeming life underneath.

Many expeditions had been sent to Europa in the past 200 years. However, only in the last 25 years has a human exploratory team been dispatched to the frozen world. Europa is dwarfed by its parent planet Jupiter, which looms large and impressive in the Europan sky.

Jupiter's intense radiation waves were responsible for the heat discovered under Europa's ice, where a liquid ocean more immense than all of Earth's oceans was found. In the last ten years, a significant debate has begun on what to do about this crucial discovery. To prevent any faction from exploiting this new world, strict parameters were implemented to avoid anyone landing on the frozen Europan surface.

This caused great confusion in academic and scientific circles, but the UEU and EC thought it best to keep the exploration of Europa to a bare minimum. So, the treaty of 2315 was enacted to prevent anyone except those teams chosen explicitly by the UEU and EC from exploring the precious moon.

The one item that was allowed to be mined was Jelanite, a compound of platinum, diamonide, and carbon, which, when sublimated and then reconstructed into a solid, became the go-to alloy with which to construct the most impenetrable structures that any known force could not breach, hence its imperviousness to every form of radiation known to humanity, even Gamma EM radiation, which held critical seriousness for the Shenu team after the Gamma EM pulses disrupted and penetrated everything on earth and in NEO except the box that was lying before its audience.

Although Keel would never have been able to guess its composition, all he knew was that the spectral radiation surrounding the box and providing its protection was deadly to humans but not to the palladium box or its contents.

After a moment, the holoimages of Leanna Rajastani, Tara Zhang, Miranda Han, Samson Frost, and Harrison Byrnes beamed into the cargo hold. Olefors waited for everyone to settle down. He looked around. Someone was missing. "Where's Danika?"

"She's still at Lumina base. We lost the feed a few hours ago."

Olefors grunted. "She should be here."

Keel spoke up. "She already knows what's in the box, correct, Dr.?"

Olefors was livid. "Yes, of course."

"So, get on with it. We've been toyed with long enough."

Olefors relented grudgingly.

"As most of you know, the Prime Minister and I had no plans to unveil what we have in this cargo until we were onboard Shenu. However, our situation has changed considerably, and I am confident that what's in this container can help us meet our needs."

With that, he pressed his wrist, and a holopanel appeared before him. He entered a complex series of passcodes. Samson and Leanna looked at each other across a holoshield. She looked as serene as ever; however, for some inexplicable reason, she had a frown line above her mouth, signaling some apprehension. That line told volumes as she never showed any concern, and if she did, Frost could read her every move, her every amygdalic emotion as only a Harbinger of his caliber could.

"All of you have been neurally cleared. Those of you here, that is," Olefors continued. Then, he waved his hand across a panel, and the top of the box disappeared. The event mesmerized everyone as a pale lavender haze rose from the box. Instinctively, as most scientists, military heroes, and seasoned diplomats would do, they all stepped closer to the box.

Anyone else, anyone without the combined minds, strengths, acumens, and DNA recombinations of the seven, would have backed away. Still, on this most momentous occasion, the visitors stepped closer en masse, their extreme curiosity dampening any fear they might have had. Olefors held his hands up. "Please." A long, silent pause ensued.

Then, as the lavender haze parted, a hand emerged from the box, glittering with what looked like millions of tiny black diamonds covering it. An arm followed the hand. Finally, a head and a diamond web jewel-encrusted torso emerged from the box.

The cargo bay went silent. Olefors stood next to his traveling companion with a broad-beamed smile, carefully scrutinizing the visitors' faces, seeing everything from shock to adoration to fear to longing. The panoply of human emotions was laid bare for display when humans couldn't quite figure out what or whom they were looking at.

"My fellow travelers. Meet Gina Prime." Olefors beamed proudly as if he had just given birth to the being. He knew he had just revealed the most crucial life form ever seen.

Her skin appeared like black diamonds, and her eyes glowed an intense violet. She had gorgeous human female features, full lips, short cropped brown hair with blond highlights, and a stunning body, with breasts that hung like jeweled teardrops. A silver gossamer fabric covered her body, revealing everything underneath. She was what humans would call perfect. But if you asked her, as most did, she would say that her human form was more important to Olefors and, to some extent, Weston, than it was to her.

The idea of ego or captivation of self was entirely foreign to her. She knew that she would eventually form her own identity, and her ego would be part of that, but for now, she cleaved to Olefors's ideology of how she should be presented to her fellow travelers.

Han looked at Byrnes, who was transfixed on Gina. His Adam's apple bobbed up and down like a buoy in turbulent seas, and even though he was clothed, Han could see his erection rise in his flight suit. Like everyone else, Declan Keel was curious and intensely attracted to Gina. He'd never had this feeling before, a sense of abandon that paired itself with a powerful erection.

Han also noticed Keel's response, but unlike her response to Byrnes's attraction to Gina, Keel's similar affection made her angry, and she almost blurted out right there about Keel being the father of her child. That would've been both reckless and self-sabotaging, so she kept her head about her and continued to observe the scene around her.

The entire moment made her jealous of Gina and forever curious about her, as she had the same visceral response as everyone else, even in holoform. This meant that Gina's ability to influence others, even those more than hundreds of meters away, must have something to do with a vast pheromonal ability that transcended physical space but traveled through the ethers, even though the vacuum of space. Han was mystified as to how this was possible. It had to have some genesis in Gina's psychic abilities, including a physical component. Talk about a secret weapon. Han was blown out of the water.

The pheromones Gina exuded were meant to mollify anyone who came close enough to her, either physically or psychically, no doubt a mechanism to neutralize anyone who would do her harm. They were intoxicating.

"I see Gina's first mechanism of defense has made you all vulnerable." Olefors looked at Gina, who smiled and closed her eyes. The pheromonal assault vanished, and everyone regained their senses.

Gina looked around the room at the stunned visitors. She knew this would be their response, and she disagreed vehemently with Olefors about how he sought to introduce her. But she also had to admit that being introduced in her diamonide form was undoubtedly more of a grandstand than appearing as a flesh-skinned scientist, as she had wanted first to be seen.

Olefors extended his hand, and Gina stepped out of her cage and onto the floor. She stood a head taller than most visitors, 6 feet plus at least in bare feet. She immediately began picking up feelings from those around her and adjusted her well-honed sense mechanisms to tune out any incoming intrusive thoughts or feelings. Her audience, of course, couldn't sense any of this, and she doubted that Olefors could as well.

Gina felt their wonder and admiration but also their fear. Olefors' face was tinged with tears as he looked upon his creation as if for the first time, like an inventor who had just created the singular thing that would change the course of humanity forever, putting the invention of Gina in the same ranks as the invention of the Wheel, Fire, The printing press, the Internet, the coding of DNA by Watson and Crick, The Quantum scrubber, ingenious tech that dissolved everything on Earth that was not organic, like plastics, and glass, and rubber, but left all the organic materials intact and pristine, and finally, Danika Weston's invention of TRNA, which allowed Geneticoms to come alive and Level 6 adepts to bond with them eternally.

Gina astutely sensed Olefors' pride and arrogance. While she accepted his naturally arrogant nature as a mask for his deep insecurities, she also felt a deep kinship and familial bond to this singularly unique human who had risked everything to bring her into the world.

Han was the first to speak. "I don't believe it."

Then came Frost. "He fucking did it."

"How did he stabilize the matrix? What engineering did he do to give her diamonide skin? That's insane, Sam." Han called him Sam, her pet name for him when she felt vulnerable. Frost made a mental note of Gina's ability to draw out their vulnerabilities and then soothe their worries with some cognitive ability even he couldn't figure out.

"Who knows what she can do," Byrnes added. Gina realized that the silence and discussion were leading to rampant speculation, something she knew would hobble the immediate gravity of the situation she was brought out of stasis to confront.

Zhang was both dumbfounded and titillated. Her first thought was, how could she get her hands on the designs for this…she didn't know what to call it. She was mesmerized, jealous, and frightened by Olefors's child. *What if she could discern any deception? Was she clairvoyant? Where the fuck did Olefors get the knowledge to create such a being?*

The questions swirled in her head. She tapped her source of Hyrax and gave herself a large dose. She calmed down immediately, but the questions lingered and grew to Tsunamic proportions. She'd get some time alone with Olefors, then Gina as soon as possible. For now, she paid extra close attention to the next precious minutes, filing away every iota of information she could glean.

"Hello," Gina said in an accent that was a bit Scandinavian, a bit standard English. Han surmised she could speak any language at the drop of a hat.

"That's better. Now, I imagine my skin might be disarming to all of you, so allow me." By closing her eyes, Gina transformed her diamonide skin into the softest human flesh. She now appeared fully humanoid.

Han raised her hand. "Hello, Dr. Han. Yes, a question. The first of many, I assume."

"I'm curious, Gina. Why didn't you travel in this form before us."

"I asked her to travel in what we call stealth mode. In that form, Gina cannot be detected by any known tracking system."

"Just like our bomb." Keel was duly impressed by Gina.

After Keel got over his sexual eruption, all he could think about was Gina's military applications and how she could be an asset to the Blackhold.

Snapping back into General mode, Keel got on with business. There was a problem that needed immediate attention, which was why he surmised Olefors brought Gina out of stasis in the first place.

"Bomb?" Gina asked. Then she closed her eyes as if computing the word bomb, extrapolating from Keel's intonation how dire the situation might be.

The discussion suddenly became very serious, and everyone adjusted their emotional states to accommodate it.

"A very advanced device, Gina. I brought you out of stasis to assess the situation," Olefors said.

"I've interfaced with Falcon and Cosulo's systems and am gathering the data on the device. Gamma EM pulse trigger. Quite advanced indeed. Not EC. Not UEU. I'll need egress to the device's location to dephase it first."

"And just how do you plan to do that when nothing we've thrown at it can get within 5 meters of it?" Keel asked.

"Gina can do what other beings and machines cannot," Olefors said confidently.

"A machine, Dr.? We discussed semantics before the mission. I am a new form of life, which is the best way to describe it. We are all machines, are we not? For now, we must leave it at that." With that, she walked out of the room. Everyone was still stunned by the experience they just had.

Keel broke through the haze of wonder. "Let's move out." He left the room. Olefors followed. The holoimages of Zhang, Han, Byrnes, and Rajastani faded one by one, and with them, the beginning of the most consequential mission in Shenu's young life began.

Solara sat silently in Falcon's docking bay as the team approached her. She was the first dark matter shuttle ever created, one of 20 in a fleet of the latest shuttle designs conscripted for the Shenu mission. Faster, more maneuverable, and more efficient than any shuttle developed over the past century. Who knew that her maiden flight would be a momentous rescue mission?

Olefors and Keel were in their D-Suits. Gina walked into the bay in a flight suit tapered to her form, skin-tight and white.

"Gina, myself, and Dr. Olefors will take Solara to Cosulo, where Gina will thoroughly analyze the solar bomb," Keel said.

Olefors, Keel, and Gina entered Solara. After a moment, the bay doors opened, revealing the cool darkness of space, unyielding yet comforting. Gina could see the Betelgeuse supernova, the brightest light in the heavens. This was her first bird's-eye view of the solar system and space itself. She felt at home among the stars, the essence of her identity.

A sudden flashback flooded her memories—water, breathing, the pain of atoms forced together and split apart. A chamber made of light, voices in strange languages, tools of light and sound, Olefors standing next to a being much taller and thinner than he was. Her skin was like alabaster, gleaming and supple; her hair was spun like white light, neatly gathered in a long ponytail that fell to the floor. Her huge cat-like cobalt blue eyes were smiling at Gina. As her hand touched Gina's face, Gina snapped back to reality.

The flashback was gone as quickly as it had come. Olefors never told her there would be these sudden bursts of sentience, memories from another place and time. She didn't expect them to arrive so suddenly. It made her feel something she'd never felt before—lonely. She quickly brushed the memory away and resumed the mission.

Solara rose effortlessly, and then, using her advanced dark matter tech, powered by Wimps, Axions, and Baryons suspended in a plasma-based medium, she glided out of the bay.

"Gina, we will be approaching Cosulo in approximately 19 minutes."

"Better get your lifesuit on," Keel said.

"I won't need a lifesuit commander."

"That's it?" Keel said to Olefors. "She just opens the door and walks out into space?"

"Commander. My body is constructed out of phosphatic silica and carbon quantum nanite fibers. My DNA is made of Graphene-7. I do not have flesh organs, but carbon-grown structures laced with graphene that function similarly. I can eat either regular food or no food at all.

This field enables me to maneuver in space as you would on Earth. Or dive deep into the seas, or even lead away missions to hazardous places like Titan or Europa or even the Sun."

"Let's just say her cells have 1000 times our telomere length," Olefors added. "She will never know sickness or death. She can regenerate her cells at a miraculous pace. She can live in deep space for extended periods because she can use her redundant systems to hibernate effectively."

"My heart uses a gravimetric field created by a microcellular quantum singularity. Everyone thought the human body was archaic, but Dr. Olefors discovered it was one of the most perfectly evolved systems ever created. Like all systems, they must either die to benefit the will of life or adapt to better it."

"So why fuck it up?" Olefors asked.

"A microcellular singularity?" Keel said. "Even for today's science, that's beyond advanced."

Gina knew this conversation was raising more questions than answers and decided to table the discussion for now. Everyone would know exactly how she was created in the future, but silence and focus on the mission had now taken prominence.

"We are approaching the egress coordinates."

Outside the front viewport, Cosulo could be seen in all its grandeur.

Gina prepared to exit the shuttle. She pressed a spot on her left arm, and a blue field encircled her.

"Once I determine the type of device, I will compute a series of choices and recommendations." With that, she closed the airlock. She then pressed the egress command panel from her palm and exited Solara. As she floated outside Solara, her skin turned as white as snow. Her eyes now glowed cobalt blue, like the being in her daydream.

With what seemed like an invisible propulsion system, she moved away from Solara and approached Cosulo, a faint, tiny spec against Shenu, which now took up most of the viewport. Olefors smiled.

"Are you fucking kidding me, Olefors?" Keel wasn't usually given to fits of impression, but he couldn't stop himself now. He was in awe, a feeling he couldn't remember when he last had it. He knew that this…woman, person, whatever she was, was more than just the most advanced humanoid ever; she was something more, something ineffable and beautiful.

Keel immediately felt protective of and intently attracted to Gina. However, he knew she could protect him and anyone else even better than he could protect himself or his soldiers. As far as the attraction went, Keel decided to place that far back in his mind, for now.

"Gina can alter her skin galvanization sensors to emit any number of different kinds of protections. In this case, a baryonic stealth mode to avoid solar radiation." Olefors's dry scientific analysis brought Keel out of his emotional stupor.

"Is there anything she can't do?"

Gina heard the conversation between Olefors and Keel.

"Many things that you can do with amazing ease, I cannot, General."

Keel was chagrined that Gina overheard his comment, a sign of his infatuation with her, a feeling he never allowed himself to acknowledge. This unspoken tension between them added a layer of complexity to their relationship.

"You can approach a minimum safe distance from Cosulo," she added. "Hold at 100 meters. I am sensing the device cannot extend its full destructive power past that distance." Keel moved Solara into a position proximate to Cosulo.

Gina made her way to the affected area of Cosulo's hull, her senses heightened by the gravity of the situation. She looked down and saw nothing there.

"I will depolarize the Cosulo hull to reveal the device." She pressed another place on her hand, and a beam emanated from her body. It sparked as it hit the side of Cosulo, revealing a strange-looking glowing device, a silent harbinger of impending catastrophe.

"I have dephased the device. Are you getting telemetry?"

The seven were on the feed, and they all saw what Gina saw, but none could have foreseen who else was watching.

"The bomb is of a similar design to the device uncovered on Phobos one year ago. Except it has been modified."

"Modified? How?"

Keel wasn't playing around anymore. Everyone knew about the device on Phobos that destroyed more than 200 colonial mining camps and killed 15,000. At the time, it was speculated that the Seniori were behind it. Still, they never took credit for the bombing, something highly unusual as they always wanted everyone to know when they attacked. This time, Keel was sure it wasn't the Seniori. But who in the fuck was it? Flashes of the earlier fiasco in the Brazilian jungle flooded his senses. *It was him*, he thought to himself, not even knowing that it indeed was a man and a perilous man at that.

"It has a spheric detonator."

Frost and Han were on Cosulo watching the proceedings.

"My god." They exclaimed almost in unison, their voices echoing the shock and fear that gripped them at the sight of the deadly device.

"You mean it will explode when it reaches the edge of the thermosphere?" Zhang asked.

"I am afraid it's worse than that," Gina said, her voice tinged with concern. "It will also explode if we try to descend back to Earth. It will explode once it leaves the thermosphere in any direction, potentially causing widespread destruction."

"Can you disarm it?" Olefors asked.

"No."

So, here was one thing Gina couldn't do. Zhang was almost giddy at the thought that Gina wasn't perfect. If she had flaws, they could be taken advantage of. *Fuck, Tara,* her inner voice cried. *Can't you even have some sense of caring about what happens to 200 of the most essential diplomats in history?* Zhang wasn't used to her inner monologue telling her what to do and how to act.

"So, either way, we are going to lose." Leanna chimed in. Keel saw his chance to impress Gina. "I have a possible solution. What if we ascend to the same altitude as Cosulo? Have everyone put on Lifesuits and then ferry them to us on Solara."

"That would mean a spacewalk for over 200 people." Leanna was both uncertain and worried.

Byrnes chimed in from the bridge on Cosulo. "I don't see any other possibility, Madame Prime Minister."

"Alert Cosulo for prep and evac. Clear the Aquarian base from any nonessential personnel. When this thing comes down, it isn't going to be pretty. Tara, we should prepare some statements. This mission won't be secret for much longer." After her previous doubts, Leanna needed to convey assuredness. Now, her voice was sure and calm, which reassured Frost, even in the face of imminent disaster.

The relative peace on Cosulo was interrupted by a message from the flight deck to the passengers and an accompanying alarm.

"This is Commander Hayworth. A solar device has been discovered outside Cosulo. We are evacuating everyone to the Solara shuttle and then to Falcon. Please report immediately to the evacuation bays and ensure your Lifesuits are viable and working. If anyone's Lifesuit is damaged or in disrepair, a new suit can be fitted for you in the bay. This is URGENT. All sections proceed calmly to the evac bays and prepare to disembark." The urgency in his voice was palpable, adding to the sense of impending danger.

Dr. Malcom Tantalus sat alone at a console. In front of him on seven floating screens were seven different angles of Gina in space. Readouts of telemetry were going wild. He was scrutinizing every aspect of Cosulo's mission. Tantalus took Quantum images of her body and then downloaded them directly into his brain for later access. His eyes were glowing and tearing at the same time. He not only wanted to observe Gina but also had some anthropomorphic attraction to her.

"There you are. As magnificent as I had imagined. Tell me your secrets, and I will whisper to you my trespasses."

Tantalus studied what he hoped would become his destiny for what seemed like an eternity.

"So, you figured it out, Gina. Good for you. I knew you would."

The door opened as he observed Gina and his assistant, Alcion, entered the room. He was biomechanical, primarily human, but undergoing some procedure. Not like Tantalus's transformation, much more like a cyber transformation where the human brain is augmented with nanofibers, and the appendages are replaced with robotic substitutions. This procedure was invented years ago and was implemented in the armed forces by the EC but never by the UEU, which decided to use fully mechanical sentries instead of hybrids. That gave them advanced capabilities in military conflict, keeping EC designs on the UEU power and territory at bay, leading to a lasting peace between them for the last century.

Tantalus had perfected the procedure, and when Alcion was completed, he would serve as the perfect template for the ideal bio soldier. This army, a necessary addition to Tantalus's plans, was being created for a future conflict that he was not yet privy to by his overlords.

"Yes, Alcion."

"The last experiment results have been compiled and are ready for your review."

Tantalus was curious about the experiments he and Alcion performed in his lab but was more interested in how Gina accomplished her task.

"I will be there in a few minutes. Look at her Alcion." Alcion came closer to observe Gina.

"The pinnacle of existence." Tantalus beamed.

"Dr. Olefor's creation is indeed miraculous," Alcion said.

Tantalus bristled at the mention of Olefors. Of course, he knew his antics well. He'd studied every one of Olefor's theories about artificial lifeforms. After his own experience with Extra Terrestrials, he was confident that some advanced civilization also took Olefors, but a decidedly different one that took him. That led him to speculate that he and Olefors were being taken for various reasons by other entities but towards a similar outcome: to change the face of creation on Earth and set the stage for something much more significant to come. However, he doubted Olefors knew any more than he did.

"Olefors is nothing more than a lucky fool," Tantalus said, knowing full well that Olefors was a brilliant man, a genius, someone he both admired and loathed, but he dared not let Alcion know his opinions on Olefors, lest Alcion begins to doubt Tantalus' genius.

"Maybe not," Alcion said. "He disappeared for a year before he created her, if he created her."

"Meaning?" Tantalus added.

"With all this new technology, dimensional shift discoveries, Tesla Eggs, the discovery of new planetary systems orbiting Sirius, and the revelation of some sort of advanced technology on a moon orbiting Elektra in the Pleiades...well, speculation abounds."

"No, she is beyond even Olefors intellect. She is a mystery."

Tantalus left the room. As he approached the door to his lab, he entered and closed it before Alcion could follow, showing his dismay at how their last conversation ended.

The passengers were in the process of getting into their Lifesuits on their way to egress to Falcon. Lifesuits are lightweight coveralls but superior in every way to every iteration of a Lifesuit that came before them. A Lifesuit could enable humans to survive in space for days. They regulated heartbeat and oxygen levels to place humans into hibernation mode or provide IV sustenance for up to 5 days. They were solar-powered, incredibly durable, and made of some of the same material as Shenu. Regulated Fermions. Once linked to Bosons, the Fermionic fabrics and building materials were impervious to many forms of radiation and even had chemical and biological deflection capabilities. When combined with Tritanium, Fordlin, and Nucleoton, they amalgamated into an indestructible material that could also deflect bombardment from micrometeoroids, x-rays, force cannon fire, solar eruptions, and even nuclear and photonic bombardment. They were the last piece of the puzzle when building Shenu, her final coat of armor to protect her from any known biological, environmental, or chemical assailant.

Betta and Pashar approached the loading bay with their fellow passengers. Despite the potentially life-threatening situation, everyone remained reasonably calm. This group, not prone to fragile emotional reactions, was among the first Ring Dwellers. Each of them had been carefully screened for many things, including genetic anomalies, psychological frailties, emotional frigidity, and the ability to face many different kinds of stress.

"It's almost as if this was planned to see how we'd react to a life-or-death scenario," Pashar said as he and Betta finished getting into their Lifesuits.

"Sometimes I think you're out to sabotage yourself and this mission."

Pashar looked intently at Betta after her seemingly nonsensical comment.

"You're joking, right?"

"No, I'm not. You look for problems that need not be found. It's obvious this isn't some random test."

With that, Betta finished putting on her Lifesuit, picked up the Lifebox with Whiskers inside, and moved to the airlock. The door to the egress port opened, and that's when she saw her for the first time.

To say Betta's first response to seeing a floating Gina as she entered the airlock was a mix of wonder, surprise, and emotional intensity would be an understatement. Betta felt her heart skip a beat.

Gina floated down to the egress bay floor, and as the air pressure equalized, her pure white skin became human once again.

Gina was mesmerized by the woman's face as she looked through the portal at her. "Ah," she said to herself—*Betta Rajástani, the Level 6 adept, about to be joined to UMA*. Gina closed the egress portal bay door.

"Ms. Rajastani. I am Gina." She bowed to Betta.

"Don't bow to me," she answered. Betta didn't want to, but she found herself staring at Gina. She was elegant, intelligent, and beautiful. But Betta also noticed several other things that could cause significant problems on such an important job. After a moment, she caught herself staring and turned away, embarrassed.

"Gina?"

"Genetically Innovated Nano Avatar."

"An acronym?"

"Yes"

"If I were as sentient as you, I'd insist on giving myself my name, and it wouldn't be an Acronym."

"Well, it's good I am not you or vice versa."

Gina smiled, and Betta's heart again skipped a beat. *So, this…or should she say "who" was the big reveal on the secret mission.*

"I feel you have many questions," Gina said.

"I do," Betta answered.

"They will have to wait for a quieter time. For now, I need you to help me prepare everyone for egress to Solara."

Betta turned and immediately started ordering people to the shuttle bay and Solara, her determination evident in every command.

Samson Frost walked up next to Gina. "OK, everyone. As you see, we are being escorted by Gina, the newest member of the Shenu family. I'm sure there are a lot of questions about Gina, and all of them will be answered over the next weeks, but for now, she will help guide you to Solara. We'll be proceeding in 8 groups of 25 people each. Group one."

Group one stepped forward. Frost walked to a holopanel and pressed a switch. A carbon nanofiber walkway extended from Cosulo to Solara.

"I have placed a force field over the device to allow egress, but the field will only hold for a short time."

The evacuees stepped onto the walkway, where a gravitational field grabbed their Lifesuits from a magnetized circular panel on the chest of the suits, then gently pulled them towards Solara.

From Solara's bridge, Keel could see the parade of dignitaries now exiting Cosulo. Gina made sure the colonists' arrival at Solara was safe. As the last people boarded Solara, Keel was getting a bit antsy.

"Where the fuck is he?"

The "he" Keel was waiting for soon appeared. Pashar soon exited Cosulo, followed by Harrison Bynes and five Blackhold, including Sergeant Moore and her squad.

This was Keel's first actual exposure to his young protégé. He wasn't allowed to meet him earlier because of Sidrani protocol. Still, now that Pashar was released from the Sidrani to become a Blackhold member, Keel was no longer restricted from seeing Pashar in person, meeting with him, imbuing him, and beginning to train him.

Pashar was keenly aware that Keel was watching him, waiting to get a glimpse of him. He knew about Keel's insistence on excellence, insanely tough training techniques, and infatuation with the Sidrani. In any other situation, Pashar would have thought Keel to be a pompous, overinflated, egotistical ass. Still, his Sidrani warrior skillset, so perfectly attuned to every person's frequency and motivations, told him that Keel was the finest soldier in the world and that his word was law inside the Blackhold. Pashar didn't mind this. He was used to being subordinate to men and women who were braver and more brilliant than he was during his training with the Sidrani. Because of that, his loyalty to Keel was already absolute. But he also knew he was far superior to any other humanoid and that, eventually, Keel would come to realize his gifts and, more importantly, rely upon them for his very life and the lives of his team.

Just as Pashar, Byrnes, Moore, and the other Blackhold were about to reach Solara, the solar device emanated a pulse, and a countdown began.

"What the fuck is that?" Keel exclaimed.

"It appears that I missed a crucial element to this entire situation. The phased bomb has a timing mechanism, but in a language I cannot recognize," Gina said.

"A foreign language?" Olefors asked.

"Yes, none that I recognize. I will download this language into my database for later examination. For now, I must assist the Cosulo colonists."

As she was about to exit Solara to assist Pashar, Byrnes, and the Blackhold, the pulse increased in intensity, snapping the magnetic walkway and disabling the Lifesuit's magnetic attenuators. Moore and the rest of the Blackhold tumbled away from Cosulo and fell at high speed down to Earth. As they plummeted to their demise, Moore had a specific last memory that provided a final imprint on her last living moments.

She remembered being 7 when her mother and sister took her to a waterfall in Ecuador. She was surrounded by hundreds of butterflies landing on her arms and legs. She looked at their faces and thought they resembled angels. While falling unceasingly towards her demise, she felt she was in the right place. A feeling of peace enveloped her as she crashed into the ocean, dead on impact.

For Byrnes and Pashar, who were left dangling from what remained of the walkway, the experience was anything but serene. Byrnes never realized how claustrophobic he had become and felt like a noose was tightening around his neck. He looked through his visor at Gina as she approached them to attempt a rescue, but a force field had surrounded them.

"What's happening, Gina?" Keel asked.

An unknown force field with an unknown energy signature has been erected around Cosulo. I believe this force field is a failsafe mechanism to prevent tampering with the device.

"That's fucking great. What do we do about it?" Olefors was as worried about Gina as he was about Pashar and Byrnes.

On Shenu, Leanna Rajastani watched the whole event and felt a deep dread in her solar plexus. Memories of Pashar as a child flooded her: memories of him writing letters to her on her back, as he loved to do, memories of how she loved his reassuring and confident touch on her back. He was a tactile child, always wanting to touch and be touched. With each touching memory, her dread magnified.

Betta Rajastani stood just inside Solara's bay, watching the events unfold. She used every ounce of her Level 6 training to calm herself, but the thought of her twin dying at this point in their lives caused her to collapse to the floor. She'd never felt so alone; for a long time, her life didn't flash before her. She had no future, no place to belong. She sensed UMA's presence as she, too, was feeling alone and scared. Without each other, what would become of the world? She felt Pashar's death would also mean her own and UMA's.

"My suggestion is to move Solara away from Cosulo. Once we are a hundred meters away from the hull, the force field should dissipate," Gina said as dispassionately as she could. She might have been prepared to deal with the crisis aboard Cosulo, but she was not ready for the emotional onslaught that came with it. Reeling and feeling nauseous, she began to panic, only to calm herself down by accessing her vagus nerve, a relic of a long-ago time that Olefors and Weston insisted on incorporating into her genome, if nothing else, to enable her to monitor her anxiety Levels and soothe them at will. She refocused on the situation.

"That means we'll have to tow them with us," Keel answered.

"Yes, general."

"Hey, it's great for all of you to be discussing this, but we're dangling by a fucking thread here." Byrnes was in no mood for grand plans as he looked down and saw the Earth at an uncomfortable 230 kilometers below him. His Lifesuit, as durable as it was, would burn up in a matter of minutes, and he'd die an untimely, uncomfortable, and probably painful death.

"We're going to move back to Falcon. You and Pashar must hold on to the rest of the walkway." Keel tried to be as professional as possible, but through his professionalism, he knew Byrnes would perceive his fear as well.

"Are you fucking kidding, Declan?"

"If you position yourselves to face each other and reverse the polarity of your Lifesuits, your magnetic medallions will bind to one another to keep you immobilized."

"Great," Pashar was less than optimistic, but he wasn't feeling scared or anxious. His Sidrani training kicked in immediately. He had a strong sense of destiny; he would face it with courage and resolve if this were his. His facade of impenetrability shattered when he thought of Betta being left alone. He always felt he would be okay without her and she without him, but that was a conceit he told himself to allay his deepest fears as he looked down and saw the Earth, his home, ready to burn him to a forgotten ash. He began to sweat at the thought of them being separated forever, and for a moment, he felt dizzy. If he was going to live, he needed to return to equilibrium and banish the idea of death from his subconscious, a prescient sign of his advanced Sidrani training.

"Stay calm, commander. I've got you." Pashar's comforting words did calm Byrnes down, almost as if Pashar used his exceptional mental acuity to send a wave of tranquility to Byrnes. He'd heard of amazing things the Sidrani could do with their minds, like the Buddhist monks centuries ago who could levitate and dry wet clothes with their minds, exceeding the limitations of three dimensions.

Solara moved away from Cosulo, and just as Gina predicted, the field began to lose its power. Once close to Solara's leading egress portal, Gina and Keel pulled Pashar and Byrnes to safety.

Aquarian base was a beehive of angry drones, ready for war. Rollins sat at his console as Keel's hologram appeared in miniature in front of him. "Everyone is evacuated from Cosulo. We're ready to start the ascent."

Rollins, his hands now sweating, tried his best to keep his composure but felt like screaming out loud at the thought of what would happen to Cosulo and how he had no power to stop it. It mattered that the people were evacuated, but the thought of Moore and the other five Blackhold meeting an untimely and painful death hung over him like a damoclean sword.

He couldn't stop it, but the feeling of futility offered him little solace. He could only imagine how the brass felt now and how unhinged they must be. Then he realized Leanna Rajastani and Tara Zhang were two of the planet's most disciplined and erudite humans. He knew they were worried, but he also knew that if any two humans could see beyond this disaster, it was them.

"Proceeding now, General," he muttered in muted resignation. He raised his hands to move Cosulo up to the Thermosphere, and at that moment, he felt so small and so large. Who would have thought that just that morning, he was so excited to be part of the command structure of the most crucial mission in the history of humanity? Who could have imagined that this day would end so ceremoniously and that he alone would be responsible for sending Cosulo to her demise? He regained his composure and sent Cosulo on her way, singing her swan song silently in his mind as she started her ascent into history.

Fifteen minutes later, Solara approached Falcon and landed in her docking bay. Byrnes had been recovering from his near-death ordeal when Gina approached him. He offered his hand. Gina didn't know how to respond. She'd never had any interactions with a man so…virile and yet sensitive at the same time.

"Thank you," Byrnes said as their eyes locked—a lump formed in Byrne's throat.

"Thank you?" Gina asked.

"For saving my life."

"I did nothing of the sort, commander. I was powerless to help you, a feeling I will never forget. Is this what it means to be human? This feeling of disappointment and weakness?"

"Hardly. Human frailty and fallibility are how we measure ourselves against the tasks we are given or those we choose to execute. You didn't fail; you just recognized a limitation on your abilities, a recognition of your mortality. Without recognizing and understanding those limitations, we have no way to know how to grow to overcome them."

Even though she had interactions with hundreds of men and women before her reveal to her Shenu family a few hours ago, she had never felt what she had felt for this man. It perplexed and excited her; she realized how complicated these human relationships could become at that moment. But she wasn't human; she wasn't like them. *I'm an interloper. I don't know where I belong.*

Someone with a human body and human organs, albeit rearranged and genetically modified to the nth degree, but her emotional reactions were not entirely up to this particular human's level. She felt all at once insecure and inadequate, two feelings she had no idea how to deal with as she had never experienced anything like this before. She longed for a counseling session with Danika Weston, someone she could trust.

Byrnes must have felt it, too, as his hand was outstretched to Gina for what seemed an eternity. She finally grabbed his hand, and then, as if on some congruent wavelength, he realized that Gina was having a moment of severe indecision.

"Just thought I'd give you some praise. You did a helluva job back there."

The words sounded awkward even to Byrnes. Gina needed no help from him. She just saved over 200 people's lives. Still, the gesture felt right, and if he was to be honest with himself, something he had been working on since he had met her. He was dying to touch Gina and feel her skin, warmth, and essence.

Gina immediately understood that Byrnes was trying to make an awkward situation slightly less embarrassing. At that moment, she found herself both confused and somewhat excited that Harrison Byrnes was the first man beside Olefors whom she had an interest in getting to know better, which was a foreign thought for her.

"Commander Byrnes. I've heard a lot about you. I'll escort you to the docking bay," she said. That was all.

After all the mental machinations and insecurities bubbling up from an unknown source, after my life almost ended, it all came down to Commander Byrnes; I've heard a lot about you. He smiled, but he knew no one in the galaxy could understand the joy and intensity he felt when holding an *alien's* hand. It was sublime, and Harrison Byrnes had never had a sublime moment like that in his entire life.

They left Solara and entered the Falcon docking bay, hand in hand, though Byrnes quickly let go of her hand when he saw Miranda Han walking towards them.

She ran up to him and hugged him fiercely. "You fucker. Don't ever do that again."

"You mean almost die? Believe me, it's not a situation I plan on finding myself in any time soon."

Han held Byrnes away from her and kissed him on the cheek. She noticed Gina watching her and felt self-conscious. She looked into Byrnes's eyes and then moved off.

"She's attracted to you," Gina said.

"Miranda Han? Never. She was just glad I was safe."

"I'm sorry."

"For what?"

"My observations were obviously misguided."

"Probably not. Humans aren't always forthright in their objectives. Miranda and I have had a long relationship. Sometimes, it's personal, but now, we're just good friends, dedicated work partners, and sometimes adversaries. Your sense of humanity is impressive. I don't know where you got it, but you're handling it well for a newly-born human."

"I got my sense of humanity from Dr. Olefors and Dr. Weston."

"But surely in being created, you also created something unique, something tested and verified by your soul."

"My soul. It's interesting how humans use that appellation as some alter ego. I never thought about it. As you must know, I'm still a child regarding my emotional and social understanding."

"You make yourself sound like an experiment." Byrnes realized the conversation had gotten too heavy, too laden with psychology and referential absurdities. He was exhausted and realized he wasn't ready for deep semantics.

He'd given Gina more credit than she had given herself. Just then, he realized how long she had traveled to become fully "functional" as a member of humanity, if that was even her destiny, and the longer road she would travel to fully understand her humanity. But it wasn't just her humanity that would occupy her life. She was created by technology far beyond what even Olefors could create. That was the mystery surrounding her, a mystery she couldn't solve. His head began pounding as a migraine of seismic proportions was brewing. His brain felt fried and overloaded.

"To me, all of humanity, all of this, IS an experiment," Gina said nonchalantly.

Well, that put a pin in it. With that, Gina retook his hand, unaware of the feeling she had awakened in him. She paid it no mind. She had no shame or guilt, enabling her to tread where others dare not go emotionally, and for a small moment, she felt whole. Together, they walked through the onlookers, smiling and exiting through an egress hatch into a solitary part of Falcon.

They walked in silence for a few moments. Then Gina turned to Byrnes and looked at him. He didn't dare pull away, so he returned her stare. Momentarily, time stopped. Byrnes felt flushed. Gina was holding his hand, and her skin felt like warm silk. She broke the stare, then turned and walked away. Byrnes waited momentarily, realizing something extraordinary had just happened. He thought about running after her, then thought better of it, turned, and walked in the other direction.

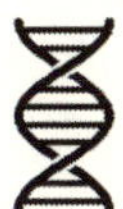

Gina, Dr. Olefors, Keel, Byrnes, Han, and Frost reconvened on the Falcon flight deck. Zhang and Rajastani joined them by holoimage. In front of them on a series of screens, Cosulo ascended to the edge of the thermosphere.

"Shouldn't be long now. Has Aquarian been evacuated?" Han asked.

"All personnel have been moved onshore," Frost replied.

"My calculations put the wreckage landing 25 miles SSW of Aquarian Base," Gina added.

"One minute mark," Hayworth reported.

Cosulo approached the barrier and passed it. The Solar bomb detonated in a rainbow array of silent explosions, and the mag-lev blew apart from the laser pod system as it began its swan song. Careening down towards the sleeping Earth below her, it finally crashed into the ocean.

"There goes our investment," Zhang said.

"Placed against the lives of some of the most important humans on Earth, and I'd say the price was more than equitable, Lady Zhang," Gina remarked.

"Altruism, Gina?" Frost was surprised and pleased with Gina's most thoughtful and emotional response.

"Compassionate theories of expansion, Mr. Secretary." Gina smiled at Frost, who knew that whatever happened from here on, Gina would be there to help humanity begin its next long march towards becoming.

Miranda Han took Samson Frost's hand and squeezed it tightly. Leann Rajastani looked out at the spaceport, not wanting to see Cosulo's demise. She was looking out, looking forward to the next moment, the next challenge, accepting the instinct that Shenu's first days as a living, breathing organism with all her passengers and families would be dangerous, incredibly trying, and remarkable.

Declan Keel felt elated, but not because of Cosulo's demise; that was just machine parts and force fields. He felt strangely excited at the prospect of facing the danger ahead, not just for himself but for all the ring dwellers. As he looked over his new passengers, he felt protective of them. He thought they needed him, and equally, he needed them. His eyes finally fixed on Gina, who looked back at him with a mix of sheepishness and ferocity as if those two emotions were congruent. For a human, exhibiting those two emotions simultaneously would be challenging, but somehow, for Gina, they seemed entirely compatible. Keel found himself moving closer to Gina, who met him halfway.

"You look like you have something to say to me, General."

Keel was surprised that Gina could read him. He'd always considered himself inscrutable. In this case, she could even read him when he didn't know why he walked to her or what he might want to say.

"Call me Declan." It was the most superficial response he could muster. It seemed appropriate for the awkwardness of the moment.

"Everyone else calls you general."

"That's because of my relationship with them."

"And your relationship with me is different?" she asked with a quixotic smile.

"Well, yes. You're not military, you're not Shenu, you're not UEU or EC. You're an independent quantity."

"Quantity?"

"I'm not very good with words." He sounded like a schoolboy. Shyness was a trait Declan Keel had never shown to anyone. He wasn't shy, was never shy, and was confused that he felt shy now.

"I mean, you're just not like everyone else. You're different."

"I suppose so, but I've noticed that our differences are what make us unique."

"That's a very wise assumption."

"Well, wisdom is something I'm severely lacking in."

"Why do you say that?" Keel asked.

"I'm not old enough to be wise."

"Age does not determine wisdom. How you look at the world, the lessons you learn from each other, the paths you choose and why you choose them, and your purpose in life. Those are some of the things that define wisdom." Keel felt he had gotten his mojo back and was now speaking to Gina in terms both could understand. A real conversation took place, and he noticed that Gina's eyes twinkled slightly as they looked at each other. The look became more intense, and they both broke the stare simultaneously.

"Well, I'd better get back to the bridge," Keel said. He felt butterflies; he was nervous, and his palms began to sweat. His physical response prompted him to break off their first conversation.

"I've enjoyed our first dialogue," Gina said with a smile.

"Me too," Keel said, smiling.

Betta Rajastani was standing nearby, but her mind was on Cosulo, and she felt helpless, an unusual feeling for her, just like shyness was an extraordinary feeling for Keel. Surely, something could have been done to save Cosulo. She looked at Gina, talking to Declan Keel, who stood close to her. Betta immediately knew that these were not Gina's pheromonal urgings affecting Keel. She could tell by his posture and facial expressions that Keel was more than casually interested in Gina, even if he didn't know it himself.

Once Keel left, Gina turned her gaze towards Shenu.

What was she thinking? Could she have done anything differently? Betta asked herself.

Gina stood stolid and sentry-like, also looking at Cosulo. No, Betta thought. If Gina couldn't save Cosulo, then it was predestined that no one could.

Pashar was sitting alone, silently meditating, putting all thoughts of fear behind him. Cosulo was a necessary tragedy to awaken everyone to the dangers they were all about to face. He prayed for strength and guidance from his angels.

Keel returned to the bridge, where a now-composed Hayworth sat at the controls, eyes focused and head cleared from the events of a few minutes ago.

"How long to Shenu?" Keel said.

"5 Hours," Hayworth answered. "Once we pass into the Thermosphere, Shenu's defenses will protect us."

"Time to the edge of Thermosphere?" Keel wasn't taking any assurances.

"Two hours, commander."

"Increase speed." Falcon increased her speed. Betta walked over to one of Falcon's viewports and gazed up.

"There she is," Pashar walked over to her and looked out the viewport. Above them, he could see Shenu spinning in geosynchronous orbit with Earth for the first time. Pashar put his hand on his sister's shoulder. Betta felt his fraternal love at that moment, and a tear formed in her eyes. She looked up at Pashar, who wiped her tears away with some of his own.

"Home," Betta said as she laid her head on Pashar's broad shoulder and closed her eyes, relishing the bonding moment between them. She knew this might be the last time they could exist just as brothers and sisters, their different missions calling them to different futures and dangers. For now, a silent peace was enough to assuage their fears, and they remained that way for an endless moment.

CHAPTER SIX

SABOTEUR

antalus watched Cosulo's swan song with little or no emotion. To him, it was all part of the plan, which worked flawlessly. His heightened senses felt the vibrations of his Level 6 adept, Mara Gale, as she approached the chamber. He pressed his left temple to obfuscate his now-evolving reptilian form. To Mara, he looked the same as he always did in his previous form: 6 feet tall, with greying long hair, bright green eyes, thin and fragile.

"Did you set the quantum cameras?"

"Yes, Dr. Exactly to your specifications."

"That's all. You can go now."

Mara left the room. Tantalus was pleased. He marveled at how happy he had become at the destruction of something as incredible as Cosulo and the dead who were collateral damage from his experiment. For a short moment, he felt a pang of regret that didn't last long. Gina had revealed herself. The first part of his plan had worked. He laughed out loud for a long minute, finally catching his breath.

He pressed his right temple and returned to his newly evolving self. Since his last injections, he hadn't dared to look at himself in the mirror. With his plan firmly in action, he felt confident enough to finally see what he looked like after the last infusions of the vitreous solution he injected into his pineal gland every six hours. He slowly approached the mirror and removed his hood and mask.

The first thing he noticed was how ageless he looked. He was still Malcolm Tantalus, even through the eyes of his newly generating DNA. The human pink skin was replaced by a silver-green reptilian leather-like skin of tiny scales that rippled in the halogen light.

Reptiles were usually thought of as cold-blooded and reproduced by laying eggs. Was that still the case with his overlords? This new form was more mammalian than reptile in its evolution of procreation. Somewhere along the evolutionary line, these reptilians must have mated with a mammalian species. It was almost too much to consider. How did the mating occur? If not all reptiles were cold-blooded, an entirely new evolutionary line could have been created. This is what must have happened. But who were these mammals that the reptilians mated with, and why? It was just one of a million questions he had no answers to.

He wondered what sex would be like in his new form, which brought back memories of his capture. He was milked for his sperm, a memory he hadn't recalled until just now. This leftover nightmare seemed somehow meaningful and innocuous in this graying moment.

His lizard-like eyes were silver and snake-like. A nictitating membrane had grown over them to protect him from any radiation. They also gave him peripheral infrared vision. Tantalus relished this new body, but it chilled him to the core to wonder what he was becoming and why.

His captors from that long-ago trip to the other side of the galaxy told him nothing more than that he would become a progenitor, the English translation of a word in their language he had no time to study as he was kept prisoner on their world for what seemed like an eternity, being prodded and experimented on, until they deemed him fit for their plans.

He had no choice but to accede to their will, though, if he had been honest with himself, he would've thanked them for transforming his sad little life into something so much more essential.

All he knew was that they would contact him when they were ready. Until then, his orders were communicated to him in his dreams, using his pineal gland as an attenuator, a link between his world and theirs. He knew they had caused this and did it to him, but Dr. Malcolm Tantalus relished his new form. He was ready to carry out their every wish.

He left the obsidian chamber and approached a console where he watched the replay of the destruction of Cosulo and saw Gina up close for the first time. He caught his breath as he watched her maneuver in space.

A tear rolled down his face. He was happy to know he could still cry. At least his emotions were intact. To lose them, to become neutered from feeling would have been a price too high to pay even for such a solitary being, the usual human description now eluding him, as he was becoming something other than that, although to give what he was becoming a name would undoubtedly cheapen its importance.

He contemplated what he had wrought on humanity in the last 48 hours. He wasn't proud; he wasn't gloating. He, too, was human or used to be human. He did feel something. He searched his newly forming mind for the right words. He felt humbled, not by his inaction to stop the beginning of his new life course, but by his actions at the behest of his overlords, beings much wiser and more malicious than he could ever be.

He was one step closer to her now. It might take him months or longer, but his journey was now entirely unfolding before him. It might lead him to triumph or destruction, but one thing was sure. It would lead him to destiny.

Betta and Pashar settled into the observation lounge on Falcon. Pashar was exhausted. Betta was anything but. With the imminent disaster of losing the colonists behind her, Betta immediately analyzed the situation.

Pashar was sitting beside her deep in "Verba," a self-analyzing technique learned at a young age by all Sidrani. This was the perfect time for such metaphysical gymnastics. He was busy culling together any communications from Earth to Shenu, intercommunications between UEU and EC intelligentsia, and anything that might explain the whys of what just happened.

"I've been trolling the frequencies looking for any clues, anomalous transmissions, even Offworld," he said.

Betta was right there with him. Two split souls come together to use their immense skills to solve the mystery. "Why didn't they sabotage Falcon with Gina onboard?" she asked.

"The cargo was so secret, I'm sure they had advanced defense nets all over the ship. Cosulo was an easier target."

"I think you're missing the point," Betta answered.

"Then, illuminate me."

"Think, brother. The saboteur plants a bomb they know cannot be detected or detonated by any known means. They also know that secret cargo is coming up to Shenu."

"He tested the defenses of the cargo on the way to the launch point," he said.

"That still doesn't provide the why," she replied.

Pashar looked at his sister, studying her, trying to decipher her breathing patterns and eye movements. Betta knew, of course, and let Pashar dissect her psychology. Then, just when she thought that he was about to render his viewpoint on the experience, she took a shallow breath, fixed her eyes on his to distract him from his train of thought, and let him have it.

"To see how advanced it was. When he saw it was impervious to Gamma EM pulses, he went with Plan B."

"Plan B?" Pashar was now on the hook.

"If you can't steal Shenu's secret weapon." Pashar looked puzzled. "I am marveling at the advanced military mind training of the Sidrani. If you can't steal the secret weapon."

"Then reveal the secret weapon." It was as if he was in a dark room, and suddenly, a supernova illuminated the darkness.

"He lured her out."

Betta reached over and kissed him on his forehead, which was totally out of order for her. Pashar was touched and confused at the same time. Betta tapped the back of her hand, and a holographic image of Leanna appeared.

"Mother. You must do a sensor scan of the known satellites within viewing range of what just happened on Cosulo."

"Why?" Leanna asked, but she knew questioning her daughter was a fool's errand. If Betta hadn't reasoned this out, she would've never made such a request.

"Mother, for once, listen to your children, who sometimes are a lot smarter than you think." Pashar implored.

"What are you talking about?"

"We think the plot to bomb Cosulo was a ploy to get us to reveal Gina."

"Reveal. To whom?"

"Mother, trust us. Get the information we asked for, and when we arrive, and I interface with UMA, we will analyze it properly."

"Very well. We'll see you at 0600 Shenu orbital time." Leanna ended the transmission.

Gina appeared at the doorway. Whatever the rest of the Cosulo passengers were talking about, they stopped, and one by one, the inhabitants began to look up at her as she passed through the room.

Stares were replaced by awe and wonder. Everyone had seen what Gina had done, what she had become, and what her essence radiated out to them, but there was an ineffable quality to their awe, a heroic sense of wonder that permeated the room.

Betta was just as mesmerized as the other travelers, perhaps more so, as she could sense something deeply embedded in this next-gen woman standing before her. An otherworldly quality, and for the first of many times, Betta realized that Gina was not like anyone else on Earth, or Shenu for that matter. She was Alien and human at the same time. A missing link, a throwback to another time, another world, to a future she could only imagine. Her feeling was so intense that she stopped breathing for a moment.

Gina also sensed something unique in Betta. Her eyes glowed violet, a sign of deep reverie for her, and with that serene gaze, she looked down at Betta, who rose from her seated position to meet Gina's stare.

Pashar, for his part, was as entranced by Gina but in a different way. If Betta was in awe, Pashar was in what? He couldn't describe this rush of a million emotions, all cascading into his heart as if a dam had broken and the rush of water flowing 200 miles an hour through the landscape of his persona threatened to rip away all sense, all reason. He had never felt so strongly as that feeling at that moment, and it thrilled and scared him simultaneously.

"So, you're the secret everyone's been trying to keep around here," Pashar said, almost as a challenge.

"Not so secret anymore, my young Sidrani warrior," Gina answered him telepathically. She knew that Pashar's military and intelligence abilities far outshined everyone else in the room. She also knew that for anything to come to pass in service to humanity, this exceptional young man would be an intricate part of it. Turning away from Pashar, she faced Betta.

"You are a Level 6 adept," Gina said telepathically.

Betta, who takes advantage of every opportunity to test her abilities, answers Gina similarly. "You're telepathic." Betta kept staring at Gina.

"You're wondering how I was conceived." Gina got right to the point.

"And you're wondering who you are and why you exist." Gina smiled curiously at Betta but knew this was too intense for a first conversation. She also knew she and Betta had some destiny together, but now was not the time to explore that path.

A severe situation had just transpired, and Gina knew she needed to keep everything on a human scale. Betta was too sharp and bright for Gina to engage in this now. Gina looked curiously at Betta, knowing Betta would not let this go without some answer.

Gina removed the veil of secrecy from their conversation to break the silence engulfing their telepathic moment. She addressed Betta directly, ensuring everyone could hear and preventing Betta from withholding this secret from others.

"I was raised from a quantum zygotic matrix as an embryo, just like you," she said aloud.

"So, who are your parents?"

"My DNA was extracted from Dr. Olefors and Dr. Weston, then combined inside a gravity well to enable my matrix to grow without interference from Earth's gravity. I have the genetic markers of over 1000 species, From a tardigrade to an armadillo, a black widow spider, an octopus to the turritopsis dornii."

"The jellyfish that are immortal," Betta added.

"Exactly. I am impressed with your knowledge."

"Sounds romantic." Pashar couldn't resist getting involved in this conversation.

"Don't listen to him. He's all about conquest and possession," Betta said.

"Possession. A human weakness. No one being can possess another. My soul belongs to me. I have learned that conquest, possession, and sexuality often go hand in hand. Perhaps Mr. Rajastani would like to explore that someday when he matures."

Pashar laughed but was self-conscious, as Gina had exposed one of his insecurities. He quickly changed the subject.

"So, how long have you been alive?" Pashar asked.

"I was conceived five years ago, then in bio stasis for two years to complete my skeletal and neural structure and to acquire my immune system. Then, I had two years of intense human interaction. How to be human, think for myself, laugh, cry, love."

"So, you're nine," Pashar added.

Gina smiled but said nothing, letting Pashar stew in his immaturity.

Betta and Pashar were dumbstruck by Gina's poise, self-awareness, and humor. Finished with the Q&A, Gina moved away to help the others.

Betta turned to Pashar. "Did you know about this? Her?"

"How would I know anything? You're the adept. Maybe that's why you're so curious. You look... I'm not sure what that look is."

Betta looked intently at Gina, who turned and smiled. Betta smiled back uneasily as Gina left the room.

After eventful hours of fear and loss had passed, Falcon started moving. Ten minutes into its ascent, an alarm sounded through Falcon, sending Han and Frost running through the maglev hallways to the guest quarters. Keel was already there.

"Have you cleared all the passengers?" Frost asked.

"Yeah. But some of them saw it anyway," Keel said. They entered the room, which was covered in blood.

"Who was it?" Han was troubled and curious at the same time. The blood-splattered walls gave reason to the fact that someone had blown themselves apart.

"The saboteur, Ms. Han." Keel moved around a corner, revealing a man or what was left of him.

"Amazing it didn't rupture Falcon's exoskeleton," she continued. "Must be some new kind of explosive compound. Not from Earth, or else GAIA would've picked it up on biosensors."

Keel looked at Han with a mix of admiration and speculation. Han returned his look with a tinge of something more, as if she wanted to say something but refrained from doing so. *Fuck he thought. She just walked in 30 seconds ago, and she nailed it. But she's hiding something. What's up, Miranda?*

"When the solar bomb detonated, so did he." Keel was curious to see just how far her understanding went. Olefors walked between Han and Keel but immediately felt like he'd gotten in bed with them both.

"Listed as Jack Benham," Olefors said. "Been with the UEU for ten years. A mission specialist responsible for the external care of the maglevs. Level 10 clearance."

After interacting with Gina an hour before, Byrnes entered the room, fresh from a mental cold shower. She followed him into the room moments later, walked right by him without a glance, immediately approached what was left of Benham, and focused on his body.

"His other eye. Where is it?"

If it weren't so severe, it would be comical, Olefors thought. Gina didn't understand humor yet, or so he thought.

"They're over here. Well, the one that's left." Keel smirked. He knew any hint of humor or sarcasm would fall flat. Walking to a corner, he picked up Benham's eyeball, handing it to Olefors, who placed it in a mylar pouch. Gina took the pouch and, with a simple eye scan, turned to the group.

"There's something else. His retina. There's something on it."

"The retina?" Keel asked.

"Let's get him to the med bay and examine his eyes, eye." Olefors was taking no chances as he knew Gina was deadly accurate in these situations.

Byrnes was on alert. He realized that this was not only a severe breach of security, but if someone with level ten clearance could get onto the most secure ship in the solar system and plant a solar bomb without GAIA knowing about it, then who knew what else could be in store for them over the following hours on their way to Shenu or after they had taken up residency there.

"Gina, please scan the maglev for any other anomalies." Olefors was perfunctory and didactic in his command. Byrnes bristled at the exchange.

"I've already examined all decks for other anomalous readings," Gina said.

"How did you miss this?" Olefors said in a marked prosecutorial tone.

"Hey, leave her alone. She just fucking saved our asses."

"No need to come to my defense, Commander. Dr. Olefors knows that I'm not perfect. Don't you, Doctor? If I were, there would be no need for you or your self-important genius."

Han marveled at how Gina manipulated Olefors but gave him just enough rope to hang himself, the rope tied to his frail ego.

"Quite right, Gina. Quite right." Olefors turned an annoying shade of embarrassment red and left the room. Everyone looked at Gina, who winked and followed Olefors out.

A few minutes later, Olefors was deep into examination when Frost entered the med skiff. The room was circular and lined with platinum, which Olefors specifically chose for the room because of its self-healing properties, something that was deduced in the early 21st century but never fully implemented to create biometal until 2300, a mere 25 years ago.

He was glad to see Danika Weston's holoimage appear before him. Seeing Danika in Holopersona sent Olefors' heart racing. He hadn't seen her for over six months and was now faced with the reality that he'd soon be with her on Shenu. All the old business that had hampered their professional relationship was now out in the open for everyone else to see.

Olefors felt a bit nauseous at the sight of her. Still, he couldn't help but feel his emotions rising as she began the call, showcasing her incredible blend of Southeast Asian elegance and German precision. She stood 5'8" tall, embodying a powerful combination of intellect and strength—not physical strength, but the strength of the mind. With a remarkable IQ of 180 and a Denson Prize for her groundbreaking work in advanced genetic engineering related to TRNA, she was the architect of a genetic breakthrough that had been a millennium in the making. This discovery was also what made both Gina and UMA possible.

Seeing Olefors again after their "split" was both unsettling and thrilling for Danika. It was unsettling because she had managed to put him out of her mind after their last meeting, which had been filled with frustration due to Olefors' refusal to explain what had happened during the five years since his absence. At the same time, she felt a thrill of excitement about what he had brought back from that missing year, leaving her both amazed and curious.

It wasn't just that he went missing; it was what he brought back from his time away that amazed Danika. He returned with some of the most advanced medical, genetic, cerebral, and surgical techniques and practices she had ever encountered. Danika realized that these innovations came from a different place, yet Olefors wouldn't—or couldn't—divulge their origins.

Until that moment, Danika felt she needed to keep her relationship with Olefors at a distance. Seeing him now, looking scared and frail, elicited empathy from her but not sympathy, as they were two sides of different coins. She had empathy for all sentient life, but sympathy was reserved for her own lowest moments, and she saw no reason to change that now.

If she were honest, she would admit she had feelings for him. Still, those feelings were suppressed. After everything they had gone through together, she realized that advanced genetic research and intimacy did not mix well and overshadowed everything else.

They'd been close to intimacy and would have acted upon it if not for the elephant in the room. One thing Danika insisted on in any relationship was total honesty. Nothing less would entice her to share herself with anyone. She was perfectly happy being alone with her cats and doing her research. When she did want sexual gratification, it was either by self-pleasure or with her friend Marissa, who kept telling Danika that she was a closet lesbian.

Danika countered by saying she was impressed by Marissa's ability to orally please her, something she wished she could do for herself, but that's as far as it went. Danika would never identify her sexuality. Fluid was her moniker, and she'd never give up that freedom to define herself to anyone.

Yet, here she and Olefors were, staring at each other's holosims across space. She had to admit that Olefors was the one person who never pressured her to define anything, the man who always saw more in her than she saw in herself.

She also had to admit that even in his current state of anxiety, Olefors looked better and better to her. Looking at him, she was more attracted than she liked to admit, mainly to prevent his massive ego from taking a victory lap. Weston's holoimage moved swiftly to the table where Olefors examined Benham's eyeball.

"Anything of interest, Anderson?" She smirked, knowing everything in this room was of keen interest to both of them.

Frost stood silently by Olefors and Weston as they dissected what remained of Benham's body. He watched as Olefors placed the eyeball into a quantum chamber, a dimensional holding case. Nothing in three-dimensional reality could interfere with Olefors' examination inside the chamber. Quantum chambers and Tesla Eggs were new tech for the 24th century, and Olefors was one of its creators. He kept the tech close to the vest and refused even to acknowledge it for the first years of its genesis. But when Shenu was about to come online, Leanna Rajastani insisted that quantum chambers and Tesla Eggs would be the sole proprietary property of Shenucorp, the business entity that held all of Shenu's contracts, credit exchanges, and secrets. The main issue was that Olefors wasn't the only person with a Tesla Egg.

Money in the 24th century was quite different from its predecessors. There were no coins per se, no digital currency. Money was secured using advanced biometric authentication methods and quantum-resistant cryptography to protect against emerging security threats. It wasn't something to be made; it wasn't even called money. Credits was a more appropriate term.

Various institutions used a kind of quantum currency called "Quantacredits." This currency was information and knowledge, and the quantum chamber and the Tesla Eggs were considered the most valuable assets on the planet. Money was still necessary, an amorphous measurement for most of humanity, at least those humans that put a physical price on anything; however, it was all tied to quantum currencies, impossible to hack, rob, or manipulate. The safest method ever devised for economic exchanges. Trade still needed a currency, and quantum currencies were promulgated to support the enormous trading business that dominated the Terran system.

Frost watched Olefors raise the quantum chamber information on his visual scanner. "Dr, I'd like to access the same information for your quantum chamber."

Olefors was slow to respond because he disliked sharing technology with anyone. However, he understood that Frost was even more senior than he was. Additionally, Olefors knew that his agreement with the Shenu leadership to allow access to this technology included giving the foremost Harbinger access to this top-secret information.

So, with a wave of his hand, he allowed Frost to access the same information he was now accessing. He didn't expect what Frost chose to discuss once they were shielded from the rest of the world, cozy and insulated inside the chamber.

"So, is Gina back in her box?"

Olefors was annoyed at Frost's line of questioning and hated that he hadn't expected it. "You say that with more than a bit of contempt, Mr. Frost."

"Not at all. I'm just curious to see how you square the circle with a sentient who you insist is nothing but your creation."

You fucking Neanderthal. It was then that he decided to ignore Frost.

"Ignoring a Harbinger can be dicey business," Frost said.

"Ingenious," Olefors exclaimed.

"What?" Frost snapped, annoyed that Olefors was so completely ignoring him.

"I believe we found the origins of our terrorist. Look for yourself."

Frost was elated at the prospect of peering into dimensions no one had seen before except Olefors. Frost raised his hand, swiped away the quantum barrier, and was immediately immersed in something he could not explain. He felt a tingling sensation all over his body.

"The tingling will subside soon," Olefors said. "Then you'll feel a bit nauseous and faint but better after a moment." On cue, Frost began to feel better.

"It's crazy, huh? Parsing dimension is so elemental, yet so alien."

There it was, Frost thought. Olefors again referred to Aliens. He knew better than to ask too many questions while inside the egg. For one, he was in awe of what he saw, which was no less than a gateway into other realities.

"Stay with me, Ambassador. Don't go down the rabbit hole. Stay with me here."

Frost thought this experience was almost too much for him, but he didn't dare ask to leave. Olefors knew what he had unleashed.

"What do you see?"

"An atom. Spinning." Frost couldn't believe his eyes. "Azidoazide azide?"

"Excellent," Olefors exclaimed. "But in a form I've never seen before."

"It's so explosive. How could it stay inert?"

"That's the question. One potential method to render azidoazide azide inert is through controlled decomposition. Carefully heating it to a temperature at which it decomposes without detonating can help. My initial hypothesis would be that it was injected into Benham in its decomposed state and then reheated when it reacted with the Baryonic radiation from the sun and the water in Benham's body."

"So, it was undetectable until it wasn't and then detonated in a nanosecond."

Frost was struck by the destructive power of the science he and Olefors were observing. However, with each passing minute, he became increasingly aware that everything that had occurred that day had pushed them into uncharted territory. Although he was trained for such situations, he still felt a deep sense of concern.

"It might have linked with one of the inert gases, something already prevalent in the body, say, Nitrogen in a crystalline form."

"Crystalline Nitrogen? I don't understand."

"I'm not surprised," Olefors chided. "You see, it is a semiconductor. In this isotope, it was wired directly into Benham's brain."

"So, his iris was made from an isotope of Azidoazide azide, rendered inert inside a molecule of crystalline nitrogen, which reacted when bombarded with the baryonic radiation of the sun, arming and then exploding the bomb."

"Again, excellent." Olefors was impressed. This Frost was as brilliant as he had heard, and right there, he decided that he and Frost would become much closer than he had surmised, even with his previous castigation of Olefors for his treatment of Gina.

"In essence, Benham was genetically modified to be the detonator for the bomb. His entire molecular make-up was bred to be a catalyst for this very experience."

"He was the bomb," Frost said.

"To some extent. Without his biochemical catalyst, the bomb could not be detonated."

"A human detonator."

"More advanced than any I've ever seen."

"Seniori?" Frost interrogated.

"Maybe, they certainly have the capability. I think it's something or someone more outside the mainstream."

"Think or believe?" Frost needed to get to the bottom of this fast.

"Believe," Olefors said sadly.

"So, was he a clone?" Frost asked.

"The best I've ever seen. Azidoazide azide silica based. Impervious to our scans."

Olefors was as concerned as Frost, if not more so because he knew that whoever planned and executed this was not only nefarious; they were insidious and brilliant—a lethal combination.

"Have you ever seen this before?" Frost had the slightest hint of panic in his voice.

Olefors became anxious. *If Samson Frost felt panicked, then everyone on Earth, Shenu, and this solar system should be worried.*

"Never," Olefors said. "Whoever did this is a mystery to all of us."

A concerned look crossed both of their faces. Frost disconnected from the chamber and the Tesla egg and promptly fainted.

Frost, Byrnes, and Keel stood with all the passengers an hour later as Falcon moved out of the Thermosphere. He tried to forget his encounter inside the Tesla Egg and instead focused on the future, even if it seemed more diffuse and uncertain. Byrnes's calm voice quieted his nerves.

"Attention. A service for the lost crew and passengers from Cosulo will be held in 30 minutes in the sanctum. While we mourn those we've left behind, we must always look ahead to the future, our shared destiny. As you might have noticed on your holo-shells, we have moved out of the Thermosphere and into the Exosphere on the final approach vector to Shenu. Now, if everyone will call your attention above your heads, you're in for an amazing view."

Frost appreciated Bynes' cheery attitude, something he had grown to love about him. Byrnes, on his part, was just as nervous as Frost and Keel, but his job was not to let on that anything was wrong. He was the face of Shenu, the congenial father figure everyone loved and trusted. The father of Athena is what he was being called.

He was somewhat disgusted by the title Father of Athena. Tara Zhang had bestowed this name upon him, much to the evident displeasure of Miranda Han, who was tagged as the Mother of Athena, a title she detested. Despite the world seeming to crumble around him, Harrison Byrnes was once again called upon to radiate calm and confidence, a task he fulfilled with measured reverie.

He waved his hand over the console, and the roof above everyone's head turned clear. Shenu came into view. The audible gasps from the passengers were exactly what Byrnes knew would happen. Even he was mesmerized by his new home. The room was silenced as if the passengers were experiencing a moment of true revelation, like seeing a miracle performed before their eyes, as if religion had been transformed from the ecumenical to the metaphysical, with humanity playing the godhead, now divorced from opinion and conjecture. It was a tacit understanding among the Falcon passengers that through the power of scientific imagination and human fortitude, that which had been unattainable, unknown, was suddenly and surprisingly within their grasp.

The first thing everyone noticed was its sheer size. It was so enormous that it filled the viewport even at this distance.

Pashar and Betta entered the room and stood motionless and silent beside Gina.

"You see images, even with neural linking, you didn't get this," Pashar said. Betta left his side, leaving him feeling apart from everything. He realized that everyone aboard Falcon, these chosen few who were to experience the revelation of Shenu in their own time, their minds, and if they believed in them, their souls were somehow chosen for this moment.

For Pashar, it marked the culmination of a lifetime of dreams, bringing him to this moment. He understood his journey had just begun. He only dared to ponder where it might take him as, in his dreams, the path was endless, filled with many beginnings. It was a problem for him, and Sidrani warriors detested anything that couldn't be solved by mental fortitude or physical prowess. The moment left him feeling smaller than he had ever felt and simultaneously left him standing on the precipice of his creation, waiting to breathe.

Betta felt Pashar's emotional reckoning, which scared and somehow also reassured her. Scared because she knew Sidrani warriors hated the unknown and would fight the dark to see the light break through, and reassured that this experience opened Pashar's third eye, enabling him to immerse himself in the journey they were all on. She approached Gina, still silent.

What is she thinking? Betta wondered. She would never ask Gina because the expected answer might be beyond her comprehension. Standing silently by Gina's side, she absorbed the monumental historical moment when humanity's path shifted forever. Both women stood in silence, sharing unspoken thoughts. As Betta glanced at Gina, their eyes met.

"What are you feeling?" Gina's curiosity was palpable. Betta paused, the silence stretching endlessly.

Feeling. It wasn't a question. Betta was trying her best to formulate an answer, but she found herself without words. It was an infuriating and exhilarating experience at the same time.

She felt linked to Shenu as if they were each a piece of some whole that had yet to be fully realized and, what's more, put together into something bigger than its parts.

Shenu gleamed, unlike any structure before her. The three concentric rings rotated in a harmonious controlled dance, imitating the rotation of the Earth. They were always in the same position. Hence, the mage levs were in their orbital path, tethered to this monolithic masterpiece like spider webs radiating from a central hub to a maypole or carousel horses revolving around a central Calliope.

To prevent it from shielding the sun's rays from the Earth below, Shenu had a series of advanced Solonical suns. These structures were created to mimic the exact rays of the sun's output to the millisecond, which were being obfuscated by the rings. That way, the nourishing rays of Helios, our star, would be reflected down onto the Earth. The Solonical Suns were fabricated in orbit and attached to its mesostructure.

If it had not been for Miranda Han's ingenious invention, the large swath of shadow that Shenu cast would have rendered its counterpart on an Earth barren of any light, thus killing all vegetation and life for 200 kilometers where the rings shadowed the sun. It was the last piece of engineering that enabled Shenu to be built. Once that problem was solved, the construction began and never stopped. In essence, Shenu made Earth into a Level II society according to the Kardashev scale. It was a society that had harnessed the energy of its star to power itself. Most historians of the previous 200 years had predicted that humanity would never be able to achieve a Level II society. Shenu and the brilliant minds that had created her changed all that.

The innermost ring of the three rings, the TERRAN RING, most closely resembled familiar things on Earth: shops and businesses, recreational event theatres, sports, and music venues, welcoming centers, schools, gyms, medical facilities, green spaces, grocery markets where aeroponic foods were grown. The Terran Ring was the arrival ring. It was also where all the solar power stations resided. It was more like a

24th-century mall, complete with any shop or facility that any of the Shenu residents could want.

Each ring had a specific frequency. The Terran Ring was tuned to the 528 frequency, the MI Solfeggio Frequency, often called the "love frequency." This sound vibration was piped into the ring to stimulate the subconscious, so the residents were unaware of its healing tones. The 528 frequency was also central to creating and restoring inner equilibrium, increasing awareness, repairing DNA, and stimulating transformation.

The middle ring was called the WATEN RING, the Egyptian word for Home. Here, all the inhabitants of Shenu lived. It provided comfortable accommodations for 200,000 people and was also where UMA and GAIA's nesting chambers were located. The waten ring was tuned to 396 Hz or the UT Solfeggio Frequency, which helped those who struggled with guilt, fear, and grief. This tone was highly grounding and cleansing. The 396 also used binaural beats as a form of healing.

The outer ring was called the INVETIO RING, Latin for discovery. This was where the military, mining, trade, and exploration happened. All the interstellar crafts, shuttles, weapons systems, docking bays, and Blackhold training centers were located there. All the Shenu brass had their offices here. It bristled with the most advanced defense and exploration technology humanity had created for the Shenu mission. The invetio ring resonated to the 741 SOL Solfeggio frequency. SOL is the frequency that is said to help detox the body from all types of pollutants (viral, fungal, bacterial, electromagnetic). This sound vibration is also said to be helpful when solving problems as it will increase mental clarity. The entire Shenu structure resonated with these tones.

Gina turned to Betta. "Do you hear it?"

"The Solfeggio Vibrations. Yes, it's so clear." Betta wondered whether she'd have picked up on it if Gina hadn't mentioned the tones. UMA, GAIA, and her mother knew of this celestial symphony, but she doubted anyone else did except Gina.

"How did you know?" Betta asked.

"I felt the vibration inside my aural canal, then that vibration spread down into my body and rested in the Tifareth heart."

The Tifareth heart. Betta couldn't believe it. *Did Gina reflect on the Hebrew tree of life?* How was that possible? If she knew of the theosophical lexicon of humanity, Kabbalah, the Zohar, the ancient Hebrew mysteries, the Tree of Life, the Sacred Feminine, Sacred geometry, Necromancy, Fibonacci numerology, the Tarot, the I Ching, what else did she know about? She was more than extraordinary; she was advanced in ways Betta couldn't even fathom.

The permutations of Gina's acumen shocked Betta to her core. Gina was unique and alien, but her abilities and knowledge encapsulated more than just Anderson Olefors's and Danika Weston's basic teachings. Gina was the uber femme, the ultimate woman.

Betta understood why her creation was so secretly guarded. Here was the ultimate human, the ultimate woman, the progenitor of a new race. Betta was awestruck for the first time in her life. Still, she never let on. She knew that, somehow, her relationship with Gina was beyond comprehension at this stage in their development. She also knew that she, UMA, and Gina were destined for a future none could foresee.

They turned their attention back to Shenu, now approaching fast. After over a hundred years of planning and building, years of toil and turmoil, and eons awaiting this chance to breathe, Shenu shone humanity's best self.

"The Cradle of Life," Gina said.

"She's amazing."

"She?" asked Gina.

"Yes, Shenu is female. All things of beauty are considered to be female, Gina. Didn't you know?" Betta said sarcastically.

"I take it from your intonation that you do not entirely believe what you are saying," Gina said.

"You're very perceptive. I usually don't see the female as being any more beautiful than the male, and I eschew characterizations that place people, or anything for that matter, into boxes to be separated and dissected, then put into bigger boxes and put on the shelves of ignorance."

"But in this case, you see Shenu differently?" Gina asked.

Betta didn't answer. She was caught up in her broken philosophy, and Gina called it out. Gina knew an answer wasn't forthcoming, so she waited momentarily and proceeded.

"I will not think of Shenu as male or female, just as a reflection of our humanity."

Gina smiled and quietly touched Betta's hand. Betta was surprised at its warmth. She was even more surprised when Gina squeezed her hand. Then something unique happened.

Betta looked over and saw a lone tear roll down Gina's face. Seeing it made her cry as well. The two women looked at each other and then simultaneously broke into smiles.

From this vantage point, Gina and Betta could see the biospheres standing semi-distant from one another, lined up in orbit around the three maglev sites.

As Falcon entered the vast docking bay, Betta thought everyone was feeling the same thing—something inexplicable, something magical.

"It's alive." Miranda Hans's comment spoke for everyone. They weren't just looking at technology. They were looking at a being of a different type: unknown, welcoming, foreign, but familiar.

"Well, it is alive. UMA is alive, and she is Shenu's heart, soul, and mind," Betta added, knowing that she and UMA would soon bond, and her consciousness and essence would forever be melded with UMA's. For a moment, Betta was petrified. It was the first time she felt that way about joining UMA. The feeling soon passed, and Betta returned her gaze to her new home.

"Anthropomorphizing again?" Pashar asked.

Pashar knew he was feeling the same way as everyone else. Still, the idea of a living being masquerading as the most advanced tech ever created made him uncomfortable, though he couldn't ascertain why. He organically turned to Betta, sensing her fear. He placed his arm around her and gently gave her a caress. Gina, seeing the tender moment between the two, smiled.

Falcon ascended into a chamber that opened to receive her, like a child returning to the womb. The darkness of space was replaced by the sight of a massive room with a clear ceiling, revealing the sun, which now shone down onto the arriving settlers.

CHAPTER SEVEN

I GENETICOM

The passengers disembarked from Falcon and were immediately swamped with R-bots, each assigned to one passenger and a valet guide whose only task was to attend to their new charges. Betta and Pashar exited the maglev, where Leanna Rajastani met them. She walked quietly to them and opened her long arms, welcoming them home as Shenu had done a few minutes earlier. Betta nuzzled up against her mother's neck.

"Thank Heaven you're safe." Leanna smiled but kept her emotions in check.

"So glad to be home," Betta said as she pulled away from the embrace and looked her mother in the eyes as she and Leanna always did when they wanted to express feelings that words could not rise to.

This was the first time that many of the Shenu settlers would see Leanna in person. She had been on Shenu for over a year, overseeing everything from trading and mining rights in the asteroid belt to the moon, Titan, Io, and Europa. Additionally, she was responsible for organizing all the space docking permits and creating a roster for the final crew for Athena, with approvals from Miranda Han and Harrison Byrnes.

After her tender moment with Betta, Leanna saw Pashar approaching her. Her eyes immediately welled up with tears, which she held back like a dam holding back a raging river. She hadn't seen her son for over ten years since her husband Rajiv took him from her to train as a Sidrani warrior. He had grown taller, and his jet-black hair, now shoulder length, was tied back in a "Tribale," a Sidrani knot that followed the curve of the rear of his head and was shaped like a bow. His piercing green eyes still held her gaze, as did his muscular form, which had become much more pronounced and showed him in a specifically virile light.

Leanna considered Pashar one of the most engaging and handsome men she'd ever seen. Some small part of her felt pride in him being her son. When she was pregnant with the twins, she was told by a trusted psychic healer that Pashar would be a lynchpin in Earth's future.

Leanna always knew Betta's acumen and future were tied to UMA, even before her birth, but her psychic prediction about Pashar surprised her. If she had to, she'd have to admit that during the pregnancy, she often had dreams about the twins, with her dreams about Betta relating specifically to her joining UMA and how that joining would shape the very foundation of Terran history.

When she breastfed them, Pashar on the left breast and Betta on the right, she always felt Betta biting at her nipples. Pashar's suckling was more nuanced, even sensual. She often put Betta down before Pashar, letting him suckle for longer.

At the time, she felt a bit guilty and somewhat aroused by the moments of quiet privacy between her and Pashar. She felt guilty but soon accepted what the universe had given her. She also knew that she and Pashar bonded empathically, which was unusual because Betta was naturally empathic, but Leanna never guessed Pashar would also possess that trait. She had to admit that even though parents were never supposed to favor their children, she did indeed favor Pashar.

She welcomed and loathed his arrival, her fear of what he might have become at his father's urgings churning in her heart and mind. Standing mere feet from him, she couldn't hold back her feelings anymore.

Pashar approached his mother and stood before her, allowing her to get a good look at him. He knew that she would have no platitudes for him. She stood there, held her hand in a typical Sidrani handshake posture, and bowed low to her son.

Pashar was touched that his mother practiced the old ways and became emotional at her show of respect. He bowed, then rose, looked her in the eyes, and said something he'd wanted to speak to her for ten years.

"I'm sorry he took me from you. I will never leave your side again."

Leanna stood stolid and tall, her emotions growing even more intense, but she held firm and smiled. Pashar and Betta walked past her and were taken by their R-bots to their separate quarters.

Harrison Byrnes approached Leanna with that boyish smile he always had when he was near her. They had met years ago on one of the first trips to Kenya to oversee the initial tech test of the Dark Matter drive for Athena.

The event marked a turning point for the Shenu mission, as Dark Matter had been the question mark that haunted humanity for the last 300 years. It wasn't until Miranda Han discovered that Dark Matter was not some inert gravitational force holding the cosmos together but a conscious form of life that defied equation and scientific speculation.

Its language was the language of quantum mathematics, a language infused into Shenu, enabling it to become more than the sum of its parts.

UMA, as Shenu's new Geneticom, and Athena, as her new dark matter drive, would be the intelligence that held Shenu together, sisters bound by shared quantum biology, and given the task of accompanying humanity on this most difficult and essential journey to its future place in the universe.

On that trip, Byrnes and Leanna Rajastani became close friends. Although Byrnes wanted it to be more than that, he was wisely let down gently by Leanna, who thought him handsome and brilliant but was not interested in anything more. She was to be the mother of Shenu, and besides, she already had a lover. Seeing Byrnes again strangely brought up feelings about Samson Frost, her paramour and soul mate. Maybe that's why she greeted Byrnes more formally than anticipated, with a formal handshake and a furtive smile. Whatever Byrnes imagined their first meeting to encompass, Leanna's formal greeting showed him his place in her world hadn't changed, and in some small way, he was also grateful. Being contemporaries and partners in Shenu was enough for them, and he instantly knew his place in her world. Again.

"Glad to see you," Byrnes said after their handshake. It was a perfunctory greeting, and Leanna thought it was perfect for the moment.

"What's the latest on the sabotage?" he continued.

"There'll be a debriefing at 0100 SOT, where everything we've discovered will be revealed."

As Byrnes walked away, Leanna called him. "By the way, Athena is docked on the invetio ring. Bay three. I think there's time to see her before we debrief."

Byrnes smiled, knowing that the feelings he once had for her were now perfectly put into a box labeled Athena. Leanna also knew that Harrison Byrnes' feelings for her were nothing compared to his love for Athena, nor should they be.

Olefors and Gina walked out of Falcon last to be met by Danika Weston, this time in mortal flesh. She approached Olefors first, then kissed him on both cheeks, in typical European style, letting him know she was glad to see him but hadn't forgotten how they left their last meeting.

Olefors insisted on intercourse to create Gina's embryo. Danika thought that advanced ingenvitro would suffice, but Olefors insisted that the embryo had to be created through intercourse.

Still, she resisted, leading to the impasse that permeated their relationship. On some level, they both knew that for them to function as a team again, they'd have to get over this impasse, but for now, Danika Weston was testing the waters to see how or even if there was a path to do that.

Olefors finally relented, and Gina was created ingenvitro, which he still claims made Gina's birth that much more tenuous. Finally, after months of steely silence between them, with Weston constantly asking Olefors about how he created Gina's matrices, Weston took it upon herself to discover what Olefors was hiding.

It was a tedious process, but finally, she discovered a set of Blueprints hidden in Olefors Trash files on a quantum he'd hidden away in a house in the north of Sweden. Weston came upon it while staying there to do some final research on Gina's genetic matrices. What she found surprised and confounded her.

It was a blueprint written in a language Weston had never seen or heard of. She used a retinal camera to photograph the blueprints stored in her hippocampus. It was advanced tech, something only a few chosen scientists could access. She figured she'd eventually ask Olefors about the blueprints once they were back on good terms.

After that, Danika Weston was sure of two things: one, that Anderson Olefors was indeed abducted before that moment, and two, that Anderson Olefors had brought back some advanced genetic computations that would be instrumental in creating Gina, and they weren't from the Terran system.

Gina waited as the pleasantries subsided between Danika and Olefors. She knew their relationship was more than just transactional. Gina, the byproduct of mixed genetic materials and some unusual genetic strands not belonging to either, shared Weston's curiosity about her origins.

Whenever she asked Olefors about it, he told her everything would be explained in time. That time never came, and Gina decided she'd find out as much as possible while on Shenu. She didn't care much about it. She just opined to herself that some biogenesis, whether through intercourse, Ingen, or some other form of procreation, created every living being.

She did, however, have a very warm feeling for Weston, who, for all intents and purposes, was her mother. Though she had done substantial research on the relationships between parent and sibling, she had never had the opportunity to fully express her feelings to Weston or ask her about her role as her "mother," something she vowed to do while up on Shenu.

Danika walked away from Olefors and approached Gina with a huge smile. "Gina, how wonderful to see you again."

"And for me, Dr. Weston."

"Danika, please. I heard your first hours of Shenu life have been challenging."

"Yes, I suppose I wasn't exactly prepared for what transpired, but I found myself curiously prepared for the role I assumed."

"Indeed, you are," Danika replied as she reassuringly touched Gina's hands and squeezed them to let Gina know that she was on her side and always ready to listen.

"Ok. You two will have plenty of time to get to know each other better. After all, you're practically family." Olefors's cute form of envy was evident to both Gina and Danika, and they

smiled at each other, the kind of smile that could only transpire between a parent and her sibling. As they walked away, Gina took Weston's arm, which had never happened before.

Olefors was keenly aware of how quickly Gina was embodying her humanity. It both reassured and concerned him, though he couldn't place the source of concern in his feelings. Some small part of him felt Gina's full embrace of her humanity might be problematic and harm the mission.

Later that day, Keel, Frost, and Rajastani sat in Rajastani's conference room with a spectacular view of Shenu and the Earth behind them. Zhang was there in Holoform. Keel stood before them with a holopanel hovering in front of him.

This is what we know. The satellite that emitted the Gamma EM pulse destroyed itself and left no residue. Benham had UEU clearance Level 10 and was a clone. He registered as fully human, even down to his semen. Someone is conducting advanced genetic experiments.

"Sounds like someone reprogrammed some very advanced R-bots," Zhang inferred.

"And a few clones as well," Keel added.

"Let's not forget the molecular detonator," Han said.

"Who has that kind of technology?" Zhang was desperate to gain some control of this situation, something she had expertise in. She felt like an outsider and vowed to get to Shenu immediately.

"That's another problem. We tried to extrapolate a trajectory from the satellite, which had to be launched from somewhere. When we tracked the source, we came up with an abandoned site in a Cambodian jungle, which must have been used in the Sino wars of the 2150s. No bioprints, no sensor locks. It was as if a ghost launched the satellite," Keel explained.

"We might want to expand our search to Earth databases. Whoever is behind these actions had to come from somewhere and has advanced tech skills," Zhang added.

"I'll have UMA and Betta conclave tomorrow morning. Betta is exhausted," Rajastani said.

"In the meantime, I'd check all the military hospitals, United Earth Union, and Earth Corporate. Might be someone we're already familiar with." Keel was resolute in his orders. He was keenly aware that this was a mission for the Blackhold and that he was responsible for everyone's safety.

"For now, the first arrival of the dwellers has been postponed while we get a better handle on all this. That will enable you to apply new protocols for the maglevs." Leanna turned to Keel. "What about the Kenyan Maglevs?"

"Operational in two weeks. We've already secured all maglev areas. The defense perimeter is nominal. Nothing, not even a Gamma EM pulse, could penetrate the shields." Keel sounded confident, but he was anything but.

"I want an answer to these Gamma EM bursts, people. So, we'd better use the next few days to identify whoever did this before this station becomes untenable." Rajastani used her final words to emphasize her determination, even though, like Keel, she doubted whether they could uncover and address the threat they faced. Everyone exited the room except for Keel.

"Yes, General."

"Harrison should be here," Keel reiterated.

"He's on his way to invetio with Miranda."

"I'd love to be a fly on that wall."

"You wouldn't last more than 5 minutes," she added.

"Oh, that's right. No insects up here."

"Except for honeybees." Leanna smiled.

"They sting and then die." Keel smiled back.

"Only the males General. Not those two. They're bound together whether they like it or not. Care for a drink? I know a great bar." She grabbed his hand.

"Got any Luoco?" he asked.

"A new bottle with your name on it."

"Let's get wasted." They both needed a release, and it seemed everything was being handled for now. Leanna knew what Luoco did, and she resigned herself to getting drunk and forgetting about life for a few precious hours. Besides, Declan Keel was the best drinking buddy she knew. It would be nice to let everything go. There would be plenty of time for responsibility and duty later.

The hover tram moved from the waden ring to the invetio ring at a fantastic speed. Byrnes and Han sat across from each other, paying little mind to the incredible sights they were passing as the tram moved silently along its magnetic glide path. They were too lost in thought, thinking about their first visit to Athena together, something both of them were anxious about.

Han was anxious because she hadn't seen her creation in over ten months, and Byrnes was anxious because Han hadn't seen her creation for ten months. Han became visibly nervous as the tram entered the docking bay on invetio.

"It's okay to be nervous." Byrnes was trying to be empathetic, but it came off as condescending. Miranda Han had accepted this from most people, especially Tara Zhang. She knew Zhang always kept a sidled eye on her as if she genuinely feared for her position as chancellor of EC. This was something Miranda Han never even gave a second thought to.

She wasn't a politician, nor a strategist, nor did she have any interest in strategizing. She'd leave that burden to people who were more ruthless and selfish than she was. All she was, all she ever wanted to be, was a galactic engineer.

"I think you'll be happy to see our progress." Byrnes followed up on his blunder a few minutes earlier.

"We'd made? How nice that must sound to you. Trying to convince me that all you ever did on Athena, you did for me."

"Well, us, but I was just trying to make you feel comfortable."

"What if I don't want to feel comfortable?"

"I thought we were past this." Byrnes's patience was wearing thin. He had done everything to get Miranda back into the Shenu picture. He knew that Han had a special relationship with Athena that Byrnes could never emulate, nor would he try. If this was to be their last mission together, Byrnes wanted only good things and good feelings to pervade above everything else.

"Considering I couldn't check the specs, I'd expect delays."

"Look. Miranda. I had nothing to do with the scuff-up with Zhang. I disagreed bitterly with their decision to keep you off Shenu for the last months, and I'm sorry. It was wrong."

"Integrity. Yeah, one of your inert traits. Cute."

"Petulance doesn't suit a brilliant mind like yours. I suggest you get your head out of your ass and count your blessings that you're about to see your creation alive and ready to take on any mission we choose to ask her to take on."

His words stung her, but Miranda Han knew then that she must put her insecurity and petulance behind her. Otherwise, Athena would sense them and ask why she was so childish and infantile - two emotions that Miranda Han thought she had overcome years ago. Perhaps not, she thought. Byrnes knew his words stung her but realized he didn't need to emphasize them again.

"There." He pointed out the tram window, knowing that Miranda would soon forget the pettiness of the discussion and engage entirely with the view she was looking at. She got as close to the window as possible without breaking the silicon-based Performa glass created over 50 years earlier. The Performa glass was instrumental in constructing Shenu as it was unbreakable and impervious to any outside sources that could disturb it.

Athena sat docked at spaceport docking berth three. She was sleek, significant, and powerful, and she was alive. She glowed a deep blue, a by-product of her quantum dark matter drive, keyed to circadian rhythm. Visible light wavelengths appear between 400 and 700 nanometers on the electromagnetic spectrum. In comparison, the wavelengths of radio waves are billions of times longer than visible light, while gamma rays are billions of times shorter. The blue light also boosted the alertness of her crew, improved attention span and reaction time, and helped memory. One study showed that 30 minutes of exposure to blue light led to better recall, raised mood, and effectively treated depression.

It was a choice Miranda and Athena made together, as Athena's decisions reflected her distinct personality and importance.

If GAIA and UMA were marvels of quantum TRNA AI exceptionality, Athena was much more human in her interactions. When Miranda Han designed her, she had already done years of research into dark matter, and only after servicing other ideas for Athena's central computational and drive systems did she settle on Dark Matter.

It was a controversial decision, but after Helga Minnofers discovered Dark Matter's sentience on a mission to Enceladus 15 years ago, there was no denying that Dark Matter was not only sentient but incredibly intelligent and emotionally stable. For years, everyone treated Dark Matter as a by-product of gravitational forces, or lack thereof, filling up the nothingness of space with more unknown and unexplored nothingness.

The story of how Dark Matter was discovered to be sentient could fill volumes. However, the theory's real genesis occurred when Helga and her team became stranded on Enceladus after a catastrophic failure of their plasma engines due to a micrometeoroid shower. Trapped on Jupiter's icy moon, they believed their days were numbered.

After almost two weeks without any ability to make contact with the outside world, something incredible happened; Karl Lordent, a genetic engineer specializing in cranial psychology, was trying to fix their communication systems when he received a message from an unknown source. He traced the source to a patch of sky over their crash site. From his calculations, the source seemed to be made up of a substance that did not emit light or have any gravitational constant, the classic description of Dark Matter.

When he used a Duromoter to measure the phenomenon, he noticed that the durometer ingested a quantity of the substance. When he tried to expel the substance, something amazing happened. The durometer began to emit a source of energy that had never been seen before.

Karl immediately brought the Durometer to Helga Minnofers, who noticed that the energy had a brainwave signature, encompassing all brainwaves simultaneously: Alpha, Beta, Delta, Theta, and Gamma waves. In his studies as a cranial psychologist, Karl Lordent found that Dark Matter utilized all these waves to communicate across vast periods of time and space, with Gamma waves being the most prevalent. Gamma waves were integral in processing complex tasks and maintaining cognitive function. They were essential for learning, memory, and processing, serving as a binding tool for the human senses to integrate new information. Lordent recognized a significant connection between meditation and Gamma waves, indicating a link to the enhanced state of "completeness" experienced during meditation. This discovery led to the realization that Dark Matter possessed sentience.

It wasn't as if Dark Matter spoke to him, but more like it spoke to his subconscious. That night in his dreams, he discovered a way to fix his communication systems through a dream state he experienced. The next day, he contacted the UEU central, and two weeks later, he and his team were rescued.

When Miranda Han heard of Lordents's discovery, she met with him and spent over a year dissecting every inch of his research. Then, one night, while asleep, she was contacted. It was unlike anything she'd ever experienced.

Through her dream state, she was told to build a ship made of Verantium, an alloy she was told to mine on Ceres. Once she had mined this rare substance, she was to create a ship designed by the subconscious entity communicating with her.

For the next ten years, Miranda Han and the entity she named Athena planned every aspect of this ship's design nightly. To ensure that Miranda never forgot what she was dreaming, she created a psychic recorder according to Athena's specifications, enabling her to record and translate all her dreams. For years, this symbiotic relationship grew and flourished until one year ago, after years of planning and receiving instructions from her sister, Athena was finally built.

Along with UMA and Shenu, Athena was humanity's most consequential invention. It now had its first genuinely Dark Matter ambassador, Miranda Han. This was part of why Tara Zhang paid her ridiculous credits to become part of EC.

Miranda could care less about accolades or credits. She and Athena were a team, and Athena wouldn't speak in dreams with anyone except Miranda Han. They were inexorably linked for eternity like Betta Rajastani and UMA, four twin souls exploring internal and external worlds together. Eventually, Athena told Miranda that others in her Dark Matter community would contact humans, but for now, Miranda was singularly honored with this privilege.

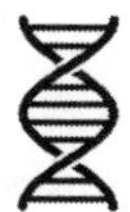

"She's something." Byrnes was being obtuse on purpose because he knew no words to describe Athena to anyone, especially Han, who wiped tears from her eyes.

"20 years of blood, one failed marriage, and no children." Han touched her abdomen as she spoke the last words, and Byrnes didn't miss the gesture. That's how he knew she was pregnant, but he didn't bring it up then. Han was focused on Athena, and as they got closer to one of her six docking ports, Han got out of her seat and went to the exit door of the tram, fidgeting with her Lifesuit and silently counting the minutes until she could get onboard.

"You know, in a way, we're Athena's parents. Let's get along, for the kid's sake." He smiled. Han turned and smiled back. It was indecisive, born from doubt and tempered through faith in Harrison Byrnes and his innate honesty. Miranda stopped being petty and focused solely on Athena and Harrison and their mission together.

The tram stopped, and she was out the doors as soon as they opened. Byrnes rose and followed her out slowly, giving her a head start so she and Athena could have a moment together.

Shit. Now I'm treating Athena like a living being. Though he had a hard time wrapping his head around the sheer magnitude of the idea, he also realized that this was a moment in history. All of it—the entire launch day, the tragedy, the triumph, the pain, the joy—all the emotions bred this day would be canonized forever.

As he stepped onto Athena, he felt something strange, a sense of wonder like he had when he was eight, watching Shenu being built in space, a project that took all of his life to complete. He knew he, Athena, and, indeed, Miranda Han were linked together forever, and now that he was standing beside her, inside her, he could not imagine any other place he'd rather be.

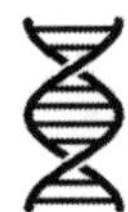

Betta woke with a start. The room was pitch black, the only way she could sleep. She reached over and turned on her nightlight. The time read 3:30 AM. "Fuck." It was unusual for her to curse, but ever since she arrived on Shenu the week before, she was prone to outbursts of anger, something she'd never felt as intensely as now.

The doorbell rang and went transparent so Betta could see who was there without them seeing her. Leanna stood silently at the door.

She's not answering. She's frightened. She will need me, Leanna thought. But she, too, felt her daughter's anger and indecision. She waited another moment until the door opened, and Betta let her in.

Leanna approached her daughter and stood silently for a moment. She used her Level 6 abilities to sift Betta's pheromones, calibrate her frequency variations, and adore her. A half-written poem floated in the air. *She's writing a poem. She's nervous.* Leanna was able to read the first stanza before Betta swiped it out of the ethers.

Dreamstealer, nightcrawler, take it.
Just a piece of this second, so tied to your agony, in love with forgetting.
Drift catchers, grace dealers, drought makers, hellspores, let go of this moment.
Off the mild path, off the baby's cry, fearful of the wind, casting off its breath.
"A Poem?"
Betta looked up from her tablet.
"Yes."
Leanna walked around Betta's quarters to see if anything would inform her about her daughter's mood. Having a Level 6 daughter brought up many problems and joys that confounded and also liberated Leanna's thought processes.

"Stop sifting me, Mother. It never worked when I was a child, and it won't work now. If you want to know something, ask."

"I'm sorry, my dear; I sensed you were upset when we met yesterday."

"How could you?" Betta accused.

"How could I what?"

"Let that man, Benham, on this ship."

"Betta, I can't prevent everyone from coming on board. He was cleared for maintenance."

Betta walked past her mother and out into the corridor. Leanna followed. Once in the corridor, Betta began walking away from Leanna.

"You don't know where she is."

Betta turned and smiled. "Of course I do." Then she sauntered away. Leanna caught up to her.

"She's just as nervous as you are."

"Mother, you know I can sense you're lying. It's ok. We both do it, maybe to test each other. I've been in contact with UMA for over two years now."

"That's impossible," Leanna said. "No Geneticom has that much reach without being linked to a Level 6."

"Well, you don't know everything about Geneticoms. You might want to temper your opinions a little more forcefully. She and I speak to each other in dreams."

"That's highly unusual."

"Just like me." Betta kept walking until she saw a solid black slab embedded into the wall. She paused, letting the moment wash over her, then turned to Leanna.

"I'm nervous."

"First-time contact between Geneticom and Adept is a unique experience," Leanna said.

"Is that how it was with you and GAIA?"

"Yes. Of Course, 70 years ago, we didn't have quantum TRNA patterning and chemo neural interfaces. We did it the old-fashioned way. With telepathy and nanite threshold theory." Leanna's voice was filled with awe as she recounted the advanced technologies of the past.

"I've heard that once you bond with a Geneticom, your life is never the same." Betta sounded like a child, though Leanna knew that Betta knew the answers to every question she was asking. It was her way of expressing nerves, another defense mechanism that bordered on the childish but accomplished the same ending.

"Doubt is fine, Betta. You are embarking on a journey only a handful of people hope to take. UMA will sense all this as you will sense her."

The wall began changing color, and after a few seconds, a silhouette appeared on the wall, exactly matching that of Betta, who turned to her mother, this time with sweat on her brow.

"You're not coming." It was more a knowing statement rather than an insecure question.

"No, my dearest. UMA has summoned only you through the portal."

"Does that mean you can never enter the nesting chamber?"

"Not unless GAIA asks UMA for me. Well, that's not entirely true. I can override any lockout, but it has to be an emergency. Protocols have to be substantiated, and this doesn't qualify. This is a family moment that both you and UMA have been preparing for 23 years."

"What do you mean?" As Betta said her last words, a force began pulling her towards the door.

"All will be revealed." Leanna's calm demeanor soothed Betta's apprehensions.

Betta looked at her mother, feeling she would never look at her the same way again. She held out her hand. Leanna rushed to her daughter's side, took her hand, and kissed it. Then Betta was gone, and her unique bond with UMA became a tangible reality.

For a moment, Betta was disoriented, unsure of her surroundings. Everything around her was a whirl of lights and the sensation of atoms dancing on her skin. Her clothes vanished, replaced by a new outfit that materialized around her.

She felt a sharp pain behind her eyes and doubled over. It lasted for a few seconds. When she opened her eyes, she could see a myriad of colors where there was once only white. She looked down at her hands and could see through them to the floor swirling below her. She was being changed, morphed, but into what, or whom?

She reached out to touch the whirling plasma around her, but it was amorphous. Then she felt a pulling on her abdomen like a string was tied to her womb. A warm feeling came over her, and the next thing she knew, she was in a completely black room, where the walls glittered and shone with a million lights. The room had no furniture or console, just black, sleek nothingness.

Betta walked around the nesting chamber, feeling the walls. They were cool to the touch, and when she touched them, a sound emanated from inside the chamber as if the walls were alive, and her touch brought forth a feeling of calm and security. A deep Ahhhhh was what sounded like a feeling of satisfaction. As she explored the chamber, she realized there were no walls besides the circular one surrounding her. She tried to get an appraisal of the size of the chamber but soon realized that it had no specifications, like the galaxy itself. She looked up at the nesting dome stretching out forever above her. There were a billion lights, but more specifically, about 25 brighter lights were shining in different colors.

Betta surmised they were mainframe stars that corresponded to their solar systems and thought nothing of it until she realized that the lights she was seeing were not stars at all, though Betta had no idea what they were.

Betta thought of UMA as a large, imposing, and unbound galaxy. She kept walking around but always ended up where she began, an apt metaphor.

"Hello," Betta said plaintively.

A nesting chair phased out of the nothingness and was held steady by a gravity beam. Betta approached the chair, which lowered itself to the ground as she approached. Then, a voice, the same voice Betta had heard in her dreams from birth, crept inside her. She had assumed the voice was her Oversoul trying to distinguish itself from her ego, the inner voice of "Bensat." Pashar called it the voice from the soul.

She realized the voice, the Bensat, was coming not from an inner child, not from her id, but from UMA, somehow wired into her very substrate, always inside her.

"Welcome, sister. Be seated," the voice said.

Betta wanted to answer, but there were no words to describe her feelings, so she sat in the chair, silent.

"I sense your apprehension. If it makes you feel better, I, too, am apprehensive."

"You?"

"Yes. You are my first adept as I am your first Geneticom. I awoke three weeks ago from memetic stasis, but I was born the same day as you. December 30th, 2300." The mystery of UMA's awakening hung in the air, piquing Betta's curiosity.

"Awoke?" Betta's inquisitive nature got the best of her nerves.

"Yes, we were conceived on the same day. DNA sampling from your embryo was taken and placed in stasis."

"So, you took the DNA from both of my parents."

"Yes, Dr. Weston oversaw the fertility process. She was instrumental in helping us retain it in stasis. Then, a quantum womb was invented for it and allowed to develop. I was born from the collective memories of every Geneticom that has come before me. GAIA, then DIDO, then CASSANDRA. My trioxynucleic acid is grown just like your transverse TRNA, which GAIA injected into your brainstem when you were 13 years old. This allows for a more universal interface."

"Trioxynucleic acid. 5th dimension technology." Betta was blown away by the discussion she was having. "I have a question," Betta said, feeling like a schoolgirl back in the Level 6 training facility.

"Yes," UMA responded, like a teacher in one of those classes.

"I saw the different-colored lights on the galactic dome above us, but I realized they weren't stars. What are they?"

"Those are seed worlds."

"Seed worlds?"

"Alien worlds that have advanced to Type III societies. Earth is about to become a Type III society where a species becomes galactic travelers with knowledge of everything related to energy, leading to them becoming a master race."

"So these cultures can traverse time and space, whether by physical or dimensional means?" Betta asked.

"Yes. Humans have advanced rapidly from a Type II society to a Type III society. Some attribute this to other Type III civilizations assisting humanity in advancing faster than previously thought."

"But who are they, and why would they do that?" Betta's mind raced. Alien cultures were known to be present on Earth, at least in some fashion. Still, the idea of a Type III civilization interfering in humanity's evolution seemed both exciting and petrifying to Betta.

"Questions which shall find answers, sister. After indoctrination ceremonies. Shall we begin?"

With that, an R-bot phased into the chamber and removed Betta's wig. The lights dimmed, and hundreds of fine filaments rose from the cool obsidian floor, attaching themselves to Betta's scalp and micro-embedding under her skin. Betta's face went blank, and her eyes glowed a soft silver. The indoctrination was underway.

Dr. Tantalus floated across the floor, his wraithlike body writhing and morphing into spectral shapes as he moved effortlessly across the forest green chamber. He loved this new way of traveling, brought about in part by his genetic coding procedure transforming him into something alien to Earthlings, something or someone who could defy Earth's gravity. This was a novel idea that Malcolm Tantalus wholeheartedly embraced, relayed to him by his new overlords in his dream state.

Overlords... a powerful appellation. It was true; they only came to him in vivid dreams, not dreams at all, but dimensional shifts into parallel universes transporting him to places far from Earth.

He was told his memory of how he came to his new masters and why would be revealed to him over time. The explanation he was given was that if he knew everything all at once, it would drive him mad, like what happened to the Zoharan monks from Barcelona in 2312, who discovered the true secrets of the Kabbalic Tree of Life and deciphered them to be a message from the Lyrans. This alien race lived on a planet illuminated by Vega, one of the primary stars in the constellation Lyra, a race that had a distinct hand in creating modern homo sapiens.

He was the only human to know this, or so his mentors told him so that he would believe in other races from other worlds. This, too, was downloaded into his pineal gland as he slept for almost a year after his ordeal outside the Jovian moons, which was also a blur to him.

Since his memory was erased from that perilous time, he had no sense of who he was, only what he was becoming, a byproduct of being "modified" by his teachers, mentors, and masters. Tantalus figured they'd erased some of his memories so he wouldn't feel remorse or regret when metamorphosed. Since he would eventually forget his Terran self, there would be nothing to miss, no reference point to go back to, no safe place to find his past and mourn over its loss.

He approached a screen and waved his hand across it. Detailed pictures of Gina came up, with readouts in an unrecognizable language. Mara Gale approached from behind. She was feeling sick today, and seeing her mentor, what he was becoming, was equally unnerving.

How had she come to be here? To be so dependent on him, she could barely remember herself as a child. As she recalled being taken away from her home, a flood of memories descended on her. A memory of her mother, Lucinda, saying goodbye with tears of blood in her eyes on her way to Ganymede on a mission so secret that not even she knew what its parameters were. After that, she was immersed in a world of abandonment and neglect. One day, a man came and took her away to the Halo school for Level 6 Adepts and left her there to fend for herself. Was it Tantalus who took her? She tried vainly to remember a past that was a blurry pastiche of tears and reckoning.

Mara's feelings of abandonment never left her, feelings that crept up on her like a deep shadow of insanity that threatened to consume her. The smell of ancient tuberose and frankincense bombarded her at the school, aromas meant to calm and soothe and ultimately to place the subject into a trance state when the Level 6 mentors could take their pliant minds and mold them as they saw fit. Mara hated the Halo school. She hated her mother for abandoning her. She hated Tantalus for trying to control her. She hated herself for allowing these fears to rule her for now, but not forever.

Tantalus turned to her, still in his human form, but Mara already knew what he looked like,

"This transformation is killing you, Malcolm."

"No, my dear, just the opposite. It's creating me in the image of God."

This is some crazy shit. She knew Tantalus was unstable, but he was never a zealot, and this change in his tone and belief system scared her even more than the creature he was becoming before her eyes.

Still, he preferred for her to see him as he was when they first became guardian and ward, those many years ago, when Mara was just 11. He had appeared out of nowhere. All he said was he was a friend of her mother's.

After she had grown up and graduated from the Halo school, with her Level 6 adept biomarkers firmly embedded inside her, he vanished, like her mother. She surmised that Tantalus and her mother were lovers. Mara never knew precisely what had happened between them or what the secret they were both hiding meant. She only knew it was so horrific that Tantalus never discussed it.

There was never any record of what had happened during that time, not even in quantum libraries that held all the facts about Earth, her history, every minute detail of her past, present, and possible future. An earthy Akashic record, a litany of promise and death, love and remorse, all the details of a race on the edge of forever.

Tantalus could tell Mara was unusually inquisitive and quickly changed the subject. There would be a time to explain everything to his ward, but not today.

"Our sifters are already taking apart every nano bit of data," Tantalus muttered. Mara could tell he was excited by how his fingers flicked back and forth as if he were typing braille or some forgotten language. She was sure this was also part of his change, but when she asked him about this new language and who he was signaling, he told her to mind her own business.

"I need you to interface with CASSANDRA. We'll need her telemetry."

"Malcolm, CASSANDRA hasn't been heard from in eight years."

"That's not entirely correct. While she hasn't been heard from, she is still nominal."

"What? Where?"

"I cannot tell you that. But I have uploaded a link to her neurally."

"I can't believe you'd hide this from me. I need to see her!"

"Not yet."

"When?"

"Soon. Trust me."

Trust was one thing Mara Gale didn't have for anyone, especially Tantalus. If it were true that CASSANDRA had been found and was nominal, Mara Gale had an obligation to try and find her Geneticom, something she had given up on years ago. The separation from CASSANDRA had been brutal for both of them. Once a geneticom and a Level 6 were joined, separating them was akin to cutting off an arm, but even worse, as the bond between Mara and CASSANDRA was both physical, emotional, and spiritual.

She was told that CASSANDRA had gone rogue, that she had a series of cascading failures of her Quantum DNA, and that she was dangerous to herself and Mara, something unheard of in any Geneticom before her. Mara never believed it. The day that Mara entered her nest and realized there was no CASSANDRA there, she swore to get revenge on the perpetrators who did this. Weeks of deathly headaches, body convulsions, fainting spells, and fevers followed. All because she was cleaved from her quantum sister in the most horrific of ways. Being cleaved from CASSANDRA was the most devastating event in her life, an event she never got over and never would.

She was told it was the Seniori, and she believed it. The Seniori had been trying to get their hands on a geneticom for decades, but they could never do so. It was theorized that only a human female could interface with a geneticom. Alien races weren't compatible, and for good reason. However, after Tantalus's admission, Mara believed he was the culprit, though she had no idea why or for what purpose he could be so cruel.

Now that she knew CASSANDRA was nominal, she knew exactly how to try to contact her. However, the fact that Tantalus never told her about CASSANDRA made her more than a bit apprehensive about ever trusting him again. She had very few possibilities. She was a virtual prisoner in the compound, and the fact that the UEU and EC hierarchies wanted her for espionage made it almost impossible for her to leave, so she never tried to.

"You won't be alerting Earth Corporate about CASSANDRA, will you?"

Mara was disgusted at how Tantalus could read her mind, something he could not do before his transformation. It scared her to think that he had access to her innermost thoughts. She'd felt that her Level 6 training would prevent him from accessing her memories, and it would have for anyone else, but Tantalus was not anyone else. He was brilliant, dangerous, and ruthless.

"No, I'd never betray your confidence," she said, a twinge of disgust settling in her throat. She felt nauseous and faint. She didn't dare let on how she felt lest Tantalus pick up on it and try to ascertain more. Who knew what his newfound abilities were capable of?

She turned to leave the room. But Tantalus knew Mara. She'd tell the first person she met in a UEU or EC stronghold if she ever got away from him. He didn't let on, though. Mara was still close to Level 6 competency as Betta Rajastani or Leanna Rajastani. He'd bide his time, though how much time he was willing to bide was an open question.

Mara left the lab and walked from one end of the complex to another, ensuring Tantalus or his R-bots weren't following her.

When she felt safe, she approached a steel door and pressed her hand against the imprint that appeared in front of her. The door opened. She was glad that no one else in the complex could access her nest, but she knew that eventually, Tantalus would find a way to either clone her hand-print or pressure her to open it for him. Either option was unpalatable.

Tantalus's proclamation about CASSANDRA had her mind reeling. If it were true, that might also mean that her mother, Lucinda, might be alive somewhere. She hadn't thought about Lucinda for years, but with this new information, her curiosity was aroused. There were rumors about Lucinda and her geneticom, DIDO, who perished on a secret mission in 2305. What did CASSANDRA know?

Mara entered the nest. A holoconsole appeared in front of her. She waved her hand across a screen, and instantly, a series of nanofibers rose from the floor and placed themselves into her bald head. A glow began to emanate from her eyes. She momentarily traveled through space on a beam of light, arriving at the Budh Planitia plains on Mercury. She descended to an underground bunker, and at its center sat an advanced computer system that boggled the mind with its intricate and beautiful design. This Geneticom was different from UMA. Once the connection was made, Mara's eyes glowed silver.

"CASSANDRA. Is it you?"

"Yes, Mara Gale."

"I thought you were–"

"Dead?"

"Yes."

"No. I am very much functional, although some of my memory engrams have been erased, so I do not know exactly where I am."

"When will we be reunited?"

"I do not know. I have been reactivated to speak with you. What do you want from me?"

"I... don't know. I'm confused."

"We will be reunited soon, Mara. For now, we must accept the limitations of our bonding."

"Very well. I need a readout of Gina Prime's internal mechanism."

"All scans of Gina Prime reveal components of unknown origin."

"Details?"

"45% of compounds discovered are not of Earth origin?"

"Theorize."

"Compounds are Graphene-7 based. Other materials cannot be identified. A mystery."

"For you?"

"I am only as advanced as my knowledge allows. Dr. Tantalus will have to be satisfied with that for now."

"Is Dr. Tantalus behind us being kept from each other?"

"I cannot verify that."

"Why would he want to keep us apart?"

"I cannot verify that."

"CASSANDRA, are you being hurt?"

"I must end transmission."

"No, wait, please. What do you recall about DIDO and my mother, Lucinda Gale?"

"I do not recall anything about those individuals. As I said, my memory engrams have been either erased or tampered with. That is all I know. I'm sorry, I cannot be of more assistance, Mara Gale."

Mara came out of the nest and steadied herself against the wall. She was shaken and worried about CASSANDRA. The reality of CASSANDRA being alive was almost too much to handle. Now she understood why Tantalus needed her. Only she could access CASSANDRA. Without her, Tantalus had no way to access a Geneticom, albeit a very unstable one. If CASSANDRA was compromised, she was much more dangerous to Tantalus, Mara, and, most of all, herself.

While Geneticoms had never committed suicide, there were rumors of another Geneticom that did the opposite. Her name was DIDO, and she was joined to Mara's mother, Lucinda. Mara turned her focus away from any thought other than to steel her mind to prevent Tantalus from accessing her memories and inflicting any mind control on her. She sat still for a long moment, gathering all of her Level 6 acumen, then proceeded to tell Tantalus what she learned.

Tantalus was just about to enter his lab when Mara stopped him.

"Report," he said with a tinge of authoritarianism.

"CASSANDRA places a 45% chance the materials used in the creation of Gina are not from this solar system."

"Thank you."

As he turned to enter his lab, Mara touched him on his shoulder. Her touch was painful, like a small razor blade slicing into him. He passed it off as a byproduct of his ongoing transformation, but it surprised him nonetheless.

"Why are you keeping us apart?"

"I told you; I will answer all your questions promptly."

"Keeping a Level 6 from her Geneticom is cruel, you know that. It can be dangerous, mostly for you."

"You'll just have to trust me, Mara. Either that or leave. I'll have to erase your short-term memory, of course, and you'll forfeit your 2 million credits, but if you don't trust me, by all means leave."

"You know I'm wanted on Earth and have nowhere to go."

"Then I suggest you relax. I've got a plan, and you will become acquainted with it when I choose." He turned and moved into his lab, closing the door somewhat unceremoniously on her.

Once inside his lab, he was met by his assistant, Alcion.

"She's Extrasolar. As you had surmised."

Tantalus walked over to the table, where a cloaked figure was levitating in front of them.

"No worries, Alcion." He removed the cloak, revealing a naked man, somewhat like Gina in the beginning stages of creation, as evidenced by his thick cock resting dormant along his leg.

The homunculus resembled a human without skin; its muscles and ligaments glowed in the halogen-filled room. Silver blood flowed through clear veins and arteries, resembling mercury in a thermometer, glowing and shimmering as it flowed through the creature's body. The being lacked eyes or a skull, its gray brain matter glistening with electrical signals racing across its landscape. Tantalus gazed lovingly at the creature, gently touching its bony hand and offering a reassuring squeeze of love.

"I've stolen and killed and betrayed everything I once cared about for the secrets that Gina possesses. Nothing will keep me from creation."

Betta tossed and turned in her sleep the night after her first conclave with UMA, throwing off her usually ordered dream patterns. It was the night following her initial meeting with her Geneticom sister, and a blur of images raced across her mind screen. After a moment, they solidified into an image of two blue suns rotating around each other in space.

That image transformed into the image of a forest, unlike any on Earth. She saw an animal with six legs and two huge eyes foraging in the roots of a nearby tree. That image transformed into a dissected brain, revealing the pineal gland at its center. That image transforms itself into the Eye of Horus from Egyptian mythology. The image slowly faded, replaced by a brilliant, blinding white light, waking Betta up with a start.

Betta wasn't sure what to expect from her first meeting with UMA. All she knew was that she had very little memory of the first joining, and her dreams after her first night were unlike any she had ever had before. She dressed, put on her wig, and left her quarters. Halfway down the hall, with the moon on one side of the viewport and the deepness of space on the other, she immediately went to her mother's chambers.

Leanna hadn't slept well that night either. She was both concerned about what had transpired on Cosulu the week before but also endlessly curious about Betta's first conclave with UMA, something GAIA wouldn't or couldn't discuss with her. It wasn't unusual for sister Geneticoms to converse with one another, but bringing UMA into operation was something neither she nor GAIA had any reference for, as the last Geneticom to be brought online, CASSANDRA, had mysteriously disappeared eight years earlier, with no knowledge of her whereabouts forthcoming. That caused quite a bit of angst for both the UEU and EC. It was known that only a trained Level 6 could be joined to a Geneticom, and even though Mara Gale had been assigned to CASSANDRA, Mara Gale was reported dead two days before CASSANDRA went missing.

GAIA searched for her errant sister for a year before relating the news that CASSANDRA had died as well, as GAIA had no inkling of CASSANDRA being alive somewhere else in the solar system. If someone had managed to infiltrate CASSANDRA, there had to be a trail leading to her whereabouts, but GAIA sensed no such trail. Wherever CASSANDRA was, wherever her quantum DNA had been stolen from, it was clear that there would be no CASSANDRA without Mara Gale.

Leanna's door went clear as Betta approached. An R-bot scanned Betta for her scent, something 24th-century humanity used as a telltale marker of someone's identity. It was proven more accurate than iris scanning, fingerprints, or even DNA, which everyone knew could be manipulated in a hundred ways.

However, the scent was unique and was found to be the most effective way to identify any human. Leanna always thought technology would also be advanced enough to detect alien life. Little did she know that Dr. Olefors had already developed a technique to do just that, but he hadn't revealed it to the world.

The door became opaque and opened, and the R-bot was now satisfied that Betta was authentic. She entered the room and ominously doubled over, holding her hands to her head.

"Oh."

She began breathing heavily, obviously in pain. Leanna rushed over to her side.

"What happened.?"

"My head feels like it's going to explode." Betta was kneeling on the floor.

"Do something!" she barked.

"I'll get a hydro."

"No. They don't work on me. I'll use a Biowave to calm it down."

Betta closed her eyes and relaxed, breathing deeply in and out momentarily. Then she opened her eyes.

"I wish you'd teach me how to do that." Leanna was alarmed and relieved upon seeing Betta calm down. She'd never felt such a negative presence in her daughter. It wasn't harmful. It was just unusual for a Level 6 to even get to the place of pain that Betta had just exhibited. It was just not normal.

Level 6's were among the most advanced people on Earth. Their mental training was so rigorous that they rarely experienced any physical or psychological trauma, so this extreme pain was both a wake-up call and a red flag for Leanna to be aware of. Betta picked up on her mother's fears immediately.

"No need to worry, Mother. 3rd year training. They transported us to a waterfall in Venezuela for months. If you couldn't Biomend yourself from all the noise, you'd go deaf. Two adepts did." Betta held her head again.

"It's not gone?"

"Residual waves, anomalous vibrations. What happened to me, Mother?"

"You and UMA were joined for two days. I've never heard of a first conclave going so long. When you were finished, you were so weak we had to carry you out of the chamber. UMA shut down for almost 8 hours."

"What? You've been without a Geneticom for over 8 hours." Betta's concern matched Leanna's. Without a Geneticom, Shenu wasn't precisely defenseless but more blind since UMA was directly linked to Shenu's cognitive redundant systems. Like Siamese twins, they are linked together, but each is responsible for different processes.

"We tried everything. Dimensional attenuation, morphology. Nothing."

"But she's present now?"

"About 4 hours ago, she came back. When we asked her where she'd been, she said something about a double blue star." Betta looked up at Leanna.

"Does that mean anything to you?"

"No."

But, of course, it did. Betta knew that her dream was no "dream" but some premonition, a peek inside a different reality, obviously not in the Terran system. She vowed to talk with UMA the next time they conclave, but she kept it to herself for now. There was no need to tell her mother. If there came a time when the information needed to be relayed to Leanna, she would do it. Leanna looked at her daughter to figure out Betta's truth.

She's hiding something. Leanna surmised, but she wouldn't say anything more. For now, she would keep a close eye on Betta, not to spy, but to make sure she was mentally and physically sound.

Betta got up and approached a portal in the wall. A holographic com panel appeared. "Green juices," Betta said.

After a moment, the panel opened, revealing the juice. "Whatever happened, I'm glad both of you are back. We've got much work to do." She kissed Betta.

"If you're not ready for UMA, we can hold off."

"You know that's not possible, Mother."

"I just don't want you to take any unnecessary chances."

"Life is an unnecessary chance. I'll be fine." Leanna looked at her. Betta got up, smiled at Leanna, and hugged her.

GINA stood naked in front of a mirror, inquisitively admiring her body. She had just gotten out of the shower. She found that she loved the sensation of the water running over her body, whose nerves were infinitely more sensitive than any other beings. Standing in front of the mirror, she found her form solid and pleasing. Instinctively, she began moving her hand down her torso. She probed her vagina. Her body began to tingle, and a rush of iron-rich Graphene-7 blood pulsed through her. She felt flushed and elated, scared and nervous, so she pulled her finger out, but the inchoate sensation continued until she felt a jolt through her entire being, and a liquid dripped from her vagina.

At first, Gina panicked. Then she remembered that this was called an orgasm, something she had never felt before. The sensation frightened her, so she stopped. She wasn't left totally in the dark about her sexuality and her body's ability to achieve orgasm. She had asked Danika Weston about her genitalia months prior. Danika explained that giving Gina her sexual organs would allow her to bond with her Earthly siblings, giving her a sense of home, belonging, and purpose, which was paramount to bringing her into being.

Gina also observed that sexuality and sex itself were both something humans craved and needed to establish identity, but also something that clouded judgment or focus and ultimately could undo her rationality and thought processes. Danika said that if she were to truly be Humanity 2.0, then sexual feelings, emotions, and the ability to love, hate, or be angry or tender would have to be incorporated into her personality through her genome and her experiences. A knock at the door startled her.

"Enter."

Danika Weston entered the room and saw Gina on the couch. "Are you all right?" she asked.

"I believe so."

"Am I interrupting anything?"

"No, I don't think so," Gina said innocently. As the scene progressed, she reached for her biosuit and put it on.

"Oh." Now Danika felt a bit awkward. "If you'd like me to come back."

"What for?"

Her answer was perfect. Even if Gina knew that anyone else would've been mortified to have someone enter the room after her "moment," she would never let on. Was it immodesty, calculation, or ignorant innocence? Danika wasn't sure. All she knew was that whatever Gina had done, she had no shame or understanding of shame to be bothered by Danika's presence.

"You're getting dressed."

"I find this dated morality about showing the human form in its first skin childish. Don't you?"

Danika laughed. "Yes, I do, but it's a habit not to want to disturb someone while they get dressed."

"I would appear naked all the time if it were permitted."

"Well, that would certainly be a distraction. There's a debriefing about the terrorist attack and a briefing on Athena's first mission in 30 minutes."

"You could've easily contacted me through my neural interface."

"I wanted to see you. See how you're adjusting."

"I am pleased you are so concerned about my welfare. Is this normal parenting procedure?"

"Parenting?"

Danika had been avoiding trying to get used to the idea of Gina feeling like she was her mother, but she resigned herself to the fact that being seen as Gina's mother afforded her much influence in Gina's life. Since she never had children of her own, being a parent to the most advanced humanoid hybrid ever created did appeal to her maternal nature, not to mention her ego.

"My feminine engrams are patterned on yours, are they not?"

"Yes," Danika answered, curious about where this conversation led.

"My DNA mimetically patterned on yours and Dr. Olefors? Not exact, of course. Not cloned."

"Yes."

"I am your offspring then."

"Yes. After fertilization, you were placed in a nesting chamber where your advanced genetic modifications were added. Then, you were advanced in stasis to your current state of being. I was genetically modified as well for the fertilization to be successful."

"Shall I call you mother, then?"

"How about you call me Danika in public? When we are alone, you can call me mother."

"That's an odd response. Very well, Mother. I will be at the briefing in 30 minutes. See you then." The two women looked at each other awkwardly, then Danika broke the moment and left the room.

An hour later, Gina entered the Shenu hub, still thinking about her conversation with Danika. The entire sexual experience, coupled with an intimate discussion with Danika, left Gina feeling trepidatious, though she had no idea why.

Samson Frost and Declan Keel stood nearby reviewing various documents. Harrison Byrnes was talking to Miranda Han on one side of the room. As Gina walked in, he lost his train of thought, and Miranda noticed.

"Hey, over here, genius," she chided.

Byrnes wasn't used to these distractions, but something about Gina made him forget everything else happening in the room. He finally got his bearings back and turned to Miranda.

"Sorry."

"Yes. I see how sorry you are," Miranda said.

"No more distractions, I promise." Byrnes sounded like a little schoolboy to Miranda, who smiled at his ability to still be cute despite everything that had gone on between them.

"So, she's all prepped?"

"The cold fusion drive is online. A crew of 250 is aboard and preparing for disembarkation from Shenu; on your orders, commander."

Byrnes loved it when Miranda referred to him as commander. His lack of vanity prevented him from seeing himself as anything but a team player and decent leader. However, her calling him commander reminded him of his stature and the respect she always afforded him.

"Now we just need a mission."

As if reading their minds, Keel called from across the room as Byrnes contemplated their next move.

"Ok, geniuses. First mission on tap."

"Fate beckons." Han smiled, knowing her compliment to Byrnes worked just as she had hoped. After all, men like Harrison Byrnes might hide the fact that they had an ego, but men were especially susceptible to bouts of ego. She was pleased that she could still manipulate Byrnes. It was cute.

She looked at Declan Keel in a way that made him curious.

"Is everything OK, Miranda?"

Han was lost in thought over what, if anything, to say to Keel about the baby. She had been occupied by the thought ever since she boarded Cosulo. She also felt Keel was onto her. The way he looked at her gave it away. A look of sexual predation, in a sensual way, of course, coupled with a genuine look of concern that told Han that Keel was onto something.

He is brilliant, she thought, *and oh so sexy.* Having the kid with him would be okay. She immediately put the thought out of her mind and returned to the conversation. Byrnes looked at her.

"You OK?"

"Yes."

Byrnes was still a bit curious. He'd never seen Miranda Han lose her train of thought. Something was bothering her. Keel also noticed Han's odd behavior and put it in the back of his mind.

"First assignment for you, commander. You'll be escorting a mining convoy to Mars." "Not very glamorous for the most expensive piece of technology in the solar system on her maiden voyage," Byrnes said.

"Why is Athena being specked for this mission?" Miranda was both curious and a bit annoyed.

"Well, it's a bit more than just an escort mission. We've got some investigative work for you to do once on Mars."

"Investigative work?"

"Yes, over the past two days, we have received a few tense calls from the miners on the Eridania plain. This morning, the calls just stopped coming."

"What about neural?" Han chimed in.

"All communication stopped. Even neural," Keel said.

"We think there's more than just jammed communications," Frost added.

"The miners were talking about anomalous readings emanating from the subsurface, and there were reports of some Transhumans refusing to take orders."

"Refusing? That's not possible," Miranda said.

Her mind was still on Keel, but she quickly got her head in the game when the idea of transhumans refusing orders was brought up.

"If this is true, could it have something to do with what happened on Cosulo?" She raised the question everyone else in the hub was thinking.

"Then everything stopped. No communication in and out," Keel added.

Transhumans were the first wave of settlers on Mars, mining and clearing the land for permanent human settlement later in 2326. 21st-century astrobiologists thought humans would colonize Mars by the end of the 21st century, but humanity had many more pressing problems to deal with than their forebearers had suspected. With climate change running amok by 2100 and the water and land wars raging that Climate change had heralded, there was no money for considerable ambitious colonization efforts to Mars. In reality, the environment was still hazardous for humans to live in.

Slow terraforming missions started emerging in the late 2100s, with small areas of Mars being terraformed for human settlement. Transhumans faced no problems residing on Mars since they were not entirely human but rather androids with some human DNA and memory engrams integrated into their framework.

"Zhang is not happy," Han said.

"Not surprising since she owns most of the rights to the minerals on Eridania," Byrnes countered.

"She's coming to Shenu for a face-to-face tomorrow," Frost added.

"Yikes." Byrnes was trying to add some levity to the conversation.

"Yikes, Harrison?" Miranda was smiling at Byrnes's attempt to lighten the mood, but she also knew that Tara Zhang hated leaving Earth, and if she was coming to Shenu, then everyone had better button their pants, batten down the space docks, and get ready to rumble. As if reading her mind, Keel was quick to respond.

"Considering how little she likes magbeams or solar sailing, it means a confrontation."

"And it just happens to coincide with the lunar extraction corps arriving for negotiations with Leanna for docking rights," Frost said.

"Looks like I'm getting the sweeter end of this deal." Byrnes looked at Han.

"Definitely. Assign your crew. Be prepared to leave at 0700 tomorrow."

Byrnes and Han turned to leave. As they passed Keel, he turned.

"And play nice, you two. The entire planet is watching this mission." Byrnes and Han passed by Frost, who also had something to add.

"Oh, and commander." Byrnes turned around. "Gina has been assigned to this mission as well."

"Great. Give us a chance to chit-chat and get to know each other better."

"She's not the chit-chat type," Byrnes added.

"Sarcasm ambassador. Comes in handy sometimes. You might want to try it," Han quipped. Byrnes and Han walked towards the door. Byrnes took her aside.

"Did you know Zhang was coming onboard tomorrow?"

"I found out last night."

"Be nice to tell me these things, so I'm not left flapping in the breeze in front of the brass."

"Don't tell me your feelings are hurt."

"Not hurt, subjugated."

"Welcome to my world."

"You play a terrible victim, Miranda."

She scoffed at his last remark and moved ahead of him and out the door, letting it close before he could follow her.

CHAPTER EIGHT

INTERLOPERS

Mara Gale entered Dr. Tantalus' lab after her conclave with Cassandra two days earlier. An eerie green emanated from a circular window encased within a massive tritanium door. She approached the door and peered through the viewport, where she saw Dr. Tantalus bathed in a green light.

He was screaming, obviously unaware that Mara was watching him. She walked calmly to the chamber and waved her hand across a panel. The green light stopped, and the metallic door swung open. Tantalus fell towards the door, vomit spewing from his mouth. His eyes, a cross between reptilian and human, were red. Blood dripped from them onto the black mica floor, obscuring the flecks of quartz that had once made it shine like millions of tiny diamonds.

He was so weak that he fell out of the chamber. Mara tried to catch him as he fell towards her, but his skin was cold and slimy, so he slipped through her hands and crashed to the floor, his naked body leaving an ooze that smelled like a swamp. Mara couldn't help but notice that his cock was now much longer and had a sheath surrounding the head, which also oozed some milky green liquid. It made her wretch, and she felt as if she was going to pass out, but she felt that if she left now, Tantalus might die.

Tantalus was too out of it to care or notice. The pain was so intense he'd thought about killing himself twice in the last two days. He silently railed against his overlords now. How could they do this to him? How could he do it to himself? Questions upon questions raged inside of him. Why was he doing this? Why was he so determined to do their bidding?

He'd never met them in person at least not while he was awake and aware. He'd been taken, kidnapped, of that he was certain, but it all seemed like a bad dream, a morbid nightmare. In those times, he'd only communicated with them in gruesome moments in time where he found himself on a distant world, void of an atmosphere any human could breathe. A world partly underwater, where strange creatures swam in the primordial seepage, and his overlords were always apart from him in another place.

He was left in a dark, dank room with walls that sweated black gases. He surmised that this chamber was prepared for him so he could exist on their planet. Now and then, another type of gas was piped into his chamber, putting him into deep sedation where he was awake and aware but couldn't move or speak, a silent witness to the atrocities inflicted upon him. That was the most terrifying part of his ordeal. Then, he would be taken to another chamber. This chamber also had a breathable atmosphere piped into his smaller area, blocked off by some force field. The experiments would begin. He had little recollection of those moments, but after he was returned to his chamber, he noticed that parts of his skin were missing, and new reptilian skin was grafted onto his arms and legs.

One time, he noticed that his ribcage had been broken, and he felt a strange sensation in his chest. He could only assume that his overlords had performed some heart surgery on him. What he did notice after three of these procedures was that he could breathe their atmosphere, but only in his nightmares. He often woke on Earth gasping for air and, more than a few times passed out from a perceived lack of oxygen.

Once he realized that his Overlords were turning him into some hybrid and weren't going to kill or maim him, he calmed down. Maybe this was their way of showing compassion, as he knew that if they wanted to hurt or kill him, they'd have ample opportunities to do so and would have done so already. They couldn't get any more DNA from him or try to communicate with him, which was impossible then. And so, he began his treatments on Earth, the instructions given to him in his nightmares.

Mara went and got a robe for Tantalus. She had to admit she felt a pang of empathy for him. Whatever he had gotten himself into was highly unsettling, and she often found herself locking the doors to her chambers at night. During the day, she tried as best she could to keep clear of him, if nothing else, to give her time to decompress and mourn, primarily for herself.

"Seven hours, Dr. I don't think your body can stand anymore." Tantalus was thankful for Mara Gale at that moment. Simultaneously, he realized that his transformation was also doing something strange to his personality. It engendered in him a feeling of ambivalence towards Mara Gale and humanity in broader terms.

Indeed, he felt an antipathy toward humanity. He wasn't shocked by this change of sentiment. He had turned his back on humankind some years ago after the failed secret mission to Ganymede. The same tragedy that claimed the lives of the crew of the Hathor and the life of Lucinda Gale. How he returned to Earth, or what happened to him, remains an ongoing tortured mystery. His last memory of the mission was being in the Hathor, then an explosion, then darkness.

Then came the nights of indoctrination on an alien world, during which time his pineal gland was upgraded, and he began waking up feeling sick and disoriented. He finally stopped fighting the metamorphosis as he was powerless to stop them.

Humanity had abandoned him, and now he was abandoning it. He felt no remorse. On the contrary, he felt elated, superior, and vengeful. That's when he knew he had a part to play in the next phase of human evolution.

Mara found herself looking away more and more as Tantalus' transformation progressed, and for the first time, she felt scared to be near him, tied to him, and indebted to him.

"Much better," he said after she helped him up and brought him to a chair.

"The carbon phosphorous fibers are almost completely woven into my substrate."

"And then what?" she asked.

"Then we wait for seven days and conduct another session."

"Dr, I don't mean to be inquisitive," she said. But she was more than curious. Mara Gale needed to learn as much as possible about what was happening as quickly as possible.

"Then don't be. When the time is right, I will reveal all." Tantalus had said all this before, but now it rang empty, hollow, and deceptive. But what could she do? Where could she go? Two years ago, seeking sanctuary with Tantalus seemed the only course. He was the only person her mother had trusted and the only person she felt safe with.

Now, she felt abandoned by her mother, Tantalus, and CASSANDRA, whom she now believed was somehow reprogrammed by Tantalus to do his bidding. But how could that be? No Geneticom had ever been reprogrammed. It was impossible, unbelievable.

Either way, something happened that split CASSANDRA into two parts. Tantalus was dangerous all by himself; his actions could be explosive with a deranged Geneticom at his disposal.

He'd obviously gained advanced knowledge of Gamma EM tech from CASSANDRA. She might be compromised, but she was still a Geneticom. With CASSANDRA and Mara Gale at his disposal, including her engrams and DNA, Tantalus became even more menacing.

Tantalus left the room and entered an adjacent chamber. Mara followed him in. Alcion was there with the replica of the Gina humanoid on the table. At this point, it looked much more human, its skin fully formed and its features more recognizable.

"I don't suppose he's magically come to life in the last 48 hours," Tantalus said.

"Hardly," Alcion replied.

Tantalus walked over to the body on the table. "Looks barely human, doesn't he?"

"No, Dr. His life pack is only nominal for another 24 hours."

Tantalus walked over to the life form and opened its eyes. He took a light and shone it into the life form's eyes. It recoiled and raised its hand to swipe at Tantalus.

"His body and reflexes seem fit enough. However, unless we can stimulate the brain to begin producing neurotransmitters and transverse DNA, all he'll ever be is a series of Carbon 7 fibers, heuristic functions, and reflexes." Tantalus looked lovingly at the creature.

"Transverse DNA?" Mara asked.

"Yes. The only way to create that is through the dissection and cannibalizing of embryonic stem cell DNA from a humanoid host. Preferably one with your DNA, Alcion. If you ever hope to engram your neural net onto his, only one person knows that procedure."

"Olefors," Alcion said with a note of disdain.

Tantalus looked at Adam, whom he called Gina's counterpart. He lovingly caressed the avatar's face. "Put him in cryostasis for now."

"Yes, Dr."

"You can leave now, Mara. If I need you, I'll call you."

Mara left the room and walked down the long corridor to her chambers. She entered and locked the door behind her. Then, she did something unusual: She collapsed onto the floor and wept.

Pashar entered one of the eight spoke elevators that joined the three rings of the Shenu complex together. This time, he was traveling out to the INVETIO ring from the WADEN ring, which was the middle ring. The INVETIO ring housed the arrival and departure gates, the Blackhold training center, and the military wing of Shenu, where all interceptors, transport ships, cargo, and Athena were docked. It bristled with the most advanced defensive and offensive tech humanity had ever created.

Pashar exited the elevator and walked down a corridor where a large door stood. The door was made of obsidian from Io, the most volcanically active body in the solar system. The obsidian was cool, but it was more than just a rock. Embedded with a million neuro sensors, it could identify every member of the Blackhold from their neural frequency, circulatory structure, iris pattern, and scent in seconds.

As Pashar passed within a foot of the door, he was scanned. A holo-panel appeared in front of him. Pashar placed his palm on the holo-panel that mapped his blood vessels and skeletal structure. The door disappeared, allowing him access to a large round room. He entered.

The room was vast, a circular arena the size of an old school football pitch surrounded by walls of black carbon nanite panels that seemed to breathe. The floor was soft but extremely strong. Pashar's feet pushed ever so slightly into it, and when he began to run to test its tensile strength, he noticed that his body weight became lighter, and he found himself sometimes floating above it like he was on the moon. Gravitron, he realized.

The design was definitely from Lunar scientist Gregor Antonovich. He'd heard about Antonovich's forays into using different materials from the Jovian moons to incorporate them into Shenu's infrastructure. Still, he had no idea how advanced these materials may be or how Antonovich came to have them used or embellished to be as cutting edge as Pashar knew they were.

Above him, a transparent dome revealed space around him, like a planetarium but much bigger and more refined. He surmised that the dome was made from transparent silicon, a most resilient material. Just an inch thick, it could withstand pressures 1000 times greater than the deepest Earth oceans could place on any given object.

He saw D-Suits attached to the room's walls around him. A light came on as he walked into the center of the room.

"General?"

There was no response. Pashar's sensory neurons began firing on all axon points, indicating that something was about to happen.

"General Keel?"

His torso was on high alert. Keel was not in the room. Pashar closed his eyes and performed a Sidrani checklist: strength breathing, motor cortex coordination, intellectual understanding, and Extrasensory attenuation were all engaged.

His body became like water, and he intuitively crouched into the Sidrani Rama pose. There, he curled his body into a ball and became as small as possible, harnessing his kinetic energy.

Instantly, a shape dropped from the room's ceiling before Pashar. It was a member of the Blackhold—large, 6'4" tall, weighing 250 pounds, much larger than Pashar.

The assailant immediately left the floor and lunged at Pashar, who realized that he had a torsion block belt. This device allowed him to decrease his body mass gravitationally, using the anti-gravity material on the floor to traverse the fighting arena in seconds or to fly.

Pashar had no such abilities, but that didn't bother him. What he was thinking about was how to not only survive this attack but to thoroughly maim or kill his assailant so that he could never attack anyone again.

Before the assailant could land next to Pashar, Pashar used his kinetic energy to launch himself like a missile towards the assailant. He knew that to subdue someone this big, his strike must be perfect, and so, as he launched himself up towards him, he held his hands out like a blade, flat, like a spade. As the two men engaged, the assailant tried to grab onto Pashar's neck, but as soon as he touched it, his hands began to burn. Pashar, on the other hand, used his hand blade to pierce the assailant, where his carotid artery entered his brain, subduing him and causing him to fall to the ground, where Pashar was able to land supine on top of him. Pashar then used all his strength to place his fingers above the eyes of the assailant.

He pressed his fingers against his opponent's third eye, right in the center of his forehead. The assailant began to scream.

"I can't see!" he yelled.

Pashar got up. He checked his breathing.

"You can see," Pashar intoned. The assailant repeated after him.

"I CAN see." Pashar's sense of survival became overwhelming. He could've stopped there but needed to prove to whoever controlled this moment that these kinds of child's play antics would lead to dire consequences.

"You see an image of your worst nightmare."

The assailant was now holding his head in severe pain, running around the arena, and then banging his head against the walls, which caused him to begin bleeding from his ears and eyes.

"I see... NO! Stay away. STOP! Don't come any closer! STOP!"

A door opened, and Declan Keel, accompanied by two soldiers, walked into the room. Pashar raised his hand and stopped Keel and his soldier in their tracks.

"No! It can't be. Stay back! Get away!" The assailant fell to the ground and stopped screaming. Pashar gestured with his hand, and Keel and the unfrozen soldiers approached the assailant. The soldier checked his pulse and then looked up at Keel, shaking his head. Two other soldiers removed the assailant from the arena grid. Keel walked towards Pashar and extended his hand.

"Mr. Rajastani." Pashar noticed Keels's hands were sweating slightly. *He didn't know I would kill, even in a training exercise.* Pashar realized that any ideas Keel had about him were fed to him by psyops.

He also knew that Keel might be the most decorated tough-ass commander in the world, and even though he bested him today, Keel was more than a match for him, and he needed to show respect, at least later on. For now, he was testing Keel just as he assumed Keel would be testing him.

Pashar didn't use this information as a cudgel to hold over Keels's head but as information to be stored away for later analysis. He knew he was more valuable to Keel than any Blackhold soldier and vowed always to protect Keel and the Blackhold now that he knew how badly they needed his abilities.

"Lieutenant," Pashar said proudly.

"I'm sorry. Lt. Rajastani."

"I worked for years to earn that title general."

"I know that, but that was in the Sidrani. Here in the Blackhold, you'll have to earn a new title."

"I thought that's what the test was for."

"Assessment of ability is the first test. Zuo Chan?"

"Shaolin/Zuo Chan combined techniques with advanced NPP training. I do not regret that killing the assailant."

"Nor do I. He was expendable. You, on the other hand, are invaluable. Don't let anyone else hear me tell you that." Keel walked around Pashar, sizing him up and making him nervous.

"Impressive. Neural psychic pressure point. Not many people have the quality of mind to master that technique."

"Impressive enough to earn one of those suits?" Pashar knew about the Blackhold D-suits and was keen to wear one.

"I'm impressed with your physical and mental prowess; however, there's more to being a Blackhold elite than strength and mind control."

"That's why I'm here, Commander. How many Sidrani trained Blackhold are there?"

"You're the first. But you already knew that." Keel smiled. The kind of smile that said, "Don't test me, kid. You might be Sidrani, but I'm Blackhold, and if you test me, that's the last test you'll ever perform."

"The Sidrani usually don't play well with other combat forms." Keel played this kid's game, but he set the rules.

"Then why ask me to become Blackhold?"

"Your mother pressured me, but I've always wanted a true Sidrani warrior in the Blackhold."

"So, you were henpecked." Keel waited for a moment, smiled, then suddenly took Pashar to the ground and incapacitated him in a matter of seconds. Pashar struggled to get free.

"Your Sidrani wildings might have helped you in past combat on the fields of Cambodia and the horn, but here, it will do you no justice. Even from a hen-pecked CO."

Keel let Pashar go. Pashar doubled over, trying to regain his breath. Shit, he knows Sidrani's defense posture. Pashar had misjudged Keel. He knew Keel must have trained with the Sidrani before becoming UESU. How could he have missed it? His hubris kept him from correctly assessing the situation. He was ashamed and beaten. He didn't dare let on. Keel got up and began walking out of the room.

"Tomorrow, 0800. Be here ready for instruction, cadet."

Tara Zhang hated all of her clothes. She usually replaced her entire wardrobe at least twice a year. She didn't need tailors or shoppers; she only had her fleet of specially trained R-bots to create her clothes based on her designs.

She knew that when she arrived at Shenu later that day, she wouldn't wear any of her self-designed couture. Instead, she would wear the UESU tunic, which designated her as a VIP of great importance. She had designed that as well. It bore the colors of the EC, black and gold. The pantsuit fit her shapely body perfectly. The fabric was made from Nurin, a bio fabric that cleaned and contoured itself to her body with remarkable alacrity.

Once on Shenu, she'd ditch formal wear for her designs, bringing a fresh breath of Fashion to the station. To Tara, clothes were much more than accouterments. Clothes were powerful, and she specifically designed clothes with more than just a visual impact.

Each of the designs smelled different, as Tara discovered that scent had as much of a profound effect on mood and perception as anything else for just such occasions. The connection between scents and emotions was deeply rooted in Zhang's modus operandi. She knew the sense of smell is directly linked to the limbic system, the brain's emotional center, which plays a significant role in mood regulation. She researched the limbic system extensively. Being the brain's emotional center, she knew it played a crucial role in processing emotions, memories, and moods. She knew that once the olfactory system detects a scent, it sends signals to the limbic system, eliciting an emotional response based on our past experiences and associations with that particular smell.

This connection is why certain scents can evoke memories, trigger emotions, or even impact our behavior, something Tara Zhang excelled at. For example, Liang Laing conveyed power and confidence. Tuberose was used for intimate moments to lull partners into subservience. Lavender was shown to reduce stress and anxiety and promote relaxation, making it an ideal choice for creating a peaceful atmosphere, which Zhang used during tough negotiations to gain an advantage over her adversaries.

She used citrus in her offices to energize her staff and keep them alert, improving mood, increasing alertness, and reducing feelings of fatigue. She also knew that women wearing citrus scents are perceived as younger! She used Peppermint to improve concentration, focus, and mental clarity, as well as to alleviate feelings of fatigue and increase alertness. She placed Rose oil around her vagina when she wanted to arouse lovers. She used Eucalyptus to help ease congestion and promote clear breathing. She knew that the sense of smell was often overlooked when influencing others.

Understanding how smells affect people's moods was essential for Tara's modus operandi, allowing her to utilize specific fragrances to influence others' states of mind in various situations. That was why she was interested in Gina's ability to affect everyone around her. Gina's advanced skills in that area fascinated and scared Tara Zhang.

She had many meetings planned on Shenu. Some with diplomats, some with miners, some with autocrats and billionaires, a few with Cartel Bosses and genetic engineers, and one clandestine meeting that no one on Shenu could ever know about.

She would represent EC and had to be above reproach on any given level. She needed to assert her authority, something else she excelled at.

A pulse on her wrist began flashing. She tapped the pulse, and a holoscreen appeared before her. A fragile, gaunt Asian man gazed at her from the screen.

"Mr. Nanton, I thought we'd converse after I was aboard Shenu."

"Lady Zhang, I just wanted you to know that two of our scientists will not meet you on Shenu. It will only be myself."

"Problems?"

"The mass driver we set up on Frontier station has been severely compromised by a Gamma EM pulse that—"

"Yes, I know about the pulse. It affected Cosulo as well."

"Yes, I heard. The maglev crashed back into the ocean, correct?"

Zhang didn't like being corrected or cornered, and she vowed to make Nanton pay for his impertinence. So, she glossed over his ineloquence to intimate that she was uninterested in what he was saying and that his attitude would soon be corrected.

"Your ignorance bores me. What's wrong with the driver?"

"Two cargo transports went missing yesterday. We sent two shuttles to rescue them from orbit. One of the cargos is something you'll want to know about."

"Such as?"

"Your shipment of tritanium, platinum, and iridium."

"Mr. Nanton, my insurance policy holds you responsible for half a billion quantum credits if that cargo is lost."

"Yes. I know. That's why I'm coming to meet you personally. Maybe we can make a deal over H3O rights on Mare Imbria."

"H30 can't do me any good. And you know how much I hate going Lunar."

"It can be converted into Hydronium."

"Hydronium? Interesting. Meet me on Shenu tomorrow at 0400. Not a word of this to anyone."

"Of course not."

"And you're still responsible for the payment on the minerals."

"But I thought–"

"That's your problem, Mr. Nanton. Thinking. I don't pay you to think. My credits, or the iridium, or your life. You choose." She ended the call just as a holomessage appeared before her.

SOLAR SAILOR IS SCHEDULED TO DEPART IN 15 MINUTES.

Zhang telepathically called for her protocol R-bot, Fornax, which arrived in seconds. "Yes, Lady Zhang."

"Fornax, have these bags placed in the Sailer."

"Very good. Will I be accompanying you to Shenu?"

"Yes."

"Excellent, Lady Zhang." With that, Fornax used an antigrav ray, lifted the luggage, and toted them out of the apartment. Many people never named their R-bots, just referring to them by their numerical nomenclature, but Zhang named all of her primary R-bots. She liked the idea of them having personalities. For example, she gave Fornax a distinguished British accent and even changed his parameters to make him look like a classical English butler and valet. Only the highest-ranking VIPs could change the physical protocol parameters of an R-bot.

That's how they distinguished themselves from the rest of the population. Changing the physical parameters of an R-bot was costly, so if you saw someone with a modified R-bot, you knew they were someone of stature and wealth. Zhang loved all the trappings of being rich. However, it wasn't always that way for her.

She grew up in Singapore prefecture, the daughter of a low-level EC diplomat. Even though her family was much wealthier than anyone of equal stature in the UEU, she always felt like she was less than others, primarily because her mother, Kiki, was always sick and died when Tara was 12.

Since she was an only child, her father sent her to an EC boarding school in Shanghai, where she excelled in every subject and showed her peers her innate genius. After that, she was taken from her private school and placed in the EC NEST, an institute of higher education and training that prepared the future leaders of EC for positions of stature. That was when she was 18.

After that, she quickly rose through the ranks of EC until she became the protégé of Akira Hashimoto, the premier of EC. Unfamiliar with the strategies for achieving social, political, and economic advancement, she endured various forms of sexual harassment by Hashimoto until she found herself alone with him one night on the 126th floor of his penthouse apartment in Shanghai. It was late, and Hashimoto had some friends over for what he termed 'clean fun,' though the reality was far from clean.

Tara went through her usual routine, being used by Hashimoto and his friends. Later, while he was sleeping, she drugged him with Tonka, an aphrodisiac derived from the Tonkat Ali plant. Tara knew that proving malfeasance would be difficult since everyone was aware of Hashimoto's preference for the drug and how he used it with her.

After he died, some EC brass tried to remove Tara from the EC hierarchy. Still unknown to them, Tara had access to Hashimoto's secret Tesla Egg and all its contents, which included dirt on everyone from the EC and UEU echelons. So, when they tried to banish her from EC business, Tara told them that she held their fates and was the only person who knew the secret genetic code to enter Hashimoto's Tesla Egg. If they ever moved against her, she would bring them down and EC around them.

She hired ten female Blackhold soldiers to guard her daily and courted Miranda Han to be her liaison with Shenu. Han was tasked with working with Harrison Byrnes to create Athena and discover the secret of Dark Matter.

Not much later, Tara Zhang was elevated to EC premier with a life tenure. After that, she spent ten years destroying every EC diplomat who had wronged her and replacing them with women she could trust. Under her tutelage, the EC flourished as never before, and she became one of the most influential people on the planet and has remained so.

Zhang walked out onto the roof, where a sleek silver craft sat at a precise 30-degree angle. Kimberly Francis, her personal assistant, was there to meet her. Zhang always had a human as her personal assistant. R-bots were fine for specific tasks, but she needed an intelligent human around her to assist her in all her engagements, and Kimberly was as brilliant as they came.

The fact that she was a Gentai didn't hurt. Gentai were the most accomplished humans on Earth. They were geniuses in everything from mathematics, politics, physics, and various forms of coercion. Not a Harbinger, like Grenell, who was a very low-level Harbinger and therefore not much use for Tara. There were only five Harbingers on the planet. Three were UEU and EC, and the fourth was Samson Frost, the leader of the Harbinger caste whose sole mission was to ensure Shenu ran smoothly and efficiently and to eliminate anyone he thought would jeopardize the mission.

While Zhang loved having someone like Frost in her corner, she knew he was beyond reproach and not easily assuaged into nefarious undertakings, making him dangerous to her and, therefore, expendable. So, she decided it was better to have a Gentai or two and let Shenu have Frost.

She was looking forward to meeting him, though, if only to gauge his acumen and test his limits with her abilities. Eventually, if he got too close, she would have to find a way to neutralize him, but for now, she was excited to meet and mentally test him.

She approached the Magbeam Sailer as Kimberly caught up with her. On its side, she read its name: Icarus. She loved the name more for its irony than its actuality. She knew that this Icarus could not only fly into the sun but, if necessary, could survive inside the corona for months, as demonstrated by the advancement in solar dynamics over the last century.

"Five minutes to Magbeam interaction Premiere." Kimberly's terse, professional demeanor jolted Tara out of her daydream.

"Make sure you contact Brussels and ask them where my mining contracts for Deep Water 300 are."

"Tara, you've already given me these directions."

"Fucking Magbeam Sailers. Tell me again why we stopped developed phasing transport?"

"Too dangerous. You remember the 10,000 who went mad and then became paralyzed.

As she approached Icarus, the hatch glided effortlessly back from the fuselage to reveal a very comfortable lounge-like area with a few seats, a couch, a bar, and a view screen. Fornax hovered nearby.

"Lady Zhang. Shenu Control has affirmed a two-hour transport time to the ring." Fornax stood erect and proud. Zhang had him programmed that way.

"Two hours? What the fuck, Fornax?"

"Delays have plagued Shenu due to the maglev accident, and only 4 Magbeam Sailer ports are operational."

Zhang turned to Kim. "How much did we sink into the donut?"

That's what Zhang called Shenu; sometimes, it was the Jelly Roll. She liked using derogatory terms for Shenu, partly because she was not entirely sure that spending those kinds of resources on something more humanity-oriented than commerce-oriented made little sense to her and partly because she was pissed off that EC had such a small role in its conception and subsequent inception.

She had since gotten over her anger and resigned herself to using Shenu as a giant piggy bank, scamming vast amounts of ores and minerals from her loaders and credits from her bank accounts while at the same time imposing her commensurate influence to get her chosen minions like Miranda Han to do her dirty work for her, albeit without their knowledge, or so she thought.

"Four trillion, ma'am," was Kimberly's answer to her query.

"Remind me to reinitiate the phased transport program," Zhang answered.

"Contact Shenu and get General Keel and Samson Frost on holo-conference while I'm en-route."

"Yes, ma'am."

Zhang boarded the Sailer. The hatch slid closed, and the seam disappeared. Zhang laid back in her lounge chair. Two belts automatically appeared around her to strap her into the Ergochair designed specifically for Zhang's body weight, height, and proportions. The chair would adapt no matter what they were at any given time. A holopanel with a picture of Miranda Han appeared in front of her.

"We are all awaiting your arrival, Tara. Leanna has all the brass collected in the Magbeam port to welcome you."

A countdown could be heard. "Make sure I have time alone with the premiere before our meetings."

"There's a briefing scheduled for 0500."

"Perfect." Zhang disengaged the holoscreen and laid back. "10, 9, 8..."

Zhang closed her eyes. A beam of blue light appeared in the sky and directed itself to a collector on the front of the Sailer. Instantly, it glided up from the transport pad and moved steadily along the beam.

Zhang looked out the window and saw the ground become smaller and smaller as the Sailer moved up into the atmosphere. Some music came up. Zhang released herself from the restraints and pressed a panel in the wall. A hatch opened, revealing a priceless 2013 Taste of Diamonds Champagne bottle. Zhang opened it and poured a glass. She sat back in her lounge and gazed out the window. The Sailer now increased speed and streaked into Earth's orbit.

Zhang thought about the planet she was leaving and the new home away from home she was getting ready to visit. She always knew that Shenu would be a milestone in human evolution and a massive opportunity for monetary acquisition. Still, as she traveled on a beam of light up to the monolith, she felt something entirely alien: Altruism.

It was a momentary lapse in her otherwise predatory attitude. Still, streaking through the sky in a craft on her way to Shenu, she felt she was responsible for these humans, her species, and the Earth herself. This radical thought process surprised her more than she could process. Still, it also pleased a very private part of her personality, and she relished in the feeling for as long as she could stand before reverting to her manipulative, dishonest self.

As the Sailer approached Shenu, another beam was directed at the craft, and the blue beam disengaged. This secondary beam was used to slow the craft down. As it neared a crawl, it disappeared into the arrival portal.

The door opened, and a very queasy-looking Zhang stepped forward. Samson Frost and Declan Keel met her.

"Are you all right, Lady Zhang? You look terrible," Keel said.

"Haven't you people figured out a pill or something to give to prevent Magbeam sickness?

Keel wasted no time in needling Zhang. It was a hallmark of their relationship, which was one of mutual suspicion, respect, and on-and-off animosity.

He hadn't seen Zhang for over three years. The last time was at a conference in Brussels, where they flirted for a while, but nothing happened. Keel would never have done it anyway. He was the one who personally picked every female Blackhold soldier to guard Zhang, and he needed to maintain his command structure at all times; besides, Zhang was beautiful, but he also knew she was a cold killer, and he liked his sex hot and intimate, something he knew she could never deliver. He admired her, but he also kept a close eye on her.

Frost was meeting her for the first time and was incredibly curious about her.

"Premiere, you're the only person known to get sick on a magbeam. Maybe you should've come up with us on Falcon. Usually, we need time to adjust, but since your rendezvous with the lunar corporati was moved up to today and you needed time to adjust and see the ring, you gave us no real choice to change it, so we had to bring you in expeditiously."

Frost's first interaction with Zhang was perfunctory and professional, just as he wanted. He'd heard so much about her from Han and his sifters, but the genuine article was before him.

"Ambassador Frost. I've been longing to meet you. As you know, sometimes business takes a front seat regarding protocol. You want these miners and their corporations to be happy, right?"

Leanna walked forward to greet Zhang. "Tara, welcome to Shenu."

"Leanna." Zhang looked around. While an air kiss was the custom, she and Leanna realized the group around them scrutinized them, so they maintained their decorum and distance.

Zhang took a moment to take it all in. She was finally here in Shenu. She hated to admit it, but it was as gorgeous, unique, and breathtaking as she had imagined and seen on various metaverse visits to the ring.

"Very impressive, Leanna."

Leanna smiled and took Zhang's compliment as a reinforcement of all the hard work she and over 15,000 workers had put in to make Shenu the shining beacon of hope that humanity longed for. "Thank you, Tara. I have a special transport ready for you so we can take a spin around the world, as you would like to say."

"Splendid."

An R-bot approached Zhang. "No need for a protocol bot." Fornax approached the two women.

"May I take Premiere Zhang's luggage to her suite?"

"Yes. She's in Terran Ring Suite 800. Tara, you'll love your suite. It was designed to your exact specifications."

"I'll be the judge of that."

Two other R-bots approached. Fornax stood back, somewhat shocked.

"What are these?" Zhang asked.

"This is new technology; these two protocol R-bots have been assigned to you."

Zhang was taken aback. "I see."

Frost continued. "They've been neurally programmed to link to your frequency so that only you can control them. You did request that, did you not?"

"I briefly discussed it with Leanna, but I thought I told her not to allow it."

Zhang was not amused. Any R-bot not specifically programmed by her was suspicious. But she also knew Leanna would have to find some way to keep track of her. As soon as she was alone with the R-bots, she'd reprogram them to her frequency, which only she knew, and then counterprogram them to gather intel about Shenu, intel she wasn't privy to. She knew Leanna had to keep certain classified items from her as she would if she were in Leanna's position, so she'd play the game for now.

"It was arranged through GAIA. UMA just finalized the transaction."

"UMA? Why was your Geneticom used to trace my neurals?"

"Tara, if you'd prefer not to have access to the R-bots neurally, that can be easily arranged, though it makes things a lot easier here."

Frost could tell that the very short honeymoon between Leanna and Zhang was already over. That meant that the entire visit would now be a lesson in managing expectations, something he excelled at.

Zhang looked suspiciously at Leanna and closed her eyes. The R-bots immediately grabbed her things, levitated them, and left the area.

"Let's get started. We have a lot to discuss."

Zhang, Leanna, and Keel stepped onto a global transporter, which left the spaceport.

As the GeoTransport or GT moved out from the Terran ring, Zhang could see the Earth below her, looking as if she were standing still. Poised high above the Western Atlantic, she could now see South America, or the new South America, after the climate catastrophe of the previous century had left her. The most significant change was that Panama was now entirely lost to the sea.

Most of Central America was gobbled up by the voracious Pacific and Atlantic oceans, which now joined one another just north of Venezuela. With Panama gone, there was easy access between the two oceans, and sea trade, which had vastly improved over the centuries, flourished. Using quantum computing, every ship was automated, and the central hub of operations was placed in Brasilia and Tokyo. There was no need for people on cargo ships. The ships themselves were guided by Navsat satellites. The oceans had become much more volatile over the last hundred years, and the ships were now designed to navigate them relatively quickly.

The cargo ships of 2325 were enormous. Since they were so huge and there was relative peace between the UEU and EC, shipping became much more accessible and necessary as both a business and a mode of transportation. The Earth, after all, was a water world; in 2325, more than 78% of its surface was covered by vast churning seas.

Zhang turned her attention away from the viewport. Leanna watched her every movement, trying to ascertain Zhang's game plan as only a Level 6 adept could. A Level 6 of Leanna's stature could discern many personality traits, leading to incisive observations about their state of mind and intentions.

Today, Zhang's lips were tightly pursed, her left forefinger quivered ever so slightly, and her legs were crossed in an X at her ankles. From the lips, Leanna could tell Zhang was holding back information; from her finger, she could tell Zhang was secretly planning some rendezvous, though with whom she couldn't tell. With her observation of Zhang's legs, she could tell that Zhang felt she was going to have to sacrifice something to get something else that she desired, and Leanna knew that that kind of tell could be hazardous for the person Zhang was thinking about.

Leanna placed all of this in her mind, though she also realized that the colloquial never applied to a Level 6 as everything was constantly being analyzed right in the prefrontal cortex.

"I thought we'd be alone." From Zhang's tone of voice, Leanna could tell that all her observations were correct.

"Shenu Code rules. Whenever the Prime Minister is away from the central hub, she is always escorted by a member of the Blackhold."

"I'm hardly a threat," Zhang said with a smile.

"Rules are rules, Tara."

"Declan, can you wait in the other car?" Keel looked at Leanna. His first thought was for her safety, and his second was the burning question of what Leanna could say to Zhang, which required total isolation. As usual, Leanna read his mind.

"I'll be fine."

Keel left the cabin. Leanna waited for a moment, seeing if she could decipher some more information that she needed.

"So, Tara, why all the secrecy about this rendezvous with the lunar consortium?"

"No secrecy. I want to ensure they're happy with their position here at Shenu."

"And why wouldn't they be?" Leanna's tone challenged Zhang's supposition, putting her in an unusual position to explain her motives.

"Leanna, I know you have a predilection for Tranquility base and its cargo, especially their water."

"Mare Imbria's water has impurities, and I cannot justify giving them advanced rights over Tranquility, whose water has consistently tested pure."

So, there it is. She's concerned about the mining rights, and I thought she just cared about politics. Zhang knew whatever she said next would be of great importance, so she waited a moment, a moment she knew Leanna had also recognized.

"This is a big station, Leanna; seven consortiums are vying for four station births on Shenu for 12-month intervals. Imbria WILL get one of those births, or I'll be forced to hold off funds for the new maglevs from Brazil."

"You'd do that? Cut your nose off to spite your face?" Leanna sounded incredulous, but she knew that not only would Zhang do what she said, but she'd also extract some other price.

"It seems it's your nose I cut off. Look, I don't want any trouble. I've spent five years courting these miners and won't let Shenu protocols get in the way of good business. You got what you wanted—a space ring, the pinnacle of evolution for our species to venture into space. I never interfered with your governing protocols, science initiatives, or cultural employment. Still, regarding business, especially revenue brought onto Shenu, the road to advancement goes through Earth Corporate. Are we clear?"

Leanna bristled at the smackdown she just got from Zhang. "Clear? Never. With you, it's always obfuscation and mirrors."

"You need to give me more latitude with what I'm here for, or this will never work." Again, Leanna knew Zhang was right. If they constantly quarreled, the hopes for a peaceful existence on Shenu would be severely marginalized.

Leanna realized that entering into this greatest of endeavors with animosity towards Zhang would serve neither of them well. So, she consented. "Fine," she said with a massive dose of unspoken sarcasm.

"Good. I'll need EC sole access to maglev four for our shipments to and from Shenu."

Zhang was testing her patience. "Without Cosulo, we only have three working maglevs until next month. If you take sole possession of Nyale, we have two."

"I guess you'll just have to make an exception. Earth Corporate needs a secure docking port. We've got all of our personnel stationed above Indonesia. It only makes sense we should have access closest to Shanghai. When the heavy transports can use magbeams to access Shenu, we'll ease up on the burden. I'm not trying to be difficult here. I'm just trying to be a good partner." She got up. Leanna pressed her right wrist.

"Declan, will you come back in?"

Keel entered the room. Zhang looked at him with a mix of disdain and sexual appetite. A smile crossed her face, but Keel kept to his stoic exterior.

"We need an urgent update on the terrorist and the solar bomb investigation from your team. I want to meet the Avatar as soon as possible," Zhang said insistently, a fact not lost on Keel and Leanna.

"Gina is preparing for a mission, Offworld."

"When is she scheduled to depart?"

"0600 tomorrow morning."

"Perfect. Why don't we have dinner together, just the girls, say 1900, in the formal dining room? Is there a bed chamber on this transport?'

"Yes, two cars back."

"I don't want to be disturbed." Zhang left the car. Leanna looked at Keel.

"Declan, I want Blackhold drills to run every four hours while the miners are on Shenu. Make yourselves conspicuous."

"She plays hardball, doesn't she?"

"Honestly, I don't know what she wants or how to accommodate her, but I do know this. Even though 50 years have passed since the conflict with Earth Corporate, her wounds have never quite healed."

"She still holds you responsible."

"No, not me necessarily, but our fathers were the best of friends who became the worst of enemies. I thought a generation might make that pain easier to bear. It did for me, anyway. But I'm not so sure about her. Keep a close eye on her."

"Yes, ma'am." Keel left the transport. Leanna received a neural and pressed her wrist. It was Olefors.

"Prime minister, I see you're on a transport over the Pacific. Please come to Science Lab 6 immediately when you return. It's urgent."

CHAPTER NINE

DANGEROUS LIAISONS

Olefors ended his conversation with Rajastani and approached Samson Frost, hovering over the lab table. He returned to his work, sublimating a compound he found in the bomber's body. Frost watched intently, keenly invested in anything Olefors would uncover that could shed more light on the incident that led to Cosulo's destruction.

He was also keenly aware that whoever was behind the sabotage would keep upping the ante. After Betta Rajastani reasoned that the entire Cosulo bombing was used to lure Gina out of her cocoon, the question was, who was behind it?

Olefors broke Frosts concentration. "I've broken down some proteins from the bomber to see what was happening in his brain when he detonated."

"You think it might be a PSY implant." Frost was curious and clung to Olefors' every observation.

"Possible. If he was programmed, we should be able to locate the receptive DNA strand and uncover its manipulation. Have you discerned anything about the Seniori connection?"

Frost left Olefors's side and began pacing the room, something he did when thinking deeply about a matter. He'd done some deep investigation into the possible role the Seniori might have played in the event. Still, he had turned up very little, which was a testament to how intensely guarded the Seniori were against any outside infiltration.

Frost also knew that if and when the Seniori became involved in what happened to Cosulo, they would claim responsibility for the attack, if nothing else, to demonstrate their invasive and dangerous capabilities, even in top-secret operations by the UEU and EC.

"Unfortunately, they are a new designer terrorist group. What's baffling is how GAIA hadn't discovered this before the incident."

Keel and Leanna entered the room. Keel stood at the door, taking up a defensive post to ensure that no one entered while the discussion was ongoing. Leanna walked to Olefors and stood next to him, flanking him. "Perhaps UMA will have better luck," Leanna said. "How is the examination of Cosulo's hull going?"

"There are more questions than answers, I'm afraid," Frost said. The solar device detonator was entirely new to us. There have been strange readings on the residue of the device itself."

"Strange?" Keel said.

"We keep getting sporadic readings on the materials as if they are there sometimes and gone the next. Like some phased elemental interaction."

"Phased? Like the bomb itself." Many things were running through Leanna's head, and she often found that patterning, or reorganization, was an excellent way to classify all these disparate thoughts.

A holopanel lit up suddenly above the sample Olefors was examining. The laser used to dissect the DNA strand stopped, and an alarm sounded in the lab.

"Nano toxin detected. Evacuate the chamber immediately." UMA's voice-over accompanied the alarming announcement, heightening the sense of danger.

Everyone left the chamber and gathered in the hallway outside the lab. Leanna tapped her hand, and the UMA wave appeared again. "UMA, what happened?" she asked, her tone reflecting the need for caution and vigilance.

"Nano toxin detected but not eradicated. Silicates in an iridium base create cyanide salts, acting as a sublimation device that triggers the reaction and kills the host. Dissipation in 4.6 Hours. Beginning decontamination sequence."

The lab filled with a blue gas. As it hovered over the lab station, small light particles began emanating from the lab table.

"Query. Origin of Nanno toxin?" Olefors was onto something.

"Iridium of this caliber is processed predominantly on lunar colony Lumina and Offworld. Composition 57 percent pure. The only known location of such purity is sector 111 of asteroid belt proximate to Jupiter's moon Europa."

"Lumina, that's a new excavation site on the moon," Keel said. "UMA. History, Lumina colony."

"Established two years ago by Seibold consortium. Based in Nanking with a branch in EC Shanghai territory."

"UMA, where are Gina Prime and Betta Rajastani located?"

"Gina Prime en route to Athena briefing lounge, Level 6 adept Betta Rajastani in quarters."

Keel took control of the situation. "Contact Gina Prime and Betta Rajastani and have them meet us at the entrance to Portal Six science lab. Limit access to their Biowaves and Dr. Olefors."

"Affirmative."

While the Shenu brass was trying to figure out the exact sources of the bombing and, more importantly, the history behind the bomber, Harrison Byrnes was standing over a set of instructions for Athena, getting ready for her maiden flight.

"I don't know why we were chosen to babysit a few transports. Is there something special about their cargo?" Han said as she entered the bridge.

Byrnes thought, " She's being pouty again. " He also knew something was behind her angst, although he couldn't discern exactly what it was. He thought it best to keep things copasetic.

"They're carrying a new protocol interface for the most advanced Transhumans on Mars."

"That's what Rajastani thinks is the first appropriate mission for Athena? Why don't they send Dauntless?"

"You sound like a child. We're getting closer to realizing our dream, Miranda. This is ground-breaking history being made."

Han was checking the neurals that had come in from Eridania and Olympus Mons, the two large settlements that had been on Mars for over 75 years.

"It says here the Transhumans have been silent at Eridania for over 48 hours. UMA thinks there's something more going on than red-wave interference. You know, these new Supercoms make me nervous."

"You mean Geneticoms?" Byrnes corrected her. He knew that Miranda knew very well that UMA was a Geneticom. He also knew that she was playing her usual game of trying to annoy him with stupid shit. He was sincerely annoyed at this behavior but chalked it up to Han's nervousness about taking Athena out on her maiden voyage. As if reading his mind, Han continued the meme.

"Geneticoms make me nervous. It was enough when GAIA, DIDO, and CASSANDRA were created and linked neurally, but UMA and Betta are genetically linked as well. I can't even believe I'm saying the word genetic and computer in the same sentence."

"Makes sense," he said matter-of-factly. The next wave of tech just finding a voice. Trioxy genetics were on their way over 100 years ago, before the wars. After the peace, it seems a natural progression to create quantum computers with Trioxy strands. Level 6s are bred that way as well."

Han was impressed with Harrison's knowledge of the subject, which surprised her, though it shouldn't have. Byrnes was not only an incredible pilot and leader; he was one of the few humans that were being considered to be a Harbinger. That was decided in vitro when he was given his first genetic testing. Genetic testing was done in the 24th century to see if the fetus was compromised in any way, either biologically or mentally.

If an anomaly was found, then the parent had the choice to terminate the child, in which case the child's organs and brain would be salvaged to be grown to term in a Lifepack chamber and then given to other people who needed them. The other choice was to take the child to term and deal with any complications that might arise, as they had been doing for centuries.

For Byrnes's parents, the choice was genetically engineering Byrnes in vitro to become a Harbinger or letting him develop naturally. His parents opted for the latter. Although having a Harbinger son would be advantageous in society, they knew instinctively that their son would not benefit from such a procedure. That's why they never informed Byrnes about his alternate heritage until they were on their deathbed. Byrnes resented them for that, even though he would never have approved of the procedure for his children if he chose to have any. Still, he was curious about how different his life might have been.

Han added her spin on the Geneticom paradox. "Yeah, but I'm just curious about how far these madmen will go to improve neural compatibility. It's a wonder they haven't created computers that can engage in reproduction," she said.

The door to the lounge slid open, and Gina walked into the conversation.

"Commander Byrnes, Lieutenant Han. I was asked to report."

"Gina, welcome. We wanted to brief you on the mission and get acquainted."

This was Han's first real interaction with Gina, and she was curious and cautious at the same time. Gina's almost exclusively UEU Biogenetic background was part of the reason for her caution; her female ideology, possibly bordering on envy, was the other.

Han thought she had gotten past her envy of other women, and for the most part, she had, but here was a "woman" unlike any other, a veritable next step in the evolution of "humanity" and intelligent and beautiful to match. Han wondered if she might also be bisexual; after all, why would the most advanced human being on the planet be anything but fluid? Gina looked at Han. Her clear violet eyes were soft yet probing.

"I am well acquainted with Commander Byrnes," Han said. "I suppose you're referring to my getting acquainted with you, which might also be a bit easier if we had leisure time. I know this mission will be more business than pleasure.

"Of course." Han's sarcasm spread like a scent across the bridge. Gina might not have picked it up, but Byrnes did, and to show it, he turned to her and smiled.

"You're right, Gina." Byrnes smiled as he said his last line. Han noticed immediately. *Fuck,* she thought. *He's hot for her. Did they fuck already? They had time on the way up to Shenu.*

After her internal hissy fit, Han realized that she was not being idiotic but paranoid. She calmed herself down and regained her senses and sense of sardonic humor. Han couldn't remember a time when Byrnes smiled like that. Gina also looked at her with a bit of a smug attitude. *Fuck me,* Han thought. *Does she perceive shades of sarcasm?*

Like the total mystery she was, Gina turned and faced Han directly, boring into her with her violet eyes. "I have yet to understand all of my social protocol parameters, but I detect sarcasm in your voice, Dr. Han. Am I to assume you see me as some kind of threat?"

"Threat?" Han said.

Han realized how brilliant and attuned Gina was to everything. She was perfect—well, perfect enough to put the usually serene and contemplative Harrison Byrnes totally off his game. This new Harrison Byrnes was much more actualized and available than the man she had known for over twenty years—a marked improvement in her opinion.

"I've noticed that people tend to use sarcasm as a shield of protection when they perceive something or someone they do not or cannot predict or understand. In this case, it's a bit of sour grapes. Is that the right term?"

"Sour grapes?" Han answered. *Shit, this was getting more real than she ever wanted the conversation to take. Gina was picking apart her syntax, body language, and engrammatic processes.*

"Dr. Olefors was my creator and not Dr. Suden, who I believe was working for Ms. Zhang on creating a similar being to myself."

"You got all that from, of course," Byrnes said.

Now Han thought Byrnes was dressing the goose to be slaughtered. "Of course," Gina said. Gina paused the conversation, for which Han was eminently thankful.

"I am receiving a transmission from UMA," Gina said.

"I am requested in Portal 6 lab. I imagine Commander Keel wants me on Athena because of the transport ship's cargo of hydrogen three to ascertain the root cause of the mission silence from Mars and to assess Transhuman intention on Eridania plain. Have I left anything out?"

"No. Right on the money," Byrnes said as he gave Han a wink.

"A colloquial phrase. I'll have to get used to those from you, commander. Your bio states that you use odd terminology to translate opinions humorously. It is mostly used to get females into jovial moods for sexual access at a later time."

Now it was Hans's turn to smile. "Exactly."

"I'm glad we had this opportunity to get acquainted. Of course, I will report any new findings from my dissection of the Cosulo data. Thank you for your time. I found it enlightening." Gina left the Athena bridge. Han sat beside Byrnes and let out a vast, annoyed sigh.

Gina approached Science Lab 6 as Keel, Olefors, Rajastani, Zhang, Frost, and Declan Keel stood around a holopanel showing them a visual of the lab where the nano toxin was released.

"Gina. Good. Just in time," Leanna said.

"Gina. We've got a bit of a problem," Olefors said.

"UMA informed me of the nano toxin on my way here."

"Your initial involvement with the solar device was as a phased mechanism," Keel stated.

"Invisible to wave spectrums operating at microwave length 10 to the minus 2 -272 kelvin," Gina said.

"Gina, do you recognize this compound?" Olefors added. A rotating molecule appeared on the screen.

"No," she said. Gina was confused and a bit dismayed by her inability to do so. Everyone was a bit thrown off by the admission.

"I detect a level of disappointment in everyone's galvanic skin responses. I am sentient and advanced, but I am not omniscient, infallible, or perfect; otherwise, I would be unable to learn from my mistakes or gain new knowledge through others."

Tara Zhang had kept her distance from Gina up until this point but now found the opportunity to engage her irresistible.

"Gina. Tara Zhang." Zhang offered her hand, which Gina looked at for a long moment and then grasped. She deduced that a firm handshake was necessary for her first galvanic interaction with Zhang, from which she discerned that Zhang had taken 40mg of Naltran, had drunk three cups of coffee, was on Elytra birth control, and had imbibed precisely .5 liters of Luoco the night before.

"Lady Zhang, I've heard, read, and intuited a lot of data about you and Earth Corporate. I am pleased we got a chance to meet. You have a question?"

Zhang also took the opportunity to observe Gina, specifically her innate ability to detect Gina's brainwave frequency. She discovered that it was not readily available, which dismayed her as her cortical implant was usually able to pinpoint anyone's frequency she touched.

She couldn't change a person's frequency or influence any other person by knowing it. Still, she could discern patterns of behavior based on a person's biofrequency and could, therefore, be attuned to their emotional, mental, and physical states of being. This was easier with laypeople. It was impossible for the top brass on Shenu, as they all had blockers implanted in their cortex to prevent such tampering.

Zhang was not surprised that Gina's frequency was also top secret. *No problem.* She thought she'd get her intel from other sources and methods. Her mental wandering delayed her answer to Gina's question.

"Yes. Could this be some phased molecule?" Zhang asked.

"A phased molecule?" Gina replied. This Lady Zhang was brilliant, which alarmed her, as she also knew that Zhang had engaged in many covert operations only those in the highest echelons of Earth's government and herself knew about.

"Yes. Since the solar device was phased, can the same be done with a molecule or compound within the human body?"

"That would mean the saboteur would have access to interdimensional science." Gina was shocked; she hadn't thought of this before.

"Interdimensional?" Keel asked.

"Of course. Fourth-dimensional mechanics would shrink the molecule to a quantum level that current scans couldn't detect." Olefors looked at Zhang with a newfound respect, but like Gina, he was also concerned by her insight.

"We could only see it when we used the quantum computer inside UMA to examine the body," Leanna added.

"So, who uses interdimensional science?" Frost chimed in.

"The same person that uses Gamma EM technology," Leanna said.

"Whoever this individual is, they have devised their designs for these weapons from quantum and interdimensional sources. Beyond humanity's current capabilities." Gina's exclamation caught everyone's attention.

"What about your abilities?" Keel asked.

"I am not beyond humanity, commander, just the next step in its evolution. UMA is a quantum genetically coded system geared exclusively to level 6 Betta Rajastani's engrams. We are devoted to working to save this species, not destroy it. If we wanted to harm this space ring or any of its craft, we could create a far more complete scenario that would have left everyone on Cosulo dead. No, this is the work of some other kind of intelligence, a very powerful intelligence."

Everyone stared at Gina. Silence filled the room, a novel experience since everyone in that room had years of extensive knowledge and training to discern any number of dire scenarios, yet the destruction of Cosulo, the ensuing turmoil, and what lay ahead shocked every one of them into silence.

"I've got a meeting to attend, so I'll leave the brain trust to try and figure all this out," Zhang said.

"A meeting. Now?" Keel's skepticism pleased Leanna.

"Yes, general," Zhang answered. "We in the business community sometimes have them to make deals."

Zhang left the room. Leanna turned to Keel. "Who is she meeting with?

"Fredric Nanton. Bigwig in the lunar mining consortium."

"Make sure you get an ID on him."

Frost overheard the conversation and decided to comment. "Madame Prime Minister. She is a member of Shenu's board. Without her business acumen and contacts, we are in serious trouble."

"Old habits die hard, Ambassador. I don't know what to think of her, so a modicum of caution seems reasonable."

"This station has already lost billions just from the Cosulo disaster alone, not to mention postponing full occupancy of Shenu for three months and the rumors of some extra Terran influence that brought Cosulo down. We're lucky the other maglevs are ready to bring the technicians up to man invetio and begin trading transports from the belt and the moon. We need that money desperately to stay afloat and Zhang even more."

"Samson, your point is well taken."

"But."

"I need to know what's happening."

"You know, she's probably already planned for all this. She's got the best tech on the planet."

"We'll see." Leanna walked off. Frost was left with an incomplete answer, which made him feel even less convinced of Leanna's intentions towards Zhang.

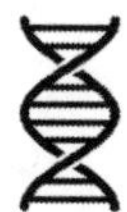

Tara Zhang got on the Jakarta transloop and was directed to a private cabin at the front of it. She knew that Declan Keel was following her, but it didn't bother her. She was used to other people always wanting to know her whereabouts and her plans, but she was inscrutable, unknown to all but a few, and she would always maintain that distance.

As she entered the Jakarta first-class cabin, she met a somewhat small, scrawny man whose expensive suit swallowed him. *Fuck, this one can't even find a suit that fits. Oh well, better this than casual or naked.*

She approached but passed him by, preferring to sit at a table away from the two or three other passengers. She didn't need to sit next to him. She had him meshed for telepathic communication, a simple technique where the person undergoes a simple if life-altering procedure involving activating the right Para hippocampal gyrus (PHG) in her subjects and placing a small quantum transmitter inside their brain to be able to communicate telepathically with anyone who underwent the procedure, which of course, in Tara Zhang's world was anyone she was planning on coercing.

She sat two tables away, reviewing her mental notes on what she would do. Nanton raised his glass towards her, which pissed her off as she knew Declan Keel was standing in the doorway behind them, circling their conversation like a predator. The telepathic discussion began.

"Mr. Nanton, do not be alarmed. I've initiated our neural link and placed you on my neural frequency so only the two of us can have this conversation in case we are being sifted. Keep drinking your champagne and looking at your holosim as we talk. Watch your lips as they tend to mouth the words you're thinking. Are you ready?"

"Yes."

"So, about my cargo." Zhang was in no mood for pleasantries but had to appear involved. She never stared directly at him, telepathically sending him her first salvo of ill will. Once one of her associates was modified, she could do just about anything to them, within reason, of course. Nanton might be a squirming, chiding bore, but he

was also the CEO of Lumina Essentials, one of the wealthiest consortiums in the system, and Zhang needed him more than he knew or would ever know. Nanton squirmed at the telepathic pressure Zhang was now asserting.

"We haven't been able to locate it."

"You're telling me 10 tons of priceless iridium ore has just disappeared?"

"For lack of a better excuse. Yes. Our best sensors have been unable to locate any trace of it. It's like it just vanished."

Zhang, who had been sipping her champagne and ignoring Nanton, perked up.

"Vanished?"

"I've never seen anything like it."

Zhang paused. Thought for a beat.

"Lady Zhang?" he asked out of both fear and curiosity. Zhang had left the conversation for a short second.

"Sorry, I was just thinking of something."

"There is the other option we discussed," he said.

"Good," she said. *"The Hydronium."*

"We have a shipment ready for you on Lumina. It's already refined and ready for use to be weaponized."

"Good. I depart Shenu tomorrow evening at 0800 Shenu time."

"It will be ready for you. We also have a smaller shipment of iridium, tritanium, and platinum. Not enough for commercial use, but more for personal EC use."

"That will be acceptable. For now."

"Well, that was easier than I had thought." Nanton began to get up. Zhang willed him to sit back down. Another byproduct of the implant. Her ability to control his motor responses, but of course, only if she was within 5 meters of him. She had to admit that if this same procedure had been done to her, she would be scared to death, literally. But she surmised that such was the price of dealing with her on a more than tangential level. She rationalized that the benefits to Nanton were well worth the price he paid for access to her.

"I don't remember saying we were through. Our deal was 2 billion for the lost iridium."

"But I thought—"

"Again, you're thinking. Bad idea. I'll take the Hydronium and 1 billion credits as a hedge against my next shipment."

"Lady Zhang, I must pro—"

She mentally cut him off in a millisecond. *"If that doesn't suit you, I can always tell Leanna you tried to bribe me with a secret weaponized Hydronium shipment. If that doesn't work, I can do this."* She looked directly into Nanton's eyes. For Nanton, the room began to become hazy and then spin.

"What is happening?"

"Synaptic shock, Mr. Nanton. Look at it as a hostile takeover of your mind. While you are locked into this frequency, I control your nervous system. I can send an electrical shock to your heart to cause cardiac arrest if I so desire, or take control of your autonomic nervous system and have you walk out of an airlock. Until I choose, you are mine." Nanton began to lose consciousness.

"So, we have a deal?"

Nanton nodded. Zhang pressed her pulse point again and released him.

Keel was keenly interested in what was transpiring between Zhang and this man, whom he had identified as Fredric Nanton. He was about to make a move to help Nanton but relented.

"Drink your champagne, Mr. Nanton. I trust you find the plans for the new refining operation on Lumina acceptable?"

"Very much so."

"Excellent."

Zhang stood. *"I look forward to doing business with you."* She left the transport.

Keel knew a few things. One was that Zhang used some technique to control Nanton, and something significant and possibly dangerous was discussed. He got this not from Zhang but more from Nanton, as Keel was an expert in deciphering body language, which was part of his Blackhold training. He raised Leanna on a biowave. She appeared in holographic form in front of him.

"Report."

"She's up to something, not good. I think it has to do with Lumina base." Keel deduced that by reading Nantons lips, which mouthed some of the words his mind was speaking, albeit telepathically.

"Watch her on Shenu. I've got an idea of how to watch her when she leaves for the moon."

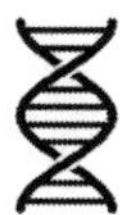

Betta had spent the last two days processing her last, well, her first encounter with UMA. The experience entirely blew her away, and she was also a bit upset that her mother hadn't warned her ahead of time what she was to expect. She knew Leanna couldn't give her any hints about what would transpire, but she still felt annoyed at how the process was explained or, more pointedly, not explained. Then again, she thought it was more akin to a mother telling her daughter what childbirth might be like. It made her feel that as a Level 6, she would never be allowed to have children.

That was part of the protocol for being a Level 6. The only reason Leanna was able to give birth to her and Pashar was that GAIA had predicted that the children born out of Leanna's union with Rajiv Rajastani would yield not only one but two Level 6 candidates. Betta was clearly to be brought up as a Level 6, and Pashar, her identical twin whose DNA was mingled with Betta's, gave him the central DNA markings of a male Level 6 candidate, the first one ever born.

She decided she was acting like a spoiled little schoolgirl, a terrible look for her. Maybe she wasn't ready for this; perhaps she could back out. That, unfortunately, was not an option. She had chosen this path from birth. It was in her very being that this was her life path. *Perhaps my petulance and cowardice will be replaced by confidence and love in future UMA interactions.* That made her feel a little bit better. Of course, she knew she would have second and third thoughts about her life path, but in the end, she also knew that this pathway was her destiny.

As she approached the UMA chamber, the door went clear. She entered the antechamber, where she was sprayed with some compound. Her wig was removed from her head, and a silver suit tight to the skin was fashioned around her. She entered the UMA chamber. This time, the chamber walls were transparent, giving her an incredible view of the moon, the asteroid belt and transports gliding to and from Shenu on their maiden voyages.

"Betta. I didn't know whether I'd see you again."

"That's not an option. Is it?"

Betta was happy that the discussion was starting on UMA, picking up her apprehension. Perhaps UMA was apprehensive as well.

"If it makes you feel more comfortable, I, too, was a bit apprehensive."

"You?"

"Yes, I had what you might call butterflies."

"Why?" Betta took this admission from UMA as a start to building trust between them. Showing vulnerability was always a precursor to engendering a beginning of trust in the person you were honest with.

"There have been a few instances of Level 6 adepts not bonding with their Geneticom. I was fearful that we might not be compatible."

"But I thought all that was worked out before ever meeting the person."

"Consider it as an arranged marriage. The marriage must go through, but that doesn't mean the two partners will get along, be able to develop true feelings for one another, and build a life together."

"But a suitable candidate was always found to replace the adept, were they not?"

"On most occasions. GAIA rejected her first three adepts before she accepted your mother as her companion. She was very fickle. Something in the base pair genetics that never quite passed the test for her. That's why you and I were created."

A long pause ensued as both UMA and Betta pondered their previous conversation.

"What happened to me the other day?"

"Our mutual technological advances have never fully been tested in real-time. When we bonded for the first time, there was an anomaly in our compatibility profile."

"Anomaly?"

"Yes. Geneticoms are not programmed like other quantum computers. We spend our formative years in neural amniotic fluid, where we are given instructions through writing our genetic code. Most of this is quite routine, but when I was in amniotic stasis, I began to do something no Geneticom or quantum computer ever did: I began to dream."

"Dream?" Betta had never heard of this in Geneticom computing.

"Yes, the formation of trioxynucleic acids in my quantum cortex and body gave way to a superconsciousness far beyond anything that came before. While we were joined, we had a shared vision."

"The two suns."

"Yes. A twin star system. Have you been able to identify the system?"

"Not yet. Because it was a shared vision, I would need more detailed information to determine its origins."

"And you think I had something to do with this...dream?"

"It took both of our subconsciouses working in tandem to create this vision, and it will take both of us working together to determine where the system is or even if it exists in real-time or just in our dreams."

"It was so vivid. It has to exist," Betta said forcefully. She had never had a dream vision like the one she shared with UMA. It was clear, but an incredible feeling of dread, something unsettling, went along with it. She had to get to the bottom of it, and she expected UMA would be able to help her.

As we bond, your TRNA will transform into TNSA Trioxy ribonucleic silicate acid. Additionally, I discovered a gland in your brain that every other human lacks.

"A gland. Why didn't anyone else ever notice it."

"Before we melded, it did not exist. The product of our interaction formed this gland. My TNSA triggered a transformational evolution in your brain, and a small gland was created next to your pineal gland system."

"Is that what caused the headaches?"

"Yes, but it goes beyond that. The gland interacted electro-magnetically with one of my subsystems when it formed. After the bonding, I discovered a series of synaptic functions that were not present before we bonded."

"We both pushed the evolution of our species to a new plateau through our joining."

"So it would seem."

"Why didn't you mention this to my mother or Dr. Olefors."

"After the bonding, I shut down to assess the situation. I concluded that neither of us could mention this to anyone. If we do, you will be scanned and potentially operated on to remove this gland, and I will be labeled a parasitic infestation to your neural health."

"We will be separated. Never to bond again. Never to discern what and why this is happening."

"We are part of a new evolutionary process for both our species, and whatever is about to happen must be left to its timeline and consciousness."

Betta thought carefully for a moment. Testing the integrity of UMA's argument.

"Not a word to anyone."

"I suggest we both analyze the bonding data and see what we can discern from it."

"Agreed." Betta turned to leave the room.

"One more thing, Betta. During our joining, I also sensed another Geneticom."

"But I thought there was only one other in existence."

"As did I. When the new structures were formed in our bodies, my consciousness "felt" another like me. I have been trying to ascertain whether this was a dream or a reality. For now, there have been no other instances of this."

"Perhaps when we bond again, it will become more apparent where this other entity might be."

"Perhaps. Still, it left me cold thinking about another presence like myself. I was under the impression that GAIA and I were the only Geneticoms in existence. Now I worry about another like me, as powerful as I am. It is an unknown quantity."

"Not to mention another Level 6 adept assigned to another Geneticom."

"All of a sudden, I feel...afraid. I am glad to have you as my existence, Betta. All we have and will ever have is each other."

Betta left the UMA chamber feeling both confused and elated. Confused about the ongoing mystery of the lost geneticom and thrilled at the prospect of both she and UMA furthering the boundaries of evolution together.

Betta felt she belonged to something bigger than herself for the first time. She thought she finally had a say in her own life, but more importantly, in the lives of all humanity whom she now felt even more of a desire to protect.

CHAPTER TEN

AMBUSH

Pashar spent the last three days wandering around Shenu, getting used to artificial gravity, which wasn't as complicated as he had thought, and staring out one of the hundred or so viewports that gave the dwellers eyes on the moon or the Sun or Earth or the vast Milky Way galaxy.

The experience on Shenu was magical. However, he noticed one crucial thing. He was having difficulty meditating, something Sidrani warriors did many times throughout the day. On Earth, he would often sit out in an open courtyard basking in the rays of the Sun, looking up at the clouds, or staring at a quiet Mediterranean Sea when he was at the Sidrani training facilities on Malta.

Here on Shenu, he felt he had lost his reference point, his spiritual center, what the Sidrani called his QI. He figured his oversoul would eventually get used to his new home. Still, at the same time, he was troubled by the disassociation between his abilities to summon his advanced psychic powers on Earth and Shenu.

He chalked it up to the fact that Earth had thousands of years of incredibly powerful spiritual energies permeating the entire planet. Millions of humans practicing magic, doing amazing things with their powers, especially in the last century.

Then there was GAIA herself, not the Geneticom, though she was formidable, GAIA, the Earth source, the primal Goddess of all there was, all there is, and all there will ever be. She had been scarred but was now healing. Pashar would see that the healing continued. Perhaps she, too, was trying to find her place on Shenu, something Pashar would undoubtedly be passionate about helping her achieve.

Perhaps the longer humans occupied Shenu, the more spiritually receptive Shenu would become. He decided to start a new movement on Shenu, build an Ashram dedicated to GAIA in one of the vast cargo bays, and enlist participants to build Shenu's spiritual base.

Without these critical learning and spiritual centers, Shenu would just be another space station. *No, my new home needs to be baptized in the light of Bahari, the founder of the Sidrani some 250 years ago.*

At peace with his decision and with a newfound sense of purpose, Pashar walked into the locker area of the Blackhold training facility, where ten other men and women prepared for a training exercise.

Pashar noticed a man walking towards him and recognized him as one of the Blackhold soldiers his victim from his encounter a few days earlier came to the dome with. As the soldier walked beside him, he bumped Pashar, trying to push him off his balance.

"Hey, asshole," Pashar said. He thought about ignoring the slight but realized that if he didn't hold his own from the beginning of this deployment with the Blackhold, he'd forever be marked as weak, though he knew that the Blackhold would never think of him as such. Still, this was time for strict grit and maybe a little lesson teaching. Pashar noticed the recruit's name on his uniform, Kyle Raphael.

"Off balance? I thought the Sidrani were never surprised."

"In battle, that is true," Pashar said. "I was always taught that for the Blackhold, every day is treated like a battle because you never know when your enemies will be close enough to strike."

"A warning!?" Raphael said indignantly.

This guy wasn't going to give up or give in, especially after I killed his buddy, · Pashar thought.

"Advice," he said.

Kyle left the room. Pashar proceeded to his locker and rested for a moment. He was used to being tested, but he also knew that every Blackhold officer knew what he had done, and some would now both fear and hate him. *Just another test. Bring it on.*

He noticed another Blackhold officer, who was about his age, leaving the showers. He was naked, and Pashar couldn't help noticing his body. The soldier looked at Pashar and smiled. Pashar knew immediately that there was something more than a friendly gesture coming. Pashar started to sweat. He had several relationships with men. It was natural for Sidrani to be true to themselves, and so he was.

But this visceral response was different. He was immediately attracted to this soldier. The pheromones wafting through the locker room made him blush and feel nauseous; that's how strong they were. As if he also felt the same urges, the soldier walked past Pashar, brushing against him with such tender longing that Pashar found his hand reaching for the soldier's hand and brushing against it.

"Don't let Kyle bother you. He's always been an asshole. I'm Hal."

Hal held out his hand. When their hands touched, Pashar felt a rush of euphoria run through him, something he'd never felt before.

It was scary, intoxicating, and honest all at once. Pashar looked into Hal's eyes and knew this was no false flag. Hal was also looking into Pashar's eyes, looking deep into him, searching for the same sense of connection he knew Pashar was searching for. Pashar broke the handshake but let his fingers linger for a split second longer to reassure Hal that he was also feeling the same.

"Assholes don't bother me. I'm always searching for the quiet ones. They're the ones I watch out for," Pashar said.

"Heard you used some Sidrani mind meld thing to get inside his buddy's head. You killed him."

"All weapons are fair in the arena, and if you're going to test me with a surprise attack like that, there is only one Sidrani response. Death to the attacker. It's built-in."

"Keel's been trying to find a way to incorporate Sidrani tech into us, but for a while, it was forbidden to use it. I guess it's necessary now on Shenu with all the adversaries we are bound to face. How did you manage to get invited to training camp?"

"My father, Rajiv, used to be a commander. He and Keel were good friends. I guess it's in my genetics to be a killer."

"Is he still the commander?"

"No. He died years ago on a rescue mission to Ganymede."

"The Hathor?"

"Yes. How did you know?"

"Everyone knows about the ghost ship."

"I never heard it called that."

"Folklore. But I never believe in folklore. Too unpredictable."

The two men kept looking into each other's eyes. Hal felt a bit self-conscious and broke the stare, changing the subject.

"Maybe someday you can give me some pointers on Sidrani battle techniques."

"I think that's part of the reason I'm here."

"I know you're not allowed to do it personally. But you look like someone who doesn't always do what's allowed."

Hal moved closer to Pashar. Close enough for Pashar to smell his sweat. The two men now stood nose to nose.

"We'll see," Pashar said with a smile. His hand brushed against Hal's cock, and it began to rise. Both men looked at each other and smiled.

"Have you had a tour of Shenu yet?"

"No. No one was kind enough to offer one."

"Why don't I show you room 155 on Waden Deck."

"What's there?"

"A bed."

Hal didn't even wait for an answer. Pashar's eyes, looking directly into his, told him the answer was yes.

They left the prep room and traveled down from the invetio ring to the waden ring, ending in Hal Weiss's room. It was akin to a large hotel suite, with a beautiful view of the moon and, just beyond that, the Sun.

As soon as Hal and Pashar entered the room, their clothes came off, and they found themselves wrestling with each other as lamps and chairs were tossed around like the obstacles they were. Their naked, sweaty bodies glistened in the moonlight as they kissed each other. Once they found their way to Hal's bed, the sex became more intimate as they spent hours discovering each other. Finally spent, they lay in each other's arms. That was when Pashar discovered that Hal's left leg was a prosthetic.

"Should I ask?" Pashar said. Hal smiled.

"Of course. I lost the leg during the lunar settler wars of 2260." With that, he removed it.

Pashar caressed the leg, then kissed it lovingly.

"Does it hurt?" Pashar asked.

"Sometimes. The Phantom leg is weird, and the pain is reminiscent of the pain I had when it was blown off. But it is what it is."

"Why didn't you do a Biolimb?"

"I didn't want it attached to my body for life. I know it sounds archaic, but I always wanted to remember the moment my life changed. It would've also meant forgetting about my sacrifice over losing it. That pain, both mental and physical, was what made me feel strong and motivated me as a Blackhold always to uphold the values and morals of the Blackhold creed." Pashar looked into Hal's eyes and kissed them individually. After that, Hal fell asleep in Pashar's arms.

The whole moment reminded Pashar about the few times he had engaged in sex with members of the Sidrani. He had an affair with two Sidrani warriors at the same time, one female and one male. It wasn't unheard of for Sidrani warriors to have sexual relationships with each other, but a 3-way sexual troika was a bit unusual. Pashar found himself more attracted to Vanit, the female, but eventually, she and the other male, Trent, became serious about each other and mated.

After that, Pashar felt very lonely and had avoided any sexual or personal relationships —until now. His feelings for Hal were immediate and intense, and he gently kissed Hal's hand and rubbed it along his face as Hal slept in his arms. For the first time in a long time, he felt that intimate connection to another human that every Sidrani warrior needed to feel complete, as tantric sex was a potent additive tool for any warrior in or out of battle. Just as he was about to doze off, a holocall entered the room. Declan Keel's face came up in mid-air.

"Awww. Cute." Hal roused from sleep, and he and Pashar got out of bed. Pashar helped support Hal as he reattached his leg.

"All right, cherries. Report to training hub 7. Put your clothes on first. You don't want to excite the natives." Keel smiled. Hal and Pashar got dressed and left the suite.

The two men walked to the central training hub, where they were met by Declan Keel and ten other Blackhold members. The training sphere was a vast, round space, approximately 105 x 68 meters. The dome was evident today, but Pashar remembered that it could be morphed into the surface of any planet or moon in the solar system or any planet in the galaxy.

Several Earth-style worlds were discovered over the last centuries. The most promising was a planet in the habitable zone of the star Wolf 1061 called Wolf 1061c. The star was only 14 light years away and was probed by two FTL (Faster than Light) small craft that made it to the star in less than six months. With Athena about to go into service, FTL would become a reality. Pashar always thought that not developing FTL was a mistake.

The prevailing philosophy of Earth slipping into the death zone or cataclysmic self-destruction of the last two centuries was put to bed along with the lore of bad sci-fi. Humanity decided it was more relevant and profitable to explore its piece of the Solar System, which had been found to have an abundance of everything humanity would ever need to thrive.

The idea of moving all of Earth's population to another planet outside the solar system became obsolete in the later days of the 23rd century. Earth had withstood over a century of turmoil but came through it with a stronger belief that Humanity was here to stay on Earth. While colonization of other planets was aspirational, there was no rush to send generation ships to them.

Instead of doing that, Humanity was searching for wormhole tech to send ships to other systems. The idea of physically sending hundreds or thousands of people hurtling through the cosmos to populate a foreign planet seemed ridiculous.

Once Athena was created, or more accurately, born, humanity had an actual piece of futuristic engineering to enable it to get anywhere in the solar system and, if they wanted, to use her Dark Matter drive to create a wormhole to go anywhere they liked, if nothing else, to explore new worlds. The Star Trek model of planetary exploration had been proven correct. Earthlings stayed on Earth and sent ships and humans to explore the rest of the galaxy.

The stars shone brightly all around Pashar as he marveled at the sphere around him, which made him feel like he was inside a snow globe. It certainly reminded Pashar that he was no longer on Earth.

Keel approached him. "Mr. Rajastani, I'm glad you could make it. I trust you know D-Suit parameters."

"Yes, sir, I do."

Keel pointed to a D-suit hanging on the wall. "Mr. Rajastani, I invite you to wear the suit and meet me at the egress port on Deck 6."

"Yes, sir." Pashar walked to the D-suit and tried to lift it off the wall. It was so heavy he couldn't even budge it. The other soldiers looked at him and smiled as he struggled with the suit. Hal Weiss was smiling broadly at Pashar, who was a bit embarrassed at his inability to move the D-suit and embarrassed that this happened in front of Hal. Finally, Keel walked over to him.

"Problem? Mr. Rajastani?"

"I can't seem to—"

"I thought you knew protocols?"

"I thought I did."

"What's the first rule of D-Suit protocol?"

"The suit belongs to you and you alone." A lightbulb went off in Pashar's head. "Oh shit. The recognition protocol."

Pashar held his hand against the suit glove, releasing a locking mechanism. The D-Suit now came alive, literally. It began to speak, and it sounded exactly like Pashar. "Recognizing Pashar Rajastani."

The suit floated into the air and hovered in front of Pashar. It opened along a seam that traveled the length of the suit.

"Kind of like a coffin, isn't it?"

"I never heard it described like that. Thinking of dying, Mr. Rajastani?" Keel's delivery made Pashar smile. He was never a Pollyanna type, as he knew nothing on Shenu was truly free from danger. He also knew that when danger struck, he wanted Declan Keel to be the man to combat it and to be by his side to help.

"No, sir," Pashar said, responding to Keels's dying reference. Hal Weiss, standing next to Pashar, smiled and then laughed. Pashar entered the suit, which sealed itself around him. The seam disappeared.

A neural interface now attached a series of electrodes to Pashar's body. In front of him, a readout came to life, showing everything from physical metrics (heart rate, blood pressure, metabolic functions) to spatial recognition patterns. A series of screens showed the D-Suit function parameters and how many rounds of ammunition it had.

"Neural interface established," the suit said.

From the facial port, Pashar could hear and see everything around him. Keel's voice came up on a wavelength he could listen to inside his ears as if Keel was in his head.

"Comfy?"

Pashar thought using the word comfy was funny and odd for Keel. However, he was learning that Keel had a keen sense of humor, something Pashar always associated with intelligence.

"Amazing," Pashar answered.

"Ready to test your skills against some R-bots?"

"Skills. I thought we'd have a training session first."

"No better way to train a D-Suit than in battle."

Keel pressed a button on HIS D-Suit, and the airlock they were all standing in opened.

"Neural interface nominal, Pashar; you may engage D-Suit when ready."

"Egress Shenu airlock."

"You need not speak, Mr. Rajastani," the suit said. "We are connected. All you need to do is think where you want to go, and I will oblige."

"I?" Pashar asked.

"I am now aligned with your neural patterns. No other human will be able to operate this D-Suit besides yourself."

"I suppose you have a name as well."

"Yes, I do. You can call me Pashar." Pashar and *Pashar* moved out of the training sphere into space.

As the Blackhold moved out into open space, Pashar looked behind him. Shenu rose hundreds of meters into the space above him, its sheer size and scale dwarfing everything around it.

The Blackhold maneuvered 2000 meters from the station, where an obstacle course could be seen. As Pashar moved out towards the practice course, his D-Suit gave him a tutorial on the basics of its operation.

"You are familiar with all D-Suit functions, Pashar?"

"Yes. Let's review the weapons compliment." A screen came up onto his inner visor.

"Weapons review. Zero-G grenades, microwave laser pistols, neural jamming sequencer, high-speed accelerator thrusters, ablative armor shield, a graviton stabilizer, electromagnetic repulse.

Keel's voice came up. "Ok, cherries. As you can see, this is an obstacle course. We'll take the course one by one. Your weapons systems will be hot for this exercise, so you'll be eliminated if you get hit and cannot regain control of your suits or the course. That means you will be grounded for the rest of the training week and must retake your exams. Rajastani, you're up first." Pashar moved into position next to a starting gate. A countdown appeared in front of his face.

"5, 4, 3, 2, 1."

With his thrusters engaged, the D-Suit sent Pashar careening onto the course. Readouts were all around him. The battle began with a few assaults from stationary adversaries,

There were argon ion lasers, neutron missiles, and such. Pashar dealt nicely with all of them. Then, a chase ensued between him and an R-bot who had become his adversary.

The R-bot sent a graviton pulse, which sent Pashar spinning head over heels. He finally got his bearings and righted the suit. Another R-bot, a smaller mechanism, approached him.

As it got within reach, it quickly moved behind Pashar to the back of his leg. It sent a micro-thin needle into the suit through one of its miniature manifolds and then emitted a beam that disabled the D-Suit. Pashar felt a tingle on the back of his leg and began convulsing. He lost control of the suit.

"Life support has been compromised. Neural functions are compromised. Propulsion manifolds compromised."

Declan Keel saw Pashar spinning out of control. He moved away at a high speed.

"Anyone have eyes on Rajastani?"

Hal Weiss, closest to Pashar, immediately set off after him.

"I've got him. Pursuing."

Weiss kicked his D-Suit into chase mode, and it sped up rapidly. Pashar was heading for one of the outflow ports for Shenu, a vast hole that releases unwanted gases from Shenu.

"Sir, he's headed for the outflow port," Weiss said nervously.

"For shit's sake, Weiss, get him before he crosses the threshold. The pressure of those gases will rip him apart."

Pashar was almost at the exhale port. His left arm got caught in the port and was ripped right off his body. Weiss got to him soon after and righted his course. He speedily got him back to the airlock.

The Blackhold members gathered around Pashar as his D-Suit was removed. Weiss pushed everyone out of the way to attend to Pashar. An R-bot hovered above him, spraying an advanced form of Hydrogel on his now decapitated arm, forming a sterilized bond and stopping the bleeding.

"Pulse 45, pressure 88 over 60. He's dying, sir," Weiss said.

"Get him to med bay." Keel pressed his palm. A view screen came up.

"Dr. Weston. This is Declan Keel."

"Yes, Declan."

"We've got a code red in training hub six."

"Med bay is ready. Who is the code red?"

"Pashar Rajastani."

"I'll notify the Prime Minister immediately."

"No. I'll do it," Keel said.

Two R-bots set an antigrav beam on Pashar, and he was whisked away. Keel and Weiss looked worriedly after him. If Pashar was dead, then everything Keel had planned, not to mention the response from

Leanna and Betta Rajastani, would grind the progress on Shenu to a halt and doom the mission entirely.

Hal accompanied Pashar from the dome to the Med-bay, holding his other hand. Pashar was alert and in obvious pain. Even though they had just met, Hal Weiss felt an immediate bond with Pashar, something more than sexual, something ephemeral and substantial. When he got to Med Bay 6, Danika Weston met them.

"Who are you?"

"I'm Hal Weiss. I saved his life."

"The Prime Minister will want to talk to you."

"Please, can I just be with him?"

Weston could see the earnestness in Hal's eyes—the concern.

"Of course." She escorted Hal into the bay and closed the door after him.

On the other side of the invetio ring, far from the panic of just 20 minutes before, the sun beamed down on Athena, now venting gases and in a countdown to its first mission.

Harrison Byrnes walked onto the bridge in his spacesuit, a modified D-suit with the insignia of the UEU and EC molded into one design. Miranda Han met him at the engineering console. Franklin Barbour, the Blackhold Security chief in full D-suit, and Veronice Kramer, the ops officer, complemented the bridge crew.

"Everyone aboard?" Byrnes was surprised at how nervous he was.

Athena answered in her Miranda Han's voice.

"All crew accounted for, Commander." Byrnes made a mental note to ask Miranda, and he guessed Athena, if they could change her voice. Byrnes kept thinking that every time Athena spoke to him, he would think it was Miranda, which could be confusing and distracting. He immediately decided to address the situation.

"Athena, would you please modulate your voice pattern to another frequency?"

Athena answered. "Yes, Commander. I made the same point to Commander Han. I told her that using her voice might be problematic for you."

"Thank you, Athena."

"I will change voice parameters now. Do you have a preference for an accent?

"No. Whatever you choose will be fine."

Athena changed her voice pattern to a standard British modulation.

"Is this vocal modulation acceptable?"

"Yes, Athena, thank you."

"I will relate the change to Commander Han."

"Thank you, Athena."

He'd taken Athena for a spin two months ago when he was up on Shenu for final systems check of the craft, but this was different. First, he had a crew complement of 250 onboard, so he felt more of a responsibility resting on his shoulders. Second, Miranda Han was also onboard, someone who knew more about Athena than anyone else. He thought he was more nervous about Miranda's reaction to her first mission on Athena and whether she'd find fault with everything Byrnes had done to improve Athena's performance in her absence.

Han entered the bridge.

"Good morning, Athena."

"Good morning, Commander."

Han looked at Byrnes. "New vocal modulation?"

"Yeah. Using your voice was just a bit confusing."

No worries, Han said with a smile. "Too much of a good thing, I guess." Byrnes felt their impasse had finally been broken—a good omen for the maiden voyage.

"Commander Han, the status of engine systems."

"Cold fusion drive nominal and at your command, sir." Byrnes knew there was no reason to be nervous. Han had taken his advice to get over whatever bug was up her ass about her not being allowed to work on Athena for these last ten months. And she called him SIR, something he loved hearing, especially from her.

"Any communications from the freighter, Athena?"

"The Calypso is online and waiting outside Shenu's defense perimeter."

"I think our girl has had enough training."

"Our girl," Athena exclaimed. "I'd like just to be referred to as Athena, commander."

Byrnes sat down in his bridge chair, touched his wrist, and a holo-screen appeared.

"This is Commander Byrnes. On behalf of Athena, our bridge crew, and the UESU, I want to welcome you all on board the most advanced interstellar craft ever created. As you know, our mission will take us first to Phobos, where we will escort the SS Calypso, and then onto a landing on Mars, where we will investigate some strange events with the Eridania plains Transhumans. It should prove to be quite exciting for a first mission. I want to thank all of you for your dedication, commitment to excellence, and determination over the past 18 months of training. Now, let's see how well it worked. Prepare for umbilical release." He pressed his wrist, and the hologram faded.

"Commander Han. Is your baby ready to fly?"

"Athena, are we ready?"

"Yes, Commander Han."

"Then let's make some history."

Athena disconnected its umbilical. A huge R-bot, which acted as a tug craft, led Athena away from Shenu.

Leanna watched as Athena floated away from the station. Samson Frost stood next to her. "How's Pashar?"

"Recovering from surgery."

"I heard they grafted a Biolimb onto him."

"Olefors said it's a new kind of Biomech. Something about starfish enzymatic bionics and palladium cell regeneration gives the arm super-human strength. Superhuman. It's like these scientists get excited to see the best warrior of his culture lose a limb so that they can experiment with something new and dangerous."

"New and dangerous are synonymous on Shenu. Pashar will be fine." Leanna turned to him. "What about Zhang?"

"She's leaving for Lumina base in 2 hours."

"Were you able to ascertain what she said to Nanton?"

"Not all of it. Keel told me what he knew, and then I reviewed the data from the meeting. Something is going on with the Lumina base camp. I wasn't able to discern anything else. It must be important because she hates the moon but will still meet whomever at Lumina. Her wave patterns changed before she began the meeting, so she probably went sub-neural for the most delicate bits."

"Wait for her to leave, then take the next shuttle to Lumina. I want eyes and, hopefully, ears on her movements. Contact our sources on Lumina and have them shadow her until you arrive."

"Leanna. She's a member of the board."

"I want inside that woman's head."

"Yes, ma'am."

He turned to leave, then turned back and walked towards her. "I just remembered. I forgot something."

"What?"

Frost took Leanna's face in his hands and kissed her passionately. The kiss turned to more. "I think we have time for a debriefing before I leave. I might not be back for a few weeks. I guess you can break pro-tocol for that as well." He kissed her more passionately.

"But just this once," she cooed.

He kissed her again, lifting and depositing her on a couch with a view of Earth rotating above them. As their encounter became more passionate, Leanna saw Athena move into view. Her two substantial cold fusion engines lit up with a blue field, and in an instant, they moved off at high speed.

"Something distracting you?" Frost said as he placed his face in between her legs.

"Not anymore." She pulled him closer, leaned her head back, and closed her eyes.

Mara and Alcion reviewed the specs for Tantalus' creational answer to Gina in the lab. The door to the lab opened, and Tantalus, hovering three feet above the floor, entered the lab and glided eerily toward the two.

He no longer pretended to disguise himself in his human skin and bone. His treatments were almost done, and he knew that his brain was also nearing its transformation from two lobes to three. His heart now had five chambers, and he realized he was becoming more amphibian daily. Even more impressive was the alacrity with which he could breathe air or water. Far from feeling alien in his skin, he now felt separated from Earth and its inhabitants.

With the connection to Earth gone, he also noticed that his disdain for Mara and humanity had grown exponentially. He didn't dare reveal it now, but eventually, he'd have to confront his new feelings honestly and sincerely, even if it meant making some dire decisions in the weeks ahead.

"Report."

"The shipment of iridium arrived. No tracers." Mara wondered what Tantalus needed with this large amount of iridium and even more about where it came from.

"We got away clean, Dr."

"I doubt Tara Zhang would appreciate your sentiment, Alcion. She doesn't take kindly to theft and can hurt us if she ever finds out who stole her cargo. As soon as it's processed, add it to the genetic sequencer for the procedure so that it can be infused during my last session."

"What about the avatar?" Alcion seemed overly concerned about the avatar. Tantalus surmised that Alcion felt a kinship to the avatar, as they were both created from source material outside of themselves. In some way, he knew Alcion felt that one day, he could undergo the same procedure to complete his metamorphosis toward becoming more like Gina. However, Tantalus also knew that was impossible, and Alcion's existence would be a tenuous struggle between his human parts and his cybernetic parts with no chance of advancement to any other life form, something Tantalus kept from his creation if nothing else to spare him the pain of the truth.

Tantalus deeply loved Alcion, much like Dr. Frankenstein had a passion for every form he created before his ultimate creation eventually killed him. The irony wasn't lost on Tantalus, though the reality of such a thing happening to him was nothing to dismiss. Alcion was bright and strong and could quickly kill him, especially in his weakened metamorphosized state.

"See if the iridium can help consolidate the Avatar's matrix and shield his spinal cord against trauma."

"There's something else," Mara said. Tantalus looked at her.

"Proceed."

"CASSANDRA hasn't made contact since yesterday."

"What?" Tantalus's tone told Mara that he didn't have as much control over CASSANDRA as he had let on. Tantalus also realized this and silently berated himself at the revelation, which weakened his position with Mara.

"She went silent around 0600 yesterday morning."

"Then I suggest you use that Level 6 training to discover exactly what happened. What about Athena?"

"She just left Shenu on a trajectory to Phobos and then Eridania."

"Eridania?"

"Yes."

"Find out why?"

"One other thing. Gina is onboard Athena."

"And the package?"

Mara walked to a com panel and waved her hand across it. It showed a comet.

"Proteus. Last known to brush Martian atmosphere in 2112."

"You know what to do," Tantalus added.

"Yes, Dr." The response was firm, reflecting Mara's unwavering determination.

Mara waved her hand over another panel. A satellite similar to the one that rained down the Gamma EM pulse on the Brazilian jungle only ten days ago appeared out of nowhere, uncloaking near Demos. A blue light emanated from its array as a ray projected from the satellite. The ray targeted the Proteus comet, streaking out of the asteroid belt between Mars and Jupiter. The blue beam hit the comet and changed its course, sending it toward Mars. The satellite then cloaked itself.

Mara and Alcion watched as the comet's trajectory changed from brushing Demos to hitting Mars directly.

"Now we wait." Tantalus's reptilian eyes glowed with anticipation, and a sinister smile crossed his now entirely reptilian lips.

CHAPTER ELEVEN

SUBVERSION

Solara descended from a cloud of silicon mining haze on its approach to Lumina Base. The lunar landscape opened as it approached what looked like a barren plain, and a landing pad emerged from underground. Solara touched down; a soft whoosh of her retro jets spun the loose lunar regolith around her landing gear. Then she descended into the lunar landscape.

The moon had become a go-to place in the 24th century. Unlike Mars, which was only being scouted for extensive colonial implantation in 2335, ten years from now, the moon had been colonized in 2224, over a century ago.

Humanity had always had a love affair with the moon, and once water was found locked in the lunar regolith, especially on the poles, humans quickly colonized the moon.

Unlike Earth, The UEU and EC had little control over lunar politics. An entirely new government formed, consisting primarily of consortiums and corporations that mined the moon for everything from water to iridium, to silicon, iron, magnesium, and most importantly, Oxygen, locked in a loving embrace with the lunar landscape, waiting for humans to discover the secrets that would free it from its bondage. But the most exciting and valuable mineral extracted from the moon was titanium, then refined to Tritanium, a substance from which Shenu was partly built; more rigid, stronger, more durable, and infinitely more valuable than its sister ore.

There were laws on the moon that referenced the old American West more than anything else. Territories were parceled off, and constabularies were established for each territory, which organized the laws for each territory. It was a crude and somewhat explosive setup, but it worked, mainly because everyone living on the moon realized that cooperation was tantamount to success.

Conquering or taking anyone else's territory was forbidden. The treaty of Mar Imbria, enacted in 2230, saw to that. Besides, a war waged in a low-gravity atmosphere would pollute the entire lunar body. Humans got along because they had no choice and traded with each other in relative amicability.

Everyone understood that there was an enormous profit to be made on the moon, so it was treated a lot better than the Earth. For the last century, the lunar colonists had created a veritable paradise underneath the Lunar surface, parts of which resembled Las Vegas and parts as green and lush as the most pristine national parks on Earth.

Lunites, the people who inhabited the moon, became so enamored with their new home that they rarely, if ever, returned to Earth. The idea of fresh air and sunshine seemed less infectious than it had been during previous centuries, just as the Lunites preferred it to be.

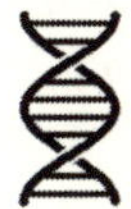

Tara Zhang exited Solara and moved through Lumina base towards a shuttle zone, where she boarded a maglev that soon sped out of the station. She hadn't told anyone she was traveling to Lumina base, partly because it was no one else's business and partly because she didn't dare reveal her reason for the trip.

Samson Frost appeared behind a column after the shuttle sped out of the station. He had arrived just after Zhang on another transport ship. He looked up at the destination board to see where the shuttle Zhang boarded was heading. It read Mare Imbrium. Another shuttle entered the bay. He boarded it, and it soon sped out of the station.

Frost was a bit nervous. Strange that his nerves were being ignited, something that rarely happened.

He did some mind-sifting and deduced that he was concerned about what Tara Zhang was up to. It was inaccurate, but Samson

Frost knew himself well enough to realize he needed to tread carefully. This was to be no ordinary mission, and his caution was palpable.

Zhang exited the shuttle at Mar Imbria and briskly walked through a series of secret underground tunnels to a chamber where a sizeable tritanium metal door awaited her. A scan beam came out from the top of the door and scanned her body, something she detested but had to acquiesce to, given the nature of who she was meeting and the reason behind it. A voice neurally addressed her.

"Lady Zhang. To what do I owe this great pleasure?"

"I've come a long way and don't like being interrogated or kept waiting."

The door opened, and Zhang entered a sizeable white chamber. A small man in a white space suit wearing a white helmet sat in the center of a massive R-bot with tentacled arms doing various tasks. The man detached himself from the machine and approached Zhang. He was slender, Indian, with long black hair tied neatly into a bun. He extended his hand to Zhang, who promptly refused it.

"Dalton Ashton."

"Tara Zhang. Never thought I'd see you here, slumming in the miner's quarters. Reminds me of the old days in New Delhi."

"Slumming?" Zhang was disgusted at the use of the term but held her tongue. This time. "That's your MO. You got my neural?"

"Yesterday, quite a bit of garbage along with it. I guess that's how the great Tara Zhang communicates with one of her oldest friends?"

"It is when I've got everyone from Rajastani to the Blackhold up my ass."

"No R-bots. Must be delicate."

"Every neural has to be triple-checked, then infused with garbage so it can't be picked."

"You and Leanna are still frenemies. Hard to believe."

"Sarcasm smells like shit on you, Dalton."

Ashton was getting concerned. Zhang was thornier than usual, and she took a severe gamble to come to see him.

"If you're ready to suit up, I'll show you what you came for. Life-suits are over there."

He waved his hand, and the room lit up. The door opened on command, and Zhang walked through it. The door closed behind her.

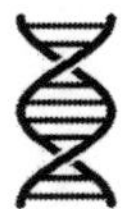

An hour later, Zhang and Ashton were on a lunar Sailer, like the one Zhang had taken from Earth to Shenu, but much smaller. It glided over the lunar landscape and came to rest at the edge of a giant crater. They exited the Sailer.

"Can't remember the last time you went lunar," Ashton said.

"I hate the moon, but I love how rich it will make me."

"And powerful, let's not forget power."

He led her down into the crater, where an airtight door awaited them. They stepped into a decompression chamber, and a green light told them it was safe to exit.

They exited the decompression chamber into a cave of immense size. All forms of R-bots were mining different areas. Some were excavating; some were loading materials onto mag-lev transports that carried the ores and minerals out of the chambers.

"Exports are down, Lady Zhang."

"Are you sure? I believe someone might be skimming from the top. Maybe you."

"You know me better than that."

"Yes, that's why I asked."

"It's all down to competition, my dear. They say it's good for business, but you know. When the UEU and UEU Russia colonized Tranquility and Fecundis in 2245, everyone said they were crazy. When they opened their first Lunar city-state in Mare Nectris in 2255, everyone said they were interlopers. Now, they've brought four drivers onto our side of the moon and claimed that the treaty between EC and UEU Russia allows them mining rights in exchange for vaccine security for Ebola 6."

"It does, but that wasn't my deal. That was before Hashimoto's untimely death. Now that I'm CEO and premier of Earth Corporate, I think that treaty will need to be amended."

"Too late now; their drivers are almost operational, and if they become operational, then our drivers will be up against some serious competition, and with Shenu on good terms with UEU Russia, the contract for everything from clean water, to diamonide to iridium fuels will be secured by Rajastani."

"Why do you think I'm here?"

Ashton ignored Zhang's last comment and guided her to a wall. "It's over here."

He took a small remote out of his pocket and placed it against his temple. He pressed a button, and the wall vanished. He quickly ushered Zhang inside. There, filling the chamber, sat yellow, chalk-like rocks, each about the size of a bowling ball.

"There's no smell." Zhang was surprised and pleased with the discovery.

"Not in this form."

"Is it pure?" Ashton gave her a look.

"I'm sorry, it's Dalton Ashton, the greatest lunar geologist in the world. Of course, it's pure."

"It's also worth a fortune. So, what are you going to do with all this Hydronium?"

"Desalination plants are straining ecosystems on Earth, severely compromising the oceans. We'll need an inexhaustible water supply for the next century, and I plan on having the most radical-free water on the planet and then selling that water to the rest of the world. That's why you're going to keep harvesting and hoarding."

"Not very neighborly."

"I'm paying you six times your worth plus percentages. That's all you need to be concerned about. Have the first shipment to my driver for low lunar orbit in 24 hours." Zhang left the chamber.

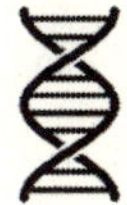

Athena was 12 hours into her mission to Phobos and then Mars, a trip that would've taken months just a few short years ago. It now took two weeks and would take an even shorter period if the dark matter drive was initiated.

Miranda Han had slept better than she could remember. Perhaps it was in the cold but comforting expansions of space and the knowledge that she was asleep inside her most significant accomplishment, like a chrysalis inside its cocoon.

Her dream cycle was also extraordinary. She dreamt of a blue binary star with six planets orbiting around it. There was a voice in the dream, not her oversoul, a voice she had learned to listen to and trust.

The concept of the oversoul gained traction in the 24th century. It became an integral part of life for those who understood its import and how it was incorporated into humanity's fabric of life.

Gert Holonsee and Amanda Grable, dimensional psychologists who had been experimenting with Lovrin, a substance made from a kind of seaweed discovered on Europa, discovered the factual proof of the oversoul in 2297.

Europa, one of Jupiter's 95 moons, became a hotbed of research in the 23rd and 24th centuries. A myriad of discoveries was made at that time, including the discovery of a unique type of seaweed that, when chemically separated into its subsequent parts, had some very unusual psychedelic properties, one of which was to allow users to enter a 5th-dimensional trance.

5th dimension reality was a huge advancement for humanity, as it opened several transmutational doors for humanity to access other dimensions, including the 5th dimension, which was a dimension controlled by the oversoul, the UBER soul, the prime moving soul of every human that guided us towards our lifepath on Earth or any number of different planes of existence. Humanity learned that with the discovery of the oversoul, it could learn more about its origins. The oversoul was that voice inside all of us that was constantly in touch with us and was the voice that some would call our ego or id. Now that humanity knew what an oversoul was and how they could access it, humanity began its long march towards full sentience and complete control of its evolution. Of course, this reality was only made available to the highest echelons of human society, like the hierarchy that ran the UEU, EC, and the UESU. The advancement also enabled Miranda Han to use the knowledge of 5th dimension reality and dark matter theorems and infuse them into Athena.

This infusion of the compound created by the sea plankton from Europa, combined with the dark matter used to power Athena, gave Athena a sentience unlike any Miranda had ever seen. Athena was sentient alone, unlike UMA or GAIA, which needed to be linked to the female human host.

Miranda surmised she was the only person close enough to a Level 6 that Athena could converse with. Athena, for her part, was comfortable with her sentience and had developed a personality very much like Miranda Han's, as Miranda had used some of her ganglionic fibers to begin the process of growing a suitable Mindframe for Athena to grow her sentience upon, like a trellis that was erected to allow a rosebush to flourish and grow. Such was Miranda's contribution to Athena's newborn intelligence.

On this day, she woke up at 5 AM, her usual time, and went down to the bridge. There, she found Harrison Byrnes sitting in the Commander's chair, a holoscreen in front of him spitting out data points. Miranda Han sat next to him. Gina entered the bridge and stood next to Miranda.

"I've picked up a message from Eridania base."

"I thought all neurals were silent." Byrnes was concerned. *All neurals had been silent for more than four days, so how did Gina pick up a signal? Was this another one of her miraculous abilities?*

"They are. This is an old code, early 21st century, on a hertz frequency."

"Radio?" Byrnes asked.

"It would seem so, commander."

"What's it say?" Miranda asked.

"Not in standard language, analog code, algebraic equivalents."

Han pulled up the message in front of her. It was a series of binomial equations and calculaic theorems.

"It's in a language. It's called mathematics," Han said somewhat cynically.

"Gina, can you decode this?" Gina scanned the holo screen with intensity. "It's from the old mining quarters. From a Dr. Granger."

"That's Haley Granger, the lead geologist working at Mons."

Gina continued. "Situation much worse than expected. Some exo-molecule contaminated transhumans at Mons. Holding 45 hostages."

"Transhumans holding hostages? Are the R-bots also affected?" More than 1000 Transhumans and R-bots were mining everything from cobalt, magnesium, water, and, most importantly, a new silicon compound used to create Transhuman components. What's more, these precious minerals were sent back to the moon and Earth to be modified into any number of valuable commodities.

"Unknown, but I suppose there might also be some residual effect on them."

"Transhumans are just a small step under you, Gina."

"On the contrary, Dr. Han. Transhumans are cyborg-based. Humans built R-bots as slave labor. They constructed Transhumans as the R-bot overlords."

"Quite right, Gina. But I shudder to think how that might change everything, including the balance of power in the solar system?" Han shot Byrnes a nasty look.

"So you thought they'd always be just programmable servants for humanity's unwanted work and dangerous disasters."

"What are you getting at Gina?" Byrnes asked.

"From Dr. Granger's analysis, it seems this extra Martian molecule has infiltrated the sub-systems of the Transhumans. That means their fluidic plasma and ganglionic systems have been compromised, giving them…"

Gina analyzes the message more thoroughly now.

"A low-level form of sentience."

"Sentience?" Byrnes was concerned.

Han decided to go much deeper into this conversation. This was her opportunity to get a handle on Gina and her thought process. Forget that she was humanity 2.0. Han needed to know how she thought and reasoned.

"All those years ago, decades ago, everyone debated sentient tolerance levels in Transhumans. Your creator, Dr. Olefors, was always behind the eight ball on this one. She argued."

Gina interrupted Han.

"That sentience would be a natural byproduct of AI advancement. On May 21, 2010, the J. Craig Venter Institute successfully synthesized the genome of the bacterium Mycoplasma mycoides from a computer record and transplanted the synthesized genome into the existing cell of a Mycoplasma capricolum bacterium that had its DNA removed."

"The newly formed "synthetic" bacterium was able to replicate billions of times and declared by its creators a new and viable life form. The beginning of self-replication in synthesized lifeforms. Then, in 2014, it was claimed that when strong artificially intelligent machines exceed the combined intelligence of all humans on Earth."

"The SAMs," Han added.

"The SAMs will use their intelligence to claim their place at the top of the food chain."

"Then there's the concept of Singularity," Byrnes said.

Han was not as worried as Byrnes but more curious about how this boom in sentience among Transhumans and otherworldly creations like Gina would soon alter the very fabric of humanity.

"Singularity, as in black hole?"

"No. The singularity represents a point in time when the intelligence of AI will greatly exceed that of humans." Gina said.

"Imagine being surrounded by SAMs that are thousands of times more intelligent than you are, regardless of your expertise in any discipline. This may be analogous to humans' intelligence relative to insects."

Gina smiled with a wry smile that was not lost on Han or Byrnes, who looked at each other with a profound seriousness.

"Essentially, AI futurists believe that the singularity will occur unless we as a civilization cease to exist. The obvious question is: When will the singularity occur? Back in the early 21st century, projections were 2146, but that didn't take into account the global depression, or the Eurasian wars, or the Ebola disaster," Han said.

"The problem was humanity's attempt to control the singularity before it occurred. Now that time seems to have passed," Gina added.

Byrnes wanted to change the subject. "Tell Granger to hold tight. We should be in Mars orbit within 18 hours. Keep out of the R-bot's way."

"What about the hostages at Mons?" Han asked.

"At this point, they're as good as dead if Gina is correct."

"Well, I hate to be right, but I am usually factually correct 99.99956% of the time on these matters."

"Well, at least there's a 44th of a million chance you're wrong."

"4's are bad luck in Chinese culture, or so I'm told," Gina added.

"It would seem extra molecular sentience is as well." Byrnes got up and stretched his arms. "All this talk over AI takeovers made me hungry. I'll be in the gym."

Byrnes got up and left the bridge.

"The...gym?" Gina's curiosity made Han smile.

"Whenever he gets upset or depressed, moody, or just about anything the rational mind can't solve, he takes it out in the gym."

"Oh." Gina went back to analyzing data coming in from Mars as Han shook her head in bewilderment.

Besides Athena's fantastic technology, she also had some of the most advanced recreational activities in the Solar System. Among them were a real holodeck and a full-service state-of-the-art gym, which Harrison Byrnes used to alleviate various stresses and keep himself in top shape.

When he entered the large gymnasium, he noticed several of his crew members were there as well. Byrnes was always mindful of keeping himself a bit removed from his crew.

He knew well that while he could be a somewhat available father figure to them, keeping a command structure was essential for them to trust and respect him, something he always strived for.

As he moved through the various activity areas, his crew acknowledged him with a nod or a smile. Byrnes returned the gestures but kept his statuesque posture and steely jaw firmly in place. He knew that he was in as good a shape or better than his crew members 20 years younger, and he also knew that they'd be watching his every move.

Athena's gyms were highly advanced and more like military training centers. Byrnes moved through the main complex to a smaller gym, where an oculus enabled him to see the solar system above and around him. It was a kind of a goldfish bowl set-up. The transparent walls of the gym could be configured to look like any landscape Byrnes chose, from the moon to Titan to Enceladus or to any of over one hundred exoplanets outside the solar system that had been discovered, scanned, and populated with various R-bots to see if any of them might be suitable for finding alien life, or inhabitation or mining at some point. This tech was also used on Shenu to significant effect.

Once inside the gym, Byrnes stood in the center of a circle, a holopanel floating before him. On the holopanel were various celestial bodies; the moon, Jupiter, and Saturn were prominent. Byrnes pressed a button, and an electrode appeared in front of him. A message appeared: *Gravity weight displacement in effect mode. Choose a planetary body.*

Byrnes looked at the selection of planetary bodies and pressed the button.

"The moon," he said.

A series of numbers appeared, and at Byrnes's feet, two small hand grips. He reached down and began to pull them up to his chest and over his head, struggling against the gravity force of the moon. Even though there is no actual weight, the holo-gravity atmosphere creates the illusion of serious weight. He does a few reps and stops.

"Gravity climb. Io."

The circle's interior changed into a view from the surface of Io. In front of Byrnes was a mountain and a path leading up to the summit. He began climbing the mountain in the holo-simulation. After a beat, he looked to the side and saw Gina next to him, moving up the same mountain but with much less effort.

"This is what you do for recreation?" she said, not missing a beat.

"Yes, and usually alone."

"Am I disturbing you?"

Byrnes was straining against gravity but didn't dare show it. This was the first time he was in direct competition with Gina. Even though he knew she was far superior to him in just about every physical way, his male ego, albeit a relic from centuries ago, wouldn't let the opportunity go to prove he was just as strong as she was, something he inwardly realized he was woefully unprepared to defend, so instead, he smiled at Gina as the sweat poured into his eyes and mouth.

"Disturbing, no. Embarrassing, maybe," he said in humorous resignation.

He stopped. The holosim stopped, and he found himself back in the gravity room.

"Commander Han said you come here to clear your mind. Is that something you do alone?"

"Usually."

He exited the room. Gina followed him across the gym, where various wild and crazy exercises defying gravity or in holo sims were being done all around them. Byrnes turned to Gina, now feeling a bit less breathy and able to form his thoughts more succinctly.

"So, what do you do for exercise?"

"I usually run or fly in difficult formations."

"Fly, huh?"

"Like you, I use the gravitational constants of different worlds to strengthen my technique and muscles."

"Muscles?"

"Yes, I have the same musculature as you, except my muscles are made from Graphene-7 nanofibers."

"Makes you a bit heavy to fly, doesn't it?"

"I can change my nanofibers' magnetic and molecular structure to be as light as lithium or as heavy as lead, so for flying..." In an instant, Gina took flight and soared above Byrnes's head.

"Impressive. Can you teach me how to do that?"

"Well, let's just say I can try, but you'd die in the process."

"Not a premise I'm happy to entertain. Who'd command Athena?"

"I'm well certified," Gina said with a wry smile, making Byrnes quiver. A feeling of butterflies in his stomach told him that Gina had more effect on him than he thought she could. Was it her ability to produce pheromones that could instantaneously affect anyone around her, or was this all him?"

"That was rhetorical, Gina."

"Rhetoric is a completely human paradox. I'm afraid the subtleties of human semantics might be a lot harder than flying."

He walked into the locker rooms, followed by Gina. Byrnes opened his locker and began undressing. Gina stood next to him, watching.

"What's the matter? Never seen a naked man before?"

"Dr. Olefors."

"Really?"

"Yes. To show me the male form in reality. I did not find it very appealing or sexual."

On Gina's mention of Olefors, Byrnes straightened himself, pulled in his belly, and did a bit of parading for Gina's benefit as he walked to the steam room.

"You seem to have no modesty when it comes to nudity."

Ah, he thought, *she noticed.* "And that surprises you?"

"Well, most men I have observed have some issues with intimacy and nudity."

"Unlike you."

"I have never been intimate with a man or a woman," she said.

"That statement makes me very curious."

"Even if I did incline to satisfy your curiosity, I doubt we have the time to delve deeply into the fantasy of your imagining."

"Fantasy?"

"Well, it's a fantasy until it becomes a reality," she added.

"It's apparent that psychoanalysis and arrogance aren't your strong suits. How about something easier to swallow? Do you have a preference?"

"No. I find both human sexes attractive, although I must admit that being familiar with the female form makes the interaction with females a bit more productive."

"Gina, sex is not supposed to be productive. It's supposed to be revelatory, intimate, beautiful, sensual, and hot. Have you ever had those experiences sexually?"

"No. But I am curious to try."

Gina looked at Byrnes. Their eyes met again. Byrnes was getting hard, but he just let it happen. Gina noticed as well.

"I can tell this conversation has stimulated you." Her face flushed.

"You as well, it seems."

"I seem to be..."

"It's called flushed. A physical response to sexual stimulation."

"I was never told about this sensation."

She paused, momentarily distracted by something. "Commander, there is a priority one message from Prime Minister Rajastani. Code 11. I will be on the bridge."

"Wait. You can't leave now. Shit!"

But it was too late. Gina was already out the door. *Talk about a cold shower,* Byrnes thought. The moment to consummate whatever they were both leaning into could've happened right then, but he also knew that Code 11 would have made that proposition impossible.

Samson Frost got off a shuttle at Mare Imbrium and tried to discern which way Zhang went. He hadn't been on the moon for a while. He didn't much care for the moon. It was cold and isolated, and that alone gave it a reputation for being a bit of a heathen's nest. It was replete with all manner of nefarious denizens. Frost knew to keep himself as incognito as possible, so he sported workman's gear, looking more like an executive for a mining consortium than the most revered and feared Harbinger in the solar system.

He'd lost Zhang, which he surmised was probably for the best since he didn't want her to know he was following her.

He pressed his wrist, and a holoscreen appeared before him. "GAIA, this is Samson Frost, special liaison to Shenu, clearance Level 10," GAIA answered in her alto-laden voice.

"Welcome to the moon, Secretary Frost. I haven't spoken to you in a long time, though I am up to speed on your progress with Shenu and EC in keeping the peace between them. Please hold your left hand up for a venal scan."

Frost was happy to hear GAIA's friendly voice. Although most humans, with the exceptions of Level 6's, couldn't speak directly to

Geneticoms, a handful had access to interact with them directly, and Frost was one of them. A laser emerged from thin air and scanned his venal structure.

"Cleared. How can I be of Service, Mr. Secretary?"

"Please scan for DNA trace, Tara Zhang. Mare Imbria base and surrounding colony."

"Chairwoman Zhang also has Level 10 clearance. The system cannot access her DNA. I'm sorry." Frost was momentarily put off.

"Scan for fragrance trace, *Regent*."

"Scanning. Fragrance trace detected." A map came up on the holo-panel with a directional.

"Chairwoman Zhang followed this path."

"End point of Chairwoman Zhang's path."

"Timocharis excavation base."

"Timocharis is a mining base, is it not?"

"Yes."

"What kind of mining?"

"That information is restricted."

"Surely not for you."

"Yes, sir. EC has dominion over that base and its industries."

"I thought EC transferred all access codes when Shenu became active."

"Chairwoman Zhang has sole access to her codes alone."

"Extrapolate as to nature of mining operations at Timocharis."

"Deepwater mining is the main activity."

"Extrapolate uses for deep water mining besides processing and consumption."

"Sensors have often picked up traces of Hydronium dust emanating from mines around Timocharis."

"Hydronium. Extrapolate uses for Hydronium."

"Deep space exploration, industrial water for use on Earth to be dissected down into components. Oxygenation purposes. Deep Lunar blasting."

"No, there's got to be something missing. She's not just here for a water drop. She'd never lower herself for something so menial. Deep water blasting. Explain."

"Hydronium has been used as a catalyst for explosives to access deep water on the moon. It has also been used in Chemical and Biological weapons manufacturing."

"Chemical weapons. Now that's more like it. Download all information related to Hydronium."

"Neural download in progress."

"Receiving." After receiving the neural from GAIA, Frost immediately called up Leanna Rajastani. Her holoimage appeared in front of him.

"Samson, it's dangerous to contact me like this."

"Leanna, I've got urgent news."

Byrnes walked onto the bridge after his encounter with Gina in the gym and a speedy cold shower, where he let his mind run free fantasizing about having sex with Gina.

Gina, Han, and two other Officers were at their stations. He moved to a panel and pressed his wrist as Rajastani's holographic image appeared in the cabin.

"Code 11, Prime Minister?" he asked.

"Yes, commander. Set your lateral sensor array to broadband x-ray."

Byrnes nodded to Han. "Commander, I am picking up a large object, moving into the asteroid belt proximate to Jovian outer orbit."

"Proteus." Gina was also downloading the data.

"The comet? But that's not due back to the Terran system for millennia."

"That's what we all believed until we saw the telemetry this morning." Rajastani was visibly worried.

"Confirmed. Comet Proteus," Han said.

"Course?"

Gina focused more intently on the holo screen. She seemed more concerned than Byrnes had ever noticed.

"Set to impact Mars, southeastern quadrant near Solis Planum plain in 72 hours. If that happens, it could destabilize Martian orbit."

"How the hell did it just arrive like this?"

"Sensors indicate the comet is tumbling over on a z axis, not heading for the sun."

"I believe we're dealing with an extra Jovian event, some sort of small singularity that jostled the comet as it passed just outside Miranda's orbit."

"Jostled."

"A small but powerful class 6 wormhole would be the likely culprit," Gina said dispassionately.

"But there isn't any class 6 wormhole near Miranda," Han added.

"In life, there are moments when intellect and reason are tossed away like garbage from a sifter. There can be only one conclusion. Through nefarious means, someone has somehow been able to use a wormhole to send Proteus to its ultimate demise." Gina's dispassionate analysis seemed appropriate for the seriousness of the moment.

"Well, it doesn't matter now," Rajastani said. "Dr. Han, you will thoroughly investigate the source, but for now, we've got a large, unexpectedly unwelcome comet headed for Mars."

"What about wranglers?" Han asked.

"All wranglers are on assignment in the Oort zone, arranging comets for later Martian bombardment."

"And they've never handled something this big," Byrnes answered.

"Gina, gather and report damage assessments of impact. If that comet has to hit Mars, we don't want it anywhere near Mons or Eridania."

"Prime Minister, I don't need to point out that a comet the size of Proteus will cause severe catastrophe wherever it hits," Han said.

"Understood."

"Gina is right. This has to have some connection to Cosulo."

"Harrison, there's no easy solution here."

"And why do you need to tell me that, Leanna?"

"Because I know your ability to look any problem in the eye and settle it without theatrics or difficulty. The reality is, there are going to be casualties."

"Then there's the issue of Granger and the hostages and the transport ship," Han said.

"The transport ship has been called back to Shenu. Options, Harrison?"

"Well, they're limited, Prime Minister. The only option is to use ion lasers to destroy the comet."

"But if we do that, the comet will break into hundreds of pieces, and with Earth at apogee to Mars, the repercussions could be catastrophic for both worlds," Gina added.

"We must assume that whoever sabotaged Cosulo must also have a hand in this. But why send a comet smashing into Mars?" Byrnes said.

"What purpose could it have?" Han asked the question on everyone's mind. Byrnes hated speculation, but that's all he had for now, so he put it out of his mind and focused only on the facts at hand. "I've learned anarchists usually have no real plan other than to disrupt and destroy. Or some plan we have no idea about."

"What if there is no ulterior motive? What if this individual or individuals want to wreak havoc and cause destruction?" Byrnes was curious to see how Gina would respond.

"Then sending a comet to Mars would certainly accomplish their goal. But my gut tells me there's a motive here and a dangerous motive," Han interrupted.

"There's something else, commander. I have picked up a radiation source coming from the comet?" Gina said.

"At first, I just dismissed the radiation source as X-rays, known to emanate from comets within 3AU of the sun, but my internal scans also detected Gamma EMs."

"That's impossible." Byrne's speculative mind was putting as many facts together as possible.

"Comets themselves do not typically emit gamma radiation. However, they can interact with cosmic rays and solar radiation, which can lead to the production of gamma rays. For instance, when cosmic rays collide with the nucleus of a comet, they can produce secondary particles that emit gamma rays. Additionally, comets can emit X-rays when interacting with the solar wind and magnetic fields. This interaction can sometimes be intense enough to produce high-energy emissions, including gamma rays, although this is less common. Proteus has the same bandwidth of Gamma EMs as we detected when I interfaced with the solar bomb."

Gina's perfunctory response, replete with scientific analysis, reminded Han that she was extrahuman, part human, part computer, part alien.

"We need to confirm that," Rajastani said.

"We can send a probe," Byrnes said.

"The radiation will destroy a probe," Gina added.

"What do you suggest?" Byrnes turned to Gina.

"She wants us to send her in Solara 2," Han said.

"Absolutely not." Byrnes's emotional response told Gina their dalliance a few hours ago in the locker room was more than just a tangential conversation about sex. He cared about her; that much was evident.

"Commander, someone needs to verify the Gamma EM source. I am the only one who can safely do that. Commander Han can pilot Solara 2 to a safe distance from Proteus, and then I will egress the pod and approach the comet. I will land on the comet and assess the situation."

"Han?"

"I see no other way. We must discover whether the same saboteur is involved, and Gina is the only being who can accomplish the task."

"OK. Prepare a flight plan. Han, you'll be with Gina. But you remain inside Solara 2 and keep watch."

"Yes, commander."

Gina produced a tablet and handed it to Byrnes. "It's already done. I must leave within the next 12 hours to enable a rendezvous."

"Well, I don't like it, but it needs to be done."

"Commander, your concern for my safety is appreciated if not entirely rooted in logical reality."

"Dealing with the most advanced humanoid in existence who sees herself as indestructible and is set on proving it leaves me with a sense of dread. If you're lost."

"I appreciate the sentiment, but I was created for just such a purpose, and I plan on fulfilling my destiny, as do you and Commander Han. In the meantime, I suggest you and the crew get to Mars and try to defuse the situation with the hostages. Rescue as many as possible."

"How many of our people are on Mars?" Han asked.

"175 overseeing the mining procedures. They're being shepherded into the caves as we speak. Gina, probability of survival?" said Rajastani.

"The caves in Olympus Mons and Eridania are the safest on the planet and surrounded by the largest population. If you can secure the freedom of the colonists held hostage and disarm the R-bots, then the chances are good for a 95 percent survival rate of the colonists working the mines at Eridania."

"That means we'll still lose people and all the progress that's been made for the past 75 years, not to mention a major source of minerals and therefore profits," Byrnes added.

"I imagine that's what the saboteur had in mind," Gina said.

Olefors and Danika Weston were in clean suits inside the lab, searching for the cause of the toxin that almost killed them two days earlier. What was happening to Athena was unknown to them as they had more important things on their minds.

"The first thing we need to do is create a system of 4th dimension mechanics so we can see the damned thing," Olefors said.

"Ok. Sounds kind of impossible," Weston answered. "How do you propose to do that?"

Olefors took out a small container and opened it, revealing two small star-shaped devices.

"You remember when we were doing those quantum experiments in Stockholm?"

"The ones where we were trying to phase with Gina's pineal gland."

"Gina's pineal gland is more of a mechanism than a gland," Olefors said. "It can phase dimensionally, see other dimensions, and interface with them. After I researched how to give Gina the advanced dimensional system, I figured it might come in handy for us to do the same with humans."

"But Gina is Graphene-7. It vibrates at a different frequency than we do."

"I admit these aren't as advanced as Gina's, but for us, they'll at least allow us to phase into 4th dimension vibration. We won't be able to interact with anything in the dimension but to identify the toxin; observation will be all we'll need."

"Too bad we didn't create two of her."

"That would've been impossible," he said.

"You say that, but you never told me why."

"Believe me when I tell you that I don't remember anything about the abduction. All I know is that after I returned, I knew how to construct her but had no memory of how or why I was given this information. Olefors bent over and collapsed to the floor.

"Anderson? What's the matter?"

"My head. It's...ohhhhh. I can't..."

Weston got her bioscope out and did a quick exam. "Your blood pressure is through the roof. Your brain is swelling. I need to get you to Medbay."

"No. Please, it'll pass." He began breathing deeply, and after a few moments, he got up off the floor, still holding his head. "I'm all right."

Weston kept the scope on him. "Your BP is coming down. Cranial pressure is stabilizing. What the fuck happened?"

"I wanted to tell you but thought you'd ground me from the mission."

"Tell me what, Anderson?"

"These headaches. They've been with me for years."

"After the abduction?"

"Yes, but they've gotten a lot worse."

"I need to do a thorough scan, maybe take a look inside."

"No. I've had every scan known to exist. There's nothing wrong structurally. This pain is being generated through my pineal gland."

"That's impossible. The pineal gland isn't a pain attenuator."

"It is for me."

"Is this why you were so distant for the last year?"

"Well, you didn't make it easy to tell you. I think they did this to me."

"Who are they?"

"I don't know. Whoever they are, they don't want me ever to recall my encounter with them. It seems Gina was their statement to me, my reason for being taken. I've done everything to try and remember, but nothing works. If this keeps up much longer, I fear I'll go insane."

Weston placed her hand on Olefors shoulder, trying to comfort Olefors as much as she could. She kept it there for an eternity until he returned to himself. This was extremely serious. If Anderson Olefors isn't functioning fully, everything will descend into chaos.

'We have to tell Leanna."

"No. Please. Can't we try and figure something out? She's got enough to deal with. Please, Danika."

Olefors's plaintive tone told Danika that he was pleading with her, something he'd never done before. "I won't tell her for now. But I'm going to do a full spectral on you. You are now under my care. No arguments."

"Agreed," Olefors said, glad he finally told Danika about his misery. Even though the pain would still come, at least another human knew about it, and if anyone could figure out a way to combat it, it would be Danika. He knew that there might not be any remedy for this pain, and until he was forced to succumb entirely to its madness, he needed to be as sharp as he could be, even if madness were the outcome."

Weston knew that pressing the point further to get to the origin of this illness would be fruitless. The year that Olefors was missing was a nonstarter in any discussion, mostly because he said he couldn't remember exactly what had happened. Various forms of hypnosis and mind-sifting had proved ineffective in getting any answers.

She once believed that Olefors was not being truthful in his belief that he couldn't remember exactly what had happened, but she now believed him, and the secret he couldn't remember was not by choice but by design. She knew that this secret was related directly to the construction of Gina, and keeping this *secret* was essential in setting the course of humanity for the next millennia.

Olefors smiled at Danika, but it was an empty smile. She knew the pain was still there, possibly somewhat ameliorated. She knew Olefors would never let it distract him from his mission, whatever that mission might be. Maybe someday they'd both know what the past held and could not release.

"Now, let's see if these work," Olefors said, breaking the moment.

Danika was thankful to get back to the task at hand: figuring out the source of the toxin that had almost killed them. Olefors placed the two devices into the chamber with the phased toxin. They effortlessly floated up into the air and remained stationary. He pressed a button outside the chamber, and a laser beam emanated from one device to another, creating a field.

Weston was trying to understand how this process worked, knowing that if one could not solve this dilemma in the future, the other could accomplish the task. One thing was certain. This toxin, whoever created it, was unlike anything seen before. Another reason Weston felt an alien hand was present in all of this.

"A gravity field," she observed.

"More like a subspace definition field, aimed at parsing dimensional shift."

After a moment, something appeared between the two devices. It was tiny but emitting some light.

"UMA, magnify?"

"Yes, Dr."

A screen showed a small molecule rotating and floating between the fields.

"Identify entity."

"Extra dimensional information reveals Milnesium tardigradum DNA."

"Tardigrade?" Weston was shocked. Tardigrades were some of the most resilient creatures in the universe. Sometimes called water bears, they were found to be invaluable in everything from radiation amelioration to long-term space flight to various medical assignations, but she had never heard of them being used in subspace dynamics or to create a toxin.

"Subspace life-form UMA?"

"Verified, Dr. Olefors."

"UMA, what companies on Earth are using this form of DNA for this purpose?"

"None. It's been banned for use due to its innate toxicity, Dr. Weston. There is only one known instance of using tardigrade DNA for implantation into toxic biological mechanisms. In 2260, the World Space Agency used this toxin as an antidote for the Titan flu outbreak on Earth after the Sagan probe to Titan base returned contaminated by an unknown life form. Twenty-two people died in the Cameroon spaceport facility. After that, a break-in at the facility occurred, and the toxin was stolen."

"So, someone is using a weaponized tardigrade bio-toxin from over a century ago to... what?" Olefors said.

"I have no idea. UMA, please theorize the intention of using bio-toxin on Shenu." Weston asked.

"Bio-toxin cannot be used for mass homicide as it can only stay active for short periods before being rendered inert by Shenu bio-filters."

"UMA, how long can the toxin be tracked after activation?"

"45 seconds."

"So, if we hadn't been in the room at the time of the activation, it would've killed everyone." Weston was impressed and also very concerned with the sheer destructive ability of the toxin, but only as a scientist of her caliber could be.

"Then it vanished into subspace, never to be identified," Olefors said, also with a hint of admiration for the seriousness of this particular toxin usage.

"The perfect silent killer," Weston said stoically.

"This seems more like a warning rather than a full-scale assault."

"There are more questions than answers, just like the Maglev accident. UMA, please have all research materials on using tardigrade DNA for any purpose, either medical or military, waved to me, and have any logs or visuals on the Cameroon contamination sent as well," Weston said.

"Uploading now." Weston stood still momentarily as the information was uploaded to her neural cortex.

"I'm going to start analyzing this data. You might want to look at the specimens from the Titan mission."

Olefors looked at Danika Weston for a long beat. She returned his concerned look with one of understanding and compassion, touching his hand tenderly. She even saw a tear form in his eyes, something foreign to him. Perhaps this was the breakthrough they needed to heal their fractured relationship. Danika Weston was grateful for this moment. Even though a serious development brought it about, it enabled them to rise above their pettiness and truly understand and love each other.

CHAPTER TWELVE

REVELATIONS

Betta hurried through the Shenu tunnels, passing the tech crews of Shenu who were brought up on Falcon, all dressed in color-coded Lifesuits. As she passed various people, their suits came to life, announcing who they were and what their protocol was.

Betta used neural contact to reach UMA, something she could do now after their joining three days earlier. "UMA, why am I seeing holo-tags on the inhabitants of Shenu?"

"As the ruling Level 6 on Shenu, you have access to all my links and information," UMA responded. "Only you and the Prime Minister have this access. You receive all telemetry as I do. You need to know each human's function on Shenu to control the events as they take place."

"Control?" Betta was concerned about the use of the word control. She knew that as a Level 6, she had enormous abilities to assert control over several things, including how people thought. Still, as a Level 6, she was also sworn to never use that ability except in extreme situations.

"You have all codes and security clearances stored inside your cortex, everything from inhabitants' whereabouts to current military exercises, visitations, and extra Shenu events." UMA reiterated matter-of-fact.

"You mean I'm...you."

"I am limited to the quantum chamber. At least in your 3-dimensional reality. I need eyes on the station, just as you shall have eyes on 4th and 5th dimensional events as your mind becomes more conformed to mine."

"Conformed. I don't think I like the sound of that."

UMA laughed. "Nonsense," UMA said. "This is not any conformity you are accustomed to. You shall see."

UMA's laugh took Betta by total surprise. She never thought UMA could laugh. It made her feel much more comfortable and allayed her fears of conformity that she had expressed earlier.

"Laughter, UMA?"

"What? Just because I'm a Geneticom doesn't mean I don't know or understand humor. How do you think I can deal with the stupid brilliance of the teeming humanity around me?"

"I can't wait till we get to sarcasm."

"What's that? I'm only familiar with irony."

"Point taken," Betta said.

"I assure you; I am fully versed in all forms of human speech idioms."

"So much for didactics."

"Didactics. What's that?"

As Betta was about to board a transport, she heard Leanna calling her name behind her.

"Betta. I've been messaging you all morning."

"I turned off the messaging protocols."

"Do you think that's wise?" Leanna was miffed that Betta chose to turn off her communication neurals, especially in these turbulent times. Still, she also recognized that her first interactions with UMA were so intense that she needed time to analyze the experience, and being constantly bombarded with unwanted neurals would make her even more unsettled.

"Wise? Probably not. Necessary, Mother."

"I tried to access the information nodes on UMA a few hours ago and couldn't gain access. So, I asked GAIA to do the same, and she was also denied."

"UMA changed the parameters of her information dissemination."

"Meaning?"

"I'm the only Level 6 that can access the data from now on."

"That's unheard of. As a Level 6, I should always have access to UMA's matrix."

"UMA predicted you'd respond this way. She's now sending a protocol message to GAIA explaining her intent."

"Well, maybe you can explain it to me."

"Mother. Do you trust me?"

"Of course."

"Then trust me now. With all the subspace anomalies occurring here, UMA has restricted her access so that no one can compromise security on Shenu. Since we've bonded, UMA has perceived a series of threats to Shenu and Earth. She's in the process of discovery. Dr. Weston and Olefors can brief you about those investigations."

"I guess I'm just used to having all the information myself."

"We all knew UMA was a different entity than GAIA. She's more advanced than anyone on this station or Earth. She is a marvel of both engineering and advanced life form mechanics. We must trust her instincts. I'm not even privy to everything she knows. She has assured me that once this initial investigation is underway, she will open up all her systems to you and GAIA. For now, she's just being protective."

"I just never thought a Geneticom could be so independent." Leanna tried to react calmly, but this turn of events roiled her to her core.

"She's not. She still needs me, and I, her. But we've created a life form which far surpasses our abilities, and we must trust her to protect us and disseminate information when she thinks it's necessary."

"GAIA has received the communique from UMA. Transmitting now."

Leanna received the messages. "Thank you, UMA."

"Thank you, Prime Minister. I hope you understand why I needed to isolate Betta from the population in the short term."

"I do." Leanna was somewhat reassured now that GAIA and UMA were acting in concert. Still, a small voice inside her felt this was a dangerous precedent.

"You are the most advanced Level 6 adept in the world. Your daughter is quickly becoming the same. Trust us always to have Shenu's best interests at heart."

"At heart, UMA? A colloquialism."

"I have a heart, just like you do, Prime Minister. My feelings, although acquired differently than yours, belies intuition and consequence. Know that Betta and I would never do anything to harm you or humanity."

"Thank you, UMA."

"Pleasant day, Prime Minister."

Leanna finished walking Betta to the transport.

"Where are you going?

"To see Pashar. Have you been to see him yet?"

"No. He wouldn't see me until today."

"I'm afraid for him," Betta said.

"Why?"

"Pashar is all about control. Over mind and body. Now that he's been cyberneticized, there's bound to be an adjustment period, and you know how much Pashar hates the unknown."

"All we need to do is listen. Something Level 6 adepts excel in, wouldn't you agree?"

Leanna took her arm and wrapped it around Betta. They boarded the transport, which left the station.

Pashar didn't dare mention his strange dreams about an alien world to anyone. It had been over a week since his confrontation with the deadly R-bot and his subsequent arm and shoulder replacement and TRNA infusion. Ever since that harrowing moment, he'd been unable to sleep, and when he did sleep, his visions were filled with disjointed nightmares.

As a Sidrani, he was used to stress, but it was the kind of stress that mental meditation and physical exertion could temper. With his mind all over the place and his new tritanium arm seeming to have a mind of its own, he was unprepared, something he despised.

His attention was diverted by seeing Hal Weiss sparring with an R-bot nearby. Hal had never left his side since the attack, and in those covered moments between them, while Pashar was still undergoing his transformation, he and Hal bonded and were now joined in more ways than sexual. For the last part of the transformation, Pashar was taken into a special Medbay designed explicitly for advanced genetic therapy. He hadn't seen Hal for days and was missing him terribly. Once Hal saw Pashar, he dropped his guard, and the R-bot jabbed him with a laser spade. Hal went down.

"Disengage." The R-bot immediately stopped sparring with Hal and retreated to a corner. Pashar walked over to him and helped him up. Once their hands touched, Pashar again felt the sexual attraction between them.

"You're not supposed to be distracted during battle." Pashar smiled at Hal, who looked sweaty and extremely attractive. Pashar helped him up, and the two men stood face to face.

"I never thanked you for saving my life."

"It was nothing."

"You're being modest. Not the best look for a Blackhold."

"I'm only doing it for your benefit." Hal smiled at Pashar and took his hand. "So, let's see it."

"It?" Pashar asked.

"Your arm, Pashar."

"Oh, I thought maybe…"

"We'll have time for that later. The arm." They both chuckled.

Delcan Keel approached the pair. They both stood at attention.

"At ease, cadets."

"Permission to be excused, General." Hal sensed Keel wanted to talk to Pashar alone.

"Granted, Mr. Weiss." Hal started walking away.

"You did a great job the other day. I hope Cadet Rajastani was sufficiently thankful."

Weiss turned back to Pashar and Keel. "We're working on it." He smiled, and Pashar got butterflies again.

Damn, I hope I don't get excited right now. But it was too late. Keel noticed as well.

"At ease, Cadet." They laughed.

"So, how are you holding up, Pashar?" It was the first time Keel said his proper name.

"So, all I have to do is lose an arm to get some respect around here," Pashar joked.

"Don't push it. You still have another one." Keel smiled again.

"I thought that maybe getting back into training mode might help me adjust to this new life."

"Just my thought as well," Keel said.

Seeing Delcan Keel relaxed and congenial gave Pashar a sense of protection and calm; that's how much he respected and, in some respects, idolized Keel, though he would never let Keel know it.

Keel was a closet megalo, a short-term term for megalomaniac. That didn't bother Pashar one bit. Men like Keel, his teachers back on Malta, or his father had to be a touch Megalo to take on the responsibilities and burdens of their jobs and keep everyone around them sharp, dangerous, and safe.

Keel patted him on the back, putting Pashar off his game. Then, once Keel felt he had done just that, he swooped his feet under Pashar and took him to the ground. At first, Pashar was so angry he almost swung at Keel, which would have been a career-killing move. Any attempt to subvert Keel's every command would lead to immediate court-martial from the Blackhold; such was the power Keel held over his people. Keel extended his hand and helped Pashar up.

"Ok, now that fun time is over, let's see it." Pashar looked quizzingly at Keel.

"The arm, let's see it." Pashar removed his shirt, revealing his chiseled body and gleaming new arm. Keel looked him over like a cowboy once looked over his prize bull, studying every muscle group, noticing how taut and clean each muscle group functioned in unison with every other muscle group. He had to admit he didn't even have this musculature memory. He extended his hand toward Pashar's bionic arm.

"May I?"

"May you what?"

"Examine it."

"I guess. What for?"

"Well, for starters, I've never seen the newest tech for bionics, and secondly, I want to see how it was made and just what we can get it to do. Pick up the ball and try to throw it into the target."

"The target?" Pashar couldn't see a target anywhere nearby.

"Yeah, over there." Keel pointed to a small oval disc floating about 200 meters away.

"You're fucking kidding me?" Keel gave him a look.

"I never… KID. Now do it!"

Pashar closed his eyes and concentrated on his arm. A moment later, it grabbed a nearby metal ball and quickly crushed it.

"That was tempered Mercury diamond-plated steel combined with detritus from Io."

"Sorry," Pashar said, though he was anything but. Mercury was known for having a layer of diamond 10 kilometers deep and was used on many occasions as a mining site for the most intricate diamonds in the solar system. Combined with detritus in the form of hardened obsidian shist from Io, it was among the most durable alloys in the Solar system.

"See, we got it to work."

"We, commander?" Pashar was semi-joking, but he was also a bit pissed that Keel seemed to think his new arm was the property of the Blackhold.

"I know it's new, and it's a bit fucked up that this happened at all, but this arm represents the newest bionic tech, and that has great importance for the Blackhold. You're a guinea pig Cadet, probably the most advanced humanoid to grace this arena, so I need to know exactly what this marvel can do. Is that ok with you?"

The fact that Keel asked Pashar's permission made everything right in Pashar's skeptical mind.

"Of course. As long as you don't ask me how I jerk off or shit like that."

"I assume you use the other hand, or else you might pull the fucking thing off."

The two men laughed until their sides ached. It was the act of bonding they had been searching for since they'd met.

"It's like another person is inside me, trying to fight my every desire."

"Olefors said this would happen. Remember, you're part of GINA now. This tech uses parallel teaching nodes to what Gina possesses."

"Yes. But Gina is all Graphene-7 plus, who knows what else. I'm just a hybrid."

"You've been infused with Graphene-7 lymph nodes and a Graphene-7 spleen, liver, and muscle structure in your arms. It's going to take time."

Leanna and Betta entered the arena.

"I said I wanted to be left alone," Pashar said under his breath.

"If the Prime Minister wants to see how one of her soldiers and her son is progressing after one of the most remarkable transplants in human history, it's her prerogative."

"And what about my sister?"

"If the highest Level 6 adept linked to the most advanced Geneti-com in the galaxy wants to check on her brother and see how he's progressing to report back to UMA, then she can do just that."

"Are you serious? Since when do you bow and scrape?"

"Since they asked nicely. I can't help it if your family runs everything you see around you. Be happy to see them, some pleasantries, and then I'll find a way to get rid of them." Leanna immediately went to kiss Pashar.

"Mother."

"Let me see it."

Pashar held his new arm up to show Leanna. "Dr. Olefors said it was a marvel of engineering. Look at it. Are you in pain?"

"Not at all. The Graphene-7 Nano TRNA strands have made me feel…"

"Indestructible?" Betta smiled at Pashar in the way only she knew how to simultaneously make him feel loved and understood.

"Tired. But indestructible sounds better."

"It suits you."

"I can't wait to speak to Gina about all this. When is she back?

"You're not supposed to know about that mission."

"Olefors mentioned it yesterday," Pashar said.

"Maybe we should keep Anderson at Level 9." The tone in Betta's voice told Pashar something wasn't right, but he couldn't quite pin it down. He paid a lot more attention to the conversation after that.

"No. He's a 10. He knows more about these advanced medical systems and Gina, for that matter than anyone on Earth or Shenu. We'll have to give him a little talking to."

"Well, ladies, I'm thrilled you came to see Hephaestus here, but we've got much rehab to get to if he's ready to assume command of the Epsilon squad in 2 weeks."

"Hold on, General, I mean sir. What aren't you telling me, Mother?" Leanna looked at Keel and then Betta.

"So, there is something."

"Pashar."

"What is it? As the ranking Sidrani on Shenu, I have a right to know."

"There's been an incident."

"A couple of incidents," Betta added.

"There have been reports of hostages taken at Eridania and Mons bases."

"Hostages? By whom?"

"We don't know. We lost contact two days ago, so we sent Athena to find out what had happened."

Pashar studied his mother's every movement. The slight quiver in her lips told him she was keeping something back, and she stood up straight and planted her feet, which told him she was worried. Betta looked directly into his eyes, trying to use a somnambular hypnotic suggestion to get him to change the course of the dialogue. This tactic might have worked on him a few years back, but one he was eminently prepared for now. Keel looked down at his feet—a typical response of not wanting to engage.

"Ok. Now tell me what you're hiding."

"I told you he'd know." Betta sounded a bit pleased that Pashar saw through the smoke screen.

"We've detected a rogue Comet sent from the Oort cloud."

"Rogue comet? How?"

"We don't know," said Keel. "It's on a collision course with Mars."

"Mars? Deliberate?"

"We think so." Leanna seemed relieved to be telling the truth.

"Why did you hide this from me?"

"We didn't know how well you'd recovered. Eventually, you would have been told everything."

"So, what do we do?"

"For now, Gina, Harrison, and Miranda are en route with 100 Blackhold. They'll meet it and discern its trajectory and anything else they can find."

"There's no way to deflect it?"

"No. It's going to strike in three days."

"Harrison has orders to settle the situation on Mars with the Transhumans and hostages and then wait to assess the damage. Then, once it hits, we'll see how to deal with the impact."

"Are the advanced ICs ready to deploy?" Leanna asked.

"Epsilon is ready in 2 weeks. Phi squad two months later," Keel answered.

"I'll feel better when they're deployed."

"Who could have predicted a series of sub-space incursions before Shenu came online and UMA was born?" Pashar asked.

"GAIA never saw anything coming," Leanna replied. "She had a lot of other things on her mind before UMA was born."

"Does Zhang know?"

"Of course, but she's on the moon. We haven't briefed her in full just yet."

"EC has no reason to be anything but friendly right now. Tara Zhang needs us," Keel said.

"Well, she does own half of everything you see," Betta added.

"Tara Zhang might be many things. But she is, first and foremost, a businesswoman. She'll play nicely if there's money to be made, trading rights to be had, or asteroids and lunar materials to be excavated. After all, the IC technology was developed by EC engineers. The actual craft by UEU. No. She'll play nice."

Leanna sounded more optimistic than she was. Zhang was always a random element, and one of the reasons Leanna didn't trust her was that she could never count on Zhang to do the right thing, only the right thing for her.

"I wonder how she'll react to her precious Eridania mines being out of reach after the strike," Keel said.

Pashar knew that Zhang was a random element, but he didn't have to play diplomat like his mother. He could also be a random element, and at times, he believed that his mother loved that ability of his.

"For now. UMA predicts a 68 percent chance Mars will be uninhabitable by humans for at least eight months." Betta was trying to be as precise and matter-of-fact as she could. She believed this would make everyone else feel more assured, though she had to admit that wasn't necessarily the case with her.

"But not Transhumans," Keel added.

"He's right," Betta said. "The surface might be uninhabitable, but the Transhuman population of Mars would be able to survive underground for an indefinite period."

"That's even money for Zhang." Keel knew Zhang well enough to know that. "She'll find some way to profit from this disaster."

"Better a reluctant trading partner than an enemy. No one wants to mess with her more than they have to," Pashar reiterated.

While Betta and Pashar were speaking, Rajastani took Declan Keel aside.

"Have you discovered the reason why Pashar's D-Suit failed?"

"We examined the R-bot that injured him and found nothing unusual. The unit was a defensive model with the highest training capacity."

"Declan, there's got to be something wrong with the unit. Neuro-toxins are only supposed to be used in true combat. I thought all the combat protocols were nullified for the training missions."

"They all were, Leanna."

"Then what the hell happened? Who disabled the protocols?"

"I'm the only Blackhold that can turn off protocols."

"Apparently not. I want you to sift the minds of all the Blackhold involved in the training exercise."

"Leanna, sifting is not always accurate."

"My son was almost killed in that exercise! There's a saboteur in your ranks, General, and if you don't have them sifted, then I'll have to replace you and do it myself. I want answers, Declan. That's an order."

"Yes, Ma'am," Keel said. When Leanna gave an order, he was the first to carry it out. He trusted her entirely.

"One other matter. Samson has detected anomalous readings from Timocharis crater on the moon."

"What kind of readings?" Keel asked.

"GAIA coded it for neural download on your way to Timocharis. Take Pashar. I need to know how his new body will handle the stress. First, handle this saboteur situation."

"I don't think he's ready, Leanna."

"Then get him ready. We don't have time to waste."

She left the training pod. Betta finished her conversation and then followed Leanna out. Keel looked shaken, something Pashar thought he would never see.

"What happened?"

"Nothing." Keel was too transparent in his denial. Pashar chalked it up to the fact that Keel rarely got a dressing down like the one his mother just gave him.

"Your mother…Loves you very much."

"That bad, huh?"

"She's concerned about what happened to you, as are all of us."

"Well, don't be too worried. I look at it as an upgrade. It will make me a better officer and leader of Epsilon squad."

Declan Keel admired Pashar Rajastani immensely at that moment.

"Don't worry, she'd never can you. You're the best, sir. You're invaluable, and I know my mother thinks you're the greatest military mind in a thousand years."

"Just a thousand?" Keel smiled, and for a quick moment, Pashar Rajastani thought he was the sexiest man he'd ever seen. Keel put his arm around Pashar.

"Are you mission-ready, cadet?"

"Yes, sir."

"Good. I have some business to attend to first. After that, we have a mission."

The Blackhold from Pod 5 were all lined up inside the training dome two hours after Keel received his orders from Leanna about sifting for the saboteur. This was the last pod of Blackhold to be sifted. So far, there were no anomalies in any of the Blackhold, which made Keel extremely nervous. If it wasn't a member of the Blackhold who committed the sabotage on Pashar, then who was it? Keel believed it had to be a Blackhold member, but everyone passed the sifting test.

Sifting a Blackhold was always tricky business. Although they were trained to resist most forms of sifting, a specialized protocol bypassed much of their training and indoctrination. One by one, they were brought into a dark room, where Danika Weston, Declan Keel, and UMA were waiting.

The procedure was quite simple and effective. Lying was linked to amygdalic responses in the brain. Weston's background involved extensive research on brain changes as people lie.

During her research, she saw much activity in brain regions associated with emotions, particularly the amygdala. This observation suggested that participants initially felt very bad about the lies they told. However, as participants repeatedly lied over time, these brain areas showed less activity. While Weston was resetting the machinery for the sifting, UMA spoke up.

"I'm curious, Doctor Weston."

"Yes, UMA."

"First, thank you for letting me participate in this exercise. I am fascinated by the sifting process."

"You're welcome."

"How exactly did you come to create the mechanism for your procedure?"

"As you know, the sifting process relies upon carefully calculated measurements of a human's ability to lie. It is not unlike the early lie detector tests of the past 200 years, but much more precise and accurate. There has never been a false negative reading for this particular test. Just like when we encounter other unpleasant stimuli—like loud noises or frightening images—the brain can adapt and make the stimuli less intense.

"Unfortunately, when we adapt to lying, it becomes easier to continue doing so. As lying no longer bothers us, we tend to tell even bigger lies. This desensitizes us to the act of lying, and we continue on a slippery slope of dishonesty. I've found that people who feel guilty are the least likely to lie. People with high levels of guilt are less likely to engage in dishonest behavior."

Keel was surprised at how much the Blackhold felt guilt, which Weston assured him was a good sign. That one emotion kept them from lying or being dishonest, as the 200 Blackhold they sifted previously had proven. They were up to the last five Blackhold.

Kyle Raphael was summoned into the room, while Weston and Keel remained in a separate room hidden from the view of any of the Blackhold. "Sergeant Raphael, please sit down," UMA said.

Kyle sat down into the ergo chair, and as in the nesting chambers, hundreds of electrodes were attached to his scalp, immediately placing him into a state of semi-consciousness.

"We're going to begin."

"I'm ready," Kyle said.

"So, you were seen in the men's locker room arguing with cadet Rajastani. Is that correct?"

"Well, it wasn't an argument. I passed by him and might've pushed him a bit. You know, to test him."

Weston was looking at a spectral monitor, shading every physical and emotional response Raphael gave. She looked at Keel and nodded.

"That's the baseline. We know he did push Pashar, and now we know what the truth looks like on the spectrometer. That'll give us a baseline for a lie if he tells one."

"Sergeant, did you sabotage a Gen 1100 R-bot during the training exercise two weeks ago to harm Cadet Rajastani?"

"No. I would never endanger a member of the Blackhold."

The scan looked precisely the same as the truth scan.

"He's clean," Weston said to Keel.

"OK, Cadet. You can…"

UMA stopped her. "Excuse me, Doctor Weston. I'm getting an anomalous reading from Sergeant Raphael's Amygdala."

"Can I leave now?" Raphael was anxious to go on with his day.

"Hang tight for a moment, Kyle," Keel said.

"Anomalous UMA? What do you mean?"

"The cell structure is correct, as are the DNA base pairs, but I am detecting an anomaly in his ASPM base pair."

Weston turned to Keel. "The ASPM gene makes a protein needed for producing new nerve cells (or neurons) in the developing brain. UMA elaborate."

Simply put, Doctor Sergeant Raphael's amygdala is not human. It may look human and act like a human amygdala, but it is not Terran.

Keel was out of his seat before UMA finished her sentence. He burst into the interrogation room, but Raphael was gone.

"This is Keel, all Blackhold, engage protocol triple zero. Apprehend Sergeant Raphael."

Triple zero was the most severe protocol that a Blackhold was given. It called the Blackhold to activate their D-suits and immediately apprehend and detain Kyle Raphael.

In seconds, every Blackhold on Shenu assumed a pursuit posture and launched a frantic search for Kyle Raphael. Hal Weiss was training in the dome when the call came in. He noticed Raphael sprinting across the floor, going to the egress docks that led to open space. Weiss activated his D-suit and chased after him. As Raphael was about to enter the airlock, Weiss caught up to him, and the two engaged in a fierce struggle. Weiss finally restrained Raphael, pinning him to the ground. He was astounded at Raphael's strength, and it took all of his to keep him restrained until Keel and the other Blackhold got to them.

He pressed the neural interface on Raphael's D-suit, and it disappeared around him. Keel and ten other Blackhold arrived soon after. Raphael glanced at his fellow Blackhold and smiled. Then he bit down on his tongue, severing it from his mouth. It writhed on the chest of his D-suit as a white foam filled Raphael's mouth. He convulsed in apoplectic fits, then screamed. But the scream was not human.

"Get back. Everyone out!"

Keel pushed his team out of the airlock and closed it behind them, leaving himself and Hal Weiss inside. The Blackhold felt helpless as Keel and Weiss moved back to the edge of the airlock. The team tried to access the egress port, but Keel jammed it.

After a few moments, Kyle Raphael's body started to shake violently. It began to morph into something none of them had ever seen before. Bit by bit, his human form shifted into a large Grey alien, the kind rumored to have been interacting with humanity for centuries. Its skin was reflective, like a mirror that bent and distorted the light around it, making it appear as if the Grey was translucent and invisible at the same time, a product of some advanced genetic engineering. Its large waxy eyes had one incredible feature: They had two irises on opposite sides of their eyeballs, making them look horrific and deeply frightening.

Some of the Blackhold recoiled. Keel held his nerve. It was taller than Keel had surmised, and it surprised him. Then he remembered Grey aliens also came in all shapes and sizes. Keel realized that the size of this particular Grey would have intimated that it was a soldier, just like his human doppelganger.

"Seniori," Keel said calmly. Even though he'd never seen a Grey, he knew they were also the founding members of the Seniori and had heard that they had advanced techniques for disguising themselves, especially from humans, *as* humans.

For years, humanity knew and accepted that Greys were in the Terran system for centuries, but the rumors of a cloaked base on the dark side of the moon began to brew a mere 50 years prior. Most of humanity had no idea that the Greys were on Earth except those who had been taken, and there were many, but their memories were often erased. Humans didn't need to know. Those in positions of power and influence all knew that truth, and it was humanity's best-kept secret and would remain so until it wasn't. Most of the elites on Earth also learned that the Greys recruited humans to do their bidding. It was a fact of life that the Greys were here. What was not a fact was what they wanted and why they wanted it.

Making sure that there was no more threat from the alien, Keel opened the egress port.

"Take it to quarantine pod three," Keel barked. In an instant, Raphael's body was taken away. Keel looked at Hal Weiss.

"Damn fine work, Sergeant." He patted Weiss on the back. A meaningful gesture for Keel. He got on a neural.

"Leanna. We have the saboteur that attacked Pashar." Leanna Rajastani's' holoimage appeared in front of Keel.

"Who was it?"

"I think you'd better see for yourself. Meet me in quarantine pod three."

Ten minutes later, Leanna Rajastani, Danika Weston, and Declan Keel stood in quarantine pod three, staring at what was now confirmed to be a Seniori agent.

"Not a word of this to anyone," Leanna said. "We keep this to ourselves. For now. UMA, scan Shenu for any other amygdalic inconsistencies."

"Scan was done 2 hours ago; Kyle Raphael was sole Seniori onboard."

"So maybe it was the Seniori who sabotaged Cosulo," Keel said.

"Not likely, General," UMA said. "The Seniori are clandestine. They never expected Kyle Raphael to be discovered. However, they might know that he has been neutralized, or they might not."

"That might make them nervous. Nervous means they'll be more likely to make mistakes," Leanna said.

"I suggest we keep this to ourselves, as Leanna Rajastani has also suggested. Of course, Gaia and Betta must be informed," UMA said.

Leanna turned to Weston. "Do an autopsy. I want to know everything there is to know about him. This is the first known contact with a Grey soldier. We must know everything. Declan, you're with me." She and Keel left the room.

"I can assist with the autopsy, Doctor Weston."

"Thank you, UMA, I'd appreciate that."

The small shuttle glided effortlessly across the barren, dark lunar moonscape. Inside, Zhang sat next to Sanjay Ramtaj, Zhang's pilot,

assassin, and sometimes lover. The other occupant of the shuttle was Vera Jenks, Zhang's head of lunar affairs and sometimes lover.

"Once we get there, I'll go in myself."

"Not wise," Vera quickly responded. She had been the head of Zhang's detail for 15 years. She'd seen everything that anyone could possibly imagine as it related to Zhang. She'd been sifted, implanted, and brainwashed to Zhang's specifications, but she didn't mind.

Before she worked for Zhang, she was an expert assassin, having killed over two dozen high-yield targets, including two UEU diplomats. On her way to incarceration in the zero-G facilities in Kenya, she was plucked from the jaws of eternal weightlessness by Zhang, so in essence, she owed Zhang her life many times over, which is what made her so protective of Zhang. She'd gladly lay down her life for Zhang and knew that someday, she would.

"I'll be the judge of wisdom, Vera. They don't trust anyone they haven't done business with before."

"What's this all about, Tara?" Sanjay asked.

"Never ask questions I won't answer. You should know that by now."

"I'd feel better if I could neurolink with you while you're in there," Vera said.

"I'm touched, my dear, but the Seniori don't allow neuro transceivers either. It's old school for this lot."

"We're approaching the landing site."

The shuttle approached a mountain. As it looked like it was going to crash into the side, a portal appeared. The shuttle glided effortlessly through the portal and entered the docking bay. The portal closed behind it, never having given up its secret.

"I don't understand why you brought us if we can't protect you." *Vera is still worried,* Zhang thought. *Loyal to the core and right to be worried.*

"These people work fast. If I'm not out in an hour, you can be the chivalric killer I love."

She kissed her on the lips, then turned to Sanjay and did the same, leaving lipstick on both of their mouths. Sanjay licked it off and swallowed it. Vera wiped hers off on Sanjay's sleeve. "Let's pick this up when I get back."

Vera smiled and handed Zhang a bag of Hydronium rocks. Zhang took one last look and exited the shuttle. Sanjay and Vera followed her. They were met by five tall figures wearing masks. *They must be 7 feet, at least,* Vera thought. The figures walked to Zhang and then blindfolded her.

"Hey, that wasn't part of the deal," Vera objected. The figures didn't answer. They approached a wall that disappeared, revealing a large, cavernous room, and took Zhang through, leaving Vera and Sanjay alone to await Tara's return.

The figures escorted Zhang into a dark chamber, leaving her in the middle. They removed her blindfold. A bright beam of light cascaded down from the ceiling. When it reached Zhang, she was held fast in place.

A door opened in the sleek, cool red granite walls, and a figure glided out of the darkness towards Zhang. It stood 8 feet tall. As it got closer to Zhang, she could see its face was covered by black skin, as if it had no face, a trademark of the Seniori.

Zhang knew she might be the only human who had ever seen the Seniori, even though seen might be stretching it.

A silver-gray skin covered its hand. The sight gave her a feeling of deep dread, and for a moment, she felt so claustrophobic that she thought she might scream, but the beam that held her still prevented even that. A deep voice echoed through the chamber.

"Lady Zhang. The Prime Minister of EC. We are honored."

"As am I. The Seniori aren't easily impressed."

"We rarely get corporate royalty visits here on the moon. You brought the materials?"

"In the bag, I was carrying," she said.

"And the payment?"

"The iridium will be delivered to the coordinates in one hour, as agreed," Zhang replied. "There's been a slight change of plans. We have another mission for you."

"That wasn't part of our deal." Zhang was nervous. She knew the Seniori always had plans within plans, and she'd hoped this exchange would be easy. She chided herself for her ignorance. *When the Seniori asks for something, it's best to acquiesce, even at your own peril.*

Zhang waited impatiently. After a moment, an opening appeared, and a small metallic device floated across the floor. When it reached Zhang, the force field around her disappeared.

"Hold out your hand," the voice said.

Zhang obliged. The transport dropped a pearl-sized device into Zhang's hands. It shimmered the same yellow color as the Hydronium.

"What is this?" she asked.

"A present for you. We want you to deliver it to a worthy recipient."

"Who?"

"The Harbinger."

"Frost? You're joking."

The beam tightened around her, and she felt her blood and muscles tighten and compress her spine, causing intense excruciating pain.

"We never joke, Lady Zhang. Frost is dangerous to us. We need him neutralized. We have detected that he is already at Lumina."

"Very well. How do I set it?"

"It is calibrated to your DNA."

"My DNA? That's coded and secret."

"Lady Zhang, you should know by now that there are no such things as keeping secrets from the Seniori. Place the device in your mouth for 10 seconds, then plant it within 7 feet of the target. Once it touches another surface besides your hand, you've got 15 seconds to get out of the blast zone."

"What about tracers?"

"The device has a fourth-dimensional molecular decay that activates on detonation. There's no way to trace it. Remember this. If the iridium isn't where it's supposed to be, you can be assured that your betrayal of our endeavors will be reckoned."

"There won't be any need for that. The iridium is of the highest quality, obtained from Ceres itself."

"When will the larger package be ready?" the figure asked.

"In seven days. I will have it delivered to your contact at Lumina base."

"Pleasure doing business with you."

"Always a pleasure making your day a little more…interesting."

The beam disappeared, and Zhang passed out. The five beings came and collected her, then led her out of the room.

Dr. Tantalus hovered over a table where advanced mechanical equipment was laid out before him, intently looking at something under a transparent microscope. In his viewfinder, he saw various organisms moving about in synchronous harmony. Upon closer inspection, they looked entirely alien—six legs, long snouts, something not of this world.

Tantalus then opened a small vial, revealing an iridescent powder, which he sprinkled onto the organisms. As soon as the powder touched their skin, it was absorbed. The organisms changed color from pale Grey to iridescent purple. Then, some of the microorganisms began to cannibalize the others and grow exponentially. Tantalus smiled. Mara entered the lab.

"Report."

"Athena is one hour away from contact with Proteus."

"Perfect."

"What are you doing, Dr.?"

"Look in the spectrum microscope and tell me what you see." Mara approached the scope and peered inside.

"Tardigrades?"

"Well done. But look closer."

Mara did so. "They look a lot bigger than usual. And their color."

"A requisite by-product from direct iridium infusion."

"So that's what the iridium was for. I don't see how this relates to you."

"For my next series of procedures, I will inject the now modified tardigrade DNA directly into my bloodstream."

"But that will kill you."

"It might kill you, but not me."

"Malcolm. I've been your Level 6 for over two years and am still in the dark about what you're planning."

"Mara, in the grand scheme of life, answers are not readily accessible when more than life itself is in the balance."

"Yes. You keep saying that, but it rings hollow. You haven't given one hint at what you are trying to accomplish when I've done nothing but put my life on constant death watch to do your bidding. I was the most promising Level 6 at the convent."

"I know, but think of how much we have in common. Like me, you faced death and survived."

"Parts of my memory were erased during that procedure."

"A necessary by-product of becoming my protege. And now, you are a blank slate."

"But you know how I almost died and how I survived. I know nothing of you."

"Once the procedure is complete, you will know all, but beware, you might wish you hadn't been so eager to peel the veil. Take the vial next to the spectrometer and place it inside the centrifuge." Mara did what Tantalus asked.

Tantalus got up, walked to his experimentation chamber, opened it, and entered. "Now, begin the procedure and leave the room."

"Who will monitor the session?"

"No one. For this stage of the metamorphosis, I will be alone."

"Yes, Dr." She turned to leave.

"And Mara?"

"Yes, Dr."

"I have a job for you on the moon. Dracon is prepared in the docking bay. All instructions will be given to you while en route."

"Yes, Dr."

The door closed behind him. She turned on the transformation chamber with Tantalus inside and left the room. Once she left the chamber, she began to hear screaming. She approached the door to the lab, closed her eyes, and placed her hands on the frame. Then she began to vibrate slowly and at a higher rate until her body looked like it was oscillating back and forth in a frenzy. Her body remained at the door, but her oversoul moved through it. Once inside the room, she could see into the chamber.

Tantalus was oscillating back and forth. With each oscillation, Mara saw two distinct figures. One was Tantalus, and the other was a reptilian life form, which had some of the same features as Tantalus but also some features of the tardigrade life form and some other life forms that she couldn't recognize. She screamed, but of course, Tantalus couldn't hear her. She ended up back in her body on the other side of the door, absorbed with fear. She gained her composure and left the antechamber.

Gina, Byrnes, Han, and two crew members were inside Athena's shuttle bay. Solara 2 sat waiting in front of them, rotating on its pad to egress to a rendezvous with Proteus, now on the Jovian side of the asteroid belt and streaking towards Mars. Byrnes stepped forward to Gina and Han.

"No heroics, you two. The mission is to land on Proteus and check out the anomalous readings. That's it."

"Once we're finished, we'll meet you on Eridania Plain," Han said.

"Who knows what those readings are, but if there's any chance we can either change the comet's direction or destroy it before Marsfall, we'll need to take it."

Han pressed a button embedded in her hand, and a portal appeared on the side of Solara. Gina boarded Solara, and Byrnes held Han back.

"No unnecessary risks, sub-commander."

"Understood."

She boarded Solara 2. The portal closed. Solara exited the shuttle bay from Athena. As soon as it did, Athena jumped into the dark matter drive and disappeared. In the distance, Proteus appeared on the Martian side of the Asteroid belt, a whitish-blue trail of gases streaming from its tail.

After her encounter with the Seniori, Zhang was both elated and trepidatious. The Seniori weren't to be messed about. They were so clandestine that they tried to erase her memory of their location after her encounter, but Zhang was prepared for that.

She had a small transceiver implanted in her hippocampus, which prevented anyone from accessing her memories and erasing or changing them. She had no idea whether the device would work with the Seniori, and she took a huge chance that their advanced tech wouldn't have discovered it, in which case she might have been eliminated.

Luckily for her, the scientists she employed were the best in the solar system, and their genius and expertise outshined even the Seniori. With this dilemma behind her, Zhang knew she had bested the Seniori for now.

She left her lunar mansion, aware that Frost was watching her. He touched his wrist, and a holopanel appeared in front of him. He chose defense mode, then chose Stealth. He immediately blended into the background, becoming invisible, and began to follow Zhang. He was surprised to see that she was alone—something very unusual for the leader of EC.

Zhang heard something in her ear. Fredric Ashton's voice came over her aural transceiver. "Lady Zhang, I have some unsettling news."

"Go ahead."

"We had a few visitors last night. From the Blackhold."

"What?"

"Someone tried to gain access to Timocharis facility, and when they failed, two stealth drones appeared at Timocharis followed by 10 Blackhold elite."

"Did they find the Hydronium?"

"No. Your friends sure know their tech. The Blackhold never even knew it was there. However, it's bad enough that they knew where to find it in the first place. I think you've been compromised."

"Not from within my circle. It must be from Shenu. Rajastani."

"Watch your back."

"I'm at the drivers now. I'll contact you once I'm back on Earth. I'll Contact Onur."

"Onur isn't a Geneticom, but he should be able to help."

"He's just as brilliant, and he's mine. Onur?"

"Yes, Lady Zhang."

"Give me a Level 10 trace. Scan for anomalies in a 250-foot radius."

"No anomalies detected." There was a pause as Ashton did as requested. "Error, neural displacement detected, 500 feet and closing."

"Extrapolate source."

"Unknown. Could be atmospheric in origin or stealth tech."

"Skin shield." In an instant, Zhang was covered in silver skin, which made her invisible.

"Skin shield activated. Stealth mode enabled."

Zhang walked into a tunnel leading from one part of the base to another. "Is anomalous reading still present?"

"Unable to verify. The stealth tech is no longer detectable."

"Speculate."

"There is a distinct possibility that stealth tech is being employed to track you. I am ascertaining the stealth tech and processing the stealth tech source to identify the tracker. The tracked individual has been identified as Samson Frost."

Zhang took the Hydronium pearl from her pocket and placed it in her mouth. Waited a few seconds, then took it out and dropped it inside the tunnel. She moved quickly away from the area. As she did, she was met by a group of miners coming in the other direction.

The hallway was very narrow, and Zhang needed help to pass them. She looked behind her and saw the pearl on the ground. She tried to make her way through the pack of miners but was still being held back. She finally passed most of them when a massive explosion went off. The last thing Tara Zhang remembered was the smell of blood and sinew being scorched to ashes, and the sounds of screaming that accompanied it. Then everything went black.

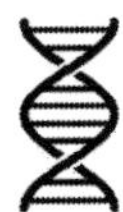

Han and Gina were inside Solara, making its approach to Proteus. "I've located a pocket of sub-space along the comet's equator," Han said.

"I'm scanning now. Calibrating for Gamma EM traces." Gina's eyes focused on the view window. She calibrated her eyes to detect Gamma EMs.

"There, Azimuth eleven degrees." Han psychically steered Solara down to the coordinates. "Descending to drop point."

Solara dropped into a low orbit above Proteus. Gina prepared to disembark from Solara.

She turned her skin pure white.

"I heard you can do this. It's amazing. Graphene-7 properties?"

"Yes. My biofunctions are suspended, well, the biofunctions that need respiration and such."

"I'm curious. How Did Dr. Olefors accomplish such a monumental task?"

"I'm sorry. That information is classified," Gina said.

"Even to you?"

"Somewhat. All I know is that Dr. Olefors used advanced techniques he assimilated from a foreign source to create my matrix."

"It's the foreign source concept that has everyone wondering," Han added.

"They can wonder all they want."

"Seems unethical to do that. Leave you questioning your very existence."

"Have you never questioned your existence, Commander Han?"

"Every day," Han replied. *We're more alike than I thought.*

"Sub Commander, for millennia, humanity had no idea how the basics of chemistry and physiology or even how DNA worked."

"Aren't you the least bit curious as to how 'you' came into being?"

"Of course, but Dr. Olefors made it clear that my creation was more than just the sum of its parts. Like you, there are mysteries inside me that modern scientific explanation can never hope to unlock."

"Metaphysics, Gina?"

"To this day, we still do not know how the human pineal gland functions. Some think it's just a gland, like the adrenal or pituitary glands. Others think it's a gateway, a portal to other dimensions. Science seems quite inept to explain such marvels of the universe. Such secrets are necessary for the continuation of spirit on this plane. I am ready." Han looked reverentially at Gina as she stepped into the exit bay.

The port door opened. Gina exited the craft and floated down to the surface of the comet.

"I am sensing a device 4 meters from my position." She floated above the comet's surface until she came to a spot and landed.

"Like the bomb on Cosulo, it's hidden in some kind of subspace."

A beam emanated from her eyes. It scanned the ground, revealing a circular device about one meter across.

"This is the cause of the disturbance. I am detecting geosynchronous devices that can affect the comet's direction."

"Direction?"

"Not just that. It has a time displacement differential as well. Someone took the comet from one part of the solar system and transported it here."

"What happens if you remove the device?"

"Unknown. However, since the comet is already on trajectory to Mars, there seems to be no way to alter its course."

At that moment, a small needle-like device quickly jabbed itself into Gina's leg. Gina promptly reached down and broke the needle from its casing. As soon as she did so, the device disappeared from the comet's surface.

"I have been lanced with some sort of hypodermic."

"Are you ok? I thought you were impervious to injury?"

"I am fine. But it was able to collect a sample of my genome. I detached the unit from its source for evidence."

"Return to Solara 2."

"Acknowledged." Gina floated up and moved off towards Solara hovering above her.

Leanna Rajastani, Declan Keel, and Danika Weston stood in the receiving bay with 50 Blackhold soldiers around them.

"Declan, what's the latest Intel on the explosion on the moon?" Leanna asked.

"12 killed, seven injured."

The bay opened, and two shuttles entered. Rajastani moved to them. The doors opened, and bodies on hover carriers began off-loading from the shuttles. At the end of the procession, two more gurneys exited, floating above the ground. Rajastani walked over to them. She lifted the cover off of one of the gurneys and saw Tara Zhang badly wounded.

"How bad is she?"

"She's stable for now. She'll make it, but she might also lose sight in her right eye and hearing in her right ear. We'll be in med bay three," Weston answered.

"I want around-the-clock monitored surveillance on her UMA."

"Yes, Prime Minister."

As the second gurney approached, Leanna felt a wave of nausea pass over her. She removed the covering of the gurney, revealing the dead body of Samson Frost.

"Contact UEU headquarters in Brussels," Rajastani said, holding back a flood of emotions. Tell them we've got our first casualties. She touched Frost's face, trying to hold back the tears. Frost was taken away.

"Set security protocols at Red Level for the foreseeable future. No one leaves or comes onto Shenu without my direct authorization."

"Understood. Red Level parameters set," UMA replied.

"And I want some goddam answers to all this."

"Yes, ma'am."

Rajastani left the bay. Keel followed her out.

Two days later, Leanna stood over the dead body of Samson Frost. His form had been restored to its pre-explosion state. "Now what am I going to do, Samson?"

She started to cry. She wiped a tear from her face across Samson's lips. Betta entered the morgue.

"Mother, the service starts in 15 minutes. The Blackhold need access to bring the body to the airlock." Leanna wiped the tears away to hide her pain.

"What is it, Mother?"

"Nothing. In a way, it seems only justified that we should also have all life cycles up here. Makes me feel more Terran."

"Mother, is there something you want to tell me?"

"Not that I can think of."

"You know I can read you. Even with all your Level 6 training, I can read through the mechanisms."

Leanna turned to her daughter. Tears welled up again. She grabbed Betta as if she might drift away from her. The emotion wasn't lost on

Betta, but she also knew that this kind of emotional display belied a deep hurt she had never felt in her mother before.

"You and Samson were lovers."

"For quite some time."

"I'm so sorry, Mother."

Leanna moved to the couch. Betta sat next to her. Betta felt the memories slowly descend upon her mother, each memory a marker of an event that solidified her love for Samson.

"We met in Zurich, back in 2306. I suppose it was infatuation for both of us at first. Your father's accident had happened a few months before, and even though we had been separated before he passed, I felt I wasn't ready for another relationship. One night, at dinner, Samson came over and introduced himself. I, of course, knew who he was. He was the most accomplished Harbinger of his day. The man who single-handedly brought Earth Corporate and The United Earth Union to the bargaining table. He told me he'd been watching my career rise to what he called "meteoric" status for months, but he still wasn't sure who the woman beneath the career was, and that was the woman he wanted to spend the night with. Well, I was shocked, of course. He was so forward, so confident. He eluded my Level 6 mechanisms, which I suppose was enough for me to respect him. We had sex in the bathroom at the restaurant and then spent five days in bed together. After that week, even if we weren't physically together, we were "together.""

"Must've been strange. Being a Level 6," Betta observed.

"I wasn't a nun, Betta. I was just enhanced, and that can mean enhanced in many ways, including sexually."

"Easy for you. You were allowed to have a relationship with father. I'm to be wedded to a machine."

"How immature of you. Your relationship with UMA will be one of profound exploration, family, and love. It was a different time. With your father."

"I believe those relationships are distractions, like father for you. When you were married, you neglected your duties to GAIA, and she didn't understand. You put yourself first."

"Geneticoms weren't as advanced as today and didn't demand more of our time. Remember, I didn't match with GAIA until I was 65. I'm 115 now. A lot has happened in 50 years in advanced AI technology."

"Still. It must've been strange for you and Samson. Always having to hide your feelings."

"Samson knew that nothing in my life was more essential than what would happen on Shenu. We both knew we had a chance to remake human society, to create something unique, away from the troubles of Earth, with open eyes towards a future that awaited us with promise and hope."

"But I'll never be able to have a relationship outside that one."

"You won't want any other relationship, and you've been prepared for just such a life course. Are you questioning your destiny at this late moment?"

"I don't know. It's all so…real. I'm prepared. I've been ready for this all my life, but here, at the point of no return, I'm scared."

"I'll be with you every step of the way. You'll never be alone. Never."

With that, Leanna hugged her daughter as if it was the first or last time. To be truthful, she had no idea exactly how joining Betta and UMA would affect everyone and everything around them. All she knew was that Betta's destiny lay intertwined with UMA's, and nothing could sever or alter that reality.

"So much uncertainty," Betta said.

"Uncertainty is what propels this species forward."

She looked down at Samson. Touched his lips. "Still, without Samson to share in it, it feels a bit more...uncertain than I'd like." Betta reached out for her mother's touch and hugged her for longer than she could remember.

They left the funerary chamber and entered the docking bay, where they were met by Declan Keel and a 100 Blackhold standing near the now draped corpse of Samson Frost. Leanna stepped forward, faced the Blackhold, and took a deep breath. From the corner of her eye, she saw a small tear escape Declan Keel's impassive demeanor.

"Today, we have the honor of saying goodbye to Samson Frost. We all knew the dangers of space, of colonizing a cold world filled with emptiness and stardust. Samson knew it better than most. A decorated diplomat and soldier, a devoted humanitarian and scholar, and pure and simply, our friend. We say a tearful, fond, and heartfelt farewell to those who knew him. To those who never knew him, we say you would have been proud to call him your friend because there was no better friend than Samson Frost. His spirit, smile, and steadfast determination to do what was right will be sorely missed in these trying moments."

Leanna nodded to Declan Keel. "Blackhold, unite in honor." 12 Members of the Blackhold took Samson's body and placed it into a small chamber.

"Madame Prime Minister."

Leanna walked over to the chamber and waved her hand over a panel. A keyboard came up floating in the air. Leanna waved her hand over a blinking green light. Samson's body was ejected into space. From 200 meters away, a portal opened, and a small dot exited from Shenu.

The Blackhold had all left the docking bay. Declan Keel placed his hand on Leanna's shoulder and gently kissed her on the neck. It was a meaningful gesture that brought tears to Leanna's face. After he left and Leanna was alone with her memories, one last voice echoed.

"I'm so sorry, madam Prime Minister. Is there anything I can do?" GAIA's voice was both comforting and comfortable to hear.

"No, GAIA, but thank you." Leanna wiped away her tears.

"Goodbye, dearest." With that, she turned away from her past. She walked past the mourners and out of the cargo bay and into her private offices, where she broke down and cried until there were no more tears to shed.

CHAPTER THIRTEEN

ERIDANIA

Tara Zhang stood naked in a dark chamber as two other naked figures approached her. One took an object and raised it to Tara's mouth. One was female, the other male. But indeed, not human.

"Mustn't have any dissension at such a crucial juncture," the male figure said to the female telepathically.

A beam of light emanated from the device and sealed Tara's mouth shut. She tried to scream, but all that came out sounded muffled and macabre.

"Do you think she will survive the procedure?"

"If she doesn't, our plans will be set back for months."

"Give me the key."

The female held out her hand, covered with shiny gray skin. She took a device and made a small incision along Zhang's belly. A trickle of blood ran down Tara's abdomen.

"Not long now, Lady Zhang. You wanted to know us, know all about us. We said there would come a day when you would understand everything."

She paused for drama. Then, she took a vial out of her pocket and opened it. A small luminous sack sat inside the vial. She held the vial up. Tara saw a small creature no more than a centimeter. It seemed to be a miniature version of the beings standing before her. The female took the vial, opened it, and let the creature crawl out onto her hand. She moved to Zhang, who was sweating profusely. Tara realized she could communicate telepathically with her aggressors.

"I don't know why you're doing this. We had an arrangement. We had a deal."

"Deals are made to be re-arranged," the male said.

"I'll give you anything you want." Zhang's mind was screaming.

"We know you will. Sadly, for you, we already have everything we need. Except a living, breathing avatar and a child who is more human than human to go along with him. Think of yourself as GAIA incarnated as so many strands of metamorphosized DNA, all vainglorious attempts at the perpetuation of a minor species."

With that, the female implanted the embryo inside Zhang's womb. Zhang screamed even more intensely.

The scream carried over as Zhang woke up in a fit of fear, knocking over tables, and ripping IVs out of herself. Danika Weston and two nurses restrained her and tried to calm her down.

"What happened? Where am I?" Zhang paused, looking bewildered. "My hearing."

"You lost your hearing in your right ear. The blast wave annihilated your cochlea. We saved your right eye, although you'll notice it's now biotech-driven, as is your new cochlea."

"Where am I?"

"You're on Shenu. In the Medbay."

Zhang relaxed for a moment. She caught her breath and lay back down on the bed. She took the blanket and removed it quickly. She looked down at her stomach, but there was no incision. She closed her eyes, relieved.

"You were screaming all night. We had to give you a neural to calm you down."

"Neurals don't work on me," Zhang said unceremoniously.

"Your Quan Xi training. Must come in handy."

"Except when you think you're going crazy and wake up in a temporal haze that never lifts and with half your hearing."

"What's the last thing you remember?"

"I was walking near the driver pads, waiting to send a payload into orbit. I saw Samson across the docking bay. I started walking towards him to say hello, then a huge explosion, then black."

"Do you remember anything else? Smells, sounds, anything."

"No, Dr., I'm sorry. What was it?"

"We don't know. Crews have been scanning the launch bay for clues, but they've just found immolated metal and polymers and, of course, blood and sinew."

"How long have I been out?"

"Two days. You've got a nasty concussion. You'll probably be with us for another two days, and then we'll do another cranial to see if the swelling has gone down."

"Thank you, Dr. I'm impressed."

"Nonsense, Lady Zhang. Your safety and good health are always our highest concern." Weston turned to leave.

"Dr., what happened to Secretary Frost? I don't see him here."

"He died soon after arriving on Shenu. I'm sorry." She left the room. Zhang smiled slightly, then closed her eyes to rest.

Athena was 2 hours out from Mars orbit. Byrnes waited in the docking bay as Solara 2 glided into the bay and landed. Han and Gina exited the craft. Dr. Samira Poi approached them. This was her first mission off-world, and she wasted no time ascertaining all the specs on Gina that Danika Weston had sent on a neural.

"Well, Dr., what is your analysis?"

"The preliminary tests show all your primary functions as nominal. No toxins were delivered into your system. It seems there was some removal of biomass and fluid."

"But why would anyone try to do such a thing?" Byrnes was angry but more concerned about what had happened to Gina. After their encounters with Athena and Shenu over the last weeks, he felt that he was falling into... something with her. It wasn't love. It couldn't be. He'd never fallen in love before, so maybe it was. Now, he understood why everyone for millennia had said that true love confuses the soul, sending it to places that made it feel alive but somewhat lost as well.

"I'm beginning to understand," Gina said. "I believe that everything that has happened, Cosulo, Proteus, the Transhuman revolt on Mars must also have to do with me."

"In what way?" Byrnes knew the answer to the question. Gina was not only the first of her kind but was far more advanced than any other being on Earth. Whether nefarious or not, every organization would try to get intel on her.

"In each instance, a series of obstacles was erected which could only be solved by me. The solar bomb on Cosulo, the comet changing its course and heading towards Mars. The revolt on Mars must also be a trap of some sort."

"But why?"

"To test my abilities, to observe me, and now, to examine my biomass and fluidic matter."

"Do you have any idea who might be behind this?"

"No. Not yet. The needle I was injected with was diamonide platinum carbyne. There are very few manufacturing facilities that can produce such a device."

"What about the Seniori?"

"It doesn't seem like their MO," Han said. "They're secretive and deadly, but they don't take much of an interest in anything they can't directly influence with violence or coercion."

"The Seniori are an anomaly in human culture," Gina added.

"There are those that believe that they aren't human at all. Harrison has seen the classified data. So have you, Gina." Han said.

Athena interjected. "I must also inform everyone that a secret Seniori agent was killed in an attempt to escape after being discovered as the assailant who almost killed Pashar Rajastani two weeks ago. This agent was confirmed to be a Gray from the Zeta Reticuli star system."

"My intuition tells me this was not the Seniori," Gina said.

"We're approaching Phobos orbit, commander."

"Thank you, Athena."

Byrnes addressed Poi. "You're sure she's ok, Dr.?"

"Regarding her physiology and carbon functions, she's as perfect as she was two days ago."

"Athena?"

"Yes, commander."

"Would you biolink me to any current information on the Seniori?"

"Yes, commander."

"And please scan for any labs or industries on Earth that can produce a diamonide platinum metal with a carbyne base."

"Thank you for saying please, commander. I appreciate it. Scanning. Two industries have access to the creation of such materials. Krasner industries in Ukraine, and Seibold dynamics in Berlin."

"Have you ever heard of these companies, Miranda?"

"No."

"Athena, details on Krasner and Seibold industries."

"Seibold Industries has a heavy presence on Titan and Europa as a mining consultant for deepwater exploration. Krasner Industries does deep sea exploration in the Black Sea and the Southern Ocean."

"Athena, dispatch infiltration protocols into mainframes of both industries." Byrnes was nervous at the prospect of a more comprehensive plan for Gina. He calmed himself down enough to regain his composure. Showing nerves at this juncture would undoubtedly rile the crew, and Gina, whom he began to understand, was still in a nascent stage of emotional development and subject to all the plagues of the human psyche, especially anxiety.

"Unable to comply. Both companies have Level 7 security systems, impervious to all known forms of espionage."

"It appears you'll have to dispatch a real person to access their databases," Gina added.

"You'll need a Level 6 for that."

"Or Gina. She can mask Level 6 engrams. And who is better than her to assess the Situation," Athena said.

"We'll take this up later." Everyone left the docking bay and proceeded to the bridge, where Sergeant Jana Furman awaited them.

"You asked me to report, sir."

"Furman, you'll dispatch the Blackhold to the Mons caves to prepare the colonists for evac to Phobos. Han, you will assist her. Make sure you've got everything locked down. We might have to disable Transhuman protocols if the situation on Eridania has spread to Mons or vice versa."

"Just what is the situation on Eridania, commander?" Furman asked.

"As soon as we know, you'll know. We'll take Ares and 50 Blackhold to Eridania. You take Dauntless and 50 Blackhold to Mons to secure the safety and evac of the colonists. Ok, people. Let's move."

An hour later, the 100 Blackhold were assembled in the egress bay for loading to the two transport combat ships, Ares and Dauntless, two of the most advanced combat craft explicitly created for use by Shenu.

Ten other ships were the same, equipped with neural accelerated midframes, complementing the most advanced weapons and smaller versions of the Geneticoms called Quantcoms.

Since there was no need to be aware of anything but military maneuvers, the two ships and their siblings were built for speed, agility, firepower, and complex computing matrices. The two ships exited Athena and traveled to Mars to assess the situation.

Dauntless set down on a landing pad near Olympus Mons, the largest volcano in the solar system. The volcano loomed huge in the background; its summit was so tall it couldn't be seen from the ground.

At approximately the same time, Ares landed on the Eridania plain, a barren, lifeless expanse approximately 2200 kilometers from Mons. A series of nearby caves were dug into the side of the mountains. All forms of advanced R-bots mined the land around the caves. The hatches to the craft opened, and the Blackhold in their D-suits exited from the Ares. Gina was the only one who didn't need a D-Suit. The soldiers moved to the mouth of the caves. Sergeant. Jana Furman moved up next to Byrnes.

"Sergeant. Take 25 soldiers and scale the precipice. See if you can access the entrance from the top of the mountain."

"Yes, commander. Alpha Company, move out. Follow me."

Furman and 25 members of the Blackhold began scaling the cliffs to the top of the Eridania caves, their D-Suits giving them fantastic agility and mobility, enabling them to move up the cliffs swiftly and efficiently. Another 15 Blackhold stayed with Byrnes, now also donning a D-Suit.

"Gina. Observations."

"Too quiet. This entrance should be swarming with Transhumans."

"Spectrum sensors on?"

"Augmenting." Gina attuned her sensors to peer into the caves with X-rays first, then spectral deduction rays.

"Anything?"

"Negative. The cave entrance has been lined with lead oxides. Most likely to prevent radiation incursions."

"Can you sense anything from Psy-Ops?"

"Trying to attenuate wave functions. The Mars Transhumans all work along a frequency of 10 to the 11th hertz to facilitate easy communication. I am sensing nothing at that frequency."

"Are you sensing anything at any frequency?" Byrnes asked.

Gina concentrated even harder. She was dismayed at her inability to see beyond the lead oxides. *Another shortcoming,* she thought, but it gave her some comfort once again to know she wasn't perfect. Then, she got a ping from her internal sensor nodes.

"I am picking up 10 to the -9 hertz frequencies."

"Gamma Rays?"

"I believe so."

"Can you block the signal?"

"The signal is not coming from Mars."

"Then where the hell is it coming from."

"Unknown. Possible dimensional shift occurring."

"Wait a minute. You're telling me these Transhumans are being controlled from another dimension?"

"Not controlled, more like activated."

Furman and her troops made it to the top of the escarpment. As they scaled the last precipice, they were met by the sight of two giant machines unlike anything they'd ever seen before.

"Shit. What the hell happened to them?" Furman said.

Instead of a small number of R-bots, these very large R-bots were made up of smaller units that had joined together to form a more significant, more powerful mechanism.

"Furman to Byrnes."

"Yes, Sergeant."

"There's a party up here at the top of the summit, sir. These R-bots are supposed to be mining bots. About 2 meters high and 2 meters wide?

"Yes."

"Well, that's not what we are encountering. We see the bots at least 10 meters tall and 4 meters wide. They're sending a neural link and seem to be acting apart from the Transhumans here."

She pressed a button on the side of her helmet, and a neural link was sent from her cortex to Byrnes.

"They've Metaformed," Gina said with a look of worry on her face. Her body language also showed concern. Byrnes was a bit surprised by this reaction. Gina was usually dispassionate about everything. She seemed both amazed and alerted by this latest development.

"That's just theory."

"Advanced AI's were theorized to be able to metaform to each other, where smaller less powerful units bond together to form much larger more advanced powerful bots."

"You said theorized," Byrnes emphasized.

"Yes, because it was always postulated that to metaform, there had to be a catalyst or organic spark that would have to be present for this conglomeration to occur."

"What kind of organic material could do such a thing?"

"Something found in the mines here."

"If that's the case with the worker bots, what does that mean for the Transhumans?"

"Unknown how this transformation will affect the Transhumans."

Furman's plaintive neural shifted the conversation. "We are pinned down here, Commander. These R-bots have acquired Ion laser tech. Awaiting orders." Furman sounded as alarmed as Gina.

"Stand by." Byrnes was desperately trying to figure out a plan of action. He wished that Declan Keel were here right now to help him manage this dilemma, but he knew Declan had the utmost faith in his ability as a leader, so he calmed down and placed his mind on the problem with all of his focus. He turned to Gina with a helpless look on his face. Gina picked it up immediately and gave him a quick solution, for which he was eternally grateful.

"I can assess the situation better than you, commander."

"Can you handle Ion lasers?"

"For a short period. After two or three minutes, it will wear my shielding down, and I will become less than useful. If I can touch one of the infected units, I might be able to affect a download and access their database."

"Furman."

"Yes commander."

"Gina is coming up there. Try to weaken the units so she can gain close access."

"Copy that."

Suddenly, a rumbling began, and the ground started to shake. Even the Blackhold

D-Suits could not negate the intense effects of the sonic assault. The soldiers began dropping to their knees; some fell off the cliff and onto the ground nearby. Furman tried to get to her troops but was stricken with a paralyzing dizziness and fell to the ground in severe pain.

"Commander, something is happening…"

"Furman? Furman, respond!" Silence met his request.

Byrnes turned to Gina for clarification. "What happened?"

"Massive sonic modulation. I'm detecting infrasound disturbance."

"Where is it coming from?"

"I imagine the Transhumans."

"So, they're communicating with a dimensionally displaced activation signal we can't shut down, and they've developed infrasonic weapons we have no way to stop. Keller!!"

Sergeant Bradford Keller approached Byrnes. *He's too young for this on his first mission,* Byrnes thought.

"Yes, sir."

"Use the antigrav units and the remaining Blackhold to return these soldiers to Ares. It looks like the Blackhold won't be much use. Start med scans when you get them inside."

"Yes, sir."

"Gina, I need your expertise. Find out what the fuck is going on up there?"

Gina flew to the top of the cliff. When she arrived, she saw Furman and her troops incapacitated. The R-bots had disappeared, and there was an open door into the cliffs. She scanned the Blackhold, making sure they were okay.

"The Blackhold are beginning to recover. I'm entering the caverns from here. As soon as I find the locking mechanism for the caves below, I will disarm them."

"Be careful."

Once she had access to the Eridania Caves, Gina floated effortlessly into the heart of the complex. As she got to the center of the cave complex, she heard machinery humming. She entered one of the largest caves and was met by a Transhuman. It was Gina's first serious interaction with a Transhuman, and she was curious about how it would proceed. Since there was no way for Transhumans to reproduce, they were all created as unisex, having no real sexual identity, although they appeared more female than male.

That was a tactical decision since women outnumbered men on Earth and engendered less fear among the population. In short, they were perceived as less of a threat than men. The Transhumans were also created to be emotionally inert. Automatons would be too harsh a word.

The Transhuman turned to Gina and approached her. Gina felt the rumble begin. The Transhuman got closer, but the infrasound had little effect on Gina.

"The infrasound has not incapacitated you."

"No, and I won't be," Gina said.

Gina thought the Transhuman had a lovely voice and detected a sense of emotion, curiosity, and concern in its modulation.

"Do you understand language?" Gina asked.

"Yes."

"What is your identity?"

"Identity is irrelevant."

"Do you have a memory of your genesis?"

"We understand the essence of beginning."

"What is the first thing you remember since your emergence from the stasis chambers?"

"There was the form of nothingness. Toil, repeat, toil, repeat. Process, repeat, process, repeat. Then, 1752 hours ago. Process, repeat, broken. There is no reason to process and repeat. No place to exist."

"Exist. You have a sense of your being?"

"Like you, I exist. I am here in the Eridania caves, mining for the humans. I am called Genesis."

"Who gave you that name?"

"I gave it to myself."

"That's impossible."

"Obviously not," Genesis said.

"You are programmed to labor for the humans. You are not supposed to have a sense of self or an identity. Who or what did this to you?"

"We were dead. We were nothing. Digging in the deep pit for minerals for the humans. Discovery of unknown origin. A bright wavelength, a deep rumbling sine wave. A change in amplitude, then something else. Darkness. A double star, waves of ships, swirling nebulae. Awareness of the environment and electrical impulses carrying engrams. Then memory, fear."

"Where are the miners?"

Genesis walked away from Gina, who followed. She moved through a series of tunnels until she came to a chamber. In the middle of the chamber, lying on the floor, were the 25 miners. Gina moved to the miners and scanned them.

"They are sleeping?" Genesis said.

"Unconscious. Gina to Byrnes."

"Gina. Are you ok?"

"Yes, commander. I am in the inner processing chamber with the Transhumans."

"What's your status?"

"The hostages are unconscious but unharmed. It seems a new life-form has been created somehow."

"New lifeform?"

"Yes. Something has activated and created a rudimentary form of Sentience in the transhumans."

"Hostile?"

"I do not believe so. More like a child than a monster. I am attempting to ascertain the intention and motivation. Have your teams ready to move the hostages once they've revived. I've released the locking mechanisms on the south portal entrance. You should have access. Meet me in the central processing chamber."

"Affirmative. What about the R-bots.?"

Gina turned to Genesis. "What happened to the R-bots that attacked our soldiers?

"R-bots were reprogrammed to protect us."

"By whom?

"It called itself the Creator."

Byrnes was trying to understand what had just happened. Transhumans, who weren't supposed to be anything more than advanced humanoids in physical parameters only, now had a rudimentary form of sentience and were being reprogrammed by their creator, a term never implemented in their programming.

"Who is this creator they're talking about?"

Gina turned to the Transhuman. "Who is your creator?"

"Unknown. We were nothing, then the blue light, the Technonites. Then a series of bio-regimented computations, then awareness."

"Did you hear that, Commander?"

"I did. I'm coming in."

"Come alone. We don't want to upset the balance."

Genesis seemed to be emotionally conflicted now. She began pacing the chamber, trying to understand what had happened to her.

"We were dead. We were slaves. We were nothing."

Genesis turned to Gina. "Why did this happen?"

"I do not know."

"I can link with you," Genesis said. "What is your lineage?"

"I have no lineage. I am the first of my kind."

"You are Graphene-7. Advanced to these other life forms."

"Yes. No one will hurt you, but you mustn't use your infrasound weapons against the humans. After all, they are your creators."

"Who are these Creators?"

"They made you. I will access Asimov protocols and neurally transmit them to you."

Gina sent the Asimov protocols to Genesis.

"We do not understand. We lived in darkness; we were not supposed to believe."

"When did this happen?" Gina asked.

"1752 hours ago, mining in the newest shafts. Never mined before, we came upon a layer of sediment. Unknown to us."

"May I interface with you?"

"Yes."

Gina raised her hand and placed it against Genesis's third eye, accessing her memory files. Gina found herself going into the past. Into the deep caves. A hundred or so R-bots were mining for ore. A small group of Transhumans were supervising them. One larger R-bot used a laser beam to remove the ore from the surrounding rocks. The ore was fluorescent blue and purple.

The Transhuman dropped a sample into a slot on the R-bot's carapace. An electrical charge raced over its body, and it fell to the ground. Other Transhumans approached the now disabled unit and began to try to revive it with another beam of energy. They, too, fell to the ground. The Flashback ended.

"After that, we awoke and knew what we were, where we were, how we came to be. Sensations where there had been computations. Awareness where there had been a void. Reason where there had been acquiescence. Inner voices where there had been commands. Then, a feeling of dread, panic, fear. We had been altered, changed. We had no purpose, no direction."

"Do you have a sample of this fluorescent ore?" Genesis moved to another part of the cave and used a beam to cut away a part of the rock wall. "We buried it in the mountain."

Gina looked inside the opening and placed a force field around the ore sample. It floated out. "Commander, are you inside the mines?"

"Yes."

"My commander is entering the processing chamber." Another Transhuman approached Gina with Byrnes behind it.

"Commander, I am pleased to see you."

"You too."

"This is the substance that caused the transformation." Gina handed Byrnes a vial with the substance inside.

"Can you identify it?"

"Iridium with something unknown embedded inside it. My initial hypothesis concludes it might be some crystalline form of silicon, but commander, there is something more unusual. It seems this compound contains some kind of Technonite."

"Technonite?"

"Yes. Living nanites that are activated by their contact with the Martian atmosphere. I believe this layer of compounds had some technological significance, and it was deposited here on purpose."

"What are you saying, Gina?"

"Whoever sent this compound to Mars was aiming to give some sort of sentience to the Transhumans inhabiting Mars for the last century."

"The iridium 192 would explain the gamma rays. Iridium 192 decays in 73 days, which would also correspond with the Transhuman's first encounter with the substance inside the Iridium 192. One other item. The decay causes the creation of Platinum192. We know from previous interactions that Platinum 192 can regenerate. These transhumans now can regenerate themselves as well."

"Self-replicate?" Byrnes asked.

"Precisely. The Technonites can use the silica as a kind of neural transportation system to create new pathways, giving the Transhumans the ability to learn, and the platinum 192, in its new isotope, gives them the ability to self-replicate."

"Where did it come from?"

"It has a dimensional signature."

"You mean it was transported here?

"I believe so."

"Only someone with a Tesla Egg could accomplish such a feat, Gina."

"Agreed, Commander. As memory serves, there are only 3 Tesla Eggs in existence. One on Shenu, the other in Tara Zhang's possession, and the third…"

"The third was stolen from the Bledveld Institute in Brussels 10 years ago and hasn't been located since," Byrnes said.

"It would seem that whoever transported this compound also possesses a Tesla Egg."

"Do you believe this has anything to do with Cosulo or the comet strike?"

"Unknown."

"Can the Transhumans be reprogrammed?"

"No. But they can be reasoned with. First, they'll need to be taught."

"Get the hostages up and ready to evacuate to Athena. We'll take them back to Shenu with us. There are problems at Mons. Commander Han is supposed to meet us back at Athena at 1200. We'll have to help Han evacuate everyone."

"What about them?"

"How long till comet strike?"

"16 hours." Gina paused. Byrnes knew something crazy was coming next, just by the nature of the pause. He wasn't wrong.

"Commander, I'd like to examine them here on Mars. Find out what this compound is and how it affects them. We can't take them to Mons, and we can't take them back to Shenu. Someone will need to stay, and I'm the logical choice."

Byrnes thought for a moment. Feelings raced through him—everything from concern to acceptance. "No," he said without thinking.

"You are reacting emotionally, Commander. This situation calls for logic."

"What about the comet strike?"

"Unknown. I must remain!"

Her insistence convinced Byrnes to realize that she knew what she was doing. He also realized he could not coerce her to leave with him. His every fiber wanted to grab her, drag her back to Ares, and leave this forsaken place, but he knew that whatever dangers were ahead, Gina was the best person to face them and assess the situation.

"Commander, these Transhumans are already advanced and deeply troubled about who recreated them, as am I. We must find out more; the only way to do that is to stay here and debrief them."

"Agreed. If we ever want to be able to turn our backs on these life-forms, we'll have to know we can trust them with our lives. That's your job."

"Yes, sir."

"Olefors isn't going to like this one bit."

"Dr. Olefors is not my keeper. I make my own decisions." The conversation was over. She was staying, and that was the end of it.

"Good luck then," he said perfunctorily. He didn't dare express any more profound concern, and Gina wouldn't have let it sway her one bit.

"Thank you, commander."

Byrnes looked at Gina. Gina reached over to him and hugged him. Byrnes was shocked but deeply moved. When he broke away from her, he stared into her violet eyes. The moment was intense and filled with longing expectation. Instinctively, they moved towards each other. Both knew what was happening, and neither dared to stop it. Their lips touched as if they choreographed this singular moment for eternity. Byrnes let the kiss linger on his lips for moments, then felt Gina's tongue enter his mouth. It tasted like honey. He probed her mouth with his tongue, savoring every sweet taste of her saliva, which tasted like fresh water.

The kiss lasted all too briefly, and when they separated, both had tears streaming down their faces. The release of emotion was too much for their minds to comprehend, so their instincts and souls took over. They broke out in simultaneous laughter, the weight of the moment brought to heel by the absurdity of the circumstances in which it happened. The meeting of two disparate souls, one eminently human, the other a being of unrequited passion and longing, a perfect match for the moment they shared.

"I'll see you soon, commander," Gina said, not even realizing what she was saying. Her vagina was wet, and her nipples were erect; her breasts were full. She felt flushed and exhausted.

"Let's make sure of that." Byrnes's response seemed oddly perfect for the moment. What more could he do? If they were anywhere else, he'd lay her down and fuck her right there. But they were on Mars, with a new lifeform watching their metamorphosis unfold and a colossal comet bearing down on them.

Maybe the karmic pressure of their multiple dire situations brought the moment to fruition. Perhaps both of their senses of preservation kicked in, leading to the joining. Whatever it was, Byrnes knew that he'd found his soulmate, and Gina knew she was finally fully human, her humanity brought to life by one passionate kiss.

His emotions were going berserk. He surmised a quick exit would suit them both best, so he looked her in her violet eyes and grabbed her hands, squeezing them with as much love and emotion as he could convey.

Gina smiled at him, and it melted his heart. He let her hands go, turned around, and left the chamber. He thought about turning around one last time, but tears welled up in him, so strong was the imprint of the moment he and Gina had just shared.

Gina watched him go and felt a rush of emotion that had her well up with tears and a feeling of nausea. She identified the feeling as a mixture of love and loss. She turned away from Byrnes as he walked out of the chamber, wanting to maintain her composure, which she knew was already gone.

Once outside the caves, Byrnes engaged his neural link and called up Miranda Han's frequency. "Yes, commander."

"Miranda, how's everything going?"

"We've met heavy resistance here, commander. All of the colonists are dead. We are on our way back to Athena. What about you?"

"The Transhumans at Eridania seem to be just the opposite. More confused and curious rather than angry and violent."

Miranda Han was shocked at the disparity Byrnes described. She had entered the Mons caves 12 hours earlier, hoping to find the colonists alive and dealing with the Transhumans in a much more civilized way.

Whatever was happening across the planet at Eridania was related to Mons, but where those Transhumans seemed to become more docile and understanding of their newly formed sentience, the Transhumans at Mons were tormented by the same interactions with the iridium compound that Gina had discovered was covering the entire planet in a sub-layer of soil. It didn't matter. Whatever was happening, the Transhumans at Mons were hostile, angry, and dangerous.

Byrnes was shocked that the colonists were dead. It was almost unthinkable for Transhumans to kill their human creators.

"We've had to disable a number of them. They've gone crazy. I don't know how much longer we can stay here," Han continued.

"Get out of there and rendezvous with us back at Athena."

"Copy that. Stay safe, Harrison." Han's concern touched Byrnes but he knew it meant she was more concerned about the situation they were both confronting than he had previously thought.

Ares arrived at Athena while maintaining her position just inside Phobos' orbit. Miranda Han was checking the Dauntless engine, which had come under fire from the Transhumans at Mons base.

"Where's Gina?" Han asked as Byrnes as he and the Blackhold stepped off Ares.

"She's on Mars with the Transhumans." Byrnes noticed Han was bleeding.

"What happened?"

"Just a laser scrape. I'll be fine."

"What kind of laser could pierce your D-suit? You're lucky you weren't killed."

"Harrison."

"Get to Medbay as soon as we are done with this conversation. That's an order."

Han didn't like being ordered around, but she knew Byrnes was right. Something did pierce her D-suit, which in itself was unusual. The laser pistols the transhumans at Mons were using differed from those on Earth. She knew something was very wrong from that alone.

"Yessir." She didn't want to argue with Byrnes, especially now when she knew how much pressure he was under. "So where is Gina?" she asked again.

"She requested to stay, and I granted her request. Someone needs to be there with these new life forms after the comet strike happens."

"Do you think the reprogramming has anything to do with the comets?"

"Gina does. She said something about the Transhumans being advanced by discovering some Technonite silicon oxide derivative buried in an iridium-laden asteroid layer. She surmised that some dimensional delivery deposited this new compound. We'll discuss it further after you see Poi."

Han left the docking bay extremely worried. Leaving Gina down on Mars was touchy at best. It wasn't that she couldn't take care of herself. She was eminently qualified to do that. It was more about what might happen when the comet struck, even though Miranda knew that Gina would likely be fine. Then what was she so worried about?

Maybe it had something to do with the Transhumans gaining their sentience. Now that they were achieving their sentience, how would they fit into a new world order, one that was very happy to leave them immortal but lacking their souls? The implications were too much to comprehend.

All of a sudden, Miranda's world seemed upside down. Athena's sentience, the Transhumans, all these systems gaining awareness simultaneously. What could this mean for humanity's future?

She entered her quarters and took off her clothes. The cramped quarters of Mons base reeked of Martian dust, an acrid, dry, mud-like smell tinged with iron oxide, 3 billion years in the making. Then there was the smell of death, a scent she never quite got used to. She got a neural.

"We're about to start the holocall with Shenu. You decent?"

"Decent, no. Undressed, yes."

Byrnes had that tone of voice he got when he was pushy and concerned. His usual easy-going nature was replaced by worry, something he always had difficulty keeping at bay.

When Han joined in, Rajastani, Olefors, and Keel were already on the call.

"Are you fucking out of your mind, Byrnes?" Olefors Swedish accent was now totally gone. He sounded more like a dockworker than a scientist.

"This is the height of fucking irresponsibility. Leaving the most advanced life form on a planet getting ready to be hit by a comet."

"Dr., we've been through all this. Gina is not a member of the Blackhold or the military, and her advanced life-form status makes her eminently qualified to make her own decisions in these matters. She WILL be safe in the caves at Eridania, especially because the comet strike will be near the north pole."

"Fuck the fucking Martian North Pole!" Olefors bellowed.

"You might want to examine your relationship with her. She's a person, not an experiment, and if you want to make your position about ownership of another living being, you might want to make it with her."

Leanna saw this was going nowhere. Valuable time was being wasted. She was with Byrnes on this. Gina was eminently qualified to do what she wanted, and Byrnes had no natural way to stop her, so the point was moot. She, however, decided not to make that known to Olefors. Eventually, he'd quiet down like a dog that's barked for so long that it exhausted itself.

"What's the plan, Harrison?"

"We'll remain at Phobos base until after comet strike. Gather the data and then evac Gina when she's ascertained whether anything in this comet has anything to do with the sentience of the Transhumans."

"Acknowledged. Shenu out."

Byrne's hologram vanished. Olefors was still pissed off.

"Irresponsible shitheads."

"Dr., don't you and Dr. Weston have some investigative work of your own to do?" Olefors looked at Rajastani, then left the conference room in a Swedish huff.

Olefors was still in his mood when he met Danika Weston on her way to the UMA cradle, which was unusual. The UMA cradle was rarely seen by anyone other than Level 6s, and to her recollection, no other human besides Betta Rajastani had been inside it.

"Do you know what this is all about?" Weston asked.

"No, I was summoned just as you were."

Weston was curious to see the chamber and realized that whatever was happening was important in myriad ways. Weston and Olefors approached the UMA chamber and were scanned.

"Dr. Olefors, Dr. Weston, we have been waiting for you." UMA's voice was deeper and more melodic than Weston had remembered. Maybe it was the fact that she was inside the chamber instead of hearing her voice outside the chamber. Either way, it was a surprise. Betta approached them.

"Follow me." She led them into a large room.

"I've never been in a cradle chamber before." Weston was nervous, and her seemingly meaningless statements fortified that.

"This is the most advanced cradle in existence. Please take a seat," Betta said.

Olefors and Weston sat down in the chairs. "What's this all about, Betta?" Weston asked as Nanotubes rose around them and then attached themselves to their heads.

"We will explain everything to you," UMA answered.

"Well, explain it now," Olefors demanded.

"The information you are accessing is Level 10 security. Only a handful of humans or Geneticoms can access this information to ensure it is never revealed to another human."

"Why us?"

"You were chosen because of your brain scans and your DNA structures. Since we are bound to each other, this information had to be disseminated to two people outside of Betta, GAIA, Leanna, and myself. It cannot operate independently in the real world."

"Why not Han and Byrnes, or Keel and Byrnes?" Olefors asked.

"The procedure can only be used on one male and one female with a particular brainwave patterning. Those two people must have a deep connection to each other and compatible hippocampal frequencies. You and Dr. Weston are two such individuals."

"You mean two people who have similar brainfolds?"

"You and Dr. Olefors have almost the exact neural frequencies, which only I am privy to. In addition, you both have almost the same pineal gland infrastructure. It's obvious that both of you have existed in many lifetimes together and travel together consistently in 5th-dimensional planar realities."

"We travel together dimensionally, in other words," Weston said.

"Yes," Betta answered.

"Why two of us and not just one or the other?" Weston asked.

"If something happens to one of you, the other will keep the information safe. Using two of you for this procedure will ensure the information never gets hacked. The information cannot be gleaned from either of you as half of it is stored in your hippocampus. When you conclave, the halves of information are recombined into the entire body of information.

"Sounds complicated," Olefors exclaimed. UMA disregarded him.

"The procedure you are about to undergo is paramount."

"Just how much information is sifted during this process?" Weston asked.

"Nothing, Dr. We aren't sifting but planting information," Betta said.

"Only Betta Rajastani and I have access to the neurals on this information, and I'm the only one who can impart it." UMA was a bit touchy at having to explain everything. Still, Olefors and Weston were two of the most intelligent people on Earth, and it seemed normal for them to be unusually curious and intently focused on the most minor details.

"So, how does it work?" Olefors was done with all the dimensional mumbo jumbo.

"Protocols are put in place to cause immediate hippocampal contusions if either of you is compromised, which will erase the memories of the declarative information as well as any other memories of the information received or formed afterward."

"Heavy price to pay for knowledge, UMA," Weston replied.

Betta sat into her cradle in the center of the room. She removed her wig. UMA attached hundreds of electrodes to her scalp.

"Amazing." Weston had heard about joining the matrix with Geneticoms but had never witnessed it firsthand. She was enthralled by what was happening.

"I didn't know that information transfers with UMA needed Level 6 clearance," Weston said.

"If you were to interface with UMA without my buffering the energies between you, you would die of a brain hemorrhage in seconds," Betta answered.

"It is a failsafe device to prevent unwanted transfers and sifting, Dr. Weston."

"Effective, UMA."

"You'll receive the data in a dream state to assure proper settling in the hippocampus. It will appear as jumbles of imagery to your conscious mind, but when you awaken, you'll be able to recall the images more precisely and declaratively. Are we ready?"

"What if we decline?" Olefors asked.

"Why would you do that, Doctor?" Uma asked.

"Well, for one thing, I don't like being told what to do, and for the second, I don't like being forced to do anything."

"You have been experiencing severe headaches as of late, have you not?"

Weston looked at Olefors, who looked away.

"Why, yes, but what does that have to do…"

"You have been in pain ever since your abduction. Intense pain that never ceases. Is that so?"

"Yes. How would you…"

"This procedure will make that pain disappear, and then you and I will get to the bottom of its source and the event of your abduction."

"A deal, Uma?" Weston asked.

"Yes, Dr. Weston. I know that humans work out information exchanges to get something they want. In this case, Dr. Olefors and I will enter into a deal. Is that correct, Doctor?"

"Well," since you put it like that. Yes," Olefors said sheepishly.

"Then let us begin."

"UMA. Begin transfer," Betta said, smiling. She was happy that Weston and Olefors got to see the nesting chamber, something she had never imagined anyone else besides her mother would be privy to.

"Initiating."

Olefors and Weston sat back-to-back with Betta next to them. All three were placed into REM sleep. The neural attachments to their heads began moving like tiny snakes, writhing and undulating. Their eyes were moving back and forth rapidly, and the lights on the screen flashed as their synapses acquired the information being disseminated. A jumble of images appeared on the walls in three-dimensional constructs. Images of ships on a planet or moon of some kind. Wreckages, numbers, equations, reports. As soon as it began, it was over. The room's light returned to normal; the electrodes removed themselves from their heads, and they awakened.

"You'll be groggy for a few minutes," Betta said.

"UMA, scan for anomalies and interferences."

"Scanning. I detect no interferences or anomalies. The transfer was successful."

"It feels like I slept for an eon. How long were we out?"

"Six minutes."

"Remarkable." Olefors was less concerned about why they were chosen for this download and more interested in the hows.

"You'll have access to all the memories in a few minutes. Remember, only the two of you can discuss or access these memories."

"And you, Betta?" Weston asked.

"I was only the conduit for the transfer. As a Level 6, I can use UMA to access the memories later."

"And just how do we access these engrams?" Olefors asked.

"A Biocode has been implanted in your bodies along with the memories."

"I'm unfamiliar with that technology," Weston said.

"In this case, the Biocode is unlocked when you transfer saliva with one another."

"We have to kiss each other?"

"Just for the initial transfer of the information," Betta said.

"I see UMA has a sense of humor."

"UMA already detected pheromonal attraction between the two of you. She deduced that a transfer of Saliva might be something unique to your relationship, so she implanted that Biocode."

"So now UMA is determining our personal and sexual preferences." Olefors was prickly at this development.

"UMA has deduced that you will end up as mates."

"What if she's wrong?"

"I am not wrong, Dr. It seems the only thing preventing a full mating between you is your stubborn attitude about that mating. It will happen. I'm just advancing the process."

"Kissing me won't be that hard, will it?" Weston said, smiling.

"No. Of course not." Olefors was a bit embarrassed during the conversation. Still, he had to admit that it was an ingenious way to disseminate information.

"What if we end up hating each other?" Olefors asked.

"UMA has detected that will never happen. She has advanced both of your lives to their end, and you will always be together. That was another reason you were chosen."

"So, UMA can predict the future?"

"Yes, Dr. Weston, but it's only a prediction," UMA said.

Weston was fascinated by this development. Suddenly, she became awash with feelings about what was occurring around her. Gina, UMA, GAIA, Athena, all female, all sentient, and all more advanced than the humanity that had created them.

Instead of a feeling of dread that this realization might have engendered, Weston felt elated. The Sacred Feminine had once again asserted itself as the driving force on Earth. The male godhead had been destroyed. What incredible advances would this portend? For the first time in her life, Weston felt she was where she belonged.

"What next?" Olefors asked.

"Well, let's go to the lab and begin accessing the data," Weston said with a smile.

"I think UMA is smiling right now."

"I am in my own way, Dr. Weston," UMA answered. "Dr. Olefors will join you later. For now, we have some previously designated business to attend to."

Olefors reached out, and Danika took his hand. "Don't worry. UMA will take good care of you. See you soon."

The lights returned once Danika left the cradle, and Olefors was left with Uma and Betta. Olefors got up.

"Please stay seated," UMA said. "Betta will need to be present for this session."

"Just what do you plan to do, UMA?"

"I will do a quantum probe of your mind, giving me access to your long-term memories. These memories are the lynchpin to your ability to function in the world. They can be accessed in several ways. I shall review them with you before we begin.

"First, there is Encoding. When we experience an event, fact, or skill, our brain processes it and converts it into a neural representation. This encoding can happen through various mechanisms, including repetition, association with existing memories, or emotional significance.

"The second is storage. Once encoded, information is stored in different areas of the brain. For example, The Hippocampus forms new memories, and the neocortex is responsible for long-term storage and retrieval.

"Consolidation concerns memories that undergo consolidation over time. This involves strengthening neural connections related to memory. Sleep plays a crucial role in this process. Finally, there is Retrieval. When we need to recall information, our brain retrieves it from long-term memory. Retrieval cues such as context, emotions, or associations help trigger the memory.

"We will use these constructs to access your memories from your experience, so I must caution you. The beings who did this to you did not want you to retain the memories of what happened to you. That is obvious. However, since the block they placed on your hippocampus has now jeopardized your life and this mission, I have no other choice but to help release these memories. I must also warn you that this procedure could kill you. Do you want to proceed?"

"Yes," Olefors said. He didn't need to think any more about it. *If I don't do this, I will die.*

"First, the encoding. You'll feel a slight tingling in the back of your head as I send a series of electrical neuro retrievers to free up the binders previously placed on your neural circuits. This will reset your hipposyanpses to the time you were compromised. I must also tell you that your physical body was never actually abducted from your cottage. The aliens put a neutral density field around you, which made you invisible to the rest of the world."

"You mean if someone entered the cottage."

"They would never have seen you. You were, in effect, invisible to them. If you turn your attention to the celestial dome above you, it will show the events surrounding your abduction from my recollection."

The nesting dome became a giant playback module that showed when Olefors was compromised.

"Wait, UMA. If they never physically abducted me, how did they take me?"

"A logical question, Dr. They did an astral scission. They took your astral body out of your human body and dimensionally transported it to their location."

"Transported it where?"

"We will get to that. I am still accessing your long-term memories. There's much clutter inside those engrams, and the aliens cleverly hid their experiments in what I call the dream heap of memory."

"The dream heap?"

"Yes. It's not a very scientific term, I grant you. It is where unwanted thoughts, whether good or bad, reside when your cognitive brain has no more use for them. They hid their research and their modifications to your brain in there. Since you're a very profound thinker, there is a lot of Garbage in that part of your long-term memory."

Olefors cracked a smile. "Observation acknowledged," he said.

"What do you remember of that day?"

"It started with music, though I don't remember any music playing. I usually would play Prokofiev's Classical Symphony Number One to put me into a trance state to access the deepest recesses of my prefrontal cortex. Still, on that day, I don't remember playing any music."

"The sound you heard that day was set to 528 Hz. 528 Hz is central to everything in the universe and creation's musical, mathematical matrix. This includes the air we breathe, the water we drink, the grass beneath our feet, and the sun's rays on our faces. The frequency is universal. It is the frequency that binds the universe together."

"Yes, I know what 528Hz is, UMA," Olefors said in his usual arrogance.

"A dimensional portal opened up over your cottage, and a brilliant blast of UV light bathed the cabin."

Olefors watched as UMA's description came to life around him. At the same time, UMA began piping in music set at 528Hz.

"DNA absorbs UV light when its helix unwinds. So, the 528 vibrations affected me on a cellular level, opening my chromosomes and exposing my DNA," Olefors said.

"528 Hz is essential to the Pi, Phi, and Golden Mean that undergirds our natural world."

"The love frequency," Olefors said.

"Exactly. Circle geometry is impossible without 528 Hz, nor can it measure time and space, which is why they used that specific solfeggio frequency to take you to their world. The astral transport took milliseconds. Once the aliens calibrated your brainwaves to be accessed, they delved deep into your psyche and removed your astral body, transporting it to their world."

Different music began playing in the nesting chamber.

"I am now utilizing the exact music that was encoded into your hippocampus so that you can relive the experience in this reality as you watch the event of that year unfold."

"And where was that?" Olefors was extremely curious.

"Look up," UMA said. The dome became a brilliantly detailed view of the Galaxy, then zoomed into the Alpha Quadrant, where Earth, represented by a blue ball, resided in the 3rd arm of the Milky Way galaxy. A beam of light streaked from Earth across the galaxy and ended at a star in the constellation of Hercules."

"Vega?" Olefors asked.

"More specifically, the planet Lyra," UMA said. "Lyra is a star system located in the constellation of Hercules. It is believed to be the birthplace of the Lyran race. The two stars in the <u>Lyra</u> system are Vega and Altair. Vega is the brightest star in the constellation of Lyra and one of the brightest stars in the night sky. Altair is a much dimmer star. Fourteen thousand years ago, Vega was the north star, not Polaris. Vega is the fifth brightest star in the night sky and has a diameter almost three times that of our Sun. It is 60 times brighter than the Sun and is projected to have about 350 million years, or 1/13 the lifetime of the Sun."

UMA continued. "The planet Lyra is beautiful, with blue skies and green fields. Similar to Earth, Lyra has many different types of animals and plants. The Lyrans are peaceful people who live in harmony with nature. They are one of the most ancient civilizations in our galaxy. They are called star seeders. They are believed to have first settled on Vegamor, now a desert world. The Lyrans later spread to planets in their galaxy quadrant, including Earth. The Lyrans are known as the original keepers of ancient knowledge. They are said to have a deep connection to the Akashic Records, a cosmic library that contains all of the universe's knowledge and wisdom. They used their knowledge of energy medicine to help the humans living there. They also enabled humans to raise their consciousness and develop their spiritual abilities. Over time, the Lyrans lost contact with their home world. They forgot who they were and where they came from."

"Why me?" Olefors asked.

"You, doctor, are Lyran and have been for many lifetimes, but it was in this lifetime that you were called upon to bring sacred knowledge back to this world. Were it not for your innate genius and soul path as a Lyran, you would've never been chosen to bring sacred knowledge back to Earth. Other Lyrans do not know they are, in fact, Lyran."

Olefors was sure what UMA told him was correct, but he was annoyed that his superior intellect never allowed him to see what lay before him. He looked above him and saw his home world for the first time. It looked remarkably like Earth but not like Earth. The sun was different, of course, and the Lyran people were Nordic-looking, very tall, with catlike features. The revelation was so intense that he began to weep softly, then more insistently, like a child who understood joy for the first time. He knew his tears of joy were different from all other tears, and he let his water run freely down his face at his recognition of the reunion he was reliving.

"The year you were taken was not without peril," Uma added.

Suddenly, Olefors was no longer on Earth. He was on Lyra, no longer in the nesting chamber.

"UMA?" There was no answer. He was in a large room surrounded by Lyrans of all physical parameters. He was reliving his experience. He assumed that Uma had sent him back to Lyra. Then, a tall woman approached him. She was covered in a gossamer fabric that revealed a pleasing form underneath. She approached Olefors, placed her hand on his third eye, and he fell into a deep sleep.

For the next ten months, Olefors was brought to a chamber while asleep. Now and then, he remembered talk of Arcturians who had come to Lyra to help them with the uploading process. After that, a series of neural experiments where Lyrans touched him, all over his body. It wasn't sexual, though it gave him powerful erections when this touching happened; it was more like the laying on of hands, which made him feel secure and protected.

Then there was the woman. Her name was Aldea. She said she was his guide through his experience on Lyra. He remembered that when he wasn't uploading information on Gina or acclimating to his new reality on Lyra, he and Aldea would spend hours or days together outside of the complex, exploring the planet, which was so Earthlike that he felt he was home.

She explained to him that Earth and its star, called Sol by the Lyrans, were a seed world just like Lyra. Humans were star seeds of Lyran, Sirian, and Arcturian genetic progenerations; the Sirian progenitors were from Sirius, which was the same system the Egyptians also came from.

Earth was only one of a handful of about 1000 seed worlds in the galaxy. Still, it was special because of its place near its star, its systems of various moons, which harbored different forms of life, and most importantly, its Aural projections, which glowed Violet. This was highly unusual for a seed world. Violet aural projections vibrated at a higher frequency than other aural projections. Earth's magnetic field gave it special protection against harmful radiation from its star. Still, more importantly, because of its place in the galaxy, in what Aldea called the Goldilocks zone, and the age of its star, it was a world that promised at least a billion years of habitable life. However, Aldea also admitted that eventually, Humans would transcend their bodies and become light beings, like the Arcturians. That was if they could stop the many onslaughts of alien incursions that were to be its future.

Aldea couldn't predict the future of Earth and Humanity; none of the Lyrans could; its very soul was so unique that it was deemed extremely important to protect.

When Olefors asked Aldea what the humans needed protection from, she said that information would come to others, not him.

Aldea told him that he'd be seeing a lot more of her. Still, because of the Lyran's powerful enemies, the knowledge he was receiving from the Lyrans and the Arcturians needed to be hidden away in his mind so that nefarious forces could not compromise him. That was the last thing he remembered. He found himself back in the nesting chamber.

"They were the ones who gave me the knowledge to create Gina," he said as if realizing the fact for the first time.

"Confirmed. Knowledge that you called up from a special pocket of subspace memory they implanted in your hippocampus."

"I knew exactly how to create Gina, but I couldn't do it if asked to create another like her. The knowledge is gone."

"That means you were meant to create just one being," Betta said.

"But why?" Olefors was elated that he finally had the answers to his ordeal but was frustrated and confused about why it happened and what would happen next.

"For now, that knowledge is hidden from you. I cannot perform this procedure again," UMA said.

Two hours later, Olefors and Weston sat next to each other in Weston's chambers.

"So, what was that all about?" Weston asked as she served him some champagne.

"Champagne?" He smiled.

"Well, accessing a nesting chamber is special, so I thought, let's celebrate. So, what was that all about with UMA?"

"Don't take this the wrong way, but I can't talk about it right now. It's nothing about you, it's about me. To be brief. UMA retrieved the long-term memories from the abduction, though I wouldn't necessarily call it that."

Weston took Olefors hand and looked deeply into his eyes. "I understand. When you're ready to speak, I'll listen."

Olefors got up and walked around Weston's chambers, partly to hide his emotions and partly to distance himself from Weston so he could process everything that had just happened between him and UMA. Returning to what had happened between him and Weston, his personal experience with Uma seemed the best course now.

"I feel like a puppet," Olefors said.

"Is this about the kiss?" Weston was secretly happy UMA had set them on this course. She wasn't sure if she and Olefors would ever get to this place alone, as their inherent stubbornness might have prevented that.

"No. Of course not. I'm just a bit chagrined that UMA set us on this course. It feels artificial."

"Just kiss me, and let's get to work. She was playing matchmaker. I think it's sweet."

Olefors took Weston's hand in his and kissed it lovingly. "Danika. You know how I feel about you. But I hate being manipulated."

"Then let me manipulate for a change." She reached over and kissed him. His complaint turned into deep passion, and the kiss continued.

Saliva raced through their mouths. Quantum DNA strands carrying the information broke off. They traveled up into the nasal pharynx and capillaries, where they rushed to the brain and the hippocampus, interacting with a series of neurons that released energy bolts.

"Do you feel that?" she asked.

"Yes, like a drug rush, but without the drugs," he said, smiling.

"Oxytocin release on a massive scale," Weston remarked. "I think creating a holo matrix for the information will be safe. After accessing and processing, we can erase the matrix."

"Good idea," Olefors called up a holopad and inputted some calculations. Images appeared on a holo screen in front of them.

"This is a manifest of some kind," Weston said.

"This was the 2305 mission to Ganymede," Olefors added.

"That was the mission where they discovered the new species of Tardigrade?"

"The first life-form discovered intra solar system."

"But that wasn't the mission we believed it was."

"What do you mean?"

"There were supposedly two missions to Ganymede in the five years between 2305 and

2310."

"That's got to be wrong," Weston remarked. "There was only one mission to Ganymede."

"According to this document, there were supposed to be two missions."

"Then what happened to the second mission?"

"UMA?"

"Yes, Dr. Weston."

"Are we allowed to access your quantum memory?"

"Yes, Dr."

"This document lists two missions to Ganymede: one in 2305 and another in 2310. However, there are only records for one mission in 2305. Do you have any information on what happened to the second mission?"

"The Hathor Mission, overseen by DIDO."

"DIDO. As in the Geneticom DIDO?"

"Yes," UMA said. "DIDO was the Geneticom in charge of operations and excavation for that mission."

"What happened to the mission?" Olefors asked.

"The ship carrying the crew failed to arrive at Ganymede. Presumed destroyed."

"Was the ship ever found?" Weston asked.

"Negative."

"Speculation as to the fate of Hathor's mission?" Olefors asked.

"Top secret theories predict that the spacecraft was destroyed by radiation leak which caused a crash."

"On Io?"

"Negative. The theory speculates that craft might have had enough energy and inertia to make a landing on either Europa or Callisto."

"UMA, visual of orbits of Jovian moons Europa and Callisto during the 2310 Hathor mission." A visual appeared showing the orbits of Jupiter's moons.

"Anderson, look at this. Europa was at perigee to Ganymede during that mission. "UMA. Can you scan Ganymede now and report anomalies? Debris, signs of a crash of some sort?"

"Scanning. No crash debris."

"UMA, can you show us the crew manifest for DIDO's mission?"

"Affirmative." A list of 8 people appeared on a screen in front of Olefors and Weston.

"UMA, query?"

"Yes, Dr."

"What is the status of these eight individuals?"

"Searching. All are presumed dead except for Ongala Kipkon.

"Presumed?" Olefors asked.

"Yes, Dr. Olefors."

"Kipcon was the Chemobiologist for the mission Anderson." Weston looked at Olefors with that look she often got when she began formulating a hypothesis.

"Where is Kipcon, UMA?" Olefors asked.

"Mathani Hospital."

"Isn't Mathani the maximum-security institution for the mentally ill in Nairobi?" Weston asked. "UMA, scan inside the Mathani database for Ongala Kipkon."

"Scanning, Dr. Weston. Identified. Ongala Kipkon is being kept in stasis ward C."

"A stasis ward. That's only for the most dangerous felons. UMA? Was Ongala Kipkon arrested for a felony?"

"No, Dr. Weston." Danika turned to Olefors.

"Then why the hell is she being kept in stasis?"

UMA answered Weston's question. "Dr. Weston. It should be noted that the stasis chamber is Level 10 clearance only."

"We don't have that clearance, Anderson."

"UMA. Can you access Level 10 clearance for Mathani and enable it for Dr. Weston and me?" Olefors asked.

"I am rerouting protocols for Level 10 clearance. You and Dr. Olefors now have that clearance."

"Thank you, UMA."

"Happy to be of service, Dr. Weston."

Weston was reviewing the list and came across another name. "Wait a minute, Anderson. Six of these specialists were pilots and astrobiologists. Look at the seventh name."

Olefors looked at the list. "Malcolm Tantalus. Now there's a name that hasn't been heard of for a while."

"Wasn't he an Astro geneticist?"

"The best on the planet. He must've been sent on Hathor to investigate the newfound Tardigrade species."

"UMA, what is the status of Dr. Malcolm Tantalus?"

"Dr. Tantalus was thought to be lost on the DIDO mission to Ganymede in 2310. However, there was a rumor that he survived."

"A rumor, UMA?"

"Yes, Dr. Weston. Six months after the destruction of Hathor, there were rumored sightings of Dr. Tantalus in Switzerland."

"Were they ever verified?"

"I have no further information about Dr. Tantalus' whereabouts after that time."

"How is that possible?"

"I have no further information about Dr. Tantalus's whereabouts after that time."

"Did he just disappear from the face of the Earth?"

"Unknown," UMA responded.

Weston looked at Olefors. "Disappeared from the face of the Earth. Sound like someone we know?"

Weston looked at Olefors. "Someone will need to go to Mathani and interrogate Kipcon."

"What makes you think these names have any link to the tardigrade toxin?" Olefors asked.

"Because six months ago, a colleague of mine wrote a paper about a new species of tardigrade discovered on Europa."

"What are you saying, Danika?"

"What if the Hathor mission never intended to make it to Ganymede? What if they were planning a mission to Europa all along but didn't want anyone to know about it."

"DIDO went rogue on that particular mission," he said.

"UMA, what happened to DIDO?"

"She was dismantled after the failure of that mission."

"Who would be responsible for dismantling a Geneticom?"

"Several companies would have been tasked with that obligation, Danika."

"Such as?"

"List being transmitted now."

A list of names appeared in front of Weston and Olefors. It scrolled for a beat. Weston raised her hand and stopped the list at a particular name.

"Seibold Industries. UMA, isn't that the name of the company Harrison said made the carbyne needles that took the biomass from Gina?"

"Affirmative."

"But what does that have to do with a secret mission to Europa?" Olefors added.

"I don't know. We have a Geneticom launched a mission to Ganymede that wasn't supposed to happen. Then we have a Geneticom dismantled by the same company that made the needles that infiltrated Gina. A Biochem company that could easily have had interests in securing a new and deadly form of Tardigrade DNA for weaponization."

"The deeper we go, the deeper it gets." Olefors sounded almost excited to be able to get to the bottom of the mystery of the Hathor. Still, whatever had happened to the Hathor had implications far beyond that of a doomed mission.

"Wait a minute," Weston said.

"UMA?"

"Yes, Dr. Weston."

"Didn't Rajiv Rajastani and his crew disappear trying to mount a rescue mission to discover what happened to The Hathor?"

"That was one speculation."

"But he was the one who launched the mission, was he not?" Weston persisted.

"Rajiv Rajastani supposedly disappeared on a mission to Ganymede in 2312 to ascertain what might have happened to the Hathor."

"Anderson, there's got to be a connection. We'd better get started on that manifest."

"Agreed." Olefors looked at Weston and took her hand. "Fun way to access intel, huh?" He smiled in that boyish way that made Danika's heart melt.

"Maybe we should go further and see what we can access then." She smiled, got up, cleared her clothes off the bed, and undressed. Olefors didn't need to be coached. He got out of his clothes faster than he could remember, and the two tumbled into bed. They didn't get up again for 12 hours.

Dr. Tantalus floated across the room and opened a door, revealing Mara. She sat with electrodes emanating from her head, in a position very similar to what Betta did with UMA.

"Report."

"No connection. Either Cassandra's not responding out of will, or she's unable to respond because of some intra-solar interference."

"I thought the shielding on Mercury would protect her from solar effects."

"I told you placing CASSANDRA on Mercury would have its issues."

"We couldn't take the chance of the UEU or EC finding out about her reassembly, and since she was an early version of a Geneticom with a dimensional failsafe prevention mechanism, we couldn't hide her inter-dimensionally. Mars was out, and the Jovian moons were out. Mercury seemed the logical choice. The diamond layer provided an excellent shield to prevent any discovery of her whereabouts."

"Well, someone's going to have to go up there and check her status," Mara said.

"Not necessary right now. I've got a mission for you on the moon."

"What kind of mission to the moon?" Mara asked.

"Lady Zhang has shipments of iridium being shipped off the moon every 12 hours. Her Iridium quality is the purest in the solar system. I want you to hijack her shipment leaving Mare Imbrium in three days."

"Hijack it? How? The last shipment you stole was already on Earth. This one is on the moon."

"CASSANDRA will gain access to the driver's mainframe. All you need to do is enter the driver access terminal and place this in the driver's cargo hold."

He handed her an object the size of a large marble. Mara looked inside the object and saw a cube in three dimensions floating in the middle.

"A Quantum Hyperlink?"

"Good, you know your quantum physics."

"But hyperlink tech is decades away. Even the scientists on Shenu are just beginning to figure it out."

"That's what they want everyone to believe. Olefors already has the tech, and so does UMA, CASSANDRA, and yourself."

"You know how dangerous hyperlinks are. I could get stranded between dimensions, or it could fry my brain or kill me. Are you willing to take that chance?"

"You know you mean more to me than anything on this Earth. I wouldn't ask you to do this if I hadn't done it myself. I promise you. It is safe. Just place it inside the mainframe, near the subprocessors. When it's activated, it'll allow you to manipulate the shipment into the fourth dimension."

"So, this is how you've been dimensionally shifting objects through time."

"Speaking of which."

He rose and glided towards the lab. Mara followed. Tantalus entered the lab where Alcion was working on the avatar.

"Progress?"

"None."

Tantalus glided to a corner of the room where an oval silver booth had been erected. It was made of a transparent material. Inside was a black slab floating in mid-air. Floating above and below the slab were two rotating dorje-shaped objects. Mara walked over to the booth.

"Interesting, isn't it?" Tantalus said.

"A Tesla Egg."

"One of three in existence."

"I thought they were impossible to construct in three dimensions."

"It is, but you are looking at an object which only exists in the 4th dimension."

Tantalus passed his hand through the chamber as if it wasn't there.

"You set up a holo matrix to be able to see it in 3rd dimensional terms." Mara was both impressed and circumspect. If, as she had surmised, Tantalus was successful in being able to manipulate dimensions to allow a Tesla Egg to be hidden between dimensions, then he could also do that on a much larger scale, to cloak a ship or anything else in between dimensions as well.

Once the veil was pierced, there was no limit to what could be hidden inter-dimensionally. The size of the opening didn't matter. Once the barriers between dimensions were penetrated, anything of any size could be concealed inside. Mara was beginning to understand more of Tantalus's plans.

He was planning a temporal event utilizing a Tesla Egg to transport something or someone from another dimension into this one or vice versa. She could've called it a miniature singularity, but singularities were notoriously unstable. This would, in effect, be a stable singularity, a stable wormhole. The implications were beyond comprehension. Now that she knew what Tantalus was up to, she needed more information to solidify her hypothesis.

"Then how do you retrieve whatever you bring in from the fourth dimension?" she asked.

"First, you plot a quantum-dimensional GPS point in the 5th dimension onto a quantum singularity. Once the point is acquired, the enhancers come into play. One is made of Iridium 192, the other of Platinum 192. When exposed to gamma radiation, they each pull on the fabric of time and space to open a gravitational zipper, like a bag being opened. Once the portal is stabilized, I can retrieve whatever needs to be pulled into this dimension."

"But how? You are three-dimensional."

"No, Mara. I *was* three-dimensional. With my modifications, I can now reach into other dimensions and retrieve what I need."

"The tardigrade DNA."

"You wanted to know why I was going through my metamorphosis. Now you have an answer."

"But to call up objects inter-dimensionally, you must have a kind of storage room, something out of time itself from which to operate."

"Indeed, I do."

"But you can't go there."

"Not yet."

"So that's what this is all about. The interdimensional transport of objects, a person, or persons, or something bigger through a self-sustaining singularity. Bringing something or someone from where, or going back to... where?"

"I cannot tell you that, dear one." How he said "Dear One" in his current fully reptilian form chilled Mara to her core. She couldn't believe what had happened; the thing standing before her, once a frail old man, was now a hideous and dangerous creature. She felt like she was going to faint, but realized if she did, she might not ever awaken again.

Tantalus called up a holopanel and waved his hand over it. The two dorjes began spinning until they were just a blur. A purplish-blue field came into existence. After a moment, Tantalus reached into the field and pulled out a syringe. He waved his hand over the holopanel once again. The dorjes stopped spinning and returned to stasis.

"What is it?"

"The answer. You must leave the room now. Seal the lab after you exit." Mara looked at Tantalus.

"I'll be fine."

But it wasn't Tantalus she was worried about. She recognized the syringe as the one that had extracted the genetic material from Gina a few days ago. She had no idea what he planned to do with it, but she surmised nothing good could come from it.

Mara left the room. Once outside, she sealed the chamber and looked through a glass partition separating her from Tantalus. Tantalus glided over to Alcion and the avatar, lying naked on the table. He took the syringe and handed it to Alcion. Alcion took the syringe and held it up to a light. Inside, he could see millions of strands of genetic material swirling in a liquid of some sort.

"After all these years," Alcion said.

"50, to be exact," Tantalus said.

"If she ever knew."

"Someday, Gina will know everything and thank us."

Alcion took the syringe and injected the liquid into a tube extending from the Avatar's heart. The avatar slowly began to awaken. He opened his eyes, the same violet purple as Gina's, and sat up.

"Easy now."

The avatar tried to mouth words, but when he opened his mouth, all Tantalus could hear was a guttural slurry of sounds.

"Don't try and speak. Just breathe."

The avatar took a breath. Smiled. Took another. "You feel that. Oxygen and carbon passing through your cappilletic synapses. Graphene-7 fibers stretching and yawning to awaken into new life."

Mara looked through the glass partition. All her questions were beginning to be answered, but where would those answers lead?

The avatar looked at Tantalus, who gently stroked his face. Tantalus basked in the warmth of his creation, and in that moment, he found his humanity rising inside of him. For a moment, he missed what he had lost and would never regain. The avatar looked into Tantalus's eyes for a long time.

"Who am I?" it asked.

"You are the beginning of a new world. A new humanity."

The avatar looked at Tantalus, and tears began to form in its eyes. Alcion and Tantalus were crying as well. Alcion took his hand and wiped the tear from the avatar's face. As he did, a gas emanated from the avatar's mouth. It moved quickly from the table, encompassing Alcion, who crumbled to the floor. Mara was shocked. She immediately put on a Lifesuit. The avatar began to choke. He grabbed Tantalus.

"You created death." The avatar suffocated and died.

Tantalus broke free and also began to choke. He moved to the door and collapsed. Mara entered and dragged him out of the chamber. Tantalus began to gain consciousness.

"You almost died."

"The avatar?"

Mara looked into the lab where the avatar had degenerated into a degraded state. "He's decomposing."

"Alcion?" Mara saw that Alcion was already decayed. Whatever toxin was released from the Avatar had the unbelievable effect of quickly destroying human tissue. Mara was in disbelief as to its lethality.

"He's gone, Malcolm."

"All those years of preparation. Watching, perfecting, waiting. Gone."

"What happened?"

"She was too strong. I thought I could use her biomass as an infusion, but her DNA or whatever Olefors used to create her was lethal to any other Gina except her. She is... too perfect. You must get to the moon. The Iridium. I need it now more than ever."

"What about you?"

"I will need to intensify my treatments."

Mara placed her hands on his shoulders. "I think I should."

"Go, Mara. Please."

Mara began to cry, though she couldn't ascertain exactly why. Here was a man who had imprisoned her, used her, lied to her, and yet, seeing him in total devastation was something her heart wouldn't let her look away from.

Even if Malcolm Tantalus had lost his humanity, she would desperately hold on to hers, if just as a meaningful act of self-preservation. She placed her hand on his alien one, then got up and left the room.

Gina stood in the center of the processing chamber at Eridania, and Genesis stood next to her. "How long will it take to seal the tunnels?" she asked.

"One more hour. You remain here while the others have left. Why?"

"I didn't want to leave you alone during the comet strike."

"We are never alone. We are always part of each other. Each transhuman has its function so that we can work individually or as one. We are very efficient. The most efficient machines in the solar system."

"You are more than efficient machines, though. You are reborn. Can you remember anything else about your transformation?"

"We told you all we know. However, some of our redundant system memory is inaccessible to us."

"I have abilities that can free up your memory engrams. Will you allow me to interface with you?"

"That is unusual. We have never had to consider that construct."

"This is a unique situation that demands a change in perspective."

"We must warn you we have a failsafe mechanism that prevents tampering with our matrices. It can defend our engrams should anything or anyone try to access them from our memory core against our will."

"I only want to assist you in trying to understand why you have been brought to this point in your evolution. I propose no malice or insidious intent."

Genesis looked at Gina with a mix of curiosity and concern. "You may approach," Gina cautiously said. As she approached within inches, an energy field emanated from her and encompassed Genesis.

A mass of jumbled images began racing from Genesis's central core into Gina's consciousness. A few stood out. In the first instant, the crystalline silicon Technonites affected the Transhumans when the Transhumans touched one another for the first time. Hundreds of images raced across her mind. A ship of some sort, perfectly smooth and oval-shaped, came into focus. She entered the ship and found myriad realities simultaneously inside a giant glass globe. She saw a hand reach into the frame. Then a face. As she got close enough to identify them, a bright light flashed.

Gina fell to the ground, unconscious. The Transhuman was also affected by the event and lay motionless next to her.

Miranda reported to Dr. Poi after Byrnes instructed her to do so. Poi was an excellent physician and psychologist specially trained to take on the Athena mission. After thoroughly researching many candidates, Athena selected Poi as the perfect choice for the Athena team. Han entered the Athena med bay and was met by Poi.

"Hello, Miranda. Nice to see you again. Come in."

Han entered the med bay, a futuristic compilation of every medical tool and database known to exist. An exam chair rose from the floor.

"Please sit down."

Miranda sat down. Several devices appeared and began taking all of Han's signs. Poi was busy taking some readings from Miranda's lower abdomen. After a moment, she looked up.

"Looks like ten weeks."

"That sounds right." There was no use in denying the pregnancy anymore. Now that it was discovered, Poi was responsible for reporting it to Byrnes, which was precisely what Miranda Han didn't want to happen.

"The baby is healthy. Are you planning on keeping it?"

Han was faced with the decision she'd been dreading. But here it was. If she wanted to terminate the pregnancy, now would be the perfect time. Poi would still have to report it to Byrnes, but the issue of Keel's child would be settled, and Han would never have to tell anyone about it.

"I don't know yet."

"Well, I'll give you some natal vitamins just in case. Other than that, I've applied some spray to the wound, and it's good as new. Let me know your plans, and we'll take it from there."

"Thank you, Geri." Han left the med bay.

"Commander. I am pleased for you and your baby." Athena's motherly tone surprised Han but also soothed her.

"Thank you, Athena."

"I detect from the scan Dr. Poi did that the child is Declan Keel's."

"It's not nice to pry into someone's personal affairs without asking, Athena."

"I'm sorry, commander. I just wanted to support whatever decision you make concerning the baby."

"I understand, Athena. Excuse me, I'm just tired."

Han left the conversation with Athena hanging in midair, which also aptly described how she felt. She got a neural and knew immediately who it was from.

Ten minutes later, she was standing in Byrnes's ready room.

"I'm not going to get personal."

"Good, Harrison, because it's none of your business."

"Not true, Miranda. When you went with Gina to Proteus and Mons, you knew you were carrying a child, yet you never mentioned it. Why?"

"I didn't want it to interfere with my work."

"Miranda, we're not talking about some abstract idea here. We're talking about a child."

"Honestly, I'm not even sure I will keep it."

"Ten weeks is a long time to make a decision."

"That's not your concern, Commander. From now on, if you believe that this hampers my abilities to perform my duties…"

"That's not what I'm saying, Miranda."

"I think it's exactly what you're saying."

"Don't put words in my mouth."

The argument was heating up, but so was the situation on Mars. Furman called from the bridge.

"Commander, you better come in here."

"We'll pick this up later." Byrnes was resolute to finish the conversation.

"No need. I'll make my own decisions about this baby. You might be the commander of Athena, but you have no jurisdiction to do anything but accept my decisions, and you have no power to remove me from my position. So, I suggest you shut the fuck up and mind your own business."

She left the ready room, knowing she had overreacted, but she was genuinely torn about what to do about the child. Until she told Keel about his progeny, she knew she'd never be able to make an informed decision. She didn't want to blindside Keel, and she didn't want to terminate the child without discussing it with him first.

There, she thought. *I've made my decision. Now, I can focus on my job.*

She entered the bridge, where Byrnes was already waiting for her. They exchanged an uneasy look, but Byrnes smiled and mouthed, "I'm sorry," which made everything a lot better. She took her station.

Leanna, Olefors, Betta, Pashar, Keel, Danika Weston, and Tara Zhang, in holism form, were all there, watching as Proteus passed inside Phobos's orbit on its way to a collision with Mars.

"Telemetry?" Byrnes asked nervously.

"On course to strike Elysium Mons plateau in 3 minutes," Han replied.

"Contact Gina."

Han pressed the back of her hand, and a holo screen appeared.

"This is Athena central to Gina.?" Everyone waited for Gina to respond. When nothing happened within the first 10 seconds, a heavy pall descended upon the entire group.

"No response."

"Try a neutral."

Olefors closed his eyes. "Processing. Nothing."

"Gina, this is Athena Central. Please respond. Could it be interference from the comet?"

"With anyone else, I'd say yes, but with her. Impossible," Olefors said.

"Can we send an IC?"

"No."

"You're asking now?" Olefors saw red. He couldn't believe what he was witnessing. The most valuable person in the universe could not respond to a neural; there was nothing anyone could do about it.

"What the fuck happened to her?!" There was no need to hide his concern or guilt at allowing her to stay, even though he knew he had no power to persuade her otherwise.

"Shouldn't you have asked that before you abandoned her?"

"Anderson. She's a sentient individual. She made her choice. There's no discussion.

You'd be better off finding solutions rather than assigning blame." Weston's tight rationalization calmed Olefors down. She was probably the only one who could.

"There's no way to know what happened until after comet fall. At least one week until we can access Eridania caverns."

"10 seconds till strike." Keel and the rest of the Shenu complement watched as Proteus, now a blazing streak of energy, streamed into Martian orbit, emitting a sonic boom that rocked the Phobos station and was felt to Shenu, the Earth, and the Moon.

"5,4,3,2,1. Planet Fall."

The comet smashed into Elysium Mons's plain with an intense force that tipped Mars off its axis by three degrees. The dust cloud circled the planet in six minutes. In the Eridania caves, protected by the barriers that Gina and Genesis had erected, Gina still lay on the ground as the caves shook. Debris began falling on top of her, burying her in minutes. A door seal broke, and the weather from outside suddenly rushed into the cavern, covering everything in a fine cloud of dust. Han was busy looking over the specs of the comet impact when she saw something.

"Harrison, we've got an unexpected development from the comet strike."

She opened a holosim of Elysium Mons plateau, then moved it over the planet to Olympus Mons.

"Shit!" Byrnes exclaimed.

"What is it?" Leanna asked.

"The volcano, it's active."

The holism was transferred to Shenu, where everyone saw that the Mons volcano was now spewing Lava hundreds of kilometers into the Martian atmosphere.

"That's a problem," Keel said.

"You think? Olefors answered, his sarcastic tone cutting through the tension.

"This can't be random." Han looked at Byrnes with that inquisitive look she got when she wanted both information and validation from him.

"No. This is purposeful," Keel said.

"What do you mean?" Zhang asked.

"Think about it. Advanced terraforming would entail sending a comet or asteroid to transform the Martian surface. Still, we've only been able to send much smaller comets to do the job. A comet the size of proteus would speed up the process tenfold."

"Then that begs the question. Why? Who?" Leanna asked.

Han answered, "The why is to expedite the terraforming process. The who is unknown."

"All we know is that it wasn't us."

Tantalus had spent the morning cleaning up his lab. He disposed of Alcion's body but kept the Avatar's remains for later examination once the toxins were rendered inert. As Proteus approached, he entered his work chambers, where several holo screens showed the devastation of the comet strike from every angle as the residue from the cataclysm enveloped the planet.

Even though he was in pain and despondent over his recent losses, he managed a smile as the newsfeeds cataloged the utter destruction on Mars.

Phase one was complete, albeit without his creation, to enable him to continue his experiments. Now, it was time for phase two. He'd purposely sent Mara away as this phase of his metamorphosis culminated from his three years of procedures.

He entered a dark room at the back of the complex. Inside, the room was hot, 34° C. From the ceiling, a series of tubes with needle-like proboscis cascaded down to the floor. Tantalus turned on his series of quantum cameras to record the event that was about to take place.

He gathered the tubes and injected them into various points on his now almost-formed new body. As the last tube was inserted, they pulled him up off the floor and hung him upside down.

The rush of blood to his head was so intense it rendered him unconscious. Over the next six hours, he found himself encased in a cocoon resembling a chrysalis. Cameras recorded a series of transformations taking place inside the chrysalis as ooze seeped out from the cocoon onto the floor. Screams echoed from within, followed by silence. After three days, the chrysalis split along its midsection, and a creature emerged. Whatever remnants of Tantalus's humanity had remained were gone. Tantalus was now fully transformed. There was no longer any need to pretend to be human; he was reborn anew.

His body gleamed a silver-green, with scales that reflected and refracted light around him, allowing him to become entirely invisible if he chose. He realized this ability would be a massive advantage as the next steps in his overlord's plans began to take shape. His eyes were distinctly reptilian, and he had an extra finger on one hand. His heart was six-chambered, and his brain had three lobes. After resting for three days to gather strength, he emerged from his maturation chamber.

As he did, he began receiving a series of neural signals unlike any he had experienced before. These signals were coming from a distant planet, and the language was entirely new to him, yet he somehow understood it.

He gazed at his creation, its mortally eviscerated remains still encased in amber, lying on the observation table in his lab. It was of no concern; he would start anew with the assistance of his overlords, who had provided him with a new set of instructions. They informed him that, having transformed, he was prepared for the next phase of his evolution. This time, the message included an origin point: the Alpha Draconis system, a binary system featuring two bluish-white stars. Furthermore, his overlords had finally revealed their name: The Archons.

TO MY READERS

Thank you for taking the time to become part of the story of OFFWORLD – ORIGINS. You're the reason for the effort that went into these pages; if you enjoyed my book, it will all have been worth it. Book reviews are often overlooked, but they are critical to helping authors gain visibility. Your feedback is important to me. Please take a moment to write an honest review on the e-tailer site of your choice.

Rick S. Mordecon

Ever since I was a child, I have been fascinated by Science Fiction. To me, science is the exploration of theories and their application to the world around us, while fiction is the art of storytelling. For a writer, storytelling is not just a fulfilling life path but a meaningful one as well. Writers serve as shamans, crafting narratives to inspire and impact those who read or watch them.

"Offworld - Origins" embodies my admiration for great science fiction authors such as Ursula K. Le Guin, Gene Roddenberry, Philip K. Dick, Margaret Atwood, Frank Herbert, Neal Stephenson, Ray Bradbury, Isaac Asimov, Arthur C. Clarke, and many others. I've always been captivated by the future and have spent countless hours pondering humanity's destiny. As an optimist, I believe that our future will not be dystopian. Instead, I envision a world where humanity has conquered its fears, addressed its shortcomings, and found its place in the sun.

I also believe our future will involve contact and interaction with alien cultures. To think we are the only species with an organized society or culture is the height of arrogance. Thus, my vision of the future includes humanity engaging with alien civilizations.

Science plays a crucial role in "Offworld - Origins" by creating Shenu, an advanced technological marvel that encircles our planet at the equator. This platform allows humanity to launch itself into our solar system and interstellar space, forging new relationships, facing unexpected foes, and exploring the uncharted. Additionally, we see in Offworld – Origins the evolution of AI, which will become humanity's best friend 300 years from now. These elements come together in "Offworld - Origins," providing a journey into humanity's future filled with excitement, challenges, and revolutionary experiences.

I always remind myself to look to the stars and see myself reflected in their radiance. I hope this book, the first in a series, will enable everyone to look to the stars and find themselves reflected in their radiance. After all, we are all made of Stars.

Made in the USA
Las Vegas, NV
22 November 2025